Jane and the Wandering Eye

ALSO BY STEPHANIE BARRON

Jane and the Unpleasantness at Scargrave Manor:
Being the First Jane Austen Mystery

Jane and the Man of the Cloth:
Being the Second Jane Austen Mystery

Jane and the Wandering Eye

~Being the Third Jane Austen Mystery~

by Stephanie Barron

BANTAM BOOKS

NEW YORK·TORONTO·LONDON·SYDNEY·AUCKLAND

Bantam Books are published by Bantam Books, a division of Bantam Doubleday Dell Publishing Group, Inc. Its trademark, consisting of the words ''Bantam Books'' and the portrayal of a rooster, is Registered in U.S. Patent and Trademark Office and in other countries. Marca Registrada. Bantam Books, 1540 Broadway, New York, New York 10036.

ISBN 0-553-10204-4

JANE AND THE WANDERING EYE

Dedicated with love to my sister,
Liz Ferretti—
she of the truest eye

Editor's Foreword

THIS, THE THIRD OF JANE AUSTEN'S RECENTLY DISCOVERED JOURNALS TO be edited for publication, finds the Georgian novelist at home in Bath for what would be her last Christmas spent in that city. It proved a time of excitement, intrigue, and loss—one of the most memorable seasons in Austen's life. She celebrated her twenty-ninth birthday and bid farewell forever to a dear friend amid a sinister web of scandal and murder.

The familiarity with theatrical and artistic circles Austen displays in these pages will hardly shock those who study her life and work, for it has long been apparent that she possessed a cultivated taste and a fondness for playacting and dramatic composition. In editing the present volume, however, I found it necessary to consult a number of works pertinent to the theater and portraiture of the day. *The Kemble Era: John Philip Kemble, Sarah Siddons, and the London Stage* by Linda Kelly (New York: Random House, 1980) was a marvelous guide to one of the most exciting epochs (and families) in British theater. *Sir Thomas Lawrence: Portraits of an Age, 1790–1830* by Kenneth Garlick (Alexandria, VA: Art Services International, 1993) and *Richard and Maria Cosway: Regency Artists of Taste and Fashion* by Stephen Lloyd (Edinburgh: Scottish National Portrait Gallery, 1995) were also invaluable to one of my benighted ignorance.

My deepest thanks, however, must go to Elle Shushan, Manhattan

gallery director of Earle D. Vandekar of Knightsbridge. Her knowledge and expertise in the world of Regency eye portraits is irreplace-
able.

Stephanie Barron
Evergreen, Colorado

Jane and the Wandering Eye

Chapter 1

Death Comes
in Fancy Dress

A ROUT-PARTY, WHEN DEPICTED BY A PEN MORE ACCOMPLISHED THAN MY own, is invariably a stupid affair of some two or three hundred souls pressed elbow-to-elbow in the drawing-rooms of the great. Such an efflorescence of powder shaken from noble wigs! Such a crush of silk! And what general heartiness of laughter and exclamation—so that the gentler tones of one's more subdued companions must be raised to a persistent roar, rendering most of the party voiceless by dawn, with only the insipid delights of indifferent negus and faltering meat pasties as recompense for all one's trials.

So Fanny Burney has described a rout, in *Cecilia* and *Camilla;* and so I should be forced to record my first experience of the same, in a more modest volume I entitle simply *Jane,* had not Fate intervened to render my dissipation more intriguing. For last night I endured the most fearsome of crushes—a post-theatrical masquerade, forsooth, with myself in the role of Shepherdess—at no less exalted an address than Laura Place, and the Dowager Duchess of Wilborough's abode, with attendant hundreds of her most intimate acquaintance.

And what, you may ask, had Miss Jane Austen to do in such company? So my father gently enquired, at the moment of my setting out from No. 27, Green Park Buildings (where all my dear family have been situated but two months, having lost our former lodgings in *Sydney Place* to the infamous Coles), my brother Henry at my side, a most formidable Richard the Third, and his wife, Eliza, done up as Marie Antoinette.

"Why, Father," I replied, with a wave of my Shepherdess's crook, "you must know that the invitation is all my brother's, procured with a view to amusing Eliza, who must have her full measure of Bath's diversion during so short a visit to the city; and in such a season Bath at Christmastide may yet be called a trifle thin, in requiring the larger crowds of Easter to lend it style; and if Eliza is not to be thoroughly put out, we must seize our diversion where we may. A masquerade, and at the express invitation of a Dowager Duchess, cannot be let slip. Is not this so, Henry?"

"Indeed," my brother stammered, with a look for his elegant wife, who appeared to have entirely swallowed her little dog, Pug, so pursed with false innocence was her mouth. Eliza is but a slip of a lady, tho' in her present towering headdress, complete with ship's models and birds of paradise bestowed about her heavily powdered curls, she bid fair to rise far above her usual station.

I must confess to a greater admiration for Eliza's queen than for Henry's king—for though both may be called cunning by history's judgement, Eliza has the advantage over Henry, in having at least *seen* Marie Antoinette in all the Austrian's former glory, and thus being capable of the incorporation of that lady's vanished style in her present dress; while Henry is dependent upon the merest notion of humped backs and twirling moustachios, or a general reputation for squintyness about the eyes, for the affectation of his villain.

"And our own dear Madam Lefroy is to be in attendance at the Duchess's party as well, Father," Eliza added. "It is to form the chief part of her final evening in Bath—she returns to Hampshire on the morrow—and we cannot part without some notice on either side. I am sure you would not wish us to neglect so amiable a neighbour, so dear a friend. For who shall say when we shall meet again?"

"But are you even acquainted with the Duchess, my dear Jane?" my father asked, in some bewilderment.

"Assuredly—" Henry began.

"—*not,*" I concluded.

"That is to say," my brother amended hastily, "the acquaintance is entirely *mine,* Father. I have performed some trifling service for the Wilborough family, in the financial line. The rout tickets came to me."

"I had not an idea of it, my dear boy." The expression of pleasure that suffused my father's face, at this indication of his son's advancement in his chosen profession of banking, made the falsehood almost worth its utterance.

"But now we must be off," Eliza interjected firmly, "or lose another hour in search of chairs, for our own have been standing at the door this quarter-hour.[1] It has quite struck eleven, and how it snows! Do observe, my dear sir, the unfortunate chairmen!"

Bath's climate is usually so mild as to escape the advent of winter, but this night at least we were subject to a fearsome blast. And thus, as my father clucked in dismay from the drawing-room window, all benevolent concern for the reddened cheeks and stamping feet of the unlucky fellows below, we hurried down to the street, where indeed our chairs had been idle already some minutes, and settled ourselves comfortably for the trip to Laura Place—or would have, had not my Shepherdess's crook refused the conveyance's close accommodation. This small difficulty resolved, by the abandonment of the offending object on the stoop of No. 27, Green Park Buildings, the chairmen heaved and hallooed, and off we went—with only the occasional bobble to recall the untidiness of the snowy streets, and the likelihood of a yet more strenuous return.

I profited from the brief journey, by indulging in a review of the causes of our exertion, for pleasure was unfortunately the least of them. However circumscribed my usual society in Bath—which is generally limited to my Aunt Leigh-Perrot's insipid card parties, and the occasional indulgence of the theatre when my slim purse may allow it—I am not so desperate for enjoyment as to spend a decidedly snowy midnight done up as a Staffordshire doll, in a gay throng of complete strangers more blessed and happy in their mutual acquaintance. Nor are Henry and Eliza so mad for rout-parties as my

---

[1] In Austen's day, it was the custom to travel about the streets of Bath and other major cities in hired sedan chairs carried by a man fore and aft.—*Editor's note.*

father had been led to believe. My brother and sister[2] had suc-
cumbed to my entreaties for support, and had gone so far as to
prevaricate on my behalf. From an awkwardness of explanation, I
had deliberately withheld from the Reverend George Austen the
true nature of our visit to Laura Place. We were gone in the *guise* of
revellers, indeed, but laboured in fact under a most peculiar commission.

Lord Harold Trowbridge, my dark angel of recent adventure—
confidant of the Crown, adversary of whomever he is paid to oppose,
and general Rogue-about-Town—is the Dowager Duchess of
Wilborough's younger son. He is also in the throes of some trouble
with a lady—nothing unusual for Lord Harold, although in this instance, the novelty of the lady's being not only unmarried, but related to him, must give the mendacious pause. In short, his niece,
Lady Desdemona Trowbridge—an Incomparable of the present Season, a girl of eighteen with all the blessings of fortune, beauty, and
breeding to recommend her—has thrown off the protection of her
family and friends; has left all in London whose interest should form
her chief consideration and care; and has fled to the Dowager Duchess in Bath. The agent of her flight? The redoubtable Earl of Swithin,
who claims an interest in the lady's future happiness. In short, the
Earl has offered for her hand—and caused the fair Desdemona considerable vexation and grief.

Lord Harold observed the flight, and respected his mother's
wishes to leave the girl to herself for a time; he remained in London,
and restrained His Grace the Duke from summoning the chit immediately back home; he forbore to visit Laura Place himself, and urge
the reclamation of sense; and when the Lady Desdemona showed
neither an inclination to quit her grandmother's abode, nor to suffer
very much from her voluntary exile, being engaged in a delightful
round of amusement and shopping in the weeks before Christmas—
he applied, at last, to me.

My niece is a lady of excellent understanding, Lord Harold wrote in his
barely legible hand, but possessed of the Trowbridge will. She is headstrong,

[2] Eliza de Feuillide was both Jane Austen's cousin and the wife of her brother
Henry, but Jane usually refers to Eliza simply as her *sister.* It was a convention of
the time to address relatives acquired through marriage in the same manner as
blood relations.—*Editor's note.*

and entirely capable of acting against her own interest. I am most concerned that she not fall prey to the basest of fortune hunters—whose attentions she might unwittingly encourage, from a misplaced sense of pique, or an inclination to put paid to Lord Swithin's plans. Is it impossible—do I ask too much—that you might observe her movements for a time, my dear Miss Austen? And report what you observe? I wish chiefly to know the nature of Desdemona's acquaintance—in whose circle she spends the chief part of her days—and the names of those gentlemen upon whom she bestows the greatest attention. You would oblige me exceedingly in the performance of this service; for tho' Her Grace might certainly do the same, she is, as you may be aware, not *the strictest judge of propriety.*

And as the letter supplied a direction in Pall Mall—Brooks's Club, to be exact—and the very rout tickets formerly mentioned, I could not find it in me to refuse—if, indeed, at present I could refuse Lord Harold anything. It is not that I owe him some great debt of gratitude, or harbour for the gentleman a more tender sentiment; but rather that where Lord Harold goes, intrigue surely follows—and I confess I have been insupportably *bored* with Bath, and the littlenesses of a town, since my return from Lyme Regis but a few weeks ago. The Gentleman Rogue and his errant niece presented a most welcome diversion.

And so to Laura Place we were gone.

I DO NOT BELIEVE I EXAGGERATE WHEN I DECLARE THAT THE DOWAGER Duchess of Wilborough's establishment was ablaze last e'en with a thousand candles. Light spilled out of a multitude of casements (the original glazing of which must have exacted from the late Duke a fortune), and cast diamond-paned shadows upon the snowy street; light flowed from the open entry-way at every chair's arrival, like a bolt of silk unfurled upon the walk. A hubbub of conversation, too, and the clatter of cutlery; a voice raised hoarsely in song; a burst of laughter. The faintest strain of a violin drifted to the stoop.

Henry paid off the chairs and presented our cards to the footmen, but I found occasion to dally at the very door, almost deterred by the glittering hordes I glimpsed within—until an exclamation from Eliza thrust me forward. I had trod upon the foot of Marie Antoinette.

The foyer was a wealth of pale green paint picked out with pink and white, the colours of Robert Adam. Pink and green silk lined the windows, and a bust of the Tragic Muse loomed before a pier glass opposite—Mrs. Siddons, no doubt, and taken from the painting by Reynolds.[3] I gazed, and beheld myself reflected as Shepherdess, a forlornly bucolic figure amidst so much splendour. Eliza pinched my arm.

"As near to Old Drury as may be, my dear," she murmured.[4]

"Indeed," I replied. "The Dowager Duchess may be living in relative retirement, but she has not yet foresworn her passions."

"Let us go up," Henry interposed with impatience. "There is a fearful crush at my back!"

The rout was intended, so Lord Harold had informed us, as a tribute to the principal players of Bath's Theatre Royal[5]—and the present evening's performance being just then concluded, the tide of humanity spilling into Laura Place from the direction of Orchard Street was decidedly at its flood. The staircase, a grand curve of mahogany, was completely overpowered with costumed bodies struggling towards the drawing-room; I hooked one arm through my brother's, and the other through my sister's, and so we stormed the redoubt.

Let us pass over in silence the travails of the next quarter-hour; how our gowns were torn, and our headdresses deranged; what injuries to slipper and glove. Better to employ the interval in relating the chief of what I know about the Dowager herself—the barest details of Her Grace's celebrated career.

I have it on so good an authority as my dear mother's dubious memory, that Eugénie de la Falaise began her ascent as a pert young chorus girl in the Paris comic opera; from thence, with a comely ankle and a smattering of English, she rose to Covent Garden; and it was there the Duke of Wilborough—the *fifth*, rather than the pres-

[3] Sarah Siddons (1755-1831) was the foremost tragic actress of Austen's day. With her brother, John Philip Kemble, Siddons dominated the London stage at this time, where it is probable Jane had seen her perform.—*Editor's note.*

[4] Robert Adam's renovation of Old Drury Lane Theatre in 1775 featured pale green and pink paint with bronze detailing—which the Dowager Duchess apparently emulated. Old Drury was pulled down and replaced by a newer building in 1794. This building burned to the ground in 1809.—*Editor's note.*

[5] This was the original Bath theater on Orchard Street, where Jane was a frequent patron. Its company divided performances between Bath and Bristol, playing houses in each city on alternate nights—Tuesday, Thursday, and Saturday in Bath; Monday, Wednesday, and Friday in Bristol.—*Editor's note.*

ent, Duke—fell headlong in love with the lady. Wilborough was already past his first youth; he had seen one Duchess into her grave, and her stillborn son with her; and thus it should not be remarkable that he might establish the beautiful Eugenie privately, or offer unlimited credit in the most fashionable shops, and a smart pair to drive her about Town, in return for the enjoyment of her favours, as Lord Derby once did with Miss Farren.[6] But Eugenie had a greater object in view. She wished to play at tragedy.

That she was unsuited for Isabella, or Lady Macbeth, or even the role of Portia in *The Merchant of Venice,* need not be underlined. *Twelfth Night,* perhaps, or *She Stoops to Conquer,* may have shewn her talents to advantage; but at the Duke of Wilborough's intercession with the Drury Lane director, Lady Macbeth she played—and opposite no less a personage than the redoubtable Mr. Garrick.

The performance—there was, alas, only one—was declared to have been lamentable. The outraged patrons hissed and shouted, threw all manner of refuse from theatre pit to stage, and forced the curtain down in the very midst of Lady Macbeth's celebrated walk. Eugenie de la Falaise was mortified, and disappeared abruptly from public view, never to return to the London theatre.

We cannot in justice fault the fifth Duke for having married her. He may be forgiven the indulgence of his folly. The pity, the generosity, the rashness her ruined career may have excited—we can have only the merest idea of how they worked upon his sensibilities. Eugenie was, it is said, a beautiful woman at twenty-four; and though she is now a grandmother these many years, and Wilborough long since gone to his reward, she is no less formidable a presence.

I say this, having found my eyes directed to the Dowager Duchess upon first gaining entrance to her drawing-room. Tho' possessed of fully seventy years, and requiring the support of a stout cane she clutches tightly in one hand, Her Grace commands immediate attention. Her narrow features and shuttered aspect recall the face of her son, Lord Harold; but where the effect is often forbidding in the latter, it may be declared devastating in the former. A lesser man than the Duke of Wilborough—accustomed as he was to the power

---

[6] Elizabeth Farren was a member of the Drury Lane company during the 1780s and the recognized mistress of the Earl of Derby, who made her his second countess at his first wife's death in 1797.—*Editor's note.*

of doing as he liked—would have braved greater scandal in pursuit of such a woman.

And scandal there was. His Majesty George II is said to have interceded in the match, which condescension was stoically declined. The Duke's political fortunes may subsequently have suffered. Certain of his acquaintance may have cut him dead. But others, made more valuable through the passage of time, accepted his bride; and accepted no less the heirs she pragmatically produced.

Bertie, who succeeded his father, bears the greatest fidelity to the Wilborough line, in character as well as countenance; Lady Caroline Mulvern, *née* Trowbridge, is the unfortunate picture of her Trowbridge aunts; but in the face of Lord Harold, the impertinent among society's loquacious have gone so far as to question paternity. Lord Harold is so clearly Eugenie's son, that the late Duke might have had nothing to do with his fashioning.

The Dowager stood in the midst of her fashionable rout last e'en arrayed in the form of Cleopatra—an Egyptian robe and a circlet on her brow, with a velvet mask held before—and beside her stood a girl so very much of Eugenie's stamp, albeit some fifty years younger, that I knew her immediately for the Lady Desdemona, Lord Harold's errant niece. She was robed to perfection as none other than *herself,* having ignored the general command of fancy dress; and her quite ordinary appearance amidst the general excess of baubles and plumage rendered her as exotic as a sparrow in Paradise. I could trace no hint of her mother, Honoria, or her apoplectic father, Bertie, in her narrow and elegant face, and wondered whether her character was as French as her countenance.

''Jane,'' Eliza cried, her visage incongruously marred by the mask that covered fully half of it, ''Henry *will* have me to dance; and though I confess the heat and crush make the prospect an indifferent one, I cannot find that sitting down should be so very agreeable *either.* Can you forgive us our desertion?''

''Go, my dear, and make as frivolous a figure as your murdered Queen may support; I shall do very well in idleness here. I find I have an excellent prospect of Lady Desdemona.''

''Where?''

''She stands beside the Duchess.''

''Ah,'' Eliza said, with the driest satisfaction, ''in the figure of an *ingénue.* She might readily be Cecilia herself, and prepared to thwart a cavalcade of admirers, whose costumed obscurity can only encourage impertinence. Let us call her Virtue, and have done."

"Indeed? I had thought her merely to disdain all pretence or disguise. And burdened as I am with so hot and ungainly an outfit"—I surveyed my multitude of muslin underskirts with a shake of my bonneted head—"I cannot in justice criticise. I fairly long for an exchange."

"Perhaps. But does her abhorrence—or wisdom—reveal a niceness of temperament and taste? Or may we judge her merely to spoil sport?"

"I cannot undertake to say, without a greater knowledge of the lady."

"Then find her out, my dear Jane, and I shall be content to think as you do. It saves me a vast deal of trouble in thinking for myself." And with a smile and a care for her overpowering headdress, Eliza left me to Lord Harold's business.

I began by surveying the company—a torrid blend of the comely and the grotesque, their colours garish and their accents brazen, relieved somewhat by the solitary interval of an elegant figure, composed against a doorframe or supporting a distant wall—engaged, it seemed, in an activity similar to my own. A Harlequin I espied, resplendent in a suit of black and red, in the closest conversation with a stately Queen Elizabeth; and a fearsome Moor, all flowing capes and harshly graven features—though *not* in attendance upon my particular Desdemona. More than one visage I detected, that when deprived of its domino might daily grace the pages of the *Gentleman's Magazine,* or one of Gillray's satiric drawings.[7]

A full quarter-hour of observation, however, could not betray to my sight the predatory horde whose idea had so excited Lord Harold's anxiety. Two men only approached the Lady Desdemona—yet *another* Harlequin, suited this time in diamonds of alternating black and white; and a fellow who might well have been Henry VIII, tho' of a corpulence supplied by tailor's padding. These two seemed as in-

[7] James Gillray (1757–1815) was the foremost political caricaturist of Austen's day. His satiric prints began to make their appearance in the 1780s. The aquatint engravings generally made sport of fashionable scandals or political missteps, much as do present-day political cartoons.

tent upon conversation with the Dowager Duchess, as with her lovely charge.

"And are you, too, of the Theatre Royal?" came a voice at my shoulder; and looking up, I beheld a Knight in the semblance of armour, complete with visored head, his identity secure in mystery.

"Of its occasional box alone," I replied, "but I may confess to admiration for good, hardened, professional acting. Are some part of the company present, then?"

"The masquerade is in their honour."

"So I had understood. But with so many figures in fancy dress, how is one to divine the true player from the false?"

My companion bowed. "You merely posit, madam, the oldest question of mankind."

I studied the visored face, which revealed nothing of the gentleman within. Could it, in fact, be Lord Harold, making sport of circumstance? The voice betrayed an echo of the Gentleman Rogue's tone. But no. He should hardly engage my offices on the Lady Desdemona's behalf, had he intended to form one of the party.

"I wonder, sir," I began again, "that you can think me a member of such exalted company."

"I merely tossed at hazard. You might be exalted in any number of ways—as I might myself. We appear as utter strangers the one to the other; but indeed we might claim the deepest intimacy, and yet pass in ignorance, so impenetrable is our garb."

"And the most accomplished actress herself must go unremarked."

"There, madam, you betray a charming innocence of accomplished actresses. It is the first rule of the stage that to go unremarked, is to go presently into the wings. Observe the Medusa in scarlet."

I looked about, though the compass of both bonnet and mask rendered all vision partial.

"By the fireplace, in converse with the bearded Pierrot."

I observed then an extraordinary woman, all vibrance and fire, her flowing black hair and tattered raiment the very soul of madness. Her beauty was such as to astonish. Her costume, however, barely merited the word, in leaving more of her person exposed than it disguised. The effect *must* draw even the most jaded attention. She had flaunted custom, and wore no mask. Whether her conversation was as engaging as her person, I could not discern; but as I watched, the bearded Pierrot threw back his head in hearty laughter.

"That is Miss Conyngham," my companion remarked.

"*Maria* Conyngham? I had not an idea of it."

"Her brother is beside the Duchess."

I turned to look for Her Grace.

"The Harlequin?"

"Henry the Eighth."

"So *that* is the famous Hugh Conyngham! I wonder I did not observe it before! Who can see his present self, and fail to trace his tragic Hamlet? His murderous Macbeth? His pathetic Gamester? The nobility of suffering is writ in every line of his countenance!"

"With charcoal, if not by nature," the gentleman observed.

"And are you then a player, sir? Claim you some acquaintance with the pair?" It was absurd in me, I own, to cry such admiration at Conyngham's discovery; but so much of my meagre purse has gone to furnish *his*, in supplying the coveted seat in a box for the actor's performance, that I may be excused my excesses of enthusiasm. I have invested as much in Conyngham as Henry in all his four percents.[8]

"I have not that distinction," the Knight replied with an inclination of the head. "I may claim the accomplishment of dancing only, and that with indifferent skill. But I must beg for the indulgence of your hand, fair Shepherdess, or suffer the charge of impertinence, in having monopolised your attention too long."

I hesitated, with thoughts of Lord Harold, and the necessities of duty; but a glance at the floor revealed the Lady Desdemona, all smiles and animation, going down the dance with her partner opposite. The White Harlequin, it seemed, had prevailed in his suit; his appearance of attention to the Dowager had been rewarded with the hand of her granddaughter. Lady Desdemona's eyes were bright, and her complexion brilliant; but how, I thought with vexation, was I to report her partner's name? For a masquerade is ill-suited to espionage; conjecture only might supply the place of the man; and I

---

[8] These were the government's public funds, one of the few reliable investments in Austen's day, which generally yielded annuities of four percent per annum.—*Editor's note.*

should be reduced to outright eavesdropping, if I were to learn any-thing to Lord Harold's purpose. To the dance floor, then, with the greatest despatch.

I bowed, my own mask held high, and took my suitor's proffered arm; and found to my relief that armour may be formed of cloth, however shot through with silver, and pose no impediment to a country dance, though it reveal nothing of the Knight within.

A FULL HALF-HOUR OF HEATED EXERCISE PROVED INSUFFICIENT TO THE fulfilment of my schemes, however; it was impossible to overlisten anything to Lord Harold's purpose in so great a throng; and so, with a civility on either side, I abandoned my partner for a comfortable seat in the supper-room near Henry and Eliza. I had divined only that the White Harlequin made a shapely leg and was a proficient in the dance, with a vigorous step and a palm decidedly moist, as he handed Lady Desdemona along the line of couples. She seemed happy in her choice of partner, and moved in a fine flow of spirits; *he* was a spare, neat figure possessed of a hearty laugh and a general conviviality, who comported himself as a gentleman; and what was visible of his hair was brown. There my researches ended.

The delights of cold fowl and buttered prawns, white soup and ratafia cakes, were all but consumed, and Henry had embarked upon the errand of refilling our cups of punch, when I began to consider of Madam Lefroy. Anne Lefroy has long been our neighbour in Steventon, being established in the rectory at Ashe these two decades at least; and though she is full five-and-twenty years my senior, she remains my dearest friend in the world. The claims of friendship had recently drawn her to Bath—her acquaintance with the Dowager being of several decades' standing—and the previous fortnight spent in her company had been one of the most delightful I could re-call. Our tastes are peculiarly suited the one to the other, and there is no one's society I should more eagerly claim in good times or in bad.

It was Madam who refined my taste in poetry, who improved my ear for music, who taught me that cleverness is far more than mere surface wit. From Madam, too, I learned that even *ladies* might converse about the nation's affairs—for as Madam feelingly says, when so great a figure as Mr. Sheridan confuses a parliamentary bench for Drury Lane, how can *we* be expected to respect the difference?[9]

Anne Lefroy was to leave us on the morrow—but we had intended a meeting in Laura Place. The crush of bodies and the bewildering array of fancy dress had quite disguised her from my sight. I craned about in search of her glorious hair—when a muffled ejaculation from the direction of the fire demanded my attention.

Two men—the White Harlequin and my unknown Knight—were arranged in an attitude of belligerence, although the effect was rendered somewhat ridiculous by the incongruity of their costumes. The Knight had removed his helmet, revealing a fair head and a sharp-featured face that *must* be vaguely familiar; and he now glared boldly at his masked opponent.

"You are a blackguard, sir, and a liar!" he cried.

The Harlequin swayed as he stood, as though influenced by unconquerable passion, or an excess of spirits. And at that moment, Lady Desdemona intervened.

"Kinny! You will apologise at once! Mr. Portal meant nothing by his words, I am certain of it. I will not have you come to blows!"

"I'd sooner fall upon my sword than beg pardon of such a rogue," my Knight exclaimed; and as if in answer, the Harlequin thrust Lady Desdemona roughly aside. She cried out; it was enough. The Knight rushed swiftly at his opponent.

A scuffle, an outburst of oaths—and the two were parted by the actor Hugh Conyngham and the stern-looking Moor.

"Gentlemen! Gentlemen!" Mr. Conyngham exclaimed. "You will look to your conduct, I beg! This is hardly what is due to the Duchess!"

My Knight, his countenance working, drew off a silver glove, and dashed it to the floor. The White Harlequin struggled in the Moor's arms, determined to pick it up.

---

[9] Richard Brinsley Sheridan, the noted Georgian playwright of *The School for Scandal* and owner of the Drury Lane Theatre, was also a member of Parliament. Sheridan first came to Jane's notice in 1787, when he made a four-day speech against her family's friend Warren Hastings, the former Governor-General of Bengal, during Hastings's seven-year parliamentary trial for impeachment.—*Editor's note.*

But it was Hugh Conyngham who bent to retrieve the glove. He tucked it deftly into his Elizabethan doublet. ''No challenge, my lord, I beg,'' he muttered, with a look for Lady Desdemona.

Eliza craned on tiptoe for a clearer view of the scene. ''But how droll!'' she whispered. ''An affair of honour! And can the lady be the cause?''

Lord Harold's niece turned and quitted the supper-room in considerable haste, her eyes overflowing with tears. As if released at a command, the scandalised guests sent up a buzz of conversation; and the Duchess moved to follow her.

''Stay, Grandmère,'' called my Knight; ''I shall go to Mona. Have Jenkins show this blackguard the door.'' And with a look of contempt for the White Harlequin, who sat slumped in a chair, he sped swiftly in Lady Desdemona's train.

My Knight, the Dowager Duchess's grandson? Then was he, in fact, Lady Desdemona's brother, and the heir to the Wilborough dukedom? There was something of Eugenie's sharpness in his features, and I could imagine him as almost his uncle's twin in another twenty years.

The Duchess halted in her path, leaning heavily upon her cane, and glanced around the supper-room. ''Jenkins!'' she called, her voice low and clear. ''Send round the wine, if you please. I shall attend to Mr. Portal.'' And grasping her cane with one hand and the White Harlequin with the other, she led him unprotestingly away.

''I might almost think it a set-piece of the stage,'' said a wry voice at my back, ''did not my familiarity with a lady's tears argue its sincerity. What think you, Jane? A lovers' quarrel? Or something deeper?''

''Madam Lefroy!'' I turned in delight, and held out my hands. ''Do my eyes misgive me? Or is the magnificent Elizabeth reborn in the form of Ashe?''

The masked figure of Queen Elizabeth, whom I had observed earlier in conversation with the Red Harlequin, seized my fingers and laughed.

''As you find me, my dear Miss Austen!—My dear Mrs. Henry! And how do you like the Duchess's party?''

''I may forgive her the disadvantage of a large acquaintance, however much it ensures I shall be crushed, now that there is a touch of scandal to the evening," Eliza declared mischievously. "Of what else might I speak in the Pump Room tomorrow?"[10]

"Eugenie should never forgo a chance to set the town to talking—but I wonder if the Lady Desdemona is quite of her way of thinking? She seemed much distressed."

All discussion of the interesting episode was forestalled, however, by my brother's return. Henry carried a chair with effort in one hand, and a glass of punch in the other; and the result of his exertions, in having raised a fine dew along his forehead, did little for his Richard.

"My poor Henry," I exclaimed. "Your benevolence is for naught. I have secured my dear Madam Lefroy, as you see, and will leave you to your lovely Antoinette, and the comforts of iced custard."

"What think you of the rout, Jane?" Madam began, as she slipped her arm through mine, and commenced a measured step in time to the musicians' playing. "I confess to some amazement at the company—a more Whiggish group I have rarely seen, and did your father know of it, he should as soon have barred you within doors as hastened you on your way. Is Henry, then, a traitor to the Austen cause?"

"Our sentiments may be Tory, my dear Madam, but our practices are not so discriminating, as to refuse a patron of the Duke's stature."

"Or his brother's?" Madam enquired keenly. "Do not I recall some little acquaintance of *yours,* and of fully two years' duration—with the disreputable Lord Harold?"

"Indeed, I have never found Lord Harold *disreputable,*" I faltered, with a sudden colour in my cheeks.

[10] The Pump Room was one of the social centers of Bath. It adjoined the King's Baths, near the Abbey and Colonnade in the heart of the city, and was frequented by the fashionable every afternoon. There they would congregate to drink a glass of medicinal spring water presented by liveried pump attendants; to promenade among their acquaintance; and to peruse the calf-bound volume in which recent arrivals to the city inscribed their names and local addresses. Austen describes the Pump Room to perfection in *Northanger Abbey,* in which Catherine Morland and Isabella Thorpe make the place their second home.—*Editor's note.*

"But his behavior towards your friend the Countess was hardly honourable. I read the accounts of that notorious trial, you know. The papers wrote of little else that winter."

"Both Isobel and her present husband were acquitted by the House of Lords." Impatiently, I thrust my mask in my reticule. "What was possible to proclaim to the public, of the sad business at Scargrave, and what of necessity remained closed to the general understanding, I am hardly at liberty to reveal. But I may freely assure you, Madam, that Lord Harold Trowbridge acted *then* in a manner that has fully won my respect and esteem."[11]

"I am heartily glad to hear it," Madam Lefroy replied, "for I should not like to be uneasy about my dear Jane's associations, at such a remove from Bath. I may well rejoice at the delay that has provided an occasion for finding you amidst the very best society this town may offer, however Whiggish its aspect. Is Lord Harold present, Jane?" Her head turned swiftly about the supper-room. "I quite long to make his acquaintance."

"I do not believe that he is. Business in Town, I understand, has detained him."

"A pity. I might almost have prolonged my stay in Bath on the hope of meeting with him."

"Prolong your visit for any whim, I beg. If the prospect of Lord Harold may serve to keep you by my side, I shall summon him from the ends of the earth!"

"I require no very great inducement," Madam replied with a smile. "There is so much of the diverting to be found in Bath! I might almost believe myself returned to Kent, and the days of my girlhood, when the Dowager Duchess presided at Fairlawn! The present Duchess entertains only rarely, you know—and her circle is hardly so lively as Eugenie's."

I drew Madam Lefroy towards a pair of chairs just then returned to liberty. "You have enjoyed a singular intimacy with the Dowager, I collect."

"She is some years my senior, of course—but her warmth must always transcend age or station. A great many changes have occurred

11 Jane refers here to the events related in the first volume of her edited journals, *Jane and the Unpleasantness at Scargrave Manor* (New York: Bantam Books, 1996).—*Editor's note.*

since first we called one another by our Christian names. How gay we all were, when the late Duke was alive, and all the world came to Kent!"

My friend's voice held a familiar note of regret. Anne Lefroy may be many years a clergyman's wife, but she has not forgot the brilliance of her father's house, or the elegant society of Canterbury in the days of her youth. She married late, and only, it is whispered, after a grave disappointment in her first attachment; and has suffered the remainder of her days in the retirement of a Hampshire village. She retains as yet the beauty that marked her youth—the fineness of bone and brilliancy of complexion that so transported Gainsborough—and hungers still for the best of the Fashionable World: stimulating conversation and the elegance of a select acquaintance. Indeed, it is her air of the great lady that inspired the affectionate title of *Madam*.

"The sight of so many ravishing young gentlemen and ladies, all accomplished in the theatrical line, must recall the days of Eugenie's youth," she continued, as she glanced about the throng.

"Had you occasion to see her play?"

"I? Good Lord, no—I was barely out of leading-strings when Her Grace quitted the boards forever. But as a girl of sixteen I *was* privileged to participate in amateur theatricals, at Fairlawn of a Christmastide—Wilborough maintained a private theatre, you know, for his lady's use—and all manner of personages were wont to parade in pantomime, for the amusement of Her Grace's guests. The young Sarah Siddons and her brother Kemble, and the elder Conynghams, were summoned one year as I recall—and very prettily they played it, too, though not yet attaining the excellence of their London years."

I looked for the Medusa in scarlet, and the corpulent Henry VIII, and found them in animated conversation with Pierrot. "I did not know you were acquainted with the Conynghams."

"I cannot claim the honour, my dear, though Her Grace was so good as to introduce them to my society. They were not even thought of, when I enjoyed the art of their parents—and their parents are many years deceased."

"How melancholy to consider of it!"

"Age *will* advance upon one," Madam observed with a sigh, "though I must remark that Her Grace seems to keep its depriva-

tions at bay! How very well she looks, to be sure! And the
Conynghams appear to have survived their early loss, Mrs. Siddons
had the raising of them, I believe. They were of an age to be thrown
together with her children—she possesses no less than five, like myself—and I cannot think but that they do her credit.''

''With such a rearing, it should be marvellous indeed did the
Conynghams abhor the stage.''

''They were bred to the boards, as they say in theatrical circles.
Miss Conyngham was educated in France, in company with the Miss
Siddonses; and her brother, Hugh, was sent to the same college as
the Kemble gentlemen patronised—a religious school somewhere in
Flanders.[12] Mr. Conyngham would be about the same age as Mr.
Charles Kemble, the Siddons girls' uncle, and both are Papists, you
know.''

''I was not aware,'' I replied. ''And do the Conynghams look to
the Siddons family to patronise their careers? Mr. John Philip Kemble is presently the manager of Covent Garden, I believe—and might
do much for his friends.''

''There has been a little coolness in their relations, it seems,'' said
Madam Lefroy, ''owing to an unfortunate love affair. Hugh Conyngham was excessively attached to the younger Miss Siddons, and
thought to have married her; but the lady turned her affections
elsewhere, and he has not yet got over the disappointment. However,
she was of a sickly constitution, and passed away some years since.''

''How tragic!''

Our exchange was broken by the clang of a gong—we turned as
one, and perceived once more the Dowager.

Her Grace had got rid of the offending White Harlequin somewhere, and now leaned on her cane at the head of the drawing-
room, as if on the point of speech. Lady Desdemona, seeming quite
recovered in spirits, stood once again by her grandmother's side. At
the Dowager's other hand was Henry VIII—or the actor Hugh Conyngham—possessed of his usual dignity. The entire rout fell silent.
''Dear guests and fellow devotees of the theatre,'' Eugenie said,
the faintest suggestion of France in her guttural tone and tender way

[12] John Philip and Charles Kemble both attended a Roman Catholic college in
Douay, Flanders. Their father was Catholic, their mother Protestant, and according to custom the sons were reared in their father's faith while Sarah Siddons
was raised in her mother's.—Editor's note.

with consonants, "the *artistes* of the Theatre Royal have honoured us tonight with their presence. It is my noble office to present the celebrated Mr. Hugh Conyngham, who will speak a short passage from *Macbeth* for our enjoyment. Mr. Conyngham."

"Your Grace," the gentleman replied, with the most elegant sweep of his hand, and the deepest of bows, "I am honoured to be of service." And with that simple acknowledgement, he fixed his gaze upon the decorative plaster of the ceiling, his aspect at once become sorrowful, brooding, contemplative, and tortured by turns.

My heart, I confess, gave way to a painful beating; I felt the impertinent blood rise swiftly to my cheeks; and was glad for the support of a chair. *Macbeth,* as Conyngham plays him, is the very soul of tragedy; and I am but too susceptible to its power.

" *'If it were done,'* " HE BEGAN, IN THE HUSHED TONE AND SLOW PACE appropriate to murderous thought, turning before our eyes like a cage'd tiger—

> *"when 'tis done, then 'twere well*
> *It were done quickly. If th' assassination*
> *Could trammel up the consequence, and catch*
> *With his surcease, success; that but this blow—"*

(Here, a swiftly upraised hand, a clenching fist, the agony of indecision in his aspect.)

> *"Might be the be-all and the end-all here,*
> *But here, upon this bank and shoal of time,*
> *We'ld jump the life to come. But in these cases*
> *We still have judgment here, that we but teach*
> *Bloody instructions, which, being taught, return*
> *To plague th' inventor. This even-handed justice*
> *Commends th' ingredience of our poison'd chalice*
> *To our own lips. He's here in double trust:*
> *First, as I am his kinsman and his subject,"*

(The nobility of his consciousness! The foulness of his thought!)

*"Strong both against the deed; then, as his host,
Who should against his murtherer shut the door,
Not bear the knife myself. Besides, this Duncan
Hath borne his faculties so meek, hath been
So clear in his great office, that his virtues
Will plead like angels, trumpet-tongu'd, against
The deep damnation of his taking-off;
And pity, like a naked new-born babe,
Striding the blast, or heaven's cherubin, hors'd
Upon the sightless couriers of the air,
Shall blow the horrid deed in every eye,
That tears shall drown the wind."*

(A long declining wail, as though uttered from within a tomb.)

*"'I have no spur
To prick the sides of my intent, but only
Vaulting ambition, which o'erleaps itself,
And falls on th' other—'"*

The last words, whispered and yet utterly distinct, came like the gentle slip of leaves from a November bough; and his lips had scarcely ceased to move, when the applause that was his due rang forth in strenuous tumult. Every throat swelled with praise, and the madness of cheering all but blotted out Hugh Conyngham's gentler thanks. The actor's brilliant eye, and the fever of his cheek, spoke with firmer eloquence, however; and I read in his looks a grateful understanding. For such an one, as yet so young in the life of the stage—for he can be but thirty—to take his place among the Garricks and the Kembles, if only in the estimation as yet of *Bath,* must seem like glory, indeed.

The cheering did not cease; the clapping hands acquired a measured beat; and it seemed as though Hugh Conyngham must bow to the desire of the guests, and speak on—when the tenor of the hoarsest cries declined by an octave, and gained a sudden accent of horror and dismay. The acutest attention o'erspread the actor's face; the crowd's mood changed as perceptibly as though an icy draught had blown out the blazing fire—and I turned, to perceive a stumbling knot of bodies caught in an anteroom doorway.

"I fear some part of the Duchess's acquaintance are but too disguised in truth,"[13] I said to Anne Lefroy. "We had best make our *adieux,* and summon the chairs, before this rout turns to a riot."

"Nonsense. It is nothing but a bit of theatre—the stabbing of Duncan, I suspect." She stepped towards the anteroom with the others, and protesting, I followed.

Craning on tip-toe, the better to discern the man who had stolen Hugh Conyngham's scene, I comprehended a small salon to one side of the massive drawing-room, done up in Prussian blue picked out with gold. Its double doors were thrown wide and obscured by a press of bodies. The late Duke's reception room?—Or perhaps a study? But all such observations were fleeting, for my eyes were fixed on *one* alone—the mettlesome Knight, my erstwhile dance partner. He strained in the grip of two stout fellows, and his reddened countenance worked in horror.

At his feet lay the White Harlequin.

The face still wore its mask, but behind the lozenge of velvet the eyes were sightless and staring. Blood pooled slowly on the Duchess's Savonnerie carpet, as though the man called Portal had wished to exchange his white-patterned stuff for the rival Harlequin's red.

I raised one hand to my lips to stifle a scream, and with the other, gripped Madam Lefroy's arm. She tensed beneath my fingers.

A woman brushed past me with a flash of black curls, and fell in supplication at the Harlequin's feet. The Medusa, Maria Conyngham. With shaking fingers she snatched at the dead man's mask.

"Richard! Oh, Richard!"

The voice of a bereaved mother, or an abandoned wife—the soul of a woman destroyed by grief. The crowd parted to admit Hugh Conyngham to the hushed circle, and he knelt at his sister's side.

"Dead!" she cried, and fell weeping on his breast.

"Kinny?"

The voice, clear and sweet as a child's, was the Lady Desdemona's. She stood just behind Hugh Conyngham, on the edge of the crowd. The pallor of her face was extreme. But in her composure and the intensity of her dark grey eyes I saw something of the fierce Trow-

---

[13] To be "disguised" in Austen's day was to be quite thoroughly drunk.—*Editor's note.*

bridge will. Without even a look for the murdered Harlequin, she crossed to the Knight.

"Kinny, *what have you done?*"

"Nothing, Mona! I swear it! I found him just as you see!"

"Then show me what is in your hand!"

Her brother started, and released the thing, which fell clattering to the parquet floor—a bloody knife, chased in gold, as curved and deadly as a scimitar.

Chapter 2

Wilberforce Elliot
Pays a Call

12 December 1804, cont.

~

THE UPROAR OF THE ASSEMBLED GUESTS WAS SWIFT AND SUDDEN. THE
Dowager Duchess of Wilborough screamed, the Knight was wrestled
into a chair, and not a few of the guests made swiftly for the door—
being disinclined, one supposes, to a meeting with the constables
that evening, and all the tedium it should require.

For my part, I had not the slightest hesitation in remaining. The
murder of the White Harlequin had rendered Lord Harold's business irrelevant; but he should assuredly be summoned now from
London, and my observation of all in the Wilborough household
should be as gold. My thoughts were suddenly diverted, however, by
Anne Lefroy's seeking a chair, her pallor extreme. Madam can never
rely upon a physical courage in the face of blood, and I feared
she should faint. *Where* were Henry and Eliza? A swift glance for a
tower of birds' nests and ship models—and I waved my sister to my
side.

"Do you look to Madam Lefroy," I enjoined, "while I attend to
the murder."

"But of course." Eliza was all efficiency. "Henry! A glass of water,
if you please—or better yet, brandy! And quickly!"

I returned to the anteroom doorway, and there found the Knight
in the midst of an outburst.

"But do observe the open window! I assure you, whoever committed this dreadful deed has jumped to the paving below! Quickly, Jenkins—to the street, or he shall escape us entirely!"

The man Jenkins hesitated, bewildered, and glanced to the Dowager Duchess.

"Go, go—and take Samuel with you!" she urged him. The footman dashed for the stairs.

The massive Moor, his face blackened with burnt cork and his turban formed of a lady's cashmere shawl, pushed his way to the fore of the pitiful scene.

"My name is Gibbs," he said, "and I have the honour to act as Her Grace's physician. I must be permitted to examine the gentleman."

"It is Mr. Richard Portal," Maria Conyngham told the doctor. She was weeping still, but struggled for composure. "He is our company's manager. Your physick will avail him nothing, however. The knife blade found his heart."

"Hush now, Maria," her brother said, and drew her to his bosom. Dr. Gibbs dismissed the pair with a glance and bent to the unfortunate Portal. He felt of his wrists and neck, then laid an ear to the blood-soaked breast. And at last, with surprising gentleness, the physician removed the black velvet mask.

All evidence of the Harlequin's former gaiety was fled. The expression of agonised horror that still gripped his countenance was distressing in the extreme. Richard Portal was revealed as a not unattractive gentleman, but well past his first youth; his brown hair was touched with grey, and his complexion reddened by exposure or drink. Dr. Gibbs closed the staring eyes, and arranged the lifeless limbs in an attitude of dignity; and then he turned to look at the Dowager.

Eugenie was huddled on a blue and gold settee. Lady Desdemona stood at her side.

"A constable should be summoned, Your Grace," Dr. Gibbs said quietly. "Elliot, the magistrate, is to be preferred, of course—but at this hour—"

As though conjured by his words, a bronze clock on the mantel began to chime. It had just gone two.

"I did not kill him, Gibbs," the Knight burst out, straining in his captors' grip. "You must believe me! I did not do this thing!"

"Be quiet, Simon." The Dowager Duchess's voice was weary. "You must save your words for the magistrate, my dear." Gripping the knobbed head of her cane, she rose a trifle unsteadily, patted Lady Desdemona's hand, and progressed towards the doorway. Her gaze she kept studiously averted from the dead man on the carpet. The hushed crowd of guests parted like a tide to permit her passage, then closed again around her.

"Your Grace," Dr. Gibbs called after Eugenie in a commanding voice. "Your Grace, I must beg your indulgence. Would you have the body removed?"

The Duchess halted in her stride, but did not turn. "Leave him, Gibbs," she replied. "Mr. Elliot will wish to view everything precisely as it was found. Later we may consider what is due to Mr. Portal—but for the nonce, I must summon the constables and despatch a letter to the magistrate's residence. Are you acquainted with the direction?"

"I am, Your Grace," Dr. Gibbs replied. "Mr. Elliot resides in Rivers Street."

"Very well. I shall write to him directly. But I must beg that no one depart this house until the constable or Mr. Elliot arrive."

The doors closed behind the Duchess—and that part of the assembled masquerade, that had not fled at the first instance of blood, commenced a dispirited milling about the drawing-room. I surveyed the ranks hastily, and could find no trace of Madam Lefroy's acquaintance, the Red Harlequin, or of the bearded Pierrot who had conversed at such length with Maria Conyngham. Some fifty guests arrayed in motley nonetheless remained. Most eyes were careful to avoid the pathetic figure felled upon the exquisite carpet, or the group of actors despondent at its feet; and Dr. Gibbs was so good as to summon a footman, and request some bed linen, for the composure of the body.

"Jane." Madam Lefroy raised a shaking hand to my arm. "I must leave this place at once. At once! I cannot bear the pall of death! I find in it a terrible presentiment!"

"More brandy, Henry," Eliza said tersely, "and perhaps some smelling salts. Enquire of Lady Desdemona."

My brother hastened away, and I knelt to Madam Lefroy.

"Dear friend," I said softly, "you must rally, I fear. Indeed you must. For we none of us may quit the household until the constables have come. At the first opportunity, I assure you, we shall summon a chaise and attend you home."

She closed her eyes and gripped my fingers painfully.

FOR THE CONSTABLES' ARRIVAL WAS REQUIRED PERHAPS A QUARTER-hour, the streets being all but deserted at that time of night. At the approach to Laura Place, however, the party encountered some difficulty—the way being blocked by an assemblage of chairmen in attendance upon the rout, and expectant of any amount of custom when it should be concluded. The news that a murder had occurred within, was incapable of deterring these hardy souls, who had braved a night of snow and considerable cold in pursuit of pence; and it was with a clamour of indignation, and the most vociferous protests, that they suffered the constables to clear them from the stoop.

I observed all this from the vantage of a drawing-room window, having grown intolerably weary of turning about the overheated room in attendance upon the Law. If Simon, Marquis of Kinsell, was to be credited—for such, I had learned, was the Knight's full title—then the chairmen must have observed the murderer in the act of leaping from the anteroom window. The prospect of that apartment gave out onto Laura Place, in company with the window at which I now stood. It should be a simple matter to question the fellows assembled below—

But I had only to entertain the thought, before it was superseded by another. Had the chairmen observed a figure to exit the Dowager's window in considerable stealth, should not they have given chase? One had only to shout out "Thief!" in any street of the city, and a crowd of willing pursuers was sure to form, intent upon the rewards of capture. But no hue or cry had arisen from below—and thus a faint seed of doubt regarding Lord Kinsfell must form itself in my heart.

A sudden hush brought my gaze around from the window—the constables were arrived, two grizzled elders more accustomed to calling out the watch than attending a murder among the Quality—and with them, Mr. Wilberforce Elliot.

He was a large and shambling man, got up in a wine-coloured frock coat, much stained, and a soiled shirt. His neckcloth was barely equal to the corpulence of his neck, and in being forced into service, had so impeded the flow of air to his lungs, that his countenance was brilliantly red and overlaid with moisture. But Wilberforce Elliot was an imposing figure, nonetheless, in that room arrayed for frivolity—a figure that stunned the assemblage to a devout and listening stillness.

"Your Grace," the magistrate said, as he doffed his hat and bowed. A clubbed hank of black hair, thick and dirty as a bear's, tumbled over one shoulder. "Your humble servant."

"Mr. Elliot," the Dowager Duchess replied. "You are very good to venture out at such an hour."

"It is nothing, Your Grace—I had not yet sought my bed. May I be permitted to view the body?"

Eugenie inclined her head, and gestured towards the anteroom. After an instant's hesitation, and the briefest survey of the appalled onlookers, Mr. Elliot made his ponderous way to the dead man's side.

I let fall the window drape, and joined my party at a little remove from the anteroom itself, but affording an excellent prospect of the interior through the opened connecting doors.

"What a devil of a man to intrude upon the Dowager's misery," my sister Eliza whispered. "He might be Pantagruel from the Comédie Française! But I suppose the Duchess is familiar with such characters of old."

"Eliza!" Henry muttered fiercely in his wife's ear. "I have told you that oaths cannot become a lady!"

With a sigh and a grunt, Mr. Elliot forced his bulk to a creaking posture by Mr. Portal's head. A quick twitch of the covering linen; a shrewd appraisal; and a forefinger bluntly probed at the dead man's chest.

"And where is the knife?"

Dr. Gibbs cleared his throat and glanced at Lord Kinsfell. The Marquis sat with bowed head and slumped shoulders, his attention entirely turned within. The physician reached for the bloody thing, which had been laid on a napkin by one of the footmen, and handed it to the magistrate.

"Ah, indeed," Mr. Elliot said through pursed lips. "A cunning blade, is it not?"

No reply seemed adequate to this observation, but none was apparently deemed necessary.

"And you, sir, would be—?"

"Dr. Gibbs, of Milsom Street," the Moor replied. "I have the honour to attend Her Grace."

"Then I venture to suppose that you will declare the gentleman dead, will you not, Dr. Gibbs? What a quantity of blood there is, to be sure!"

Mr. Elliot sat back upon his massive haunches, and surveyed the body with a rueful look. "To come to such a pass, and in such a suit of clothes! I fancy you should not like to end in a similar fashion, eh, Gibbs? —A similar *fashion*, d'you see?" The corpulent magistrate laughed heartily. "Aye, that's very good."

A sudden whirl of skirts brought the black-haired Medusa furiously to his side.

"Mr. Elliot—if *that* is how you are called—I would beg you to comport yourself with some decency and respect! A man has been foully murdered—and you would make witticisms upon his attire? It is intolerable, sir! I must demand that you apologise immediately!"

"Apologise?" Mr. Elliot heaved himself painfully to his feet, and regarded Maria Conyngham with penetration. "And to whom must I apologise, pray? For the gentleman in question is beyond caring, my dear. And now tell me. Are you not Maria Conyngham, of the The-atre Royal?"

"I am, sir."

"Enjoyed your Viola most thoroughly. Now be a good girl and stand aside. Your Grace!"

"Yes, Mr. Elliot?"

"I should like an account of this evening's amusement."

The Dowager glanced about her helplessly.

"I shall tell him, Grandmère," interjected the Lady Desdemona. She had been seated near her brother, her hand on his, and now rose with an expression of fortitude, her countenance pale but composed. "Mr. Portal is the manager of the Theatre Royal, whose company we intended to celebrate this evening. The masquerade was some hours underway, when we were so fortunate as to enjoy a recital from *Macbeth*, performed by Mr. Hugh Conyng-ham—"

"Mr. Conyngham is where?"

"At your service, Mr. Elliot," the actor replied, stepping forward.

"And in the recital you were positioned where?"

"In the drawing-room opposite, before the fire."

"The assembly regarding you?"

"Of course."

"And Mr. Portal was—?"

Lady Desdemona broke in with an exclamation of annoyance. "But that is what I am telling you!"

Her brother stood up abruptly. "Mr. Portal was within the anteroom where his body now lies. I know this, because I thrust open the door in the midst of Mr. Conyngham's speech, and found him expired upon the floor. His assailant must have escaped through the anteroom window."

Lord Kinsfell's eyes were blazing as he conveyed this intelligence to the magistrate, but he swallowed painfully at its close; and I guessed him to labour under an excess of emotion all the more pitiable for its containment.

Mr. Elliot's gaze swept the length of the Knight's figure. "Do I have the honour of addressing the Marquis of Kinsfell?"

"You do, sir."

"Heir to the Duchy of Wilborough?"

"I may claim that distinction."

"—and possessor of the knife that murdered Mr. Richard Portal?"

A hesitation, and Lord Kinsfell bowed his head. "The knife has long been in our family's possession, yes. It is a decorative blade from Bengal, bestowed upon my father by the directors of the East India Company."

The magistrate looked puzzled. "Might any person have come by it so readily as yourself, my lord?"

"I must suppose so. The knife was generally displayed upon the mantel of this room." Lord Kinsfell gestured to a small platform made of teak, ideal for the positioning of a decorative blade, now forlorn and bare above the fireplace.

"Am I correct, my lord, in assuming that you pulled the blade from Mr. Portal's breast?"

A muffled cry broke from Maria Conyngham.

"I did, sir," Lord Kinsfell retorted, with a glance for the actress, "but I was not the agent of its descent into Mr. Portal's heart." He passed a trembling hand across his brow. "I was discovered in the attempt to aid or revive him only—and should better have pursued his murderer."

"Ah—his murderer." Mr. Elliot turned his back upon the Mar-

quis and paced towards the mantel, his eyes roving about the panelled walls to either side. ''The fellow, you would have it, who
dropped from the window. A man should require wings, my lord, to
achieve such a distance from casement to paving-stone. But perhaps
your murderer came disguised this e'en as a bird. Or an imp of Hell,
intent upon the snatching of a soul. We may wonder to what region
Mr. Portal has descended, may we not?''

''Mr. Elliot!'' Maria Conyngham cried. ''Remember where you
are, sir!''

The magistrate bowed benignly and crossed to the anteroom window. A quick survey of the ground below, and he summoned a constable with a snap of the fingers.

''You there, Shaw—to the chairmen, and be quick! You are
to enquire whether any observed a flight from the sill of this window.''

''Very good, sir.''

''Mr. Elliot,'' the Dowager broke in, ''my footmen, Jenkins and
Samuel, attempted to pursue the assailant some moments after his
flight. But having little notion of the villain's appearance or direction, alas, they could not find him.''

''Naturally not. Their slippers,'' Elliot rejoined with a critical air,
''are hardly conducive to pursuit. Lord Kinsfell—''

''Mr. Elliot?''

''For what reason did you follow Mr. Portal into this room?''

''I did not follow Portal anywhere,'' the Marquis objected hotly. ''I
thought him already thrown out of the house.''

''Indeed? And upon what pretext?''

A brief silence; the exchange of looks. Lady Desdemona attempted an answer.

''Mr. Portal had so far forgot himself, Mr. Elliot, as to behave with
considerable impropriety before Her Grace's guests. My brother
thought it best that he be shown to the street before his actions
became insupportable.''

''That is a gross prevarication!'' Hugh Conyngham burst out.
''Had your brother not seen fit to challenge poor Portal to a duel,
my lady, he might yet be alive!''

''A duel?'' Mr. Elliot enquired with interest. ''And what could
possibly have inspired a duel, pray?''

Lord Kinsfell drew himself up to his full height—which was not inconsiderable. He was a very well-made young man. "I am not at liberty to say, Mr. Elliot. It was a matter of some delicacy."

"An affair of honour, in short."

"As all such matters must be."

"Of that, my lord, I am hardly convinced. Duelling is murder, as you must be aware."

"In cases where one of the opponents is killed, perhaps," the Marquis replied dismissively.

"Are you so certain of your aim, my lord, as to intend to miss? Or so contemptuous of Mr. Portal's?"

Lord Kinsfell did not reply, but the colour mounted to his cheeks. "It is of no account whatsoever what I intended, for Portal is dead, and by an unknown hand."

"Is he, indeed? And why, may I ask Your Grace," the magistrate continued, with a glare from under his eyebrows at the Duchess, "was Mr. Portal *not* conveyed to the street?"

"Whatever my grandson's feelings, I deemed it necessary to comport myself as befits a hostess," Eugenie replied with dignity. "It seemed to me more suitable to allow Mr. Portal an interval of rest and quiet, until some member of the company should be able to escort him home."

"Yes, I see." The magistrate's beady black eyes, so reminiscent of two currants sunk in a Christmas pudding, moved from the Marquis to the Dowager and back again. "And so you entered this room, Lord Kinsfell, in the very midst of Mr. Conyngham's declamation?"

"I did."

"And to what purpose?"

"I meant to pass through it to the back hall, and proceed thence to my rooms. I was utterly fagged, if you must know, and desperate for quiet."

Mr. Elliot glanced around. "Pass to the hallway *where*, my lord? For I observe no other door than the one by which you entered."

Lord Kinsfell strode impatiently to the far side of the fireplace, and pressed against a panel of the wall. With a creak, it swung inwards—a barely discernible door. "It is intended for the ease of the servants, but it makes a useful passage when the main door to the hall is blocked."

"As it would have been during Mr. Conyngham's recital."

"Obviously. The door from the drawing-room to the back hall

stands to the right of where Mr. Conyngham was positioned. I should have had to force my way through the greater part of the company to attain it. And that I did not wish to do.''

''Commendable, I am sure. Mr. Conyngham must certainly regard it thus,'' Mr. Elliot said slowly, and reached a well-fed hand to the silently swinging door. ''Very cunning, indeed. May I request a taper, Your Grace?''

The taper was duly brought from the fire, and held aloft in Mr. Elliot's hand; the magistrate leaned into the passage, and snorted with regret. ''How very disappointing, to be sure. Not a cask of gold, nor an abducted princess can I find—nothing but a cleanly-swept hall of perhaps a dozen yards, such as one might see in any well-regulated household. You are plainly no friend to intrigue and romance, Your Grace. For of what use is a passage, if it be not dank and cobwebbed, and descending precipitately to a subterranean cell?''

Not even Maria Conyngham found strength to protest at this; but her looks were hardly easy. She followed Mr. Elliot's every move, as he closed the passage and threw his taper into the fire. To Lord Kinsfell he turned at last, and enquired, ''And who among Her Grace's household is familiar with this passage, my lord?''

''Everyone, I must suppose,'' replied the Marquis.

''Very good, my lord—you will please to sit down, Mr. Conyngham!''

''Mr. Elliot?''

''Were you long intending to declaim your passage from *Macbeth*—or spurred to the act by the whim of the moment?''

''I was requested to perform by the Dowager Duchess, when first the invitation to Laura Place was extended.''

''So it was a scheme of some weeks' preparation, I apprehend?''

''To recite a part of which I am so much the master, must require a very little preparation, sir,'' the actor replied stiffly.

''Quite, quite—but you do not take my meaning, Mr. Conyngham. The interval of the speech was intended as a piece of the evening's entertainment—in short, it was *planned*?''

''It was.''

''Capital! And how long did you spend in prating and posing?''

''Mr. Elliot!''

''Oh, God's breath—answer the question, man!'' Hugh Conyngham's air of contempt deepened visibly. ''I should judge that I spoke for no less than five, and no more than ten, minutes, sir.''

"During which time Mr. Portal met his end.''

"So we must assume.''

"Any cries? Any scuffle?"

"Nothing of the sort—until, that is, Lord Kinsfell entered the room.''

Mr. Elliot heaved a sigh, and threw his corpulent frame onto the settee. It creaked beneath his weight. One blunt-fingered hand caressed his chins, and the other lay limp upon his knee. He seemed to be waiting for something—divine inspiration? But no—it was the return of the constable named Shaw. The man appeared and claimed the magistrate's attention.

"Well, my good fellow? Was our Devil's imp observed?''

Constable Shaw shook his head. In so anxious a moment, the gesture *must* be eloquent. I felt my hopes to sink.

"Lord Kinsfell!''

The Knight inclined his head.

"You persist in refusing to offer some explanation for your conduct?''

The Marquis's colour was high, and I detected the effects of anxiety in his countenance. "I do not understand you, Mr. Elliot. I have offered the only possible explanation under the circumstances.''

"Rot!'' The magistrate grunted, and slapped his knees with decision. "Very well—come along with you, my lord.''

"I beg your pardon, sir?''

"To the gaol!''

The Dowager Duchess cried out with horror, and staggered at her granddaughter's shoulder. Lady Desdemona's arm came up in support, but she uttered not a word.

"I am very sorry, Your Grace,'' the magistrate continued, "but there it is—we must have Lord Kinsfell along to the gaol! For one man is dead, as you will observe, and another must pay for it; and in the absence of the unseen fellow at the window, I cannot think that anyone will do nearly so well as his lordship!''

"But I am innocent!'' the Marquis cried.

"Perhaps you are, my lord,'' Mr. Elliot responded kindly. "Perhaps, indeed, you are. But what does that signify, if you cannot possibly prove it?''

Chapter 3

The Tiger Rampant

12 December 1804, cont.

~

I AWOKE THIS MORNING RATHER LATER THAN IS MY WONT, BEING entirely overset by the events of last evening and the weariness of my return from Laura Place. Thus I made my way to the breakfast-room in every expectation of finding it quite deserted. But here presentiment failed me—for at the sound of my step upon the threshold, the assembled Austens each turned a countenance suffused with false innocence. From their eager looks it was apparent that word of the murder had preceded me.

"Well, my love!" my mother cried, waving her napkin with some animation, "make haste! Make haste! We have been expecting you this quarter-hour. I will not be satisfied until I have heard it from your own lips. A lovers' quarrel, so Mr. Austen's paper says, but with theatre people, it might have been as much a joke as anything. There is no accounting for an actor's taste."

"Although in this instance," I observed, as I pulled back my chair, "it is the manager who is dead."

"There, now!" My mother rapped the table triumphantly. "And so we cannot hope ever to learn the truth of the matter from *him*. All dispute is at an end. But I cannot be entirely mute upon the subject, Jane. I cannot turn so blind an eye to the comportment of my youngest daughter. *How* you can find diversion in such a business—"

"Diversion, ma'am?"

"You have a decided predilection for violence, my dear, and if the habit does not alter, no respectable gentleman will consider you twice. Only reflect," she admonished, with a pointed gesture from her butter knife—"you are *not* growing any younger, Jane."

"Nor are we any of us."

"Jane, dear, let me pour out your chocolate," said my sister Cassandra, reaching hastily for my cup.

"Tea, rather—for my head *does* ache dreadfully."

"Gentlemen of discernment," my mother continued, warming to her subject, "cannot bear a young lady's being too familiar with blood. I have always held that a girl should know as little of blood as possible, even if she be mad for hunting. When the fox is killed, it behooves a lady to be busy about her mount, or on the brink of a pretty observation regarding the landscape's picturesque. So I believe, and so our James agrees—and he hunts with the Vyne,¹ you know, and must be treated to refinement in such matters on every occasion. Blood, and torn flesh, may only be termed vulgar. Are not you of my opinion, Mr. Austen? Was it not very bad of Jane to have remained in such a place, once the knives were got out?"

"Oh, there cannot be two opinions on the subject, my love," my father replied with a satiric eye. "A knife will always be vulgar, particularly in the drawing-room. The kitchens and the dining-parlour are its proper province; but when it seeks to climb so high as a Duchess's salon—even a Dowager Duchess's—we may consider ourselves on the point of revolution."

"Dear madam," I intervened, "be assured that I quitted Laura Place as soon as it was possible to do so. The general flight of guests rendered chairs remarkably scarce, and it was a full hour before Henry could obtain a suitable conveyance—a chaise summoned from his inn—which *would* set Madam Lefroy down in Russell Street before returning to Green Park Buildings. We hastened home as swiftly as our means allowed. Do but pity poor Henry and Eliza, who faced a longer journey still to their rooms at the White Hart, before

¹ The Vyne, in Sherborne St. John, Hampshire, was the ancestral home of the Chute family and their entailed heirs; Jane's eldest brother, James Austen, was vicar of the parish from 1791, and frequently hunted with William-John Chute, master of the Vyne foxhounds.—*Editor's note.*

finding the mercy of their beds. They cannot have arrived before four o'clock."

"Well," my mother said with some asperity, "since the matter is past all repair—the *vulgarity* endured—you might favour us with a report of the affair."

"Was Lord Kinsfell truly taken up for murder?" Cassandra enquired. So the papers had printed that much.

"He was," I replied sadly, "the knife having fallen from his grasp before an hundred witnesses. The manager of the Theatre Royal, one Richard Portal, lay bleeding at Kinsfell's feet, all life extinguished. The knife point found his heart. Or so said Dr. Gibbs, who examined the body. He is the Dowager Duchess's physician, and was present last evening at Her Grace's invitation, in the guise of a Moor."

"But is it likely that the Marquis of Kinsfell would stoop so low as to murder a common actor?" My father was all amazement.

I sipped at my tea and found that it was grown disappointingly cold. The virtuous Austens had lingered long over the cloth in expectation of my intelligence.

"Mr. Portal was hardly a common actor, Father. He has had the management of the company since Mrs. Siddons's day, and has won the respect of all in Bath. It is at Portal's direction and expense that the new theatre in Beauford Square is being built.[2] Mr. Portal was possessed of high spirits and considerable address—a tolerably handsome gentleman, in the flood tide of life. I may hardly credit the notion of his murder, much less Lord Kinsfell's guilt; but I must suppose that the magistrate, Mr. Elliot, will very soon find the matter out."

"You presume no such thing," my father retorted testily. "You abhor justices with a passion, as I very well know. 'They seek only to make a case against some unfortunate innocents, while the true culprit goes free.' Is not that a quotation, my dear Jane, from one of your very own letters? A letter written from Scargrave Manor?"

"I will not pretend to an unalloyed admiration for English justice," I ventured, "but I may, perhaps, have spoken then too warmly. I do not abhor such respectable gentlemen as Sir William

[2] This opened for the 1805 season, despite Portal's death.—*Editor's note.*

Reynolds.³ Nor may I assume that Mr. Elliot is entirely incapable. Mr. Elliot is a singular fellow, assuredly—both gross in his humours and repulsive in his person—but a shrewd and cunning intellect nonetheless."

"If Lord Kinsfell was found with the knife," Cassandra innocently observed, "what doubt can possibly exist? Does his lordship deny the murder?"

"Naturally!" I said, with more attention to my plate than it deserved. "He should be a fool to do otherwise, whether he be guilty or no."

"Though he uttered a falsehood? Such wickedness!"

It is remarkable, indeed, to spend all of one's life in the company of a lady so thoroughly *good* as Cassandra. Never mind that a falsehood, at such a juncture, should be as nothing to the shedding of blood—the slightest misstep is capable of causing my sister pain. It is well, perhaps, that the untimely demise of her beloved intended should have left her pining in the single state. The vicissitudes of marriage—with that frailest of creatures, a *man*—should certainly have been the death of her.

"Lord Kinsfell insists that in the very midst of Hugh Conyngham's declamation—a passage from *Macbeth*—he was overcome with an excess of heat and spirits, and intended to seek his bedchamber by passing through the little anteroom at one side of the main party. Upon throwing open the double doors, he observed Mr. Portal in his Harlequin dress, prone upon the floor with a most hideous blade protruding from his breast. Kinsfell gave a shout, and leapt to Portal's side; he felt for a pulse, and then effected the removal of the knife; but was swiftly overpowered by two stout fellows convinced of his dangerous intent. It was only then that I observed him myself."

"And this Portal? Had you remarked his figure before?"

"I had." The memory of Lord Kinsfell's bitter words to Richard Portal brought a frown to my countenance. I pushed aside my cup of cooling tea and toyed hopelessly with a piece of bread. Cook had allowed it to grow stale again.

"And did he betray any morbid sensibility?" Cassandra enquired.

³ Sir William Reynolds, a former schoolmate of Austen's father at Oxford, was the baffled justice last encountered in *Jane and the Unpleasantness at Scargrave Manor.—Editor's note.*

"Of what, my dear?"

"Of his impending death! Did he comport himself as might a marked man?"

"Indeed, Cassandra, I might fancy you to have indulged too much the taste for horrid novels! Portal seemed no more marked than *any* eligible gentleman at a rout full of ladies!" I hesitated, uncertain how much to divulge. "I *did* observe him to dance with Lady Desdemona Trowbridge, Lord Kinsfell's sister, and somewhat later, he treated the better part of the company to a scene of some belligerence."

"On the point of blows, was he? And with whom?" my father asked.

"With Lord Kinsfell, I regret to say."

He touched his napkin to his lips, eyes averted.

"An actor! Well!" my mother cried, as though picking up a thread of conversation quite lost long ago. "They are always coming to blows, with swords or pistols or ruffians for hire. One sees it constantly in Orchard Street—*Hamlet* is nothing but a brawl, though it pretends to treat of adultery. I never leave the theatre without feeling I have been pummelled from one end to the other."

"But did Kinsfell perceive no one else in the room?" my father enquired.

"He did not. He persists in believing the murderer exited by the anteroom window, which stood open at Portal's discovery." I gazed soberly at the Reverend Austen's lined and kindly face. In three-and-seventy years, my father had seen much of the evil men may do, though from so retired a vantage as a Hampshire parsonage. "But Lord Kinsfell's assurances are open to doubt, Father. Not one of the chairmen assembled in the street below admitted to having observed a similar flight; and if they had, the man should certainly have been taken. The drop from window to pavement, moreover, must be full thirty feet. For any to attempt the ground—in darkness and in haste—is madness. The man should surely have broken a leg."

"But you forget the heavy snow, my child. If there were a drift to break the fall—"

"The Dowager's footmen were assiduous in sweeping the pavement, for the accommodation of her guests," I replied wearily. "It seems unlikely that anyone quitted the house in so heedless a manner."

A brief silence fell over the breakfast table, and I saw once more in memory the Duchess's horror as Kinsfell was led away. But for Lady Desdemona, I believe Eugenie Wilborough should have sunk to a heap on the floor, her seventy years quite suddenly writ upon her face.

"Some toast, my dear? Or perhaps a muffin?"

"I believe I shall walk out, Mamma." I thrust my chair from the table. "A breath of air will do my head a world of good."

DESPITE THE HEAVY FALL OF SNOW LAST E'EN, THE SUN HAD CONSENTED to shine, with a brilliance that dazzled the eyes. I found that my own poor orbs, much weakened from years of plying my needle and pen in the indifferent light of a sitting-room candle, could barely sustain the force of the light, and so kept them fixed upon the paving-stones. Here the snow had begun to melt, and the water ran in rivulets along the gutter. In my cumbersome pattens, I picked my way around the puddles, clicking and clattering in company with every young lady so stout as to venture out-of-doors. Sydney Gardens should be impassable on such a day; my accustomed walk along the verge of the canal must be foresworn for drier weather. And so I ignored the roads leading down towards the river, and determined upon the much shorter distance through Queen Square, in the direction of Edgar's Buildings.

Edgar's Buildings are fine, respectable establishments, offering lodgings for respectable families who come to Bath yearly in the pursuit of health and marriageable young men. They comprise as well, on their ground floors, a group of respectable shops—and in one of these, I had remarked a very fetching demi-turban of apricot sarcenet, adorned with ostrich feathers, such as one might wear with a gown of the same fashionable shade. I had just such a gown in view—indeed, had one as yet in pieces, at a formidable mantua-maker renowned in all of Bath for her artistry.[4] My peach silk confection, so clearly suited to a Duchess's rout, or a night at the theatre, or a concert in the Upper Rooms—a gown that should be utterly too

[4] Mantua-maker was the eighteenth-century term for dressmaker. Jane betrays her age by employing it here. It derives from the mantua, a loose style of gown common in the second half of the eighteenth century, made of silk from Mantua, Italy.—*Editor's note.*

fine for my usual diversion of Aunt Leigh-Perrot's insipid card parties—should be the sole spoil of recent misadventure. Not two
months ago, I had purchased the stuff from smugglers in Lyme. By
such small sacrifice of Miss Austen's judgement and integrity was a
vicious murderer apprehended; and I may confess to no great unwill-
ingness to revel in the gain.

With very little fuss, and only the negligible discomfort occasioned
by over-hasty coachmen and their great splashing beasts, I soon
achieved Edgars Buildings. My enquiry as to the cost of such a thing
as an apricot demi-turban, arranged cunningly with plumes, was the
matter of but a moment; and the acknowledgement that it should be
too dear for my purse, required but another. I turned away, lost in
contemplation of how a similar headdress might be contrived,
through the remnants of my own cut-up silk, and the loan of my
sister Eliza's feathers—when a loud hallooing from the street
brought my attention to bear.

Outriders, in a gorgeous livery of black and gold, with Bengal caps
and tassels; postilions, mounted on the wheelers,[5] similarly arrayed;
and the coach-and-four, magnificent and sleek, the horses as black as
night. A spirited team, chuffing and tossing their heads as they
turned down Milsom Street—bound, no doubt, for the Bear or the
White Hart. I strained to make out the coat of arms on the coach's
door—but it was unknown to me. Certainly *not* the Wilborough device; and so the conveyance could hardly hold Lord Harold. That the
Gentleman Rogue was posting towards Bath, however, upon the early
morning receipt of an express from his mother, I little doubted.
Perhaps in the company of his brother, the Duke.

"The Devil's own cub," muttered a gentleman not three paces
away. He stood similarly arrested on the pavement, his eyes following
the careening coach.

"Who is it, guv'nor?" cried a small boy, skipping and bouncing
with excitement.

The gentleman turned angrily away, as though offended, and strode
briskly towards Gay Street. His small persecutor kept pace, dodging the
vicious stab of a walking stick with effortless grace. "Come on, now!
Tell us who 'tis, guv'nor! Ol' Prinny, maybe? Or the Queen?"

---

[5] *Wheelers* is a term connoting the horses closest to the carriage wheels—in a
team of four, the two harnessed first within the traces.—*Editor's note.*

"The Earl of Swithin, you unfortunate cull," his quarry spat out, "and now I suggest you take yourself off. Swithin's hardly the sort to throw you a penny for carting his dunnage. He's more likely to eat you for breakfast."

The urchin chortled, doffed his cap, and sped off in the direction of Cheap Street.

After a pause for consideration, I sedately did the same.

My sister Eliza was firmly ensconced in a suite of rooms at the White Hart, her maid, Manon, and her little dog, Pug, comprising fully half of her establishment, while the remainder—bedchambers for herself and Henry, with a sitting-room in between—might all be taken as Eliza's to rule, so little evidence of my brother could I find. Such an apportionment of space at the White Hart must be very dear, and I wondered at the expense, and at my brother's having failed to take lodgings in some retired square. The Henry Austens intended a visit to Bath of some three or four weeks, and it was unusual in such cases to remain more than a few days at the coaching inns. But Eliza, though accustomed to luxury, is singularly careless about convention—the result, perhaps, of her itinerant childhood. She moved with her mother, my aunt, from India to England and thence to Europe—fixing, at last, in the environs of Versailles. Even in London, Eliza is rarely at rest; she has occasioned the removal of my brother's household several times already, and fully intends to continue the practice as long as a suitable establishment should offer.

Even her grave, I suspect, will be a temporary domicile.

"My dear Jane!" she cried now, throwing aside her netting and smoothing her hair. "And are you quite recovered from the Duchess's rout? I am on the very point of venturing to the Pump Room. You will accompany me?"

She was dressed today in bottle-green silk, far too fine for morning wear, with small puffed sleeves and a plunging neck. A large green stone glittered on her finger.

"Is that an emerald I see, Eliza?"

"Oh, pooh," she cried, "it is nothing of the sort. A tourmaline merely—a gift from my godfather, Mr. Hastings. We met with him only last week. You will never guess, Jane, who has come to the inn."

"The Earl of Swithin?"

"The Earl of Swithin! How did you know? You will have seen the coach, I suspect, with its device of the snarling tiger. The Swithin fortune was made in India, you understand—my mother was intimate with *his,* Lady Swithin being one of the few who did not reproach Mamma for the attentions of Mr. Hastings—and the tiger was ever their device. I should know the coat of arms anywhere. He is a very fine-looking young man. Though not *too* young. I should put him at thirty."[6]

"Eliza," I said, in a tone of mock reproof. "You *will* not flirt in the very midst of an inn. Have a care!"

My sister shrugged her lovely shoulders. "I only hung about the stairway for a time, the better to observe his ascent; and I may fairly say that *nothing* should induce me now to trade a coaching inn for hired lodgings, be they ever so grand, and in Camden Place!"

"You may be certain that Lord Swithin will do so."

"Then we must hasten away, my dear, if we are to have a glimpse of him! I heard him charge his manservant to await his return from the Pump Room!"

It is the Pump Room, in truth—situated only steps from the White Hart—that makes the inn so convenient to Eliza; she is forever looking into the place, to meet with her acquaintance, or to spy upon those who are newly arrived. My rented lodgings in a retired square should be insupportably dull for the little Comtesse; and I understood my brother Henry the better. A bored Eliza is a petulant Eliza—a complaining and a declining Eliza, who fancies herself miserable with all manner of mysterious ailments. She should never last a fortnight in retirement.

•　　•　　•

[6] Eliza Austen was born Eliza Hancock, the daughter of Philadelphia Austen (the Reverend George Austen's sister) and Tysoe Saul Hancock, a surgeon with the East India Company. While in India Philadelphia Hancock was rumored to have "abandoned herself to Mr. Hastings." Warren Hastings, the Governor-General of Bengal from 1772 to 1785, served as Eliza's godfather and placed 10,000 pounds in trust for her; Eliza later named her only son Hastings. It was commonly believed, though never acknowledged, that Eliza was Warren Hastings's daughter.—*Editor's note.*

IT IS MANY MONTHS SINCE I LAST ENTERED THE PUMP ROOM—FOR being little inclined myself to the waters, I could find no purpose in an errand to that part of town, beyond an idle promenading about the lofty-ceilinged room. That the better part of Bath was engaged in that very pursuit, I immediately observed upon the present occasion; a hum of discourse rose above the clatter of pattens and half-boots, as a gaily-dressed Christmas crowd trod the bare planks of the floor. Pale winter light streamed through the clerestory windows. When last I had entered the Pump Room, I now recalled, the warmth of August had turned the dust motes to gold. I had been taking leave of a friend, before journeying south to Lyme.

"Jane!"

I shook myself from reverie, and espied Eliza hard by the pump attendant, a glass of water in her hand.

"Do not you mean to make a trial of the waters?" Eliza exclaimed.

"How can you think it possible, my dear?" I replied. "You forget the example of my Uncle Leigh-Perrot, and his two glasses per day these twenty-odd years. Never has water done so little to improve a faulty constitution, or to cure a persistent gout. I shall place *my* faith in a daily constitutional. It may claim a decided advantage in scenic enjoyment, and cannot hope to impair the bowels."[7]

"Pshaw. Come and examine the book," Eliza rejoined comfortably, as she turned back the pages of a calf-bound volume, in which the most recent visitors had inscribed their names and directions. "We must learn who is come to be gay in Bath. Mr. John Julius Angerstein and Mrs. Angerstein. *Well.* And so they have left their home in Blackheath, and abandoned the Princess of Wales to her scandalous beaux. The Honourable Matthew Small, Captain, Royal Navy. Well, we want none of *him,* do we? For a naval man torn from the sea cannot, I think, be very agreeable. Officers are always labouring under the influence of a wound, or a gouty manifestation. Mr. and Mrs. Jens Wolff. Capital! He is the Danish Consul, you know, and *she* is nothing short of a beauty. They lodge in Rivers Street. I have not seen Isabella Wolff this age!"

[7] James Leigh-Perrot was Mrs. Austen's brother. He added the surname Perrot to Leigh in order to inherit the Perrot fortune. Although his principal seat was Scarlets, an estate of his wife's in Berkshire, he spent half of every year in Paragon Buildings, Bath, for his health.—*Editor's note.*

And so, as Eliza exclaimed and brooded, I allowed my mind once more to wander. My eyes I permitted to rove as well, in search of a nobleman of imposing aspect. I lacked Eliza's knowledge of the Earl of Swithin's past, but I had heard enough of that gentleman's reputation to believe him stern and unyielding. His suit had driven Lady Desdemona Trowbridge from her home in London—had driven her, perhaps, into the arms of Mr. Richard Portal, who now lay dead. For what else but the theatre manager's impropriety towards the lady could have so excited her brother's contempt?

"I beg your pardon, ma'am, but if I am not mistaken—are you not Mrs. Henry Austen?"

We turned—and observed a gentleman of some sixty years at least, and quite extraordinary in his aspect. He was short, and lithe, and fussily dressed, in a sky-blue jacket of sarcenet, a lavender silk waistcoat overlaid with bronze cherries, and light-coloured pantaloons well tucked into glowing Hessians. The stiff white points of his collar were so high as to disguise his ears, and render any effort at turning the head quite beyond his power; and the arrangement of his neckcloth must surely rival the Beau's.[8] But all this would be as nothing—merely the trappings of a dandy more suited to a gentleman half his age—in comparison with the excessive ugliness of his features. The man resembled nothing so much as a baboon.

"Mr. Cosway, to be sure!" the little Comtesse cried, and extended her hand with every affectation of delight. "What felicity, in finding oneself not *entirely* without friends! How come you to leave St. James, my dear sir, in such a season?"

"A touch of the gout, Mrs. Austen, which I must forfend—though I confess, with the end of the world so close upon us all, it hardly seems worth the trouble."

"Indeed," Eliza replied smoothly, with barely a flicker of an eyelid at the gentleman's singularity of address. "One should meet any eventuality, extraordinary or commonplace, at the absolute pitch of health. But I *must* have the honour of acquainting you with my husband's sister, Miss Austen. Jane—Mr. Richard Cosway, the principal painter to His Majesty the Prince of Wales."

My senses were all alive; for though I may despise the Prince with

[8] Jane refers here to the most celebrated dandy of this period, George Bryan "Beau" Brummell (1778–1840), who set the trend in male dress.—*Editor's note.*

every pore of my being, I am not so determined in dislike as to learn nothing of a gossip. In silence, I made Mr. Cosway a courtesy. The face, the figure, were comprehensible to me now, from several de-cades' worth of caricatures in the papers. *This* was the extraordinary Cosway—whose cunning art at portraiture, particularly of a minia-ture kind, had swept the fashionable world; whose weekly salons in Pall Mall had been the sole entertainment worthy of fashionable attendance, throughout the past two decades; whose pretty little wife, full twenty years his junior, had so captivated the great with her accomplishments on the harp and at the easel. This was Richard Cosway, who followed Mesmer, and practised Animal Magnetism, and all manner of superstitious folly—now hard upon the brink of old age.[9] Trust my dear Eliza to claim acquaintance with every nota-ble oddity in the kingdom!

"And have you any news of your delightful wife?" my sister was enquiring, with becoming solicitude. "Maria is quite a prisoner, I presume, in the Monster's court?"

"Alas, I fear that she is—and it seems that any transport between England and the Continent is at a standstill. The outbreak of hostili-ties has overthrown my poor Maria's labours entirely. She had em-barked, as no doubt you know, upon a project of sketching the vast collection in Buonaparte's Louvre, for the edification of mankind. And hers was so admirable a project—the Prince of Wales himself subscribed, my dear Mrs. Austen—but it has come to naught. And so Mrs. Cosway has entirely quitted Paris."[10]

"But when is she likely to return? Can nothing be done for her present relief?"

Mr. Cosway hesitated. His eyes roved the room as if in search of acquaintance. "I may say that my wife is not without resources. She has made the best of her situation—and has gone to Lyons, for the

9 According to historian Roy Porter, both Maria and Richard Cosway indulged in the vogue for hypnotism, and subscribed to the lectures of John B. de Mainauduc, a pupil of the French Dr. Mesmer (1734-1815), who founded "ani-mal magnetism."—*Editor's note.*

10 Napoleon's wholesale confiscation of great works of art throughout Europe, and their assemblage in Paris, had occasioned Maria Cosway's project of record-ing for posterity every item in the newly opened Louvre. She embarked on the effort in late 1801. A proficient artist in her own right, Mrs. Cosway was at this time estranged from her husband. She did not return to England until 1817, when Cosway was in his dotage.—*Editor's note.*

purpose of founding a school for the education of young ladies in the Catholic faith. You know, of course, that she was born in Italy, and has always been a subject of Rome."

"But of course," Eliza replied dubiously. "And how long do you intend, sir, to dazzle Bath with your presence?"

"Not above three months, I assure you. I am bound for Brighton at Easter."

"How delightful!" Eliza cried. "I long to visit Brighton! What schemes and dissipation—the chariot races on the shingle! The breakfasts out-of-doors! The fireworks and expeditions—the crush of the balls! How vast an acquaintance one must cultivate, too, in the Prince's household train. The demands, I fear, are unending."

"The amusements of Brighton are as nothing to *me*, who must suffer from the want of solitude that such a pleasure party demands; but I cannot *help* be a slave to the Prince," Mr. Cosway observed, with a grotesque smile. "The decoration of the Pavilion, the maintenance of his collections—the imperative of Art!—are the foremost objects of my soul. My own poor daubs must be as nothing. I have not the nature for self-interest, I own—I am all devotion to the people I love."

"I am sure it does you very great credit, Mr. Cosway," the Comtesse replied, with what I thought to be admirable forbearance. "We must hope to solicit your society a little, perhaps, while yet you remain in Bath."

And with a bow and a flourish of his handsome grey melton hat, Mr. Richard Cosway left us.

"What a ridiculous fellow, to be sure," Eliza told me, "though quite accomplished in his line."

"How come you to be acquainted with him, Eliza?"

"My godfather, Mr. Hastings, sat to Cosway for a miniature some years past," she said carelessly, "but I formed a true attachment to the enchanting Mrs. Cosway. Maria had all of London at her feet, you know, in the 'eighties. We met in France, I recollect, in '91 or '92—just after the birth of her little girl, whom she abandoned to her husband's rearing."[11]

---

[11] While in Paris in the 1790s, Maria Cosway enchanted no less a personage than Thomas Jefferson, who is thought to have fallen (platonically) in love with her. The two corresponded for years after both had returned to their respective countries.—*Editor's note.*

"How very singular!"

"It was. He suffered from the conviction of Maria's infidelity, and thought the child to be anyone's but his own—and so she left him, for nearly four years."

"Four years! And the child?"

"She fell dead of a fever not long after Maria's return—in '96, or thereabouts." My poor Eliza's voice *must* tighten; for she knew what it was to lose an only child.

"I have always observed, Eliza, that those who seem to possess a life graced with distinction, and every comfort or happy mark of Fortune, may conceal in fact the deepest sorrows," I reflected. "How unhappy for the entire family!"

"Yes—but as Cosway can never survive a tragedy without turning it to account, he painted a portrait of the child on her deathbed, poignant in the extreme; and had Maria not forbidden it, he should have sold the engravings in the very streets! The man is the soul of self-promotion, Jane—has sunk art in the mire of commerce—and yet can protest that he is all selflessness and sacrifice! Were I shockingly ill-bred, I should laugh aloud! But it is of no consequence. Now his wife has deserted him, all his fashionable friends have quite thrown him over, I believe."

"And yet the Prince appears to support him still."

"The Prince! Yes, I believe he does. Whatever else Mr. Cosway may be—doomsayer, apocalypst, and practitioner of every kind of superstition—he is nonetheless possessed of the most exquisite taste in the arrangement of interiors, and is a connoisseur of the first rank. The Prince, they say, would be utterly lost without him, and should spend far more money to far less purpose than he already does."

"Indeed," I replied. "And how comes a mere painter to so elevated a place?"

Eliza did not scruple to abuse my stupidity. "Richard Cosway! A *mere* painter! Would you speak, my dear, of the great Cosway, who captured the likeness of Mrs. Fitzherbert, so that the Prince might wear it about his neck? The cunning miniaturist whose tokens in ivory are all the rage! Pray do not tell me you are ignorant of *this*, as of so much else in the fashionable world!"[12]

---

[12] The Prince of Wales illegally married the Catholic and twice-widowed Maria Fitzherbert in 1786. Ten years later he married his cousin, Caroline of Bruns-

We had commenced to pace about the room in company with all of Bath, and I gave barely a moment to Eliza's abuse, so intent was I upon glimpsing the Earl of Swithin.

"Jane! Are you attending?"

"I confess I care so little for the Prince and all his set, that I have never endeavoured to follow his example in anything, Eliza. This cannot seem so very wonderful, even to you."

"But Cosway's taste has set the mode of the age!" she protested. "He may look like a monkey, my dearest girl, but he is a cunning fellow, even brilliant in his way. Cosway would have it that every *objet d'art,* every fold of drapery, every touch of gilt in Carlton House is placed at his direction.[13] There can be few, I suppose, with so just a claim to having influenced fashion. In past years, of course, this was recognised—and barely a great name throughout the world failed to pay him homage, and seek his advice. But hardly anyone calls in Stratford Place, now that Maria has run away."

"And yet he is such a figure! —Better suited to ride bareback at Astley's, I should think, than to promenade in Bath!"[14]

"Indeed he *does* pay too much attention to matters of dress," Eliza conceded. She was vulnerable on the point, in having made her attire the primary occupation of her life these twenty years at least. "I learned only last month that he possesses no less than forty waist-coats."

"It is fortunate, then, that he is much at Carlton House—where such profligacy may go unremarked."

"But you must own, Jane, that the notion of capturing the likeness of an eye in oils is utterly singular. In this, at least, you must confess Cosway's peculiar brilliance. For it was entirely his own invention, I believe."

"The likeness of an *eye?* This has become his particular art?"

"Of course! He began it with Maria Fitzherbert. The Prince conceals the image of her eye in a golden locket, that he is said to wear next to his heart. Even *you* must be aware that such intimate like-

---

wick, who became the Princess of Wales. The Waleses were notoriously incompatible, and Mrs. Fitzherbert remained the Prince's favorite.—*Editor's note.*

[13] Carlton House was the Prince of Wales's London residence. It now forms part of the British Museum.—*Editor's note.*

[14] Astley's Amphitheatre, which Jane visited on several occasions in the company of her brother Edward and his children, was a London riding arena that specialized in mounted shows, rather like a circus.—*Editor's note.*

nesses of a *chère-amie*, when worn about the person, are the last word in fashion. Observe." She unbuttoned her dark grey pelisse and drew forth a pendant chain. "I myself have taken to wearing an eye."

"Eliza! You *would* not!"

The Comtesse shrugged with infinite grace. "It is no more than any lady of good society would undertake, I assure you. And isn't it fetching? Though Richard Cosway is much above my touch, I fancy that Engleheart is equally presentable.[15] I particularly admire the set of the brow. Quite a rogue, he must have been."

"Who, pray?"

"The gentleman who sat for the miniature, of course!"

"Then you are wholly unacquainted with him?"

"Naturally!" she rejoined blithely. "Would you suspect me of an intrigue against your dearest brother?"

"But, Eliza—to wear such a token, is to suggest to the world that you carry a *tendre* for a lover! I wonder Henry can bear it!"

"It was Henry who made a present of it to me," Eliza retorted equably. "And he thinks the notion very good fun, I do assure you." Her expression of amusement faded, and I saw that her interest was already claimed by another. She seized my arm in pleasurable agitation. "There, Jane! By the Visitors' Book! It is the Earl! But to whom does he speak with such urgency?"

I followed the direction of her eyes. "To Mr. Hugh Conyngham, Eliza—the principal actor of the Theatre Royal."

---

15 George Engleheart (1750–1829) made a virtual profession of eye portrait painting, and broadened the fashion from the nobility of England down to the gentry and eventually, to the middle class.—*Editor's note*.

Chapter 4

The Eye in Question

12 December 1804, cont.
~

THE EARL OF SWITHIN, IN CONVERSE WITH MR. HUGH CONYNGHAM! Were they, then, acquainted? And was it the actor alone who had drawn Lord Swithin in such haste to the Pump Room?

I stood as though rooted to the broad plank floor, transfixed by a shaft of wintry light. It fell directly upon the Earl's fair head, as though in benediction, and revealed him as a gentleman not above the middle height, but powerful in his frame and general air of address—a commanding figure, much hardened by sport and exercise, and tailored to within an inch of its life. Lord Swithin's countenance might be said to be handsome, for there was not an ill-made feature in it, but for the coldness that lurked in his bright blue gaze and the suggestion of bitterness about the mouth. This was not a man to be lightly crossed—and I could not wonder that Lady Desdemona had fled to Bath, rather than brook the tide of rage occasioned by her refusal.

"Jane!" Eliza hissed. "Pray turn your eyes away from his lordship, or we shall both be detected in the grossest vulgarity!"

But I was insensible of Eliza's anxious looks, so compelling were the Earl and his interlocutor. With heads drawn close together and a flow of speech that suggested some urgency of matter, the two men *must* be canvassing the murder in Laura Place.

"Eliza," I murmured, "is the Earl likely to recollect your acquaintance, so many years since in Bengal?"

"I should think not," she replied stoutly. "It was his mother, you know, who called upon mine. I do not think he was even born before we quitted India entirely."

"That is very well. Let us stroll about the room with as unconscious an air as possible."

"We may attempt the stroll, Jane, but should abandon the unconscious air at the outset. You are not equal to it, darling girl. You have not the necessary schooling in deception."

"Fiddlesticks," I whispered viciously. "Speak to me of something diverting."

"I have heard," Eliza attempted immediately, "that though the Earl of Swithin's title is of ancient pedigree, his considerable fortune has been amassed through trade."

"You shall not horrify me, my dear. I am no respecter of snobbish distinction. He retains the claims of a gentleman."

"But perhaps the nature of his trading may surprise you. The Earl is given to running opium, no less, out of Bengal to China, and using private ships to do it. He learned the habit of his father, and since that gentleman's demise has greatly increased the activity. Henry heard the tale only last week, while lunching at Boodle's."[1]

"The Earl? An opium trader? I may hardly credit it!"

Eliza's dark eyes glinted deliciously. "Do not sound so astonished, my dearest Jane. You must know that the Honourable Company has long employed opium as an antidote to tea.[2] We import so very much of that leaf, and can sell little to advantage in China; our debt in trade—or its imbalance, as Henry might put it—for many years bid fair to sink us; the kingdom bled bullion as from an open wound; but matters of late have righted themselves, and all on account of the Chinese taste for opium. Such men as the Earl must receive our thanks, however much the Government officially abhors their activity. And so the world turns round—we import tea from China;

[1] This was (and remains) an exclusive men's club.—*Editor's note.*

[2] Eliza refers to the Honourable East India Company. The private trading consortium effectively ruled India throughout the eighteenth and part of the nineteenth centuries. Her birth in India and ties to Warren Hastings, the most influential and effective governor the company had ever appointed, probably account for her knowledge of its trade.—*Editor's note.*

China imports opium from India; and India imports woolens from Manchester! Admirable, is it not, how the yearnings and vices of the multitude provide Lord Swithin with a dashing carriage and four?''

"Admirable or otherwise, it cannot be very agreeable to claim the opium trade as occupation," I observed. "I wonder whether His Grace the Duke of Wilborough is cognizant of the Earl's activity?"

We had progressed very nearly to a position opposite the Visitors' Book, where the Earl and the actor were as yet engrossed. I halted in our promenade, and turned my back upon the pair. Their voices drifted very faintly to my ears—a word or two only. "Continue conversing, Eliza, I beg—but speak of lace, or the price of muslin, in as audible a tone as you may manage."

Of all things required, my sister was equal to *this;* and she prated on happily about the number of flounces so necessary to a fashionable gown for evening, and the appearance of epaulettes, in deference to the heightened military style inevitable in such a climate, while I endeavoured to overlisten our neighbours' conversation. It was the Earl's voice, acute and low, I first discerned.

". . . must have the letters."

"I tell you they are not . . ." (indistinguishable words) ". . . and . . . is most disagreeable at present. I cannot assure your lordship . . . influence with her."

"Then I must see her myself."

"That would . . . unwise. I cannot answer . . ."

". . . is due to me! I have wasted . . . a handsbreadth to the gallows!"

". . . time."

"I have had enough of your *time!* Time has brought me only grief and vexation, sir!" This last was very nearly shouted, so that the enraged Earl was rewarded with the shocked glance of several in the Pump Room; and after an exasperated sigh, he lowered his voice once more. The next words were almost inaudible.

". . . expect you to . . . method of securing my . . ."

Had I truly heard it aright? Securing *what*—the Earl's freedom? His reputation? His interest?

His letters?

". . . well. Good day, my lord."

"Good day." All private business concluded, the Earl achieved a more civil tone.'' ''And remember me to your sister, Conyngham, I shall be in attendance at Orchard Street tomorrow.''

The actor bowed; the Earl received his deference with a faint air of irritation; and so they parted. Lord Swithin quitted the Pump Room by the door immediately opposite the Visitors' Book, apparently intent upon returning to the White Hart, Hugh Conyngham plunged towards the opposite end of the vast hall. There was an expression of anxiety and despair upon his countenance I could not like.

''I must leave you, Eliza,'' I said. ''Forgive me. My compliments and best love to Henry—we hope to see you this evening in Green Park Buildings to drink tea, if you are not otherwise engaged.''

''What have you heard, Jane?'' Eliza enquired with penetration.

''I hardly know. Everything—or nothing. Who can say?''

''Jane—'' My sister reached a hand to my arm, restraining me when I would depart. ''Had you not better leave such things to the magistrate, Mr. Elliot?''

''I do not understand you, Eliza,'' I retorted.

''And as for tea—''

The Henry Austens were to attend the concert that evening in the Upper Rooms—a recitation of love songs in the Italian by Mrs. Billington[3]—and Eliza was pressing in her invitation that Cassandra and I should make an addition to the party. Though I may accomplish a Scotch air on the pianoforte with pleasure, I am in the general way no friend to music. Singing, I own, induces a tedium that may be relieved only by a thorough review of one's neighbour's attire and conversation. And for the present, all thought of love songs, Italian or otherwise, must be banished by the interesting notion of the Earl and the actor united in intrigue.

But I promised Eliza most faithfully to propose the scheme to my sister—and with a kiss to her cheek, ran thankfully away.

•   •   •

[3] Elizabeth Billington (1768–1818) was a celebrated soprano of Austen's day, who usually appeared in Bath at concerts conducted by Vincenzo Rauzzini (died 1810). Despite her disclaimers, Austen attended these concerts often, as is evidenced in her letters. They were generally held on Wednesday evenings, so as not to conflict with the theater on Tuesdays and Thursdays, or the Assemblies on Mondays and Fridays.—Editor's note.

IN COMPARATIVE SOLITUDE I PASSED THROUGH QUEEN SQUARE, WHERE the first golden glow of an unfashionably early dinner hour now shone through the modest windows. My mother will persist in hankering after the square—it was the most select address that Bath afforded, in her girlhood—but the narrowness of the rooms will never do for so large a party as ours. She must be content with a weekly visit to the Queen's chapel, where we hear divine service of a Sunday, and a passage through its park when business draws her to that part of town. We are treated, however, to a daily recitation of Queen Square's advantages, and must allow it to be superior to every other location in Bath if we are to achieve any domestic peace.

I thrust my mother from my mind in the present instance, however, and saw again in memory the Earl of Swithin. What could such a man—of so lofty an establishment, and so recently descended upon the town—have to say to Hugh Conyngham? Who, however admirable his skill as a thespian, is as yet a provincial player, without birth or connexions to recommend him? I had expected to hear Richard Portal's name, or at the very least Lord Kinsfell's—and yet the two had spoken only of letters. Whose? And who was the mysterious *she*?

Maria Conyngham?

The actress's magnificent form limned itself on the paving-stones at my feet, like an enchantress materialising out of the common snow and dirt; and I knew her immediately for a woman any man might die to possess. Maria Conyngham had fire, beauty, and all the spirit to be expected in one untrammelled by society's conventions. I should not find it remarkable if her charms had ensnared a legion heretofore unknown to me—not least amongst them, the redoubtable Earl.

And then I sighed. Upon reflection, I should never be privileged to learn the truth—for my part in the drama must surely be at an end. With the Earl come in haste to Bath, and Lord Harold not far behind, any office I might have fulfilled, as silent duenna to Lady Desdemona, should be for naught. The unfortunate girl would be sent away to London, as soon as attention could be spared her, while the efforts of her relations should be turned to the vindication of the heir. The charge of murder brought against Simon, Lord Kinsfell, must throw his sister's private troubles entirely into the shade.

And so it was in no very great humour that I pulled the bell of

No. 27, in Green Park Buildings, and awaited the advent of Mary, the housemaid. She opened to my summons before the last peals had entirely died away.

"Ooh, miss," she said, with a look of mingled terror and awe, "there's a gentleman here as is *that* grand. He's been waiting on you above a half-hour."

"In the sitting-room, Mary?"

"Yes, miss. In the Reverend's chair."

I hastened upstairs to my visitor's relief, and found none other than Lord Harold Trowbridge, standing erect and silent before the window, his back turned to the room. My poor father gazed at him helplessly, while my mother—in full flood upon the subject of actors and their pugilism—ran on unabated.

"Sir!" I burst out. "This is indeed an honour!"

He turned, one eyebrow raised, and bowed. "Miss Austen. The honour is entirely mine."

The gravity of his tone might have impressed me less, had it not been wed to an equal command of countenance. Lord Harold was in no mood for civilities or folly—and I determined upon the removal of my mother from the room as swiftly as convention might allow.

"Jane, my dear," my father said, "your mother and I have been expecting you this half-hour, as we assured Lord Harold. What *can* have occasioned so protracted an absence?"

"Only a Pump Room acquaintance of Eliza's, Father," I replied, my eyes on the Gentleman Rogue. "And a general buzz of gossip concerning a new arrival. The Earl of Swithin has come to Bath. Only fancy!"

"The Earl of Swithin? And what is the Earl of Swithin to *us*, pray? Come, come, Mrs. Austen." My father rose slowly from a stiff-backed chair at some remove from the fire—*not* his usual seat. "If we are to have a whiff of air before Cook sets the dinner bell to ringing, we must away!"

"I am certain we have not time enough," my mother objected, "and that I shall catch a chill. Moreover, the gloom is *not* prepossessing. We shall stumble over ourselves, in attempting the pavement."

"That is always the way with December, my dear, but I must have my exercise. Mr. Bowen is most insistent."

At this, my mother submitted, for my father's health has been indifferent of late, to our great anxiety, and the surgeon—Mr. Bowen—is punctilious on the matter of a daily airing.

Lord Harold bowed to them both, and I heard the sitting-room door click behind them with palpable relief.

"These are comfortable lodgings," he said, with a glance about the room.

"Indeed. Although a trifle damp—in the kitchen and offices particularly."[4]

"You have been here how long?"

"A few months only—since our return from Lyme."

"Ah, yes. Lyme." The barest suggestion of a smile twitched at the corners of his mouth. "It is in my power to inform you, Miss Austen, that our friends reached America in safety. They have taken up residence in the state of New York."

A rush of feeling welled suddenly within me, and as swiftly died away. Geoffrey Sidmouth and his cousins might as well be on the moon, for any likelihood I should ever have of seeing them again.[5]

"That is excellent news, indeed," I managed, and felt my cheeks to burn.

"But you cannot rejoice in it as you might," Lord Harold said gently, "having occasion to regret the acquaintance—or perhaps, the gentleman. I comprehend."

I averted my eyes in some embarrassment. "Will you not sit down, sir?"

"No—I thank you. I have been sitting already too long today."

"You journeyed from London."

"As swiftly as a coach-and-four might carry me. I am arrived but a few hours." He clasped his hands behind his back and turned from the window to the fire. Lord Harold might always have been called a well-made man—he is tall enough, with the leanness born of exercise, and a shrewdness of countenance that becomes the more engaging the longer one is acquainted with it. His silver locks are worn

---

[4] Green Park Buildings was newly built at the time of the Austens' lease, and known for the high water table at its foundation; Jane herself rejected lodgings here as unsuitable in 1801, when her family first removed to Bath, but the high cost of their first home at No. 4 Sydney Place forced an eventual change.—*Editor's note.*

[5] Jane's encounter with Geoffrey Sidmouth is detailed in the second Austen journal, *Jane and the Man of the Cloth.* (New York: Bantam Books, 1997.)—*Editor's note.*

as negligently as the scar from a sabre cut that travels across one cheek, and though he commands fully five-and-forty years of age, the youthfulness of his demeanour has always cast the sum into doubt. But as I studied his lordship's form, dark against the blazing hearth, I perceived a subtle transformation. If it were possible for a man to age a twelvemonth in but a quarter of that time, then Lord Harold had assuredly done so.

Since our last meeting—on the rainswept Charmouth shingle of a September dawn—the Gentleman Rogue had acquired a weary set to his shoulders, and his aquiline features were drawn with something akin to pain. His lordship's hooded grey eyes, though cold and unthinking when in contemplation of evil, were wont to brim with amusement as well; but now they seemed quite devoid of emotion altogether. These subtle changes might be ascribed, I supposed, to the distress occasioned by his nephew Kinsfell's misadventures. There was a severity in Lord Harold's looks, however, that called to mind the ascetic—or the penitent. It was as though his lordship nursed a private grief, or suffered from infinite regret. As I surveyed him thus, he reached for the irons and prodded viciously at the fire—a betrayal of the unease within. A restless distraction held him in its grip; the evident desire to be *doing something*, I must not presume upon his patience with trifling pleasantries; the greatest despatch was in order. I seated myself upon the settee.

"If you have spared an hour to pay this call, sir," I began, "I can only assume it is with a view to learning what I might tell you of events in Laura Place last evening. But let me first offer my heartfelt expression of concern for your family, and the terrible misfortunes they have endured."

A smile flickered briefly over the narrow face. "My thanks, Miss Austen. I have indeed come to your door in the hopes of learning something to my nephew's advantage. I know you too well to fear that any part of this unfortunate affair is likely to have escaped your attention. But first—you must tell me. Is it true? Is Swithin indeed come to Bath?"

"I regret to say that I have not the pleasure of acquaintance with his lordship. But if he travels in style, with the device of a snarling tiger upon his ebony coach—"

"He does. You have seen him yourself?"

"I have seen a tall, well-made man with fair hair and a haughty expression on his noble brow, a gentleman of taste and a decided air of refinement, to whom every eye in the room is turned as a matter of course. He is accustomed, I should judge, to the power of doing as he likes; and employs it frequently."

"That is the man," Lord Harold said with satisfaction. "But how has Swithin learned so swiftly of our misfortune? And what does he mean by coming here? He abhors Bath. There is nothing to interest him in this quarter. Except—" The silver head bent slightly in thought, and after an instant, Lord Harold wheeled around. "He means to bring my niece to a stand."

"Does he? And will he achieve it?"

"I cannot undertake to say. But there is no man like Swithin for forcing a point. My niece, Lady Desdemona, has gone so far as to reject him; she has thwarted his ambition; *she has spit in his eye,* and all the world has seen it. He is not the sort of man to take such behaviour lightly. He means to break her."

The casual grimness of his tone caused my heart to sink.

"But you will not allow it!" I rejoined stoutly. "You *must* be seen to object."

"I object to everything that appears as undue influence over those I hold most dear. Rest assured, Miss Austen—I would not have Mona thrown away." He settled himself in my father's chair and gazed broodingly into the flames. "Now let us have the entire history. Tell me all you know."

And so I launched into the neatest summary of the Duchess's rout that I could manage, a summary entirely free of conjecture or surmise. And when I had done, Lord Harold was silent for several moments together.

"You have no notion as to the cause of the dispute between my nephew and Mr. Portal?" he enquired at last.

"None. Although I assumed it was the result of some insult, in word or action. Lord Kinsfell referred to Portal as a blackguard, I believe."

"That might cover all manner of offence—from cheating at cards to coarseness towards a lady. I shall have to force the admission from Simon myself—though it will prove a piece of work."

"Cannot Lady Desdemona enlighten you?"

"Alas, it is impossible. She merely attempted to part the two, when their behaviour grew too reckless, and was served with some very rough treatment herself, I understand."

"Mr. Portal's behaviour *did* seem to offend her. She quitted the room in tears. But I cannot believe her distress the cause of a murderous attack on the part of Lord Kinsfell, as Mr. Elliot fain would do."

"But consider the oddity of the attack!" Lord Harold countered. "If any desired the end of Richard Portal, why not draw the knife in the darkness of a random alley? There are an hundred places where such a deed might be done—the foetid rooms of a public house, or the shadow of Westgate Buildings, or the banks of the Avon itself.[6] Why choose a duchess's drawing-room?—*Unless* the knife was drawn in a moment, on the spur of anger and drink. I begin to see it as Mr. Wilberforce Elliot might; and should have taken up my nephew without a second thought."

"But if Portal was murdered with deliberation—and with deliberation *in the Duchess's household*—then the killer must find a purpose in publicity," I observed. "He may mean your nephew to take the blame. Or he may hope, Lord Harold, that your *niece* will suffer in the knowledge of her favourite's end."

There was a silence. "Lord Swithin," Trowbridge said.

"The thought has occurred to me."

"You think him so consumed by jealousy and pique, Miss Austen, as to plan his rival's murder? And under Mona's very nose?"

"Is the notion so incredible?"

"He was far from Bath."

"And he is the sort of man who might summon a legion to do his bidding—from any distance this side of the seal?"

"But would he resort to murder?" Lord Harold rejoined. "I cannot believe it. It is far more in Swithin's style to call a rival out—and cripple him for life. A masked stabbing would not be at all the thing."

---

[6] Westgate Buildings is best known as the home of Anne Elliot's school friend, Mrs. Smith, in *Persuasion*. It was by 1804 considered an unhealthy and danger-ous neighborhood, fronting the River Avon; rats, pickpockets, and prostitutes frequented it, and it would be ravaged by cholera in the 1830s.—*Editor's note.*

"And yet," I persisted, "I observed him today at the Pump Room, barely a quarter-hour after his arrival, already in conference with Hugh Conyngham."

"The actor? I comprehend, now, Swithin's early intelligence of the murder. I did not know his lordship claimed acquaintance among the company of the Theatre Royal."

"The Earl was most intent upon his conversation with Conyngham—and I overheard a little of it. It seems that the actor was charged with a duty towards Lord Swithin, concerning the retrieval of some letters. The Earl was quite put out at Conyngham's failure to fulfil his commission—and declared he was within a handsbreadth to the gallows! Singular words, are they not?"

Lord Harold sat very still. Firelight flickered off his sharp features. "And what would you say, Miss Austen—was Lady Desdemona in love with Mr. Portal? Enough to occasion Swithin's alarm?"

"In love? I confess I cannot tell! She consented to dance with him gladly enough—but I did not remark any particular sign of affection. Had you enquired of Maria Conyngham . . ." I hesitated.

"Yes?"

"She appeared as destroyed by Portal's death as any woman might possibly be."

"I see. That is, perhaps, no more than I should have expected. I had understood her to be attached to the man. A motive for murder, perhaps, did he turn his affections elsewhere."

To Lady Desdemona, for example. "Does Her Grace know nothing of your niece's regard for Mr. Portal?"

Lord Harold shook his head. "My mother considered the manager an acquaintance of long standing. She had no idea of a presumption to Desdemona's hand. Of far greater import, in Her Grace's estimation, was the friendship Portal so recently formed with my *nephew*."

"But I thought Lord Kinsfell held Portal in contempt!"

"Thus ends many an unequal friendship."

"So this public display of poor feeling was quite out of the ordinary way."

Lord Harold rose and began to pace before the fire. "As was the manager's violent end. I propose we consider of events in a rational manner. It is possible to divine a jealous motive for both Swithin and Miss Conyngham to commit this murder—a motive that depends upon my niece's affections. Others may exist, for parties unknown. But how was the deed effected?''

''At least two possibilities are open to us, my lord. Firstly, that Richard Portal was stabbed by a person who fled through the ante-room window.''

Lord Harold shook his head. ''It is a precipitous fall.''

''Agreed. But I have been turning over the matter in my mind. Were there a conveyance beneath the window—a common waggon, and filled with hay—might not an intruder leap from house to street, and suffer nothing in the fall?''

''If the waggon were allowed to stand but a little, and to look unremarkable in its delay.''

''An altercation with the chairmen, perhaps, who rendered Laura Place all but impassable that night, in attendance upon the Duchess's guests. The constable did not enquire whether a carter had come to the point of fisticuffs. He merely asked if any had observed a cloaked figure leap from the window.''

''That is true. I will enquire among the various stands of chairmen in the city. But you mentioned *two* possibilities, Miss Austen—pray continue.''

''Portal's murderer may have vanished through the anteroom passage, and left the window ajar as a ruse. He had only to return, then, to the drawing-room, and discover the body in company with the rest of us.''

''Then the murderer might be anyone. There were an hundred guests last night, I believe.''

''But some dozens fled before the constables' arrival, and of those who remained, but a few are worthy of consideration. I would posit, my lord, that the murderer might be found among the company of the Theatre Royal—or among the intimates of the Conyng-hams.''

''How is such an assertion possible?''

''Have you considered the *nature* of the killing? A stabbing, and in the midst of Hugh Conyngham's declamation from *Macbeth*, describing the same? It bears a sinister aspect. '*If it were done when 'tis done, then 'twere well/It were done quickly*' . . .''

''So my mother is willing to believe,'' Lord Harold admitted, with the ghost of amusement. ''She found in the scene a grisly example of life in the imitation of art; and such things must always impress her, who has confused them these seventy years."

"The speech may have served as signal, to a henchman among the guests; and thus we have only to study the players for the penetration of the affair."

"But is Mr. Elliot, the magistrate, likely to agree?" Lord Harold mused. "What think you of Mr. Elliot, by the by?"

"I found Mr. Elliot a disturbing blend of parts. He is burdened with an unfortunate want of tact, and a superfluity of wit; he is disgusting in his manners and person—but his mind is shrewd enough. I would judge him to be lazy, and amoral, and devoid of even the faintest degree of respect for the peerage; and I would watch him within an inch of his life. Your nephew's may depend upon it."

Lord Harold's brows lifted satirically. "Harsh counsel, my dear Miss Austen—but not, I think, formed of the thin air of conjecture, nor motivated by untoward malice. I know your penetration of old. No charlatan may deceive, nor sycophant charm, your wits from out your head. Little of a human nature eludes your admirable penetration. Indeed, to solicit your opinion of the man has been almost my first object in calling at Green Park Buildings. I shall approach Mr. Elliot with the utmost circumspection, and thank you for your pains to set me on my guard."

I considered of the Gentleman Rogue and the bearish magistrate, and concluded that despite their apparent differences, Lord Harold and Mr. Elliot might well deal famously with one another. They should each delight in the game of confusing and astounding the other. "You are as yet unacquainted with the magistrate, I perceive?"

Lord Harold inclined his head. "I regret that I have not yet had the pleasure—though I might have forced myself upon his attention this morning. Mr. Elliot was within the household upon my arrival, engaged in an examination of Lord Kinsfell's private papers. He thinks to find some sign of guilt, I suppose, amidst a drawer of unpaid bills."

"And your opinion of his intentions towards the Marquis?"

Lord Harold shrugged. "I have formed none to disagree with yours in any respect; but I pay no very great attention to magistrates in general. Mr. Elliot's task is simple: He does not need to discover

Portal's murderer, but only to make a case against my nephew. If the truth is to be found, it is unlikely to be at Mr. Elliot's undertaking."[7]

"Have you seen Lord Kinsell, my lord?" I might almost have looked upon the Marquis himself, I thought, in gazing at his uncle; but for the differences of age, the two were remarkably alike in form and countenance. When last I saw Lord Kinsell, however—borne away to gaol in all the inelegant discomfort of his Knight's apparel—the outrage of his sensibilities was writ full upon his face. Lord Harold, I surmised, should never betray a like emotion, even were he kneeling before the block in London Tower. His lordship wore in-scrutability as other men might their court dress, assuming it when occasion demanded.

"I went directly to the gaol upon my arrival in Bath," he replied. "Simon will not remain there long—the inquest is to be held on Friday, the conclusion of which must be beyond question; and he will then be conveyed to Ilchester, to await the Assizes."

An inquest. But of course. I knew too much of the painful recti-tude of coroners' juries to believe them capable of imagination re-garding events. Once such simple men as the coroner should summon were told that Lord Kinsell was found standing over Mr. Portal's body with a knife in his hand, they must return a verdict of wilful murder against him.

"And how are the Marquis's spirits?"

"Too low, I fear. He was much sunk in melancholy and despair, and was arrayed, as yet, in the garb of a knight. My first object upon returning to Laura Place, was to charge a servant with an exchange of clothes." Lord Harold turned abruptly to his greatcoat, and fished among its pockets. "And now we come to the chief of this murder's oddities, Miss Austen. Pray attend to what I am about to show you."

He drew forth a small object wrapped in brown paper, and laid it in my lap. "Open it, if you please."

I undid the parcel with eager hands. And there, winking dully in the candle-flame, was the portrait of an *eye*—dark grey, heavily-lashed, and fully as arresting as the roguish ornament my dear Eliza

[7] The criminal justice system of Austen's time was somewhat cruder than our own. Defendants charged with capital crimes were presumed guilty until proven innocent.—*Editor's note.*

had borne about her neck. It was an oblong pendant the size of a guinea, strung on a fine gold chain, and quite surrounded by seed pearls—beautiful, and undoubtedly costly. I lifted the thing and dangled it before the candle, at a loss for explanation. The eye returned my regard, as stormy in its expression as paint and art could make it.

"My nephew tells me he found this resting on Portal's breast, quite near his wound, as though left by his murderer in silent witness. Simon hung it undetected about his own neck, and succeeded thus in bearing it away to the gaol."

"But why did he not leave it for Mr. Elliot to discover?" I exclaimed. "For surely this miniature can have nothing to do with Lord Kinsfell! Indeed, its existence might divert suspicion from his head!"

"I cannot offer an explanation." Lord Harold's voice was heavy. "But I surmise that Kinsfell has not told us *all*. No more intelligence of the portrait or its meaning could I wring from his lips, than the plea that it be prevented from falling into the magistrate's hands— and from this, I must assume he would shield another, to whom the portrait points. He consented to place it in my keeping solely out of fear of its discovery while he remains in gaol."

"And does he expect you to shield that person also? Or are you at liberty to solicit the magistrate, where Lord Kinsfell would not?"

"Having failed to entrust the eye to Mr. Elliot *then*, we cannot with impunity reveal it now," Lord Harold said thoughtfully. "Mr. Elliot would be forgiven for believing it a foolish fabrication, and accord it no more significance than the anteroom's open window. No, Miss Austen—if we are to fathom the portrait's significance, we must do so ourselves."

"Only consider, my lord, the wonder that its disappearance must have caused," I murmured. "Our murderer expected the portrait to be revealed—to point, perhaps, to the incrimination of another. But not a sign of the bauble has the magistrate seen!"

"Then we may hope the villain's anxiety will force his hand," Lord Harold replied with quiet satisfaction.

I turned the portrait again before the candle-flame, and felt the movement of the eye's gaze as though it were alive. "It *is* a lovely thing, and must be dearly bought. I should think it far beyond the means of most."

''The setting is very fine, the pearls are good; and the portrait itself is excellent. I have known Mr. George Engleheart to charge upwards of twenty-five guineas for a similar likeness—and that would never encompass the jeweller's bill. Such a bauble would indeed be well beyond the reach of the common run. It is to Engleheart in London I must go, Miss Austen—for I believe he keeps a log-book of his commissions; and if this pendant fell from his brush, he will have recorded the identity of its subject. Such knowledge should be as gold, in revealing the meaning of Portal's death.''

''Stay!'' I cried, and sprang to my feet. ''Of what use is London, when the foremost painter of such miniatures is already come to Bath?''

Lord Harold surveyed me narrowly. ''Of whom would you speak?''

''Mr. Richard Cosway! I made his acquaintance this very morning, while promenading in the Pump Room. He intends a visit of some duration—three months, I believe. I have only to enquire of my sister Eliza, and his direction is known!''

''Capital. We shall call upon him tomorrow—let us say, at two o'clock. Have you leisure enough to pay the call?''

''My time is at your disposal, my lord.''

''That is very well, Miss Austen, for I would beg another favour of you. There is an additional visit I feel compelled to make.''

Lord Harold sat down beside me and reached for my hand. The intimacy of the gesture quite took my breath, and I fear my fingers trembled in his grip. He said, ''We must go to the Theatre Royal, as soon as ever may be. I expect the magistrate to search Mr. Portal's lodgings, but I do not think he will soon consider the manager's offices at the theatre itself. A perusal of Portal's private papers might tell us much.''

''His papers?'' I said with a frown. ''Surely there can be no occasion for such an abuse of privacy.''

''I have known a good deal of blackmail, my dear Miss Austen,'' Lord Harold said drily, ''and I cannot help but observe the marks of its effect throughout this unfortunate history.''

''Blackmail!'' I cried, freeing my fingers from his grasp.

''I sense it everywhere in Richard Portal's sad end. Lord Swithin's anxiety regarding some letters, overheard by yourself in the Pump Room; Lord Kinsfell's argument with Portal, and his assertion that the man was a blackguard; his own reluctance to speak fully of events that evening; and now, the curious portrait, returned like a bad penny to Portal's breast. Blackmail, Miss Austen—as plainly as such dark arts may be seen!''

''I confess I had not an idea of it,'' I said.

''You must understand that the practice is familiar to me through long association. I have employed it myself,'' Lord Harold said equably, ''when no other tool would serve; and have been in turn the object of necessitous importuning—a mad decision on the blackmailer's part, for never was there a fellow with so little regard for public opinion, or so great a contempt for its deserts, as Harold Trowbridge.''

''A more hardened object I cannot conceive.'' I was amused despite the gravity of his words.

''But tempting, regardless.'' He jumped up and began to turn restlessly before the fire. ''I have, in the past, acted in ways that may be judged reprehensible. I have sacrificed the reputations of my confederates, my mistresses, my dearest friends, in pursuit of those ends that have, *to my mind alone,* required such sacrifice. I have cared nothing, in short, for how my character is judged—except as regards one particular: That I am held in trust and esteem by certain men in high Government circles. It is as lifeblood to me, in ensuring the continuance of that activity which—alone among the pursuits of my life—is capable of stirring my interest, and of relieving the unutterable tedium of my existence.'' At this, something of animation enlivened Lord Harold's tone; but it was the animation of coldest anger. ''Should any man attempt to queer my relations with the Crown, or with the very small number of men who direct its concerns, I should be entirely at his mercy. That, to date, has never occurred; and I pray God it never shall. I could not answer for myself in the eventuality.''

One glimpse of his set features was enough, and I averted my gaze. Lord Harold overset—Lord Harold denied his life's blood of peril and intrigue—was Lord Harold divided from his very soul. I should not like to be within twenty paces of any man who attempted it.

''But my familiarity with the blackmailer's art has at least taught me this,'' he continued. ''Among those who can profess no stern disregard for public views or public morals, it is the aptest means of persuasion. More lives have been ruined—more spirits broken—from a fear of idle gossip and report, than are numbered on Napoleon's battlefields, Miss Austen. Portal's death may be the result of a similar campaign."

And if it were, I thought, the tide of scandal should reach even so far as a ducal household. "I comprehend your meaning, my lord, I shall be happy to assist you by whatever means are within my power."

He reached for his hat, and smoothed its fine wool brim. "Will you do me the very great honour of attending the theatre tomorrow evening, Miss Austen, in the Wilborough box?"

"With pleasure," I replied.

"It will require—forgive me—a certain subterfuge on your part."

"I am at your service, my lord."

"You will understand that any in the Trowbridge family must be known among the company. Even Simon had *not* been taken up in Portal's death, our intimacy with the Conynghams—our attention to the Theatre Royal—must make us too familiar; and at present a tide of ill-feeling is directed against us all. But as for yourself—"

"Of course. What would you have me do?"

"I intend a visit to the wings upon the play's conclusion. It is my hope that you might then create a small diversion—a faint, a mishap, something along the female line—that should draw the attention of the principal parties."

"And in the flurry, you shall investigate the manager's rooms?"

"Exactly."

I bowed my head to disguise a tide of mirth. "I have always dreamed of performing in the Theatre Royal, Lord Harold. To tread the boards was the dearest ambition of my vanished girlhood. I may hope to do you credit."

"You have never failed me yet. It will be something merely to parade you in the box."

There was a grimness to his tone I readily understood. All of Bath must be hoping for a glimpse of the notorious Trowbridges, so deeply and publicly embroiled in a violent murder; and the appearance of the Earl of Swithin in Bath must only fan the flames of speculation. "You hope, then, to show the scandal-mongers your bravest face?"

"And damn their eyes."

"Sir!" I cried. It has not been my province to know much of swearing, however I may subject my creatures to it.[8]

"Tut, tut, my dear Miss Austen—do not grow missish on me, after all we have sustained!" Trowbridge seized his greatcoat and gloves. "Expect me tomorrow at two, about the interrogation of Mr. Cosway!"

[8] Here Jane may be thinking of Catherine Morland, in *Northanger Abbey,* a clergyman's daughter much incommoded by a suitor's swearing; or of Mary Crawford, an admiral's niece in *Mansfield Park,* whose glancing familiarity with adultery, naval sodomy, and a sailor's tongue is designed to shock her less sophisticated country circle.—*Editor's note.*

Chapter 5

A Call in
Camden Place

Thursday,
13 December 1804

~

THE THEATRE ROYAL IN ORCHARD STREET IS HARDLY SO GRAND AS
Covent Garden or Drury Lane, being cramped and overheated in
the extreme; its single entrance ensures a dreadful crush at the play's
commencement and close; and indeed, the space is so incommodi-
ous, as to have prompted the building of a new theatre in Beauford
Square, immediately adjacent to Chandos Buildings, that is to open
next season. But even the unfortunate nature of the present accommodation, and the possibility that my dress should be mussed, if not
torn, in the attempt to gain my seat in Lord Harold's box, could not
dispel my intention of being as fine this evening as possible. Having
condescended to escort a Miss Austen to the play, Lord Harold
should not be suffered to blush for her appearance.

I own but three gowns that are suitable for evening engagements—a sapphire muslin;[1] a white lawn with puffed sleeves; and the
aforementioned peach silk, as yet in pieces with my fashionable *mo-
diste*. It was *this* I determined to wear—it being in the latest style, with

[1] The color sapphire, in Austen's day, referred to pale rather than dark
blue.—*Editor's note.*

a square neck sloping down slightly to the bosom; an underskirt of cream-coloured sarcenet; and negligible capped sleeves, very slightly off the shoulder. It was the gown most likely to do me credit—and so to Madame LeBlanc's in Bath Street I went, immediately after breakfast this morning.

The poor woman wrung her hands, and declared my request impossible to fulfil; the gown could hardly be pieced within a fortnight; but at the last, upon receiving the intelligence that I was to be on public view in the Wilborough box—to which all eyes in the theatre should undoubtedly be turned—she consented to set three of her seamstresses to making up the gown.

I consulted her clock—perceived it to lack yet a half-hour until noon—and hastened my steps towards the White Hart. I must visit Eliza before receiving Lord Harold, and on so fine a morning I should be lucky to find the little Comtesse within doors.[2] Were I in her place, and free of all obligation in a city wholly given over to pleasure, I should take a turn in Sydney Gardens, or promenade about the Crescent, or commission Henry to hire a carriage for a drive about the countryside.

And upon achieving the White Hart, my premonitions were rewarded, as such fears usually are, in finding the Austen rooms deserted of even the little dog, Pug. I turned away in some annoyance, and determined to look into the Pump Room on the chance of finding her—when a light step was heard upon the stair, and Eliza's delicious laugh wafted towards the ceiling.

"Good gracious, my lord, are you so determined in flattery? I have not heard its equal since I quitted Versailles. You are too wicked for Bath—you shall put the gentle invalids to flight in their chairs—and I shall not rest easy until you have secured your lodgings and left us in peace!"

An indistinct murmur of male conversation—another musical laugh—and the little Comtesse tripped gaily towards her rooms, an

[2] Jane's description of *morning* may confuse a modern reader. The word *after-noon* was not commonly in use in 1804, as the morning was considered to run from the hour of waking until the dinner hour, which might begin anywhere from four to seven o'clock. The *evening* began well after dinner, with tea, and ran until supper, a light repast sometimes taken as late as eleven o'clock. A morning call, then, generally occurred in what we would consider after-noon.—*Editor's note.*

enormous muff upon her delicate hand, and a fine glow of spirits animating her countenance.

"Jane!" she cried, and halted on the landing. "But how very fortunate! I was intending to come in search of you; and now you have saved me the trouble. But then, you are always saving me a vast deal of trouble, are you not? A delightful quality in a relation."

"Good morning, Eliza," I rejoined. "You look excessively well. Some handsome rogue has been turning your head, I fancy."

"Only the Earl of Swithin," she confided mischievously. "How I *love* the proximity of an inn! I shall be quite desolate when he goes into Laura Place."

"Laura Place? Lord Swithin intends a visit to Lady Desdemona?"

"He intends to land in her very lap, my dear. The Earl is taking the residence opposite the Dowager's for the remainder of his stay."

"Such impertinence!"

"—for a man of Swithin's position and means, to hire a house in one of the most distinguished squares in town? I do not understand you, Jane. Camden Place might possess a smarter air, of course, but—" Eliza swept past me and opened the door to her room.

"Eliza! Only consider of it! To perch like a bird of prey upon the stoop of a lady who has refused him! Surely Lord Swithin's arrogance admits of some limit!"

"But perhaps not his taste for abuse. One might wonder why he comes to Bath at all." She threw down her muff and gave her spencer into the maid's keeping. "Never fear the machinations of the Earl, my dear Jane. Now your Lord Harold is come to be gay in this splendid watering-place, I cannot find anything in Swithin to frighten Lady Desdemona."

"He is not *my* Lord Harold," I retorted crossly, "but if I were the Earl, I should hesitate before invading the gentleman's square."

Eliza's smile widened. "So he *is* come! I heard the rumour in the Pump Room. And have you seen Trowbridge, Jane? Is he bent upon the routing of his nephew's enemies? Shall you have a chance of engaging your energies in the matter? I own, I am excessively hopeful of some diversion in that quarter—there was nothing like the Scargrave business a few winters back, for wonderfully piquing the senses, and varying the dull routine of the day-to-day! Even Henry dined out on the strength of your particulars for weeks on end!"

"Eliza, Eliza—"

She collapsed upon one of the inn's hard wooden chairs and breathed a sigh of relief. "Lord, Jane! I *do* find that length of stair a trial!"

"Did you hurry less rapidly into speech, you might have breath enough for a thousand such!"

"And yet it would never do to lodge in the ground-floor chambers," she continued thoughtfully. "Such noise and smoke—and only last evening, a woman gave birth in the kitchens, if you will credit it!"

"You would affect the complaints of the aged, my dear, to confuse your husband's family—the better to conduct your flirtations unmolested." I scolded her fondly. "Do not attempt to prevaricate with me. I see the cunning of your design, and know it for a sham; you have never been in better looks, and I warrant you are well aware of it. For certainly the Earl of Swithin has not allowed your beauty to go unremarked."

She laughed, and reached a tentative hand to her hair. Though it had been cropped grotesquely in the late summer, it was now growing out, the short curls caught up behind and the whole surmounted with a band across the forehead, *à la grecque*. I should feel silly in emulating such a style myself, and thought it better suited to a girl half Eliza's age; but I could not deny it quite became her delicate features.

"Are you famished, Jane? Shall I send for cold meat and cheese?"

"For yourself, by all means—but do not trouble about me. I must be away directly, and tarry only to beg of you a favour, Eliza."

She sat up immediately. "But of course. Anything within my power."

"Might you see your way clear, I wonder, to penning a note of introduction on my behalf?"

"Nothing should be easier. But to whom? For your acquaintance in Bath *must* be larger than my own."

"Mr. Richard Cosway."

"Richard Cosway!" Eliza exclaimed. "Jane, you astonish me! Can you possibly desire to spend so fine a morning in the company of so tedious a man?"

"But I had thought him a painter of the first water."

"He is."

"And a renowned collector."

"As to that—"

"I greatly desire to consult him, Eliza, on a matter of some personal importance." This was no more than the truth, and I might utter the words without a pang.

"I perceive your method, Jane," the Comtesse observed with a roguish twinkle. "You intend that Mr. Richard Cosway shall so admire your *fine eyes*, that he shall not be gainsaid in taking their likeness. I see how it shall be. In a very little while Lord Harold Trowbridge will be the talk of the *ton*, for the pretty token he wears upon his waistcoat. But I warn you, Jane—Mr. Cosway's services are dearly bought."

"I have no intention of sitting for my likeness," I protested, "merely of enquiring as to Mr. Cosway's method and usual fees." It must be impossible to invoke the curious pendant Lord Kinsfell had found on the murdered Portal's breast without explaining the nature of its discovery—and such frankness, even to Eliza, was beyond my power.

"I might come with you, did you spare me an hour," Eliza said, with an eye to the parlour clock. "Eccentric though Cosway is, his conversation at least bears the charm of absurdity; and I should dearly love a glimpse of his rooms in Camden Place."

But the little Comtesse's company, in general so welcome, should quite incommode me in the present instance; for Lord Harold's making of the party a third, should confirm her worst invention. I started up and laid a hand to hers.

"That is impossible, Eliza—I mean to say—I am engaged to—to—"

"—Walk out with an unnamed gentleman in some secluded grove of Sydney Gardens? La, Jane, you are a secretive soul! I shall not presume to o'erlisten your conference with Mr. Cosway for a thousand pounds. But I expect a glimpse of your token in private, once he has seized the likeness. Your eyes are so similar to my dearest Henry's, that I doubt not I shall find the portrait ravishing."

She rose, and crossed to a travelling desk propped up on a table, and drew forth some paper and a pen. A few lines sufficed to commend her respects to Mr. Cosway, and beg of him the indulgence of a few moments on behalf of her sister, Miss Austen, whose acquaintance he might remember having made in the Pump Room yesterday. It closed with some very pretty, though insincere, compliments upon his taste and person, and begged that the sender should be remembered to his wife when next he corresponded with dear Maria.

"There! If that does not melt the miscreant's heart, and win you a triumphant place in his studio and salon, I have grossly misjudged my powers." Eliza folded the note and sealed it with a wafer. "Go with grace and fortune, my dear—and trust me to speak not a word!"

CAMDEN PLACE HOLDS A LOFTY, DIGNIFIED POSITION ON THE SOUTH-east slope of Beacon Hill, such as becomes a man of consequence. It was built some fifteen years ago or more, and the building abruptly halted by the inconvenience of a series of landslips in the area. That part of the Crescent sited upon solid rock is at present habitable, but presents a ludicrous facade to the world's view, in having fourteen houses erected to the left of the central pediment, and only four to the right. The north-east pavilion remains, a picturesque ruin perched atop a crag of rock, in mute testament to the triumph of nature over the ingenuity of man.[3]

The Fractured Crescent takes its name from the Marquis of Camden, whose elephant crest surmounts the keystone of nearly every residence's door, as though an entire herd had condescended to winter in Bath. As I laboured up the long approach by Lord Harold's side, glorying in the exercise, I contemplated the nature of lodgers and lodgings. The precarious ground of Camden Place might readily serve as metaphor, for all in mankind that prefer false grandeur to a more stable propriety.[4]

"An excellent morning for exercise, Miss Austen."

[3] This ruin has been demolished since Austen's time.—*Editor's note.*

[4] Austen may have recalled this metaphoric quality of Camden Place when she made it the temporary home of Sir Walter Elliot in *Persuasion*—a man whose emphasis on personal elevation ignored the fact that his fortune had a some-what shaky foundation.—*Editor's note.*

"Indeed it is, my lord."

"I had considered employing my curricle, or perhaps a brace of chairs—but reflected that neither man nor beast, when burdened with ourselves, should be expected to labour the length of such a hill. I felt certain you would feel the same."

"Are you possessed, then, of prescience as regards my thoughts and feelings?"

Lord Harold cast me a knowing look. "I flatter myself otherwise. You remain one of the few ladies whose thoughts I *cannot* read. But perhaps, having found a virtue in this once before, I prolong the effect for the sake of my enjoyment, when, in fact, it is no more than illusion."

"Then pray tell me of what I am considering *now.*"

"You are abusing me for a very unhandsome escort, in having failed to procure either a carriage or a chair, for the salvation of your half-boots," he rejoined.

"Your illusion may be sustained yet a little while," I replied with satisfaction. "I was considering, rather, the Earl of Swithin's intended removal to a residence opposite your own."

"That minor intelligence is circulating about all of Bath, I fancy," Lord Harold observed, "even as the Earl's carters were circulating about Laura Place this morning. Lord Swithin's descent has not escaped my notice—nor, I might add, the fact that any wheeled traffic must immediately come to a halt, when Laura Place is choked with even the slightest conveyance. For though the streets in the newer part of town may command a wider breadth than those within the old walls, they remain sadly narrow; and any might come to blows over the rights of passage. The night of Her Grace's rout, the assemblage of chairs must have considerably clogged the square."

"I believe they did."

"And thus inspired by the Earl's display, I embarked upon my enquiries among the chairmen not long after breakfast."

"Excellent despatch, my lord. You adventured Stall Street?"[5]

"Both the stand near the Pump Room and the one closer to the

---

[5] Chairmen waited for patrons in Stall Street in much the fashion that taxis presently do—in "stands," or queues. The last Bath chairman did not retire until 1949.—*Editor's note.*

Abbey, I questioned every chairman present, to no avail; of those who had indeed been in Laura Place two nights ago, none could recall an altercation with a waggon or carriage; and so I turned my steps to the Gravel Walk."

"The better to contemplate the problem?"

"The better to examine the chairmen in their resting huts along Queen Place Parade, my dear.[6] There were ten fellows at least, quite splendid in their blue greatcoats and peaked caps, divided between the two fires and blowing upon their chapped fingers."

I stopped a moment, from a desire to draw breath in the midst of my exertions, as to pay heed to Lord Harold's words. "And what did they tell you, my lord?"

"Amidst much contradiction, abuse, and bestowing of oaths—and a remarkable expense of coin, I might add—something of no little worth. One of the chairmen—a broad Irishman who stood well back in the crowd attending the end of my mother's rout—claims to have seen something to our advantage. He will have it that an open carriage attempted to pass through Laura Place in the wee hours of Wednesday morning; and after hesitating some moments, the driver was forced to descend to the horses' heads, and back his pair the length of the street. The chairmen closest to Her Grace's door were unlikely to have observed the debacle—which accounts for the ignorance of the men I questioned in Stall Street."

"An open carriage? But it snowed!"

"And so the chairmen observed. It must have been, they affirmed, a party caught out late by the weather—a party that had not considered of snow, when they undertook to drive about the country-side in a curricle. But as they were happily in possession of a wealth of blankets, in which one passenger at least, was effectively cocooned, we may congratulate them on having sustained no very great evil."

"Our murderer!" I exclaimed. "He had only to drop from the Dowager's window to the open carriage, while the driver was abusing

[6] The Gravel Walk bisected the Royal Crescent Grounds, a common parading lawn for the fashionable of Bath; in *Persuasion*, Austen sends Anne Elliot and her beloved Captain Frederick Wentworth to the Gravel Walk to converse privately. The resting booths Lord Harold describes may still be seen on Queen Place Parade—two small huts with fireplaces that served as shelter for the chair-men.—*Editor's note.*

the chairmen—and conceal himself among the lap robes within. Did the chairmen remark the driver's face?"

"He was heavily muffled against the snow, as should not be extraordinary. But he did approach their stand, and exhort them in the foulest language to clear a passage; which engaged their attention so thoroughly, they could say nothing of the equipage's passenger."

"And the curricle itself?"

"Indistinct in every respect. No coat of arms, no device upon its doors—a common black carriage, such as might be offered for hire at one of the inns."

"And so it might, indeed," I thoughtfully replied. We walked on some moments in silence, and then I added, "Did the murderer depart the anteroom by the open window, my affection for the cunning passage must be entirely at an end. I think, Lord Harold, that we should examine it thoroughly at the nearest opportunity, the better to dismiss its claims upon our attention."

"It shall be done directly we have consulted with your Mr. Cosway, my dear. I should have attended to it before, but that I believed the passage already searched by Mr. Wilberforce Elliot."

"I cannot be easy in my mind, regarding Mr. Elliot's searches," I replied firmly; but further speculation was at an end. We had achieved our object.

Mr. Richard Cosway had taken up his abode in no less than the foremost residence of Camden Place—that distinguished by the broad central pediment and coat of arms of the Marquis of Camden. The artist's taste, as Eliza had assured me, was exquisite in this as in all things.

We mounted the steps, pulled the bell, and were speedily admitted to the foyer, which was dominated by a spiral stair ascending to the drawing-room. A footman in sky-blue livery, and possessed of the chilliest countenance, received Lord Harold's card together with Eliza's hasty scrawl, and made his stately progress towards the first floor.

I profited from the interval in surveying my surroundings—and found them unlike anything I had encountered to date. Even so humble a space as this entry was marked by the hand of the collector. What appeared to be excellent Flemish tapestries of considerable age depended from the ceiling, the richness of their hues fired by the light of the clerestory windows. Two chairs, carved and gilded as thrones, offered the weary their damasked laps; and at their feet lay a veritable tide of Turkey carpet, its design at once intricate and bewildering. Surely the house had been hired furnished? Or had Mr. Cosway seen fit to travel with his belongings, like an Oriental potentate?

"Mr. Cosway is at home," the footman told us with a bow. Lord Harold inclined his head, I took up my reticule, and we followed the man above.

The drawing-room itself was more akin to enchantment than anything in my experience—Mr. Mozart's seraglio come vividly to life. Everywhere about were scattered small ivory cabinets and mosaic tables inlaid with curious stones, their feet carved in the form of fantastic animals. Groups of ottomans, upholstered in the richest damask, were set off by Japanese screens; a profusion of Persian rugs ran the length of the marble floor; and poised for appreciation and display were choice bronzes, artists' models in wax and terra-cotta, specimens of antique Sèvres, Blue Mandar, Nankin and Dresden china. I blinked, and turned about in wonder—and caught at the last the amused smile of the painter himself, as comfortable as a monkey in a jungle of his own making. Richard Cosway was half-hidden by a suit of armour, but a flash of sunlight revealed a waistcoat of cerise and yellow to my eye, as surely as exotic plumage betrays an elusive bird.

"Lord Harold," he said, coming forward with a bow, "and the delightful Miss Austen." He was so diminutive a figure, and possessed of such awkward features, as to seem almost a gargoyle stepped down from the piers of Winchester; but I made him a courtesy, and took the hand he extended in greeting. "It is a pleasure to see you again."

"The pleasure is entirely mine, sir," I replied. "You are very good to receive us on so little notice, and we are sensible of the charge upon your time."

"The notice of the Comtesse de Feuillide—forgive me, of Mrs. Henry Austen—is hardly little," he assured me with becoming grace. "She is one of the few women of fashion who retains both her understanding and her heart—and is thus to be prized as the rarest porcelain."

"I see you value her as I do."

He inclined his head, and gestured towards two of the formidable chairs. "My deepest sympathies, Lord Harold, at your nephew's present misfortunes. Shocking how little the authorities are to be trusted in a matter of this kind! But, however, all earthly authority must give way to a Higher Power in a very little time, as I have presumed to instruct His Royal Highness. All mortal concerns are fleeting, when the world is near its end."

Lord Harold glanced enquiringly at me, then bowed to the painter and seated himself without a word.

"The Comtesse suggests, Miss Austen, that you are desirous of having your likeness taken in miniature; and knowing that such is my primary avocation, you have sought my talents and advice."

"Indeed, sir, I fear that she has imposed upon you," I said hastily. "It is not the matter of my own portrait, but another's, on which we have come."

One eyebrow was suffered to rise, and the great man settled himself upon an ottoman, his splendid coattails arranged behind. I observed he had chosen his seat with care, to accommodate his short legs; for they should have dangled from the height of the chair upon which I perched.

"Pray tell me how I may be of service."

Lord Harold withdrew the small paper parcel from his coat and set it on a table close at hand. "We had hoped, Mr. Cosway, that you might recognise this piece—or perhaps, its subject."

The slight foolishness of expression instantly fled. It was replaced by an appearance of the most intense interest. Cosway undid the paper, and drawing forth a quizzing glass, examined its contents minutely.

"Yes," he mused, "a lovely thing, to be sure. Probably a woman's eye—you will remark the delicacy of the brow, the excessive length of the lashes, and the provocative glance. I should think it is a French piece."

"French?"

"Observe the hazing around the portrait's edge—the suggestion of the eye's suspension in a cloud of mist. It might almost seem to float, like an image in a dream. I devised the style when I painted Mrs. Fitzherbert's eye for His Royal Highness, of course; but it has long since been abandoned among English painters for a more realistic representation. It is usual, now, to frame the eye in a curl of hair, or to suggest the bridge of the nose.''

''Might not it be an older portrait?'' Lord Harold enquired. ''Executed in the 'eighties or 'nineties, perhaps?''

''Such things were not quite the fashion then.'' Mr. Cosway mused, ''for I only painted Mrs. Fitzherbert's eye in 1790. Had the portrait dated from so early a period, I should have recognised it instantly as one of my own. Engleheart adopted the practice, of course, and turned it almost from art to commerce—*anyone* might have an Engleheart eye for the asking—but he is often given to working in enamel, and this is clearly done in watercolours, and painted on ivory. Besides, Engleheart paints in a far more realistic style, and signs the obverse with the initials G.E.''

''So enquiry in that quarter would avail us nothing,'' I said in some disappointment.

The painter shook his head. ''May I enquire, my lord, how you came by the item?''

''Upon the death of its owner,'' Lord Harold replied, without a blush; and indeed, his words were not very far from the truth. ''I thought it possible that the lady whose eye is here represented would wish to know of the gentleman's demise; and that in returning it to its subject I might attempt to perform some final service on behalf of my friend. Miss Austen was so kind as to suggest an appeal to yourself, who must be acclaimed the acknowledged expert in such things.''

''And this *friend* conveyed to you nothing of the portrait's history before his death?''

''He did not. It came to me, as it were, in all the silence of the tomb.''

''A pity. We may suppose that the gentleman preferred to shroud the circumstances of the portrait's commission in mystery. That is not uncommon, my lord, I may assure you, with miniatures of this sort. They were devised as tokens for illicit lovers, and many a possessor has gone to his grave with the name of the subject sealed upon his lips. Pray forgive me—I risk a gross impertinence—but why should you struggle to betray the grave's confidence?''

''My friend died suddenly, in the flower of his youth, and I am certain that he would not have wished his beloved to go unremarked at his passing. A legacy, perhaps, conveyed anonymously—I feel it incumbent upon me to do *something*."

"Though your nephew's affairs are so sadly entangled at present?" Mr. Cosway's protuberant eyes were fixed steadily upon Lord Harold's face. "It is singular that so active a benevolence, on behalf of another wholly unconnected to your misfortunes, should possess you at such a time."

"And now I believe, sir, that you *do* risk impertinence," Lord Harold replied evenly.

"It is very probable. But I cannot think you approach me with any degree of frankness, my lord, and every kind of deceit is my abhorrence. Good day to you—and to you, Miss Austen. My compliments to the Contesse."

"Mr. Cosway—" I sprang up, a most beseeching expression upon my face. "Do permit me to speak a word, I beg. Lord Harold is perhaps too discreet. But I may inform you that a greater knowledge of the portrait's particulars, might swiftly avert his nephew's misery."

"I thought it possible," Mr. Cosway replied, and smiled faintly. "But I cannot like the want of confidence his lordship betrays."

"Your pardon, Mr. Cosway," Lord Harold managed, with a quelling glance for myself; "I spoke perhaps too hastily."

There was a lengthy pause, in which the painter took up the miniature once more and examined it narrowly. At length, however, he set it aside, and folded his hands upon his knee.

"I should like to propose a method of enquiry, my lord."

"Pray do so at once."

"My wife, Maria, of whom you may have heard—"

"And who has not? She is very nearly as celebrated an artist as yourself," Lord Harold acknowledged.

Mr. Cosway bowed. "My wife, Maria, is presently resident in France—and acquainted with the principal painters of the Emperor's circle. Though she makes her home in Lyons, I know that she is often in the capital, and might readily make enquiries regarding your portrait. She might first locate the hand that captured the likeness—and from him, the name of the subject."

"I am afraid it is beyond my power to part with the pendant," Lord Harold said, frowning. "Affairs are too delicate to risk its seizure, through some misadventure of war."

"But you need not give it up for longer than the space of an hour,'' Mr. Cosway cried. ''I shall sketch the piece, front and back; shade the whole in watercolours—and we may have the sending of it by the next packet that serves!''

Lord Harold paused to reflect; but Mr. Cosway's enthusiasm was at a considerable pitch. He hastened to support his first inspiration with another.

''You are intimate in Government circles, my lord. It is everywhere acknowledged among the fashionable of the *ton* that none may move heaven and earth so easily as Lord Harold Trowbridge—and the insertion of a letter in the mail pouch of a secret craft, such as plies the Channel in defiance of blockades and shot, should be the matter of a moment, for one of your influence!''[7]

''Your notion has considerable merit, Cosway,'' Lord Harold replied, rising to his feet, ''and I believe I shall avail myself of it. I shall call for the portrait in exactly one hour, and receive from your hands the coloured sketch, along with a letter of explanation intended for your wife—and may I ask, my good sir, whether His Majesty's Government might offer any favour to the lady in return? Papers of safe conduct for a voyage to England, perhaps?''

''I shall extend the offer to her with pleasure and gratitude.'' Mr. Cosway said; but a sadness suffused his ugly countenance, and I did not believe that his Maria should find safe conduct necessary. ''It is much to think that she shall have news of home with all despatch! I have been sadly vexed by the trials of the foreign post—and so we serve each other a turn, my lord. I shall expect you in an hour!''

He rang for the footman, and bowed us to the door; and I departed Camden Place with a heightened respect for Mr. Richard Cosway. For any man may possess a heart, and the most wounded sensibility, though he parade like a peacock and grin like a monkey.

[7] Not only mail, but passengers frequently passed between France and England despite the state of war. Letters of safe conduct allowed civilians to cross the Channel on packets that were deliberately ignored by the navies on both sides.—*Editor's note.*

Chapter 6

Lovers' Vows

13 December 1804, cont.

~

THE MORNING WAS WELL ADVANCED WHEN WE QUITTED CAMDEN PLACE. I had arranged to return to Madame LeBlanc's for a final fitting before dinner—Lord Harold must wait upon Cosway in an hour's time—and the theatre beckoned for the evening's investigation. No visit to Laura Place, with the intention of thoroughly searching the panelled door's passage, was accordingly possible; and so we parted in the Lansdowne Road with hasty protestations of goodwill and thanks on either side.

Madame LeBlanc had worked wonders on my peach silk in the interval. I observed myself as one transformed by a faery godmother—and in some little exultation, tripped my distance home in time for dinner. I availed myself of an hour at its conclusion, to record these thoughts in my little book; and at six o'clock exactly, when I had commenced to fret, a messenger appeared at Green Park Buildings, with Madame LeBlanc's glorious box beneath his arm. I tore at the wrappings quite heedless of decorum, and unveiled the gown to the Austens' wondering eyes.

"It is very bad of you, I declare," my mother cried, as she saw me pink with pleasure at the lovely drape of stuff. "You have spent this quarter's pin money entire, I daresay, Jane, and will be playing the pauper for months on end. And so you are off—and without a thought for the rest of your dear family! You were always a head-strong, selfish girl! I am certain Cassandra would never behave in a like manner. Had you shewn a more becoming consideration, and pressed Lord Harold for the invitation, *we* might have gone as well. The Wilborough box undoubtedly holds eight. Who is *Jane*, that the Duchess must so distinguish *her?* I confess, *I* should never be easy in the enjoyment of a pleasure denied to others; but my character has always been remarked for its delicacy.''

''Lord Harold, indeed?'' my father exclaimed, with a roguish look. ''And have you made a conquest, my dear? He is a very fine fellow, I declare—though perhaps a trifle lacking in conversation. I cannot remember that I have ever heard anything of him that does not disconcert—he is a sad reprobate, in the world's estimation, and fully fifteen years your senior—but I recollect you are an avowed intimate of old Mr. Evelyn, so perhaps there is nothing very shocking in this.''[1]

''Indeed, Father, I owe Lord Harold no greater gratitude than the preservation of my beloved Isobel, as I think you know,'' I replied. ''Were it not for his efforts, she should surely have hanged; and a lifetime of recompense, in the attending of plays in the Wilborough box, might not be taken amiss.''

''—if it were in fact your Isobel who danced attendance.'' My father's amusement reigned unabated; but his gaze was searching when it met my own. He knew a little of my Lyme adventures—enough to have feared for my safety, tho' not so much as to comprehend Lord Harold's involvement in *that* scheme as well; and it was possible that he had formed a suspicion of the present intrigue. The murder at Laura Place was so much talked of, on the streets and in the papers, that my sudden intimacy with the family would excite an understanding far less brilliant than my father's. I hastened to turn the tide of conversation, lest it drown me entirely.

''I would not have gone for the world, indeed, but that I felt this obligation. And there is Henry to think of.''

[1] William-Glanvill Evelyn (1734–1813) was an old friend of the Austen family; he maintained a second home in Queen's Parade, Bath, and was suspected of adultery. Jane liked him almost as much as his bewitching phaeton, and enjoyed joking about the damage to her reputation sustained from driving out alone with Mr. Evelyn.—*Editor's note.*

"Henry?" my mother enquired.

"Henry," I said firmly. "He has great hopes of the Wilborough fortune. He has performed some little service on Lord Harold's behalf, in the financial line, and an improvement in my acquaintance with the entire family might further Henry's interest."

"Oh, in that case, you had much better go," my mother cried. "Eliza is such a sad, heedless housekeeper—so extravagant in her ways—and poor Henry has never had much of a head for business. Only do not be saying so to the Duchess, I beg, Jane. You must do for your brother what you can. For I very much fear that if you do not, our Henry may end with skulking in the Savoy, or running for Parliament. And we cannot have politicians in the family. They have so little conversation, being given to incessant speeches, that they induce my head to ache dreadfully."[2]

And with this obscure remark, my mother hastened away, to see to the brushing of my gloves.

AT SEVEN EXACTLY THE WILBOROUGH CARRIAGES ARRIVED—ONE A chariot-and-four, which contained the Duchess, her niece, and her companion, Miss Wren; and the other, a curricle, with Lord Harold at the reins. The Gentleman Rogue himself descended in pursuit of me; and his appearance was at once so elegant and daring, in his fashionable black pantaloons and coat, that my father's expression of gravity increased. My mother was all but overcome; and my sister, after the briefest of introductions, retired forthwith to her room.

Were it not for the gravity of circumstances surrounding the Trowbridge family, I should have been entirely gay; but an oppression of feeling could not be overcome. Lord Harold, tho' possessed of admirable qualities, might never be said to move in a high flow of spirits. He was grave, and I was contained; and so we made our progress to the theatre, with a few sentences only exchanged on either side. I ventured to enquire whether Mr. Cosway had fulfilled his commission, and learned to my satisfaction that Lord Harold

[2] Persons pursued for debt could be seized at any time or place, *except* in the Liberties of the Savoy, a few square blocks in the heart of London, where debtors were accorded sanctuary. Similarly, a member of Parliament could not be taken up for debt.—*Editor's note.*

waited but for the receipt of certain necessary papers, to be fetched from London by an express, before sending the packet to Ports-mouth.

The first play was to be Kotzebue's *Lover's Vows*, with Miss Conyng-ham in the role of Agatha; her brother was to play at Frederick.[3] The public taste for German sentiment, first fed some years previous by Mrs. Siddons and her brother Kemble in *The Stranger*, reigns un-abated in Bath; but I must confess to a preference for Sheridan's comedies, or for Shakespeare's work, so elevated in its expression and refined in its feeling. There is a maudlin note in Kotzebue that borders on vulgarity; an artificiality of speech and an excessive dis-play of sentiment that I cannot like. My taste in theatre had gone unsolicited, however—and the purpose of the evening's entertain-ment being so far above the enjoyment of the play, that I determined to express only gratification, and turn my energies from the stage to the probing of Lady Desdemona.

Orchard Street was entirely blocked with traffic, and the Wilborough equipages spent a tedious interval in attempting the entrance.

''I fear the public's enthusiasm for the present drama, though necessarily large, has found an increase in the players' notoriety,'' Lord Harold observed. ''So great has been the sensation at poor Richard Portal's death, that many who should never venture into Orchard Street in the course of their usual pursuits, are present this evening.''

''It puts me in mind of a Siddons night in Drury Lane, when first she played at Isabella,'' I observed. ''I have had to suffer such indig-nities on that lady's behalf, in my attempts to gain a respectable seat, as might occur at a Tyburn hanging.''[4]

[3] It was the custom in the theater of the time to stage two performances each evening. *Lover's Vows* was produced no less than six times in the year's Jane spent in Bath; her dislike of and familiarity with the play, as well as its immense popularity, probably caused her to use it for the Bertram family's amateur theat-ricals in *Mansfield Park*. In that novel, Mary Crawford is Amelia and Edmund Bertram is cajoled into portraying the morose clergyman Anhalt.—*Editor's note.*

[4] Public hangings in Tyburn (now Marble Arch) were a thing of memory by 1804, with most such executions taking place before the gates of Newgate prison; but Jane refers to the public crush and brawling for seats that hangings had formerly occasioned.—*Editor's note.*

Lord Harold turned, one eyebrow lifted. "You are a hardened devotee, then, of the Dramatic Muse? I should have suspected it, Miss Austen. You possess a decided flair for role-playing."

"It was my family's custom to stage an amateur theatrical at Christmas, throughout my tender years in Steventon; on certain occasions we employed our barn for stage, and at others, our neighbours the Lefroys were wont to offer their double parlours for proscenium and pit. I cannot, in truth, consider drama as divisible from Christmastide." I forbore to mention, however, that I had attempted the composition of a play or two, and had determined it was not my particular art—for of my writing I never spoke with Lord Harold.

"What think you of the divine Siddons?" the gentleman enquired, his attention divided between myself and the turbulent street.

"She is possessed of a decided majesty, that none who attempt to play at tragedy may approach. There is nothing, I believe, to equal her Lady Macbeth. But I wonder if I should enjoy her company on a less exalted plane—the drawing-room, for example, rather than the stage? She seems a chilly creature. And her brother Kemble is worse! How he prates and turns about the boards, as emotive as a block of marble! Until I had seen him play at *Pizarro,* I could never like him; but there his figure gained in animation."

"Perhaps tragedy is not your predilection. For there can be few performances to equal Kemble's Hamlet."

"I do confess, Lord Harold, that with so much of sorrow to be found in the everyday—tragedies, perhaps, of a smaller scale—I can but wonder that we *pay* so often for the privilege of enduring it. When I exert my energies towards the theatre, I hope to be transported—to leave such griefs and disappointments behind. I do incline to a preference for Mrs. Jordan."

"Ah, the cheeky sprite," my companion rejoined. "She is no friend to Kemble either—but, being happy in the protection of still greater men, she cannot have cause to repine. Perhaps our own Miss Conyngham may rise so high in the world's estimation."[5]

We had achieved the entrance; Lord Harold leapt down, and

[5] Dorothy Jordan, a comic actress of great renown, unwillingly shared the stage at Drury Lane with the Kemble family throughout the 1780s and '90s. Jordan was the mistress of the Duke of Clarence, George III's third son, and bore him ten children before he abandoned her in her old age.—*Editor's note.*

handed the reins to a waiting footman. He managed the several duties of attending his family and myself with competent grace; and our introductions having been made in all the bustle of the foyer, we had very soon left both snowy street and cloakroom behind, for the relative quiet of the box.

Lord Harold ensured that my place should be at his niece's side; himself he seated by the Dowager; and Miss Wren was forced to suffer in isolation, at the farthest remove from the stage. She is the sort of poor relation that I shudder to think I shall become—dependent, decaying, and despondent in her aspect. An unfortunate creature in her middle years, without strong affection or security to protect her, and necessitous to the point of enduring the Duchess's caprice in exchange for daily bread. Her sunken cheeks, sharp nose, and respectable grey muslin proclaim Miss Wren the soul of abject decency; and I averted my eyes from the pitiable sight, lest her circumstance destroy my brief happiness in my new gown.

"You are very fine this evening, Miss Austen," Lord Harold observed, as he cast an eye over his niece and myself. "You must always go about in exactly that shade, regardless of weather or season. It becomes your dark hair and eyes extremely."

I blushed, and expected every moment the weight of the Dowager's stare, and some unease regarding her son's attentions to a mere nobody—but in a moment, all discomfiture was at an end. Eugenie had so far ignored Lord Harold's remark, being absorbed in a perusal of the program, that it might never have fallen. She was this evening a confection of diamonds and ebony lace, her carriage erect and her sharp-featured face held high; and as she leant towards the rail, an ebony cane grasped firmly in one hand, her brilliant eyes narrowed in a manner that was strikingly familiar.

"Harry," she declared in a peremptory tone, "I cannot find Miss Conyngham listed in the program. Can it be that she is indisposed?"

"Perhaps the death of her colleague has affected her too deeply."

"Then I shall be greatly amazed. I confess I detected no affection in the case."

"Indeed?" Lord Harold's interest quickened. "Then I have been labouring under a misapprehension. I had understood them to be lovers."

"Lord Harold!" squeaked Miss Wren. "How can you speak so! And in front of the young ladies!"

"Most of Bath has thought the same," his mother replied crisply, as though Miss Wren had never spoken, "but I persist in denying the attachment. It seemed, to my mind, but an affair of convenience. We must descend upon the wings, Harry, when the play is at an end, and make Hugh Conyngham tell us how she does."

Miss Wren let out another squeak, and jumped slightly from agitation. "Would that be entirely proper, Your Grace? I cannot think that it should, particularly for Lady Desdemona—"

"I am at your service, madam," Lord Harold replied to his mother. "I confess to an active interest in Miss Conyngham's condition myself."

In an apparent effort to turn the conversation, Lady Desdemona said, "You are privileged, Miss Austen, in calling Bath your home?"

I stifled a barbed retort—Bath being the very *last* place I should honour with that sentiment—and took refuge in the notion that there was nothing like a pleasure place for diverting one's attention from one's cares. Did Lady Desdemona claim a broad acquaintance in Bath? She did not; and confessed herself quite lonely.

"Then the addition of your uncle to Her Grace's party must be a happy one," I observed. "With such a gentleman to escort you to the theatre and the Rooms, your enjoyment of Bath may only increase."

"Oh, yes," the lady replied, with a grateful look for Lord Harold, who seemed engrossed in observing the crowd through his quizzing glass. "I do so esteem my uncle! He pays the least mind to what is tedious in social convention—quite unlike Papa, who is forever preaching about a lady's proper place—that I am entirely easy in his company."

"He is an excellent man."

"Do you think so?" She laughed in delight. "How relieved I am. I hear such scandalous reports of Uncle's conduct, as to suspect that he is very little admired in the world."

"Then we may assume he is but little known. For those who comprehend the depth of his character, cannot but honour it." I spoke from the heart, and too late regretted the force of my words.

"But of course!" Lady Desdemona cried. "I had quite forgot. You are *Uncle's* acquaintance, not Grandmère's." Her grey eyes, so like Lord Harold's, took on an aspect of calculation; and I knew her to be wondering at my friendship with the man, and all that it might imply. At nearly thirty, and never entirely able to consider myself handsome—lacking birth or fortune to distinguish me—I cannot have seemed at all in the Trowbridge line.

I hastened to disabuse her.

"Our acquaintance is quite recent. It is my brother Mr. Henry Austen, who claims a nearer friendship with his lordship. I only met your uncle a few weeks ago."—(though this was hardly true, I had no wish to detail the tragic events at Scargrave)—"at Henry's London residence. I can only suppose that Lord Harold has learned I am a great enthusiast for Kotzebue—and so extended his very kind invitation to make another of your party."

"Then I am happy of the addition," she replied simply, "I very nearly refused to show my face abroad this e'en—but one cannot hide within doors forever. Poor Kinny's affairs are so sadly entangled—" She faltered, and compressed her lips.

"I am certain Lord Harold will soon put them to rights."

"You were present, I understand, at Grandmère's rout?"

"I had the honour of dancing with your brother well before supper."

Her face brightened. "Then you must see it as I do! You will know how impossible it is for Kinny to do anyone a mischief!"

"Was he long in residence at Laura Place before the sad events of Tuesday?"

"He was arrived but a fortnight."

"Lord Kinsfell," Miss Wren interposed with an important air, "was come on an errand from His Grace the Duke. He intended the removal of Lady Desdemona from Bath, and I for one must deeply regret that he did not carry his point!" At this, she cast a withering look at the Dowager Duchess; and I concluded that Eugenie had refused to give up her granddaughter. "But then, in my forty years, I have often observed, that a world of misfortune will result from the too-great indulgence of a wilful mind. I—"

"Oh, Lord, Wren, will you have done?" Lady Desdemona cried in evident exasperation. "Would you have me sent off, against my express wishes? Returned summarily to that dreadful prison?"

"Wilborough House may certainly be draughty, and its decoration of a vanished era, but no bars does it boast, nor turnkeys at the door," Miss Wren replied with pointed reproof. "Whereas Bath cannot be safe for your reputation, my dear Mona, in its present climate of opinion. You are well launched on your first Season—but we cannot sink in complacency. You would do well to seize what opportunity offers. We are none of us growing the younger."

Lady Desdemona trembled with indignation, and colour mounted to her cheeks. I may say that she appeared to even greater advantage this evening, being dressed all in white and with pearls in her hair, than she had in the midst of the rout. At eighteen, her figure was already formed; she was fine-boned and elegant, and her countenance glowed with the outrage of her feeling.

"Grandmère," she pleaded, with a hand to the Dowager's arm. "It is beastly of Wren to speak to me so—as though Kinny's misfortune were entirely my fault! Tell her that she is *not* to interfere. Tell her I may stay with you always."

"Of course, my darling," the Dowager replied indulgently. "You shall grow old in retirement—nay, retreat to a convent if necessary—for the discouragement of Lord Swithin. Not a new gown shall you have, nor any amusement, until a more respectable man begs for your hand."

"But Lord Swithin is a man of parts!" Miss Wren spluttered. "I wonder, Mona, that you should slight a gentleman of his consequence; but it is ever the way with headstrong youth. You cannot know your own interest."

"And is *interest* the sole consideration upon which I must judge exactly how I am to be happy?" Lady Desdemona exclaimed, with a quickening in her looks. "Lord Swithin is a man of *far too many* parts, by my way of thinking—and he has bestowed them far too widely about Town."

"Mona!" Miss Wren cried, in shock. "What *will* your uncle think?"

"The Earl may be capable of intrigues, and dissipation, and schemes of the most pernicious kind—but as to comporting himself respectably, and in a manner that might ensure *any* woman's love—"

"*Brava,* my dear," the Dowager said comfortably. "You speak the part well. How I wish that a grandchild of mine might respectably tread the boards!"

"With respect, Your Grace," Miss Wren interposed, "the Duke of Wilborough sees nothing objectionable in Lord Swithin—and in *my* day, a father's approbation should have been enough. It is unbecoming in a lady to think so firmly for herself. It smacks of stubbornness and caprice, and neither may recommend her to the stronger sex. When you are as blessed with experience as I, my dear Mona—"

"—I shall undoubtedly be the happier, in having followed my heart," Lady Desdemona concluded. "I may wonder, Wren, that having presented so biddable a nature *in your day*, you failed to find a husband."

The mortification of this last remark was admittedly shocking; but I could not suppress a smile, nor a quick look for Lord Harold, whose countenance betrayed a smothered animation. The unfortunate Wren retreated hastily in a dignified silence, but declared from her looks that all enjoyment in the evening was at an end. A moment's reflection seemed to chasten the Lady Desdemona; her cheeks flushed and her eyes found her lap; and so the curtain rose.

MISS CONYNGHAM, AS IT HAPPENED, WAS NOT INDISPOSED.

To the Dowager Duchess's delight, the actress appeared in the very soul of Agatha—arch, too-intimate, and vulgar by turns—with a heightened colour and a depth of intonation that must captivate even the stoniest of hearts. Lord Harold, I observed, was most keenly aware of the lady—and fixed his quizzing glass upon her for the duration of the first act.

We had borne with the diverse fates of the inhabitants of a small German village—their incestuous proximity, their fantastic doubts; had heard love proclaimed, rejected, denied, and at long last embraced—and had, with relief at least for *my* part, achieved the space of an intermission. Lord Harold let fall his glass at last—and his countenance, to my surprise, was a study in abstraction. What quality in Maria Conyngham could so enthrall his thought?

"If you will excuse me, Mother, I believe I shall take the air," he said abruptly, and bowed his way from the box.

"The devil tobacco," Eugenie declared with an indulgent smile. "It is the sole influence he cannot master."

"Are you comfortable, Your Grace?" Miss Wren enquired anxiously. "I am sure you must be warm. It is decidedly overheated—dreadfully close—and such odours as will rise from the pit—"

"In truth, Wren, I am feeling a trifle cold," Eugenie replied serenely. "Perhaps you will fetch my shawl."

The Dowager's shawl—a formidable square of cashmere—being hung even now in the cloakroom, Miss Wren let slip a martyred sigh, and went in search of the stairs.

I turned my attention to Lady Desdemona. "The excellence of this evening's performance must do Mr. Portal credit. The company might almost have exerted themselves to honour his memory."

"Indeed," the girl replied. She glanced at her grandmother, who gave every appearance of dozing behind her fan, and lowered her voice. "It is a pity, is it not, that he was denied the pleasure of witnessing their glory? The success of this theatre was his dearest concern, and Kotzebue his delight. It is incredible that he should be with us no more—he was so full of life, so animated with hopes for the season, and the new theatre in Beauford Square! Mr. Portal looked to the mounting of *Lovers' Vows* to quite ensure his success; for it cannot fail to fill the stalls."

"And so he has done. By the simple act of dying in so sensational a manner, Mr. Portal has brought all of Bath to Orchard Street," I observed with deliberate coldness. "Were he on the brink of bankruptcy, we might accuse him of having staged his death merely for the sake of profit!"

"Miss Austen!" Lady Desdemona cried in horror; but horror swiftly gave way to amusement. Not for Lord Harold's niece, Miss Conyngham's outraged sensibility; and this alone could tell me much. She looked again at the dozing Dowager, and then dropped her voice to a whisper. "Had Mr. Portal suspected there to be money in the act, I do not doubt he should have entertained the notion. He prized riches above all things—even, perhaps, the glory of his company."

"Did he, indeed? And did he possess considerable means?"

"I cannot undertake to say. He was hardly murdered for his purse, if that is what you would suggest, Miss Austen. For it was discovered upon his person."

"I merely wondered how such a man—with reputation, wealth, and every consideration of good society—should have occasion for making enemies. For someone must have despised him enough to end his life. *You* were acquainted with the gentleman, my lady— surely you must have formed an opinion on the subject. What can Mr. Portal have done, to warrant his violent end?"

"I do not know," Lady Desdemona replied. Her brow furrowed.

''I have worried at the subject like a terrier at a bone. My acquaintance with Mr. Portal was hardly so intimate, as to permit me to form anything but the most cursory judgement of his character. He perpetually ran in a high flow of spirits; he was fond of company and of wine; he possessed energy enough for ten; and was rarely so nice in his sentiments or expression, as to render him the safest of companions. In short, he was boisterous and crude, and sadly wanting in tact.'' She shook her head. ''I could imagine him to offend any number of persons without the least intention of doing so, and forget the insult as readily as he ignored his engagements—which was repeatedly, I assure you.''

''Does want of tact, then, explain the gentleman's scene with Lord Kinsfell?''

Her eyes slid away, ''Of that I may say even less. For Kinny is chary of taking offence, particularly among his friends; and so I must believe the injury to have been a peculiar one. My brother was excessively grieved.''

''Mr. Portal does not seem an ideal lover for Miss Conyngham,'' I mused. ''I wonder what she saw in him to recommend his suit?''

''Was he to marry her, then? How come you to know of it?'' A quickening of interest, and a faint blush to the lady's cheeks. ''I had not heard that rumour.''

''Nor had I. I speculate, that is all. Miss Conyngham was sadly shaken by Mr. Portal's murder—and must have felt the loss quite deeply.''

''—Though not so deeply as to forgo her present performance,'' Lady Desdemona retorted. ''She would sacrifice everything to the goddess of success, I believe.''

''You do not esteem her.''

My companion shrugged. ''I cannot claim any great knowledge of the lady. But I have observed, Miss Austen, that they who earn their bread in the performance of a role, have often difficulty in quitting the stage. They dissemble, as it were, in everything—and the truth of their characters is difficult to seize. I should never be certain whether Miss Conyngham were dying of grief at Mr. Portal's loss—or if her feelings were quite the reverse.''

I had not looked for such penetration in a girl of eighteen; but she was, after all, Lord Harold's niece.

''You do not endure a similar sense of ruin?'' I enquired gently.

"My brother, indeed, is sadly circumstanced—but I can have no occasion for despair. Now Uncle is come, all shall soon be set to rights."

I was prevented from pursuing this interesting line of intelligence, by a circumspect cough from the direction of the box's door. Lady Desdemona's head swung round, her grey eyes widened, and involuntarily, she seized my arm.

The cold blue glare of a fair-headed gentleman, arrayed in all the brilliance of fawn knee breeches and a bottle-green coat, met my interested gaze. The very Lord Swithin. He was a remarkable figure of a man—and yet the good looks of his countenance were undoubtedly marred by the arrogance that suffused them.

"Lady Desdemona." He bowed with exquisite grace, but the hauteur of his glance might have guttered a candle-flame. "I am happy to see you. Your Grace—"

The Dowager Duchess awoke with a start, glanced about, and then held out her hand with all the appearance of cordiality. "Swithin! I declare! It is like your insolence to come to Bath at such a time. I could wish that *all* our acquaintance were as careless of convention."

If he took the measure of her ambivalence, the Earl betrayed no sign. He bent low over the Dowager's hand.

Eugenie patted the empty place beside her, with a look for Lady Desdemona, who sat stiffly upright in her chair. "Do sit, Lord Swithin, I beg. We have not talked this age."

"I fear that the honour is beyond my power at present to indulge, Your Grace. A large party of friends awaits my attention."

"Of ladies, you mean?" Lady Desdemona cried, and lifted her glass to peer about the theatre. "Now where is your box? I should dearly love to see the rogues' gallery you've carried in your train."

"You have quite failed to acquaint me with your friend, Mona," said the Earl in a tone of quelling severity.

"And are you due any such civility, Lord Swithin? I am not entirely convinced. But since you shame me to the courtesy—Miss Austen, may I present the Earl of Swithin. Lord Swithin, Miss Austen."

The gentleman bowed and clicked his heels. "You are visiting Bath, Miss Austen?"

"A visit of some duration, my lord," I replied easily, "since it has been prolonged now these three years and more. You are only just arrived, I collect?"

"I am."

"For the Christmas holiday?"

"I may, perhaps, remain so long, I cannot undertake to say."

"You do not attempt a trial of the waters, then? For their effects cannot be felt, I am assured, in less than two months."

My brilliant line of chatter had not so entirely engrossed my attention, that I failed to notice Lady Desdemona's furious regard for the Earl, nor the intensity of his returning stare; and the evident unease of the Dowager Duchess, as she surveyed the pair, did little to soften my anxiety. All attempt at forestalling a dispute, however, was as naught; for rather than responding to my gentle interrogation, the Earl abruptly broke out with—

"What the devil do you mean, Lady Desdemona, by throwing yourself in the path of a common upstart, who must necessarily get himself killed in your grandmamma's house, and involve us all in the very worst sort of scandal?"

"*Scandal?* Is that now to be laid at my door?" Lady Desdemona retorted indignantly. "And what, might I ask, were *you* thinking, my lord Swithin, when you threw down your glove at poor Easton's feet not a month ago—and all for the impropriety of having named your mistress in my hearing?"

"Easton is a fool." The Earl replied with contempt. "He observes me riding with a married woman in the park, and suggests the greatest calumny. When I consider the injury that poor pup visited on Mrs. Trevelyan—I should have killed him when the opportunity served. But such vengeance, even in an affair of honour, is beneath me. Having no desire to flee the country on Easton's account, I barely winged the fellow at twenty paces.[6] And what of Easton, indeed? It is hardly *Easton* who has driven me to Bath! Your conduct and impropriety, madam, have so involved my reputation, that I am forced to require an explanation."

"And I shall certainly never give it!" Lady Desdemona cried. Her face was pale with anger. "I cannot conceive how my private affairs

[6] The fighting of duels between gentlemen like Colonel Easton and the Earl, although very common in Austen's day as a means of settling disputes, was nonetheless illegal. If a duelist were mortally wounded, his assailant was liable for murder. A common circumvention of this result was escape to the Continent—although with England at war with France, such havens were dwindling.—*Editor's note.*

should *involve* a gentleman so entirely a stranger to my interest and happiness as yourself. But if ever I require your opinion, sir, regarding the intimates of Laura Place, I shall not hesitate to solicit it."

"You may attempt to brave this out, Mona," the Earl retorted in a warning tone, "but you shall not do so by abusing your friends. You will require as many as you may command in the coming weeks. Do you remember that, when the faint among them desert you. I could do a vast deal for Kinsfell, did I choose. You would do well to remember that also."

"Your concern for my brother quite overwhelms me, Lord Swithin," Lady Desdemona observed with a sneer. "Had you formed no intention of profiting by the Marquis's misfortune, I might almost have credited the sincerity of it."

The Earl bowed with frigid care and turned for the box's door.

"Whatever they may say of Richard Portal," Lady Desdemona threw at his retreating back, "he at least attempted to *play* the gentleman—in which guise you appear, my lord, as the merest caricature!"

Chapter 7

Performance
of an Ingenue

"OH, GRANDMAMMA—HOW DISTINCTLY *ODIOUS* SWITHIN IS!" SIGHED
Lady Desdemona despairingly, when the Earl had left us. "That a
man may seem the very soul of elegance—possessed of understanding, education, and knowledge of the world—and yet be so utterly
abominable!"

"He is a hateful fellow, indeed," the Dowager replied with a
soothing pat. "He would have us all fear and love him to distraction,
for which no one can forgive him."

"Perhaps," I said thoughtfully, "if he *expected* that adoration a
little less—"

"I am sure I can have given him no expectation of the kind,"
Lady Desdemona said stiffly. "I made every effort to assure him of
my indifference."

"And so appeared as spiteful as a cat," the Dowager observed.
"Your comment about his rogues' gallery was far too broad, my
sweet. I can detect no other ladies in the Swithin box than his sisters,
Louisa and Augusta. You are far too attentive to the company he
keeps. I might recommend, *pauvre* Mona, that the best way to turn a
man *enragé*, as I suspect you mean to do, is to ignore him completely."

"That should not be difficult," her granddaughter retorted.

"Ah, Wren," said the Dowager, "there you are at last."

Miss Wren was revealed as drooping in the doorway, Her Grace's wrap in her arms; and so the interesting discourse on Desdemona's heart was allowed to fall away.

The young lady herself sank into her seat, lost in contemplation of the deserted stage; I guessed her thoughts to be wandering along the paths laid out by her helpful grandmamma. But at last, with a look for me, she attempted to elevate her spirits.

"You must be thinking me a terrible shrew, Miss Austen! I behaved just now with the height of incivility. I find that I cannot see Swithin without I abuse him hatefully."

"I cannot think that Lord Swithin comported himself any more admirably; and he must be held to a higher standard. He is, after all, some ten years your senior—and yet you seem to have reduced him to the querulousness of a schoolboy!"

"I dread meeting him," Lady Desdemona confessed. "It is excessively awkward to be thrown in the way of a man one has refused! It was to avoid scenes of that kind that I quitted London. And now—Swithin is come to Bath! What can he mean by it?"

"Perhaps he hopes to persuade you of the brilliance of his suit," I suggested gently.

"Then I shall have to use every means within my power to convince him of my indifference!"

"By encouraging the attentions of other gentlemen, for example?"

She started up hotly, as though to protest, and then subsided in her chair. "I had entertained the notion," she murmured.

"And chose Richard Portal as your primary object?"

"Mr. Portal *does* seem to have thoroughly enraged Swithin, does he not? It is too delicious! For the abominable Earl to accuse *me* of inciting scandal—and with such a man!"

Any answer I might have given was forestalled by Lord Harold's return to the box, and the sounding of the bell that signalled the recommencement of the play.

WHEN THE CURTAIN HAD AT LENGTH RUNG DOWN ON *LOVERS' VOWS*, and risen again for the gratification of the players' vanity, and was at last required to close forever the scene of that forsaken German village—the Dowager Duchess thrust herself to her feet with some difficulty, and the assistance of her ebony cane. "Wren!" she cried. "Make haste! Make haste! To the wings, I beg you, with our felicitations for Miss Conyngham! Lord Harold and I shall follow."

I linked arms with Lady Desdemona, and we proceeded in company towards the stairs.

What a soaring infinity may be hidden by a proscenium curtain! What shifting worlds, in sliding panels of scenery—what hustle and bustle of figures to-ing and fro-ing about the business of the play—and what odours of beeswax, powder, paint, and scent! I stood upon the threshold of the stage's wings, and felt myself at the border of another world. The most democratic of worlds, too—for any may rise to greatness in treading the humble boards. There is a nobility bestowed by art that mere birth can never imitate, as Mrs. Siddons and her brother have shown. Would Maria Conyngham achieve a similar elevation one day, and be celebrated in word and deed? Or would she end a discarded drab—full of blasted hopes, and riven dreams, and the oblivion drunk from a cup of gin?

"Your Grace," called a voice from the obscurity of a screen.

Our party turned, and discovered the figure of Hugh Conyngham, arrayed still in his paint and court dress, a formidable Frederick. A slim, lithe figure, with a cap of dark curls arrayed in the fashionable Brutus; a sulky line to his mouth; restless blue eyes the colour of the sea. He bowed stiffly, but offered no other word.[1]

"Our deepest felicitations, Mr. Conyngham," the Dowager cried, with all the energy of an enthusiast. "It was nobly played, sir—you do our Kotzebue great credit, I am sure."

"And Mr. Portal as well, I hope," the actor returned. His eyes were fixed upon Lord Harold; but he seemed disinclined to an introduction. It was as though, I thought, the actor wished to be anywhere but in the presence of the Wilborough clan.

"I am Lord Harold Trowbridge, Mr. Conyngham," the Gentleman Rogue offered smoothly. "I must join my congratulations

---

[1] In Austen's day, theaters existed by permission of the monarch. Actors and actresses were still expected, as a result, to perform in court dress, as though in the presence of the king. Although this habit had begun to give way to period costuming in such places as Covent Garden and Drury Lane, it remained the convention. Men who sported the Brutus wore their hair brushed forward along the temples like a Roman of Caesar's day.—*Editor's note.*

with my mother's. For a company so thoroughly bowed in mourning, you comported yourselves with the utmost distinction. I was particularly struck by Miss Conyngham's performance. She was as unmarked by grief as the Comic Muse.''

''Then I may thank the excellence of my art, my lord.'' Maria Conyngham abandoned a small knot of fellow players at the nether end of the stage, and drew close to her brother. Her colour was high and her countenance stormy. ''I should think you guilty of the grossest presumption, sir, had I not already learned to expect it of the Trowbridge family. For any of you to show your faces here *must* excite comment—and we have drawn the public eye far too much already!''

''Maria—''

She stayed Hugh Conyngham's words with a look. ''My brother is too noble to reproach you, my lord. But I cannot claim so admirable a restraint. Your family has reduced us to our present misery—has nearly accomplished our ruin—and yet you would burden us with your attentions! This is hardly kind, sir; and it cannot be met with civility. I would beg you to quit the theatre as soon as may be. Any notice from the murderers of Richard Portal must be an insult to his memory.''

Her brown eyes blazed with indignation, and perhaps a film of tears; but the wonderful carriage of her head—courageous, unbowed, determined—must quell the most impertinent.

Lord Harold parted his lips as if to speak, a curious expression on his countenance—but at that moment, Maria Conyngham started forward, the Trowbridges forgotten.

''My lord!'' she cried, and dropped an elegant curtsey. ''You honour us, indeed.''

The Earl of Swithin brushed past our party, his eyes fixed on the actress, a bouquet of hot-house flowers in his arms. ''My dear Miss Conyngham,'' he said with a smile, ''I cannot remember when I have been made so thoroughly happy by any theatrical performance. Your servant, ma'am.''

And while the Dowager Duchess looked on, aghast at the myriad discourtesies visited this evening upon the house of Wilborough, her favourite *ingénue* received the blossoms with a cry of pleasure, and the most ardent look. Mr. Conyngham, however, was less happy in the Earl's attentions; for he paled, stepped back a pace, and swallowed convulsively.

But all speculation must be deferred a while, for at my side the Lady Desdemona had commenced to seethe. "What insufferable insolence!" she muttered, her hands clenched within their delicate gloves. "What a despicable display!"

Whether she spoke of the actress or the Earl, I could not bother to learn; for if ever there was a moment for feminine diversion, surely *this* was such a time. A crowd of well-wishers had gathered in the wings at our backs, and in an instant must inundate us entirely.

I stepped around Lord Harold, and hurried forward with a little flutter of breathlessness, as though all but overcome by the proximity of the great; rushed towards Mr. Conyngham with words of appreciation bubbling upon my lips; caught my heel in the hem of my new gown (to such sacrifices a heroine must be resigned), and pitched headlong at the actor's feet. A shriek of agony, and a clutching at my ankle, amply completed the picturesque.

I was gratified with a chorus of exclamation, and the swift despatching of a prompting-boy for compresses and ice. Maria Conyngham set down her flowers, and wrung her hands in dismay; the Earl of Swithin looked all his indignation and contempt; and Mr. Conyngham himself carried me to his dressing-room, which proved the nearest to hand. Lady Desdemona Trowbridge followed hard upon his heels.

"I hope you may be more comfortable here, Miss—"

"Austen," I supplied, all humble gratitude, as Conyngham deposited me upon a settee. "I cannot think how I came to wrench the joint so dreadfully. But I was in such transports at the excellence of your performance, sir—I can only think that the headiness of the experience—my *utter* delight in Kotzebue—undid me sadly. I shall not attempt the theatre again, until I may command a greater restraint of feeling."

Hugh Conyngham knelt down at my foot, then hesitated. "May I be permitted to ascertain whether any bones are broken?" he enquired.

"I cannot see how that is necessary, sir," Lady Desdemona interposed. "We shall attend to Miss Austen when once we have got her into the carriage. My uncle has gone to summon it even now, I believe, and will have it drawn up to the entrance near the wings."

Blessed child! The falsehood was uttered, of necessity, in clearest innocence; but I was certain Lord Harold had embarked upon his scheme of searching Mr. Portal's offices. I must, at all cost, detain Hugh Conyngham.

"If I might have a little water, sir," I said in the feeblest accent.

"Of course—Smythe! You there—Smythe!"

The door was pulled open, and a massive, bearded fellow entered the room. Hardly a player, for he lacked even so much refinement as an actor might claim; a labourer about the wings, perhaps, adept in the joining of scenery. Smythe looked from Conyngham to myself, and then at Lady Desdemona, with the most surly expression; and I started involuntarily under the weight of his gaze. For the man possessed a most peculiar aspect, in having one brown, and one blue eye. A hundred years since, it should have been called the mark of the Devil—and might still be considered so, in the remoter villages of the kingdom.

"A glass for the lady. Quick, man!"

Smythe turned without a word, and the door slammed behind him.

"And now I come to think of it—perhaps some brandy?" Mr. Conyngham exclaimed.

"The pain *is* excruciating. Perhaps a little would not be amiss—"

"I should have a bottle to hand, somewhere beneath this chaos of props." He began to shift among the piles of playbills and swords, horses' heads and kingly sceptres, that littered the tiny space. Lady Desdemona sat disconsolately at my side, her thoughts quite distant. The Earl and Miss Conyngham, I noted, had not seen fit to follow us to her brother's rooms. The man Smythe, however, reappeared, and noisily deposited several glasses upon a little table before quitting us abruptly.

"Capital," Mr. Conyngham declared, and lifted high a bottle. "The last of my stores from France. Brandy, Miss Austen?"

I accepted a glass from his outstretched hand. "You are very good to take such prodigious care of me, Mr. Conyngham, and in the midst of all your trials and sorrows. The company is much cast down, I suppose, at Mr. Portal's sad demise?"

"How could it be otherwise?"

"Naturally. A dreadful business. I gather it was entirely unexpected?"

"But of course, madam! What other possibility might there be, in such a case?"

I shrugged and sipped at my brandy. "When a man is murdered, one must suppose him to possess some enemy."

"One at least, of that we may be certain," the actor replied, with a painful look for Lady Desdemona.

She flushed hotly. "If you would mean my brother the Marquis, Mr. Conyngham, I must declare you to be mistaken. Lord Kinsfell is entirely innocent."

"I wonder, sir, whether you might not elucidate matters for Lady Desdemona and me," I said with a conspiratorial smile. "You were placed to advantage at the moment the murder occurred, were you not? For though *we* were trained upon yourself, in attending your declamation—and it was admirable, by the by, as is every performance you attempt—*you* were facing the anteroom door. Did you observe anyone other than Lord Kinsfell to enter it, pray?"

He turned pale, and fixed his piercing blue gaze upon my face as though intent upon reading my thoughts; and then shook his head in the negative. "I did not."

"How unfortunate. Perhaps we should enquire of your sister. But I gather she is presently engrossed in the delightful Earl. Their acquaintance is of some duration, I collect—for Lord Swithin is only lately come to Bath. He cannot have met Miss Conyngham *here*."

"No—that is to say—I believe they became acquainted in Ramsgate last summer," Mr. Conyngham replied, backing towards the door, "and I thank you for reminding me of my duty. I must not delay in expressing my thanks to the Earl for his attention; and the pantomime, too, is about to commence. Forgive my desertion, Miss Austen, and pray accept my best wishes for your swift recovery—" And with that, he fled the room.

"Oh, *where* is my uncle?" Lady Desdemona cried. "Was there ever so villainous an evening? I am wild to be gone!"

"And so you shall be, Mona, in a very little while," Lord Harold said, appearing at the door. "The coach is even now drawn round to the wings, and I am come to convey Miss Austen thither."

The glint of satisfaction in his hooded grey eyes did not escape my scrutiny. He had discovered something of worth in the manager's office, then.

"Place your hands about my neck," he whispered, as he gathered me into his arms, "and do not even *think* of blushing. It would be too

much of a performance altogether, my dear, even for *your* considerable talents."

"WHAT A QUANTITY OF CORRESPONDENCE OUR MR. PORTAL DID
conduct, to be sure." Lord Harold gripped the reins, gave a nod to
the boy at the horses' heads, and chucked the team into motion. We
had tarried just long enough in the wings to avoid the greater part of
the departing crush, and Orchard Street showed tolerably clear. "By
the by, you did not truly suffer an injury, I hope?"

"To my pride alone, I assure you. We may dismiss the event upon
the morrow, when I shall declare my ankle much improved from the
hasty attentions and fortuitous brandy of Mr. Conyngham."

"He is more solicitous of strangers than his sister."

"Indeed. She was consumed with the attentions of her friends—of
whom Mr. Conyngham appears more than a little wary."

A swift glance, sharp with interest. "You think him no friend to
the Earl?"

"I think him most uneasy in Lord Swithin's company. He certainly
did not meet the gentleman with composure; and I believe he fears
his lordship's influence with Miss Conyngham. I chanced to enquire
when the acquaintance was formed, and so discomposed Mr. Conyngham with my curiosity, that he summarily left the room."

"You interest me exceedingly, Miss Austen. I had not observed
Mr. Conyngham at the Earl's entrance."

"Naturally not. Your gaze was fixed upon the lady."

Lord Harold seemed about to speak; hesitated; and fell back upon
the gesture of snapping at the reins.

So he did not contemplate Maria Conyngham with tranquillity. To
my extreme surprise and displeasure, the slightest finger of jealousy
stirred along my spine.

"I profited from the moment to enquire whether Hugh Conyngham had observed any to enter the anteroom in the midst of his
speech, and from his dreadful reaction, I may assume that he did
so—but finer arts than mine must be deployed, before he leaves off
denial. But tell me, I beg, of the manager's office—how went your
researches there?"

"It was as I assumed," Lord Harold replied with satisfaction. "The
magistrate has no more considered of its existence than he has been

to the moon. I cannot claim to have been the first to venture within its walls—but I may congratulate myself upon having carried with me those little props so requisite to the occasion.''

"I do not understand you, my lord."

"I would guess that some part of the theatre's company has already sorted out Mr. Portal's personal belongings. It should be astonishing, indeed, did they not give way to the temptation. Some few have been at the cash box, which bears the marks of decided ingenuity about its locks, unhappily to little purpose—it is a fearsome thing, and quite impregnable—while others have tumbled his books and what papers he left to hand. I wanted leisure for a thorough perusal of the damage, and leisure I did not have; and so I bent my efforts to an assault upon Mr. Portal's cunning little desk."

"His desk! But had not others been there before you?"

"Possibly they had. But I alone possess the means to open it."

Lord Harold thrust the reins into his left hand, and with his right, fumbled in the pocket of his greatcoat. A slim iron ring was deposited in my lap.

"A quantity of picks, my dear Miss Austen," he said exultantly. "One should never travel without them. Occasions invariably arise in which this single device will prove as gold. As it has certainly done this evening."

"Your resources must astonish me, my lord," I replied with conscious irony. "Is any claim of privacy impervious to your seeking mind?"

"Where it springs from virtue, perhaps," he conceded. "But I would counsel you never to attempt a conscious deceit, my dear Miss Austen—for from my confederates I demand the most ardent truth."

Something in his tone—a harsher tenor than I had experienced of late—brought my gaze to his face. In the faint glow of a moon beset with clouds, the narrow features were utterly unreadable, as fixed as a mask of death.

"And so you opened the desk?"

"It bore an admirable lock—French, I should think—and required no less than five attempts with my picks; but in the end, it surrendered to my hand."

"Then make haste to share your discovery, my lord! We are nearly come to Green Park Buildings!''

Lord Harold permitted himself a snort of amusement—for, in truth, we had barely achieved Cheap Street, with the lights of the White Hart aglow around us. ''I was so fortunate as to find a packet, Miss Austen, bound up with ribbon and innocent to the naked eye. A swift perusal of its contents, however, revealed it to contain copies of Mr. Portal's correspondence. I had only moments to shift the papers, but saw any number addressed to at least one gentleman among our acquaintance.''

''Do not keep me in suspense, I beg.''

''The Earl of Swithin.''

''—whom we know to be most anxious on the subject of letters. And what was the nature of Mr. Portal's discourse?''

''I cannot undertake to say, without a more concerted study of the documents. I may presume, however, from the tenor of Portal's words, that they present one overriding aim—the extortion of funds in return for silence.''

''A blackmailer, as you supposed.''

''Could you doubt it would be otherwise?''

''But how despicable!''

''Say *commonplace*, rather, and I shall be entirely in agreement.''

''Then we have found our man!'' I declared with sudden hope. ''It is the Earl who must have schemed for Portal's death—and now labours under the most acute anxiety, for fear of the letters' discovery! *This*, then, is the meaning of his injunction to Hugh Conyngham, overheard by myself in the Pump Room yesterday.''

''Not so hasty, if you please, my dear,'' Lord Harold cautioned. ''There were others consigned to infamy among the packet's pages. My nephew, Lord Kinsfell, is one.''

''But what possible ill could Mr. Portal have known of your nephew?'' I cried—and too late bit back the incautious words. ''Forgive me, Lord Harold. The Marquis's affairs can form no concern of mine.''

In the darkness beside me, he inclined his silver head. ''I greatly fear, however, that they must command all *my* attention. If Simon has sadly involved himself, I shall never be easy until I comprehend the whole. But perhaps he has considered of his silence, and I shall learn something to advantage before the inquest tomorrow.''

I lapsed into silence, in contemplation of inquests, and of the rakish Mr. Portal; his cheerful air, his fondness for wine, his general conviviality. That such hearty good looks might disguise an extortionate heart! It was gravely troubling, and confirmed my general observation of mankind—that they who appear too plausible by half, are generally consumed with iniquity.

"The packet of letters might be deemed treasure enough, but I was so fortunate as to locate another item of interest," Lord Harold continued, with a glance in my direction. He eased the curricle around the corner of Charles Street into Seymour, and I espied the bulk of Green Park Buildings looming to the fore. "A small, leather-bound volume, which a hasty survey suggests is Mr. Portal's account book."

"In which he records the fruits of his correspondence, no doubt."

"I have learned to hope for it—yes."

"And you bore all away?"

Lord Harold patted the breast of his greatcoat. "I did. The better part of the small hours shall be spent deep in the manager's accounts." He slowed the team to a walk, and drew up before my door.

"I could wish, sir, that your activity might profit you more than the unfortunate manager," I said lightly, as I gave him my hand. He eased me down from the curricle's step, his aspect suddenly grave.

"Wish me more of courage, Miss Austen. I dread what I may find. For once we risk Pandora's box, we cannot shut it up again."

Chapter 8

The Dangerous
Mr. Lawrence

I SPENT THE FIRST PART OF THIS MORNING—THE MORNING OF LORD Kinsfell's inquest—in composing my account of last evening at the Theatre Royal, and inscribing it here in my little book. I had determined, however, to spend a few hours after breakfast in the society of my sister Cassandra, embroidering a flannel waistcoat that should serve as my father's Christmas gift. I am a decided proficient in the satin stitch, and may offer my work to the most discerning without hesitation or blush; and though I detest flannel in general, the damps of Bath in January are so penetrating—and the Reverend's health so very indifferent—that no other cloth would do. And so I took up my workbasket and sought my dear sister in the little dressing-room that adjoins our bedchambers.

Cassandra's head was bent over a muslin cap of her own design, intended for my mother.

"So you did not think well of *Lovers' Vows*," my sister enquired, "though the Conynghams were quite in form last evening?"

"The entire company might have played the truant, Cassandra, for all my notice—as I think you very well know. I am no friend to Kotzebue."

Cassandra was silent at this, her eyes fixed on her cap and her needle flying. "Lord Harold is a very—a very *imposing* gentleman."

"Imposing? I suppose he is, upon first acquaintance. But his manners grow more easy with time."

"And are they pleasing, Jane?" My sister fixed me with a look, part entreaty and part frustration. "Are they such as might be capable of winning your affection?"

"My affection! Indeed, Cassandra, I cannot think that my affection should be necessary to Lord Harold's happiness. He is sufficient unto himself—"

"Then *why* do you accept his invitations? Why seek out his society? It cannot be profitable to either your heart or your reputation, Jane. He is a man of whom every ill thing might be said—and *has* been said—by the world in general. He is accused of the most atrocious part in all manner of affairs—adultery, betrayal, and no doubt treason!"

"Hardly treason, Cassandra," I observed mildly, "or he should never be employed by the Crown, on affairs too delicate to be breathed. Of the rest, however, I can say nothing. It is true he is regarded as a formidable opponent, in affairs of honour; and such duels are rarely fought without cause."

"How *can* you speak so lightly, Jane! I begin to believe I do not know my own sister!"

I sighed, at that moment, for Eliza's more liberal humour. Cassandra's goodness may be said to verge, with advancing age, upon prudery; and however respectable my sister's motives in the present case, her methods recalled the schoolroom.

"And you know that he is far above our station," she persisted. "So great a man cannot make *Miss Austen* his object from any other motive than dalliance. You are too wise to play the fool, my dear—though his consequence may be gratifying, and his attention a boon to vanity. You know how you will expose yourself—to the derision of the world for disappointed hopes, or worse."

"Cassandra! These are serious words indeed! Where *can* you have heard ill of Lord Harold?"

"From yourself, Jane. But two years ago."

This brutal truth must give me pause.

"There was a time, I recall, when you did not scruple to name him as the very worst man in the kingdom," Cassandra continued. "Are you so blinded by elegance and means? Are you so fearful of ending an old maid, Jane, that you would sacrifice the respect of the people you love, merely to go about on the arm of such a man?"

"My dear—" I laid aside the waistcoat. "In the first instance, I very much doubt that Lord Harold intends to make me the object of dalliance. He merely seeks my society on behalf of his niece—who cannot claim a large acquaintance in Bath, and who is sadly grieved by her brother's present misfortunes. I may assure you that I feel for Lord Harold no more tender sentiment than friendship. I have grown to esteem him with the passage of time, for reasons I am not at liberty to relate; and if the world continues in benighted ignorance of his honourable character, then fie upon the world!"

"But from such ignorance, Jane, the world will include you in its contempt. The warmth of your nature—its impulsive regard—has misled you in the past, to your regret. Are the delights, now, of an overcrowded rout, or of an indifferent play in the splendour of the Wilborough box, worth the risk of such censure?"

She was not to be persuaded; in Lord Harold's very name she read an evil; and so I threw up my hands.

"We must persist, Cassandra, in dividing our opinions upon the subject. As long as my father and mother decline to censure Lord Harold's society, I shall continue to accept it with gratitude; and hope that a greater acquaintance with the gentleman, will increase your regard and esteem."

"That must be impossible, Jane—for I intend no greater acquaintance with Lord Harold." And at this, she snapped her thread with a vengeance, thrust aside the cap, and quitted the room.

I PUZZLED OVER MY SISTER'S BEHAVIOUR LATER THIS MORNING, AS I walked towards Pulteney Bridge. The weak light of a fitful sun turned the limestone face of Bath to faintest yellow. A weak, a dysenteric face, as though the town had languished too long in an unhealthy clime—but I am no ardent admirer of Bath, it must be said, and can never see its beauties in the proper light. I set my heart against the place from the first moment of settling here, and I have endured its customs and frivolities nearly four years, as others might submit to exile. It is in the country that I am happiest; the habits of a simple life most suit my retiring nature; but while my father lives, in Bath we shall remain. In this city was he wed to my mother, and here they suffered their first days as man and wife—so that in the last ebb of fading strength, George Austen has sought comfort in Bath, as an-other man's wits might return to childhood.

I achieved the bridge, and spared not a moment for its shops; looked back over my shoulder at the hills and winding crescents of the town; then turned my face to Laura Place, and the Dowager Duchess's abode. Cassandra should shudder to see me here, I knew—but from whence arose her decided disapproval? From com-mendable anxiety for my standing in the world—or from envy and fear of desertion? We had grown up together in the greatest love and friendship—my mother had once observed of us as children, that if Cassandra were to have her head cut off, I should beg to have mine taken, too—and any hint of discord in our opinions and thoughts was unsettling in the extreme. But perhaps the spectre of Lord Har-old—of his consequence quite dazzling my senses—had caused Cas-sandra's nose to turn?

I had dressed with care for this journey to Laura Place, in a rosy muslin and spencer that were not unbecoming. I thought it only right, that the great civility of Lady Desdemona's attention last eve-ning—and indeed, the condescension of the entire Trowbridge fam-ily—should be met with some equal exertion on my part, in paying a morning call in Laura Place as soon as decency would allow. I must confess as well to some suspense regarding the inquest, and an anxi-ety for the earliest particulars of Lord Kinsell's fate. It being now hard on one o'clock, I felt fairly certain of finding Lady Desdemona at home, and well-disposed towards visitors. And so, with an indrawn breath, I pulled the bell.

Daylight revealed the Dowager's abode as a magnificent establish-ment constructed of Cotswold stone, undoubtedly designed by Bald-win, and maintained in all the elegance that easy circumstances will allow.[1] The interior, however, was much as I remembered it from Tuesday's fateful rout—albeit greatly improved by a dearth of heat and company.

---

[1] John Wood (1704–1754) was Bath's principal architect. He and his son of the same name (died 1782) envisioned and built the city's principal landmarks, the crescents of houses constructed of similar materials and designed to appear as a single great estate. Laura Place, however, was constructed in 1788, well after Wood's time, according to plans laid out by Thomas Baldwin.—*Editor's note.*

I handed the footman my card, and enquired whether the lady was within; he departed to learn the answer; and returned as quickly, followed by Lady Desdemona herself. She was arrayed as though for a ball—in tamboured white muslin, pink slippers, and long silk gloves. A spray of diamonds glittered in her hair. If she had so much as thought of her brother's inquest this morning, I should be very much surprised.

"Miss Austen! And quite recovered from your injuries of last evening!" she cried with animation. "But how divine! You are just in time to observe Mr. Lawrence!"

"Mr. Lawrence?"

"The painter! He is above, in the drawing-room, about the business of my portrait."

I blushed in confusion. "I had not an idea that my visit should so incommode the household, Lady Desdemona. Pray, do not tarry below for my sake! Stay only to accept my heartfelt gratitude—for last evening's amusement, and the pleasure of your company. I shall look for your society another day, at a more favourable hour."

"Nonsense! You might divert me while he paints! It is the very last word in tedium, I own, to strike a pose for hours together. One's nose is certain to itch; and to give way to the impulse is quite impossible. Mr. Lawrence is extremely strict on all such matters—I daren't move an inch!—and he has *such* a satiric eye. I confess," she added in a conspiratorial whisper, "that he makes me quite *wild* with the penetration of his looks."

And with that, she turned and hastened up the stairs; and I felt myself compelled to follow.

I had heard, of course, of Mr. Thomas Lawrence. I had even gone so far as to gaze upon his more celebrated subjects, having visited the Royal Academy exhibitions of past years in Henry and Eliza's company. Who can forget his portrait of the Queen, or of the actress Elizabeth Farren, or of Sarah Siddons herself? These are perhaps his most famous pictures; but many a less notorious head has submitted to Lawrence's gaze, and appeared again as recognisably itself, upon the humble canvas. Of a sudden I wished for Cassandra—who alone of the Austens may claim a talent for drawing. She would have profited from a meeting with the great man, and studied his manner of wielding the brush.

"Mr. Lawrence," Lady Desdemona said, as she advanced into the room; and I started at finding the object of her address to be a fairly young gentleman, of a fine figure and noble head—no more than thirty, perhaps.[2] I had assumed that celebration in the world of art was predicated upon an advanced age, if not virtual morbidity; and so displayed my astonishment in my countenance. Mr. Lawrence was arrayed in a very fine wool coat, the most fashionable of trousers, a neckcloth assiduously-tied, and a collar of moderate height—which latter suggested, I thought, some soundness of mind. He might rather have been a suitor for Lady Desdemona's hand, than a painter in oils; and I understood, of a sudden, that a sort of rank in its own right attends a member of the Royal Academy, whom all the world is desperate to secure, that must be denied the fellow accustomed to daubing at innkeepers' signs, or attempting the likeness of a squire's prize horse.

''Miss Austen, may I beg the honour of introducing you to Mr. Thomas Lawrence. Mr. Lawrence, my friend Miss Austen.''

''It is a pleasure, madam.'' He bowed abruptly and then turned back to his easel. ''Lady Desdemona, if you would regain your place I should be deeply grateful. I am never blessed with a surfeit of time, and I have expended already more than is strictly necessary.''

''But of course, sir,'' the lady replied, with stifled amusement, and settled herself in a chair.

''Turn slightly to the left—*my* left, Lady Desdemona—lift the chin—now gaze at me adoringly, as though I am the only man you could ever esteem—yes, that is capital—'' And so saying, Mr. Lawrence reached for a bit of charcoal and swiftly moved his hand across the canvas.

I was prepared to be suitably silent some minutes, but a very little time indeed was required, before I detected the faint suggestion of Lady Desdemona's form. It was breathtaking to observe the man—so effortless, so certain, was his crayon—and the results were quite extraordinary. While the Duke's daughter sat with smile fixed and eyes unblinking, save when necessity required, the master painter all but seized her ghost. Twenty minutes, perhaps, and Mr. Lawrence then released her.

''That is sufficient for today, my lady,'' he pronounced, with a step

---

[2] Thomas Lawrence (1769–1830) would actually have been closer to thirty-five in 1804. Although Austen describes him as having a fine head, and a surviving self-portrait suggests he was quite handsome, he eventually went bald.—*Editor's note.*

backwards to survey his canvas. "I could not improve upon it were I to labour a fortnight."

"But are we not to work in oils?"

"Lady Desdemona," Mr. Lawrence said, with an impression of great forbearance, "it is not my custom to take a likeness so immediately as you would wish. I am far too besieged with work. I have come to you from no less a personage than the Princess of Wales, whose portrait is drying even now in her salon at Blackheath; I must wait upon a gentleman of my acquaintance in London tomorrow, among four or five others; and there remains an endless supply of infants whom, I fear, are not likely to grow any younger before their likenesses are taken. The ledger in which I record my commissions is so long, I confess, that I wonder if any person in England is *not* upon it! You have paid your half-commission; I have taken the underdrawing; and in due course we shall hit upon a suitable occasion for further application."

"Of course, Mr. Lawrence. I am deeply grateful."

The painter cast his gaze upon me, and scowled. "Your opinion of the work, Miss Austen? For you certainly stand in judgement of it."

"No, indeed!" I replied, tearing my eyes from the easel in some confusion. "I am simply all amazement at the rapidity and skill of its execution."

"But is it *like*?" Lady Desdemona moved to study her image. "I confess I cannot tell."

"Be assured, my dear," I said fondly, "that it is yourself as you look in dreams—and as you will revel in appearing, long years hence, when the bloom of eighteen has quite deserted you."

A look of grateful surprise, from Lawrence and the lady both, served as my reward.

"He is quite wickedly handsome, is he not?" Lady Desdemona said in a half-whisper, when Mr. Lawrence's assistant had folded the easel with care, and followed his master to the street below. "I nearly swoon at the thought of spending hours under his stare."

"He is very well-looking, indeed, my lady," I replied, "but who are his parents? His connexions? His station in life?"

"His father kept an inn at Devizes—the Bear, you must know it—"

"Ye-es," I said doubtfully.

"—but was many years ago declared a bankrupt, and died not long thereafter. Lawrence maintains his mother and sisters, I believe. He lives in some style in Piccadilly, and keeps a studio adjacent."

"I see. A man of some means, then."

"I should say! He will charge my father full two hundred guineas for my portrait alone—and he must turn out dozens each year!"

A faintness overcame me. So much money, for a mere likeness in oils! He might be the late Mr. Reynolds himself! "But can you hope to progress upon the project while resident in Bath? Surely Mr. Lawrence cannot mean to attend you here for each of the sit-tings?"

"No," she admitted, her brow crinkling. "If I am ever to wrestle the piece from his grasp, I must do so in London. Perhaps after the New Year, when I am spoiling for amusement. Mr. Thomas Lawrence should do nicely for a heartless flirtation."

I must have registered my dismay, for Lady Desdemona burst out laughing and took my hand between her own. "I have quite excited your anxiety, my dear Miss Austen, and to no very great purpose altogether. Be assured that I have no intention of making a fool of myself over Mr. Lawrence—though I could not blame any young lady who did. He is far too fond of ordering people about, for my taste; and I should not last a fortnight under such manage-ment."

"No, indeed."

"But even the most cautious sentiment cannot make him any less charming to look upon—nor less respectable in the Dowager's drawing-room. He was present, you know, at my grandmother's un-fortunate rout."

"The masquerade?"

"Yes. He came as Harlequin—though in a costume of red and black, unlike poor Mr. Portal. I believe he slipped away before the constables arrived."

"I *did* espy Mr. Lawrence," I said slowly, "now I come to consider of it—he was in conversation with my very dear friend, Madam Le-froy. Are you acquainted with the lady?"

"I have not had the pleasure. She is one of Grandmère's inti-mates, no doubt. Is she resident in Bath, like yourself?"

"In Hampshire, to my great misfortune. I can account the loss of

Madam Lefroy's society as one of the chief miseries of having quitted that part of the country." I said this with feeling.

"And has she sat to Mr. Lawrence, then?"

"I cannot think it likely! She is not a lady of fashion—that is to say, she lacks a considerable estate, such as must be necessary for the meeting of that gentleman's fees. But she cultivates all manner of artists and literary figures—or did, in the years before her marriage. Her brother is Mr. Egerton Brydges, the novelist."

"The author of *Fitz-Albini*?"

"The same—although I cannot think it the wisest piece he has ever done. It was intended as a cleverly-disguised portrait of his early trials and disappointments—though both the cleverness and the disguise were sadly lacking. He managed to abuse several of his dearest acquaintances, and outrage the remainder. I may declare it the only work of which his family is entirely ashamed."[3]

"I thought it to offer very little in the way of story," Lady Desdemona observed, "and that, told in a strange, unconnected way."

"Then let us not waste upon Mr. Brydges another thought. I mentioned him only as an exemplar of Madam's connexions. She may, perhaps, be acquainted with Mr. Lawrence through her brother."

Any reply Lady Desdemona might have made was forestalled by the drawing-room door's being thrust open with considerable violence. The Earl of Swithin strode into the room, his fair brows knit and his blue eyes snapping.

"Lady Desdemona," he declared, with a click of his heels. "You are well? No—never mind—do not trouble yourself to answer. I observe you are well enough. In such excellent spirits, in fact—despite the deprivation of your only brother—as to have been entertaining the despicable Mr. Lawrence."

Lady Desdemona's curtsey was as chill as her countenance. "Lord Swithin. I am all amazement to find you are thus come upon me unannounced. What possible business could bring you to Laura Place?"

[3] This description of Sir Egerton Brydges's *Arthur Fitz-Albini* is very similar to one Jane gives of the novel in a letter to Cassandra written soon after its publication, in 1798. The Reverend George Austen had purchased the book, and Jane felt a little guilty in reading it, given Madam Lefroy's poor opinion of the work. See Letter No. 12, *Jane Austen's Letters*, Deirdre LeFaye, ed., London: Oxford University Press, 1995.—*Editor's note.*

"Convenience," he retorted. "Had you spared a thought from your own concerns, Mona, you should have observed the carters and waggons opposite."

She studied him with calculation, then crossed swiftly to a window whose prospect gave out on the square. The curtains twitched wide, and we were treated to a vision of her figure outlined against the glass. Then she wheeled to face the Earl.

"And so you have taken the lodgings opposite, for the express purpose of spying upon me?"

"No other house could be hired, for all the money in the kingdom; and I am not in a temper to suffer the abominable accommodations of the White Hart even a single day longer."

"I cannot believe you are utterly without acquaintance in Bath, sir, that you must hire a palace for the *accommodation* of your needs! Surely some lady—Miss Maria Conyngham, perhaps?—should be willing to find you room."

A smile flickered over the Earl's set features, but there was little of benevolence in it. "Tit for tat, my dear. Miss Conyngham for Mr. Portal. Or should I say—Mr. Lawrence? You are exceedingly fine for so early in the morning."

"I shall dress in any manner I please, and see whomever I choose, in Laura Place, my lord—though you *do* overlook my drawing-room. You will be gratified to learn that Colonel Easton has also called upon me this morning. He is recovering slowly from the effects of your pistols. I was happy to observe that though served with shocking brutality by yourself, the unfortunate Colonel remains the soul of gallantry." She eyed Lord Swithin with a gleam of amusement. "Easton has also got rid of his whiskers somewhere, and looks remarkably well."

The Earl dismissed the unfortunate Colonel with a wave of the hand. "Clean-shaven or no, it matters nothing. I know you too well, my dear Mona, to regard such a pitiful pup as a rival. But I would counsel you to beware of Mr. Thomas Lawrence. He is a charming rogue, I will allow, and not ill-favoured—but he has a taste for married women, and the ruin of young ladies not yet out. You will have heard of Lady Caroline Upton, I presume?"

"If you refer to Mrs. James Singleton—then yes, my lord, I have had the pleasure."

"'And when no more thy victim can endure/But raging, supplicates thy *soul for cure/Then, act the timid unsuspecting maid/And wonder at the mischief thou hast play'd,'* " Swithin declaimed. "That is from 'The Cold Coquette.' A chastening verse, is it not? Particularly for young ladies too fond of flirtation."

"I am unacquainted with the poet, sir—but I must hope him better suited to his chosen profession, than he appears to be to verse."

"Unacquainted with Mr. Lawrence? But he was dancing attendance upon you only a few moments ago! That is your painter's doggerel, my lady, intended as a rebuke to Lady Caroline Upton—who refused his presumption in seeking to elope with her some two years past."[4]

"That must be the grossest falsehood!" Lady Desdemona cried, her countenance reddening.

"Forgive me—but it is not. I had it on authority from Templetown himself—the young lady's brother—while he was decidedly in wine. I see that Lawrence has quite recovered from the affair; and from the daughter of an earl, has progressed to the daughter of a duke."

"He merely takes my likeness for a portrait, Lord Swithin, at His Grace's commission. It is, after all, Mr. Lawrence's path in life."

The Earl laughed harshly and threw himself into a chair near the fire. "Would that he followed his path with greater fidelity. But instead Mr. Lawrence has chosen to play the man of fashion—adopted all manner of intrigue and display—and is sadly embarrassed for funds. He must very soon contract an advantageous marriage, Mona, if he is to survive. Old Coutts—his banker in Town—has pled his case these three years at least, to little purpose. The man's creditors are at his throat. He will presume upon the acquaintance, do you allow him."

"I believe, Lord Swithin, that it is *you* who presume upon acquaintance," Lady Desdemona replied evenly. Two spots of colour burned in her cheeks, and her eyes were dark with rage. "It is a presumption familiar now these many months; but hardly one I wish to prolong."

I reached for my reticule hastily. "I have trespassed already upon your kindness, Lady Desdemona. I hope—"

"—that Lord Swithin's unexpected arrival will not deter me from

[4] Thomas Lawrence's 1801 portrait of Lady Caroline Upton, coiffed fashionably *à la grecque,* hangs in the Sterling and Francine Clark Art Institute, Williamstown, MA.—*Editor's note.*

our plans of walking out?'' she hurriedly supplied. ''Not at all, Miss Austen. I shall attend you directly. Only stay for the exchange of my gown, and we shall pursue our scheme as planned. My apologies, Lord Swithin, but it is quite beyond my power to—''

''Don't be such a fool, Mona,'' the gentleman replied wearily. ''We have a great deal to discuss. I have been to your brother's inquest.''

Lady Desdemona sat down abruptly upon a settee, the wind quite gone from her sails. Though propriety instructed I should take myself off, I lingered for Lord Swithin's intelligence.

''Why is not my uncle come?'' Lady Desdemona said in a voice barely above a whisper. ''I have been expecting him this half-hour. Well, Swithin? What was the verdict?''

''The jury returned a charge of willful murder against Lord Kinsfell. He is to be conveyed to Ilchester in a few days' time.''

She uttered a cry, and covered her face with her hands; and silently abusing the Earl for an oaf and a fool, I hastened to her side.

''The jury could hardly do else,'' Lord Swithin added brutally. ''Death by misadventure—or wilful murder by persons unknown—just aren't in it. But nothing more shall happen to Kinny until the Assizes, my dear—and they cannot sit until the middle of January at the earliest. That gives your brother several weeks.''

Unbidden, the portrait of a smouldering grey eye revolved in memory. ''Was any new evidence presented, my lord?'' I enquired.

His cold blue gaze rested pensively upon me. ''I cannot undertake to say, having been absent from the rout myself, and thus ignorant of what passed that evening. Lord Kinsfell was called, and questioned about his discovery of the body; and then a Dr. Gibbs, a physician in Milsom Street, who attended the deceased; two of Her Grace's guests, who seized poor Kinsfell as he attempted to revive Mr. Portal—and one of the chairmen, dragged in off the street by your uncle, Mona, and quite put out at the interruption of his commerce.''

''A chairman!'' Her head came up, and surprise warred with hope upon her countenance. ''Whatever can Uncle have been thinking?''

The Earl shrugged with exquisite grace. ''He thought to show that a murderer *might* have dropped from the Dowager's window to an open carriage—which was then driven out of Bath. The chairman professed to have seen a like equipage in Laura Place that night—

but could not swear to the time, nor vow that a man had entered it by any other means than the carriage door; could tell us nothing of the occupants, and was indeed of so little credit in his appearance and expressions, that he rather weakened Lord Kinsfell's case than improved it. I am afraid the intelligence was all but dismissed."

"Poor Kinny," Lady Desdemona murmured. "And had he nothing to add in his own defence?"

"The coroner *did* enquire rather narrowly regarding the nature of his dispute with Mr. Portal," the Earl said, his regard fixed steadily on Lady Desdemona, "and could get nothing from him but a disquisition on his sacred honour."

"Kinny? *Honour?*" Lady Desdemona started from her place and began to turn before the fire, in a manner so like her uncle, Lord Harold, that I half-expected to hear that gentleman's voice. "Then there must be a lady in the case."

Swithin smiled; but the expression was quite devoid of good humour. "The lady would not, perhaps, be *yourself,* my dear?"

Lady Desdemona's head came up magnificently, and she stared him down in turn. "You are despicable, Swithin. Do you think that if I might aid my brother with any intelligence in my power, that I should hesitate to do so? Your ill nature cannot do you credit. It leads you into folly."

"Gentlemen are wont to speak of *honour* when they are bound by oaths or pledges, are they not?" I hastily submitted.

"They are," Lord Swithin replied, "and are ready, more often than not, to defend such pledges with their lives. So I take Lord Kinsfell's determination in the present case. I very much fear that he will go silently to the gallows, rather than betray his sacred trust."

"Oh, Lord!" Lady Desdemona breathed, and pressed a hand to her brow. "Where, oh, where, is my uncle?"

"You have but to enquire, my dear, and he appears." Lord Harold spoke from the drawing-room doorway. To my most active surprise and interest, Mr. Wilberforce Elliot stood at his back. "Miss Austen— a pleasure. Lord Swithin—an honour I had hardly expected. You are not, I think, acquainted with Mr. Wilberforce Elliot, a magistrate of Bath."

Introductions were made, and then Lord Harold continued, "You have disdained the wares of the hot-house this morning, Swithin. But perhaps your restraint is intended to pay tribute to my niece's unassuming simplicity. She is not the sort to take pleasure in gaudy display. You are quite right, I think, to bestow your flowers elsewhere. Others may be less nice in their tastes than Mona.''

''—Except, one supposes, when she is sitting to her portraitist.''

Lord Swithin replied.

Lord Harold's eyebrow shot upwards. ''Really, my lord, is that intended as an insult, or a rebuke? Were the lady affianced to you—or even, forgive me, did she regard you with favour—this little display of temper should be accorded as your right. But in the present circumstances it is entirely untoward.''

''Then you may name your day, my lord, and I shall name my second with pleasure.''[5]

Lord Harold smiled condescendingly. ''You are remarkably quick to offer a challenge, Swithin—but perhaps you expect me to jump at the chance to show my mettle, like poor Colonel Easton. In this, I fancy, you suffer from a misapprehension. I would never make sport of a fellow young enough to be my son—particularly when I have been as intimate with his mother as I have been with yours.''

The Earl paled, and stepped back a pace. ''I would beg you to remember where you are, my lord. Your niece—''

''Oh, *will* you both have done,'' Lady Desdemona cried in exasperation. ''What have I to do with matters in any case? You circle each other like two schoolboys on the green, while Kinny sits festering in gaol!''

''And he is unlikely ever to emerge, Mona, if your uncle will have the handling of his affairs,'' the Earl retorted contemptuously, and reached for his hat and gloves. ''I have no wish to remain where I am served with such incivility. Good day to you, Lord Harold. Your servant, Miss Austen. I trust I will not find you in the Lower Rooms this evening, Lady Desdemona?''

''Whyever not?''

''Would you dance, then, while Lord Kinsfell is deprived of liberty?''

"I am sure I cannot hope to assist him by remaining quietly at home! In such a pass, it behooves the Wilborough family to comport itself with style! Besides—poor Easton is most pressing in his desire to dance."

Lord Harold smiled, the Earl snorted—and quitted the room without another word.

"Capital!" Lord Harold cried, and gestured the magistrate towards a chair. "We have rid ourselves of a dangerous distraction. Mona, darling, would you be so good as to fetch your grand-mother—I require her presence immediately."

"Uncle," she said, hastening to his side, "the inquest—! It is in every way horrible!"

"Yes, my dear; but I hope all is not lost. You will observe I have brought the magistrate in my train. His interest has been exceedingly piqued by the notion of an open carriage halted some moments beneath the anteroom window; and though the proofs of a murderer jumping to safety in its depths are impossible to gather, Mr. Elliot is nonetheless willing to reconsider the case."

"Your servant, my lady," Mr. Elliot said with an affable smile; and then retrieving a handkerchief from his breast pocket, he blew his nose most energetically.

Lady Desdemona went in search of the Dowager Duchess; and roused from her letter-writing, Eugenie proceeded slowly to the drawing-room with Miss Wren for support. Not five minutes had elapsed, before an expectant circle gazed silently at Lord Harold.

"You remember Her Grace, I am sure, Mr. Elliot," the gentleman said, "but I do not think you are acquainted with Miss Austen or Miss Wren."

The magistrate peered at me narrowly, and nodded once. "The Shepherdess," he said.

"Miss Austen is a particular friend of my niece's. Miss Wren is so kind as to serve as Her Grace's companion."

"Indeed, it is an *honour*, not a kindness, Lord Harold," Miss Wren simpered. "When I consider the extent of Her Grace's affabil-ity—"

"Now, then." Lord Harold clapped his hands together with ener-getic purpose. "I would propose the amusement of a novel parlour game—an amateur theatrical, if you will. Let us set about the staging of Mr. Portal's murder."

"I cannot think that even *one* performance of a similar tragedy is necessary for our amusement, Harry," the Dowager protested sternly. "How should I seek another?"

"For the purposes of science, dear ma'am, Mr. Elliot has allowed the seed of doubt to enter his formidable soul, and we must do everything in our power to ensure the seed will grow. Miss Austen!"

"My lord."

"Please to adopt the attitude of Hugh Conyngham before the drawing-room fire. Desdemona! You shall play at Miss Conyngham. Her Grace shall be, as ever, Her Grace. I shall be Portal, Mr. Elliot will merely observe, I beg, and draw what conclusions he may. And you, Wren—*you* shall be poor Simon."

"I shall do no such thing!" she countered hotly. "A more decided want of taste I have never observed. And the Marquis deprived of all freedom, while we sport with his circumstances!"

"Do as Lord Harold bids you, Wren," the Dowager commanded. She grasped her cane firmly with her left hand, and Lord Harold with her right. "You should endeavour to stumble, Harry, when I lead you to the anteroom."

"Stay, Mamma—I must speak a word to Mona." Lord Harold drew the lady aside, and whispered a few phrases; at which she nodded, and grew pink with excitement. "Very well, Your Grace—lead me to my doom."

The Dowager conducted her son unsteadily to the little salon done up in Prussian blue—and left him reclining in apparent stupor upon the settee.

Delighting in my role, I advanced to the head of the room, adopted a pose by the fireplace, and set about declaiming from *Macbeth*, with many an inadvertent stumble and fault.

Lady Desdemona made her way to the anteroom door, and effected an entry; Lord Harold emitted a ponderous groan; and before I had accomplished even half the length of Hugh Conyngham's speech, the lady stood before me once more, to all appearances enraptured by my art. She had achieved the drawing-room by the panelled door's passage.

At that moment, urged by the Dowager, Miss Wren advanced upon the anteroom; and in all the horror of exclamation and dismay, fell upon the dying Lord Harold as he lay stricken on the blue and gold carpet.

"It is done," he said briskly, springing to his feet and adjusting the set of his coat, "and with admirable efficiency. I do not think we need enquire whether a lady pressed for time, with agitation to give her wings, could not have managed it better."

"And the crowd of guests must disguise even Maria Conyngham, despite her costume of red," I mused. "For I confess that on the night in question, I did not observe Lord Kinsfell's approach to the anteroom door."

"Nor did I," Lady Desdemona supplied. "I was unaware of it until a hue and cry broke out, and I turned to observe Kinny standing over Portal's body. Any number of guests might have passed from room to room without the majority remarking upon it. But why would you have it be Miss Conyngham, Uncle? Was not she in love with Mr. Portal? She can hardly have served him with violence!"

"Only Miss Conyngham may know the truth of *that* conjecture," he replied, his hooded eyes inscrutable. "But I would suggest, Mona, that her precipitate appearance at Mr. Portal's feet, before the regard of all the assembly—her wanton weeping, and her costume of red—may have been intended to fix in observers' minds, the fact of her presence in the drawing-room itself. Miss Conyngham forced her person upon our attention only *after* Portal's body was discovered— and at such a moment, the scene she played must be intriguing."

"That's all very well, my lord," Mr. Elliot interjected benignly, "but you cannot prove the lady guilty without you extract a confession. And the use of the passage does nothing to advance your scheme regarding the open carriage."

"True, my good man—but I could not be happy with the descent from the window, until I had tried the passage and found it wanting. I have not found it so. There was time enough and to spare, for the effecting of the deed; and for a lady accustomed to moving about on a darkened stage, the exit along a poorly-lit back hall should be as nothing. She might accomplish it at twice Desdemona's speed."

"You cannot prove it, my lord," Mr. Elliot said again, and scratched determinedly at his club of black hair. "And consider of the risk! For Miss Conyngham could not presume her movements should be disregarded; any one of the guests might have turned in the midst of her brother's speech, and observed her to enter the anteroom."

"But you forget, my dear Elliot. Nor could she have anticipated Lord Kinsell's passage through the room. Miss Conyngham expected the deed to remain obscure some hours, with Mr. Portal dis-covered when the rout should have been accomplished and the last of the guests departed."

"I remain unpersuaded, my lord," the magistrate said with a smile, "and though I've no formal training in the barrister's art, I cannot believe you'll find a jury as will agree with you. Do you hold to your open window, and the carriage below, if you will have it the Marquis ain't guilty—but leave Miss Conyngham in peace, I beg."

"Would you care to adventure the passage, Miss Austen?" Lord Harold said, ignoring Mr. Elliot's gibes. He took up a candle and pushed open the door.

We paced the length of the passage connecting anteroom to back hall, and observed the choice of direction—to the left, the servants' quarters and stairs to the kitchen; to the right, the drawing-room's far door. Then we returned the way we had come, our eyes intent upon the passage's floor. Nothing to be seen; not even dust.

"You had hoped for a scrap of fabric, perhaps?" I enquired.

"Preferably in scarlet."

Lord Harold swung the panelled door closed—and there in the space between door and passage wall, winking in the dim light of the taper, was a small figure in gold.

Lord Harold whistled softly beneath his breath, knelt to retrieve it—and the taper went out, with a parting scorch to his fingers. He muttered an oath and pulled open the door once more, freeing us both from the oppressive dark.

"I must beg your indulgence, Mamma," he said indolently. "Does this brooch form a part of the Wilborough stones?"

The Dowager turned the pin over in her palm, a slight frown between her eyes. "It does not, my dear Harry. I have never seen it before."

"Mona?"

She looked at the brooch—paled—and sat down abruptly on the anteroom settee. "Good Lord, Uncle, what does this mean?"

"Perhaps we should enquire of your friend," Lord Harold replied; but the gravity of his looks betrayed his careless tone.

For what he held in his hand was a snarling gold tiger, its eyes formed of rubies—the device of the Earl of Swithin.

Chapter 9

Into the Labyrinth

14 December, 1804, cont.

~

HAD LORD HAROLD BEEN ADEPT IN THE ARTS OF THE CONJURER, HE could not have produced a more stunning effect. For a full thirty seconds, no one spoke a word, while he observed us all in sardonic silence; and then Mr. Wilberforce Elliot stepped forward.

"I take it this brooch belongs to one among your acquaintance?"

"The Earl of Swithin—though I last saw it worn by his remarkable mother," Lord Harold replied, and fingered the tiger gently.

The magistrate's eyes widened in his large face. "The same earl who has just quitted the house?"

"His lordship is unlikely to have gone very far. Did you wish to speak to him, you have only to enquire for Lord Swithin at the residence opposite to this. His sister, Lady Louisa Fortescue, is presently serving as his hostess, and would ensure your every comfort."

"You are greatly pleased with yourself, my lord," Mr. Elliot observed drily, "but you know it will not do. The Earl might have lost that bauble at any time in this house—and have not the slightest part in Mr. Portal's death."

"I should concede the point with alacrity, Elliot," Lord Harold said with a nod, "had his lordship ever set foot within Her Grace's establishment before his visit this morning. Did Swithin go anywhere near the passage, Mona, while conversing with you?"

"I am sure he did not," she said faintly. She was pale, but contained; and the fever of her thoughts was evident upon her countenance. "Miss Austen? Can you recall him approaching the anteroom?"

I shook my head.

"Then perhaps he was present on a previous occasion without our knowledge—in the guise of one of Her Grace's guests at Tuesday's rout, and moving all unknown by virtue of a mask." Lord Harold said. "Mr. Portal's death is amply explained, Mr. Elliot, if effected by a jealous lover. For you must know that the dead man's attentions to my niece—whom the Earl has sought to marry—were quite obvious that evening."

The magistrate was silent a moment. "Is it impossible that a similar pin should be worn by another?"

"The device is Swithin's. You will find the figure of a tiger painted upon the doors of his coach."

"But you cannot *prove* the present object is his lordship's."

"Prove, prove—you grow tiresome with your proves, Mr. Elliot. That must be the magistrate's office, not mine." Lord Harold looked to Lady Desdemona. "I would swear that this tiger was once worn by the late Countess of Swithin—but have you ever seen the pin on the present Earl's person, my dear?"

She shook her head. "Though I can think of no one else whose coat of arms is so like—nor who should leave it in Grandmère's household."

"That is, after all, the point," her uncle replied thoughtfully. "Very well, Mr. Elliot—it would seem the only proper course would be to enquire of the Earl whether he has ever seen this tiger brooch; and then to establish his movements on the night in question. If his lordship was seen to be in London by a company of White's stoutest clubmen, and was playing at whist in the very hour of Portal's death—I will regard the cunning tiger as a phantasm brought about by the strength of my desire to clear my unfortunate nephew. But if the Earl was absent from Town . . ."

". . . then I shall be very well pleased, my lord," Mr. Elliot replied, to my astonishment. "I have had occasion to doubt the security of my arrest, or indeed of the entire fabric of this case—for it is exceedingly odd for a gentleman to murder a guest in his own home, in the midst of a rout, however much in wine and fired by argument.

Too convenient by half, you might say; and yet what choice did I have, but to seize the Marquis, him having been found with the knife in his hand?"

"I quite appreciate the difficulty," Lord Harold replied, "and if you will only undertake to set these London enquiries in train, Mr. Elliot, I shall forgive the hasty nature of your justice and afford you every accommodation within my power."

"Such as the fees for the stage?" Mr. Elliot's beady black eyes assessed his lordship shrewdly. "I'd be wishful of carrying a few constables along, and there's housing and victuals to be thought of."

"So there are, indeed," Lord Harold said smoothly. He drew forth a roll of Treasury notes from within his coat, and peeled away several for the magistrate's use. "If you move with despatch, Mr. Elliot, you might yet have time to visit the Earl across the way, before you must catch the last London stage at the Hart."

"So I might, my lord, so I might." He beamed around the room, and enquired casually, "And where in London shall I find the Earl's residence?—For I should not like to have to ask the direction of his lordship, and lose the element of surprise."

"In St. James Square," Lady Desdemona replied. "Fortescue House. I daresay there are many who would be willing to show you the way."

The magistrate bowed, and departed without further delay. Very well satisfied with the events of the morning—though conscious of a certain despair in Lady Desdemona's looks, and anxious for her spirits—I quite soon did the same.

LORD HAROLD EXPRESSED HIMSELF AS DESIROUS OF ESCORTING ME HOME to Green Park Buildings, but I had hardly achieved the street in his company, before he steered me away from the river. "Come, Miss Austen! We must take a turn in Sydney Gardens," he said. "Fine weather in Bath is as rare as Tuesday's snow, and we cannot let the opportunity for exercise fall by the way."

I should hardly call the present cloudy aspect *fine*—but I knew better than to quibble with a man of Lord Harold's understanding. He intended a *tête-à-tête*, and chose the gardens for his venue.

Sydney Gardens Vauxhall is one of the few areas of Bath that I may regard with complaisance and pleasure. For three years I lived happily enough at No. 4 Sydney Place, just opposite to the gardens' entry, and was able to take a turn almost daily in its shrubberies, and look fondly upon the various waterfalls, and pavilions, and Chinese bridges over the canal. The sham castle I can forgo without a pang, and I profess no great inclination for the various swings or bowling greens; even the Merlin grotto I may be said to despise; but I cannot do without the Labyrinth. What heroine could abuse so splendid a natural amusement, conducive to the most delicious assignations, the most intriguing conversations overheard, the unexpected presentation around a turning in the path, of an Unknown Gentleman of Distinguished Appearance? Many are the wanderings I have undertaken in the Labyrinth, while lost in the pleasant fancies that are the peculiar delight of young ladies; and our sixpences paid to the attendant at the gate, it was to the Labyrinth I led Lord Harold on the present occasion.

''I must confess I was astonished at the discovery of his lordship's pin,'' I mused, ''but to you it does not seem so very extraordinary.''

''That is perhaps because I have acquired a certain intimacy with the Earl's affairs,'' my companion grimly replied, ''by the expedient of having read his mail. I did not wish to reveal the extent of Swithin's embarrassments or machinations before my niece, Miss Austen; it was enough to start Mr. Elliot upon the track of this particular hare; but with you I shall not scruple to disclose the whole.''

''You believe Lady Desdemona to feel more for Swithin than she acknowledges?''

''She certainly did not meet the evidence of his deceit with composure. What is your opinion on the subject?''

''I confess I cannot tell. She proclaims herself utterly disinclined to encourage him—and then proceeds to do so, by a frequent display of temper and the jealousy it presages. Of *his* heart I can determine even less. He offers coldness, and pique, and a quelling tendency to favour others in her sight—and yet, to Laura Place he returns, as outraged as a bull at the thought of a rival!''

''There may be more than one interpretation of such behaviour,'' Lord Harold said equably. ''Swithin may hope to secure my niece for reasons of private gain alone.''

''You suspect him of mercenary motives? But I thought him possessed of easy circumstances. Indeed, my sister Eliza—'' I stopped, in recollection of the nature of the Earl's trade.

"I quite long to pursue your sister Eliza's acquaintance," Lord Harold remarked. "She seems a most engaging lady—on terms of intimacy with the entire world, but too strong in her understanding to be duped by it."

"Eliza knew something of the Swithin fortunes in India, I believe. She is a native of the region herself."

"And did she comprehend the nature of that fortune's present increase?" Lord Harold enquired keenly.

"She thought it due to the trade of opium with China."

"And so it is. I might add that Swithin has put his profits from opium sales into the finest gemstones the Company might obtain; and it is *these* he sends in cargoes home to Great Britain. But I very much fear that his wealth has run afoul of politics."

I frowned. "The present Government would put a halt to the opium trade?"

Lord Harold shook his head. "But Buonaparte will not hesitate to do so, I fear. Lord Swithin's fortune is much exposed, in traversing the Indian Ocean. You may have heard from your naval brothers that the French hold some islands in that clime, and have harried our shipping in recent months."

I endeavoured to recall the respective French and British holdings in the Indian Ocean. "The Ile de France, is it not? What we call the island of Mauritius?"

"The very same. We must destroy the French base in those waters if the Indian trade is to sail in security; and upon the fate of the Indian trade rests an entire web of investments and fortunes, touching nearly every family in the kingdom. The expense of the Crown's war with France could not be sustained, to name but a single venture; and yet a vast deal of English goods and bullion has lately gone without a murmur into the Empire's hands. I fear that Swithin's ships have been served a similar fate. If rumour may be taken for truth, it is many months since the Earl's merchantmen were heard from."

"And might Lady Desdemona's fortune alone preserve his lordship from ruin?"

"It should at the least supply his present want. My niece possesses no less than fifty thousand pounds. A man might murder for less. And then there is the inducement of silencing his blackmailer! The Earl perceives Mona's enjoyment of Portal's attentions—feels his influence is waning—she has already refused him once—and so he despatches the dangerous rival at a single blow, and leaves Kinsell to supply his place. I like the stratagem very well."

We had achieved the Labyrinth, and with an instant's hesitation at its mouth, plunged within.

"Is this a favourite among your walks?" Lord Harold enquired.

"It is, my lord. I may safely claim to have braved the twists and turns of its charms, a hundred times or more. Like yourself, I delight in cunning blinds and stratagems, as I believe you comprehend."

"And have you then fathomed the maze's heart, my dear Miss Austen?"

"But that should defeat enjoyment entirely!" I replied. "We do not adventure the Labyrinth with conquest in view—rather the reverse. Did we achieve the center with celerity, we should as swiftly lose interest."

We came to a turning in the path, with two possible avenues at our disposal. Lord Harold chose the right-hand way.

"And there, perhaps, may be the answer to Swithin's motives," he concluded. "He may pursue my niece for gain—or more simply yet, because she persists in denying him the prize."

"He would not be the first gentleman since the dawn of time to behave in as absurd a fashion. But tell me, my lord—do Mr. Portal's letters paint the Earl so thoroughly black? Is he quite lost to all goodness, that you should regard him as capable of every infamy?"

Lord Harold was silent a moment in reflection. "Lord Swithin is much entangled with a lady, whom Mr. Portal did not deign to name, but whom we may assume is Maria Conyngham, from the manager's proximity to his company and the Earl's appearance in the wings last evening."

"Forgive me, my lord," I said, "but are not a nobleman's attentions to a rising actress comparatively commonplace? Surely the history of the theatre is littered with examples, both scandalous and tame."

"As I have very good reason to know. But how disadvantageous a moment for his lordship's exposure! Mr. Portal's intimacy with Laura Place must have taught him how intent was Lord Swithin upon the attachment of Lady Desdemona; and so Portal's threats to reveal his lordship's liaison with Miss Conyngham could not fail to find an ear. Such knowledge was as gold in Portal's hands."

Our chosen path ended abruptly in impenetrable hedge, but I knew this way of old—and with a cry of satisfaction, showed Lord Harold a passage quite hidden behind a monolith of green. We had only to slip around it, to find the path continuing; and I discerned in this a useful lesson.

"—For what may appear to be a blank wall, my lord, may very often prove a door."

"In life as well as mazes," he mused.

"What possible necessity could have driven Mr. Portal to the extortion of so much money?" I enquired.

"An embarrassment in his circumstances. I have had the opportunity to consult Mr. Portal's account book. I found to my satisfaction that all he possessed was mortgaged several times over. The Theatre Royal Company has not been paid in months. The theatre may be profitable, of course, but Portal was sorrily profligate; and the building of the new establishment in Beauford Square has demanded increasing sums. He faced ruin and seizure by a host of creditors, did he fail to obtain relief."

"And who better to solicit than a wealthy peer? It is clear, now, from the Earl's words in the Pump Room, that the letters he would have had Mr. Conyngham retrieve, were the self-same ones you have pilfered with your cunning picks. There is an unfortunate explanation in the offing, I fear, when the letters are discovered to be missing."

"As they may already have been. I left the desk unlocked behind me—from a design of striking fear in the hearts of the complicitous. Mr. Conyngham will search for the letters; he will be unable to find them; and anxiety at the letters' discovery will force him to divulge the whole to Swithin. Thus may we provoke the Earl's hand."

"Did we observe him in such a pass, we should learn much to our advantage," I thoughtfully said. "It may save endless trouble on your nephew's behalf, my lord, if we await the natural progress of events."

"I believe I am of your opinion, Miss Austen." Lord Harold hesitated between two branching paths, chose the left, and walked on. His eyes were fixed upon the gravel walk, as though he might read his future in the stones. "I long for some betrayal on Swithin's part. For he has certainly managed the affair with miserable *éclat*. Would it not have been wiser, for example, to secure the blackmailing letters *before* dispatching their author with a knife? And what does he mean by arranging the deed in my mother's house? Did he intend for Kinsfell to fall into his trap, and take the blame? And if so—was my nephew lured to the anteroom where Portal's body lay, by the agencies of the very person whose name he now refuses to divulge? Is this why poor Simon clings to the claims of honour?"

"But what can be his purpose in so complete a destruction of your nephew, my lord?"

"I may hazard a guess. Maria Conyngham."

We turned into a path that led to an abrupt wall of green—a decidedly dead end. Lord Harold turned, and retraced his steps, glancing about for the most likely direction. Having chosen it, he waved to me. I joined him hurriedly.

"I do not understand you, my lord."

"Mr. Portal's documents revealed a more troubling matter to my unwilling eyes last evening, Miss Austen, than the involvement of the Earl. For my nephew, it seems, is most ardent in his pursuit of one among the company. The very same Maria Conyngham."

"She has been active, indeed, in cultivating admiration! At Mr. Portal's behest, perhaps? Does she play with hearts in innocence—or for a share in the blackmailer's spoils?"

"That is a cunning thought, indeed. I cannot undertake to say."

"Her present disdain for Lord Kinsfell may be taken as a sign."

"Or as a clever subterfuge to divert attention from herself. Full many a guilty woman has found refuge in righteous indignation."

"But how was your nephew to be worked upon?"

"My brother Bertie intends Kinsfell to make a brilliant match; and regardless of the consideration due to the Dowager Duchess and her former career, His Grace should consider an actress quite below the ducal touch. Simon would be at pains to present the lady in the most virtuous and commendable light; and if her liaison with Swithin were bruited about—"

"I comprehend. Mr. Portal's scheme was complete, indeed. But might this have been the subject of his dispute with Lord Kinsfell at the Dowager's masquerade?"

"I cannot doubt it."

I considered in memory the outraged Marquis; his tearful sister; his drunken opponent. In the shadows beyond their circle stood the Earl and Maria Conyngham, like pieces on a chessboard regarding their pawns. Did Lord Swithin or his agent thrust home the knife in

Portal's breast, he should be rid in a single stroke of both his black-mailer and his rival for Lady Desdemona's fortune.

"And since the Earl is undoubtedly jealous of his mistress's favours," Lord Harold said, as though reading my thoughts, "and resentful in the extreme of Kinsfell's attentions to Maria Conyngham, my unfortunate nephew was left to discover the body, and shoulder the blame for Portal's murder. Fiendishly clever!"

I came to a halt upon the path, my mind in a whirl. "But this is madness, my lord! For we know Miss Conyngham to be united by affection to Portal himself—her present grief must make it so." Unless—

I saw again in memory the scarlet-clad Medusa of Tuesday's rout, her black locks tumbled and her countenance made ugly by grief, as she keened over the slain Harlequin. Maria Conyngham *then* might almost have felt the knife to pierce her breast along with Portal's, so great was her suffering. But was her display in fact the consummate expression of art—merely Conyngham the Tragedienne, with deceit her chief ambition?

"Perhaps Mr. Portal valued wealth far more than love," Lord Harold suggested. "Or perhaps Miss Conyngham merely affects the bond—and her present grief—for the foiling of her enemies. She is accomplished in the art of dissembling, recollect."

I shook my head, bewildered. "Then how, my lord, in the midst of such a maze, do you intend to proceed?"

"I propose to make love to the lady in turn," he briskly replied. "For from intimacy much may be discovered."

"She is unlikely to allow any of the Wilborough line within a mile of her person!"

"I beg to disagree, my dear Miss Austen. If she and her brother know aught of this crime, and fear discovery, Miss Conyngham will cultivate my attentions as ardently as a watchdog. She will find in me a necessary evil, for the preservation of her peace. And I shall exploit the impulse ruthlessly."

His resolve caused my heart to sink. I could not be sanguine regarding even Lord Harold when confronted with so formidable an enchantress; and I mistrusted a something in his tone, and look, that called to mind the Theatre Royal. Miss Conyngham had worked upon him strangely as he sat in the Wilborough box, his glasses fixed upon her form.

"I intend to learn a vast deal from increased proximity," the gentleman continued, oblivious of my anxiety, "and I should relish the prospect in any case, were my nephew's name already cleared. Lord Swithin is spoiling for a challenge—but there are many ways of defending one's honour, and only a few involve pistols."

We followed a turning sharp within the maze, saw daylight suddenly before us—and were deposited at the Labyrinth's very heart. It remained only to find our way out again.

Chapter 10

The Comforts
of Cooling Tea

DANCING OF A FRIDAY EVENING IN THE LOWER ROOMS BEGINS PRECISELY at six o'clock, and runs no later than eleven—which custom we owe to the autocratic tendencies of the late "Beau" Nash, that arbiter of all that is genteel in Bath society.[1] Accordingly the Austens put in our appearance at precisely ten minutes before six; paid our respects to Mr. King, the present Master; and the Reverend George then abandoned the ladies of the party for the delights of the card-room. My father being happily taken up by a rapacious set of whist-players, we were free to move about the Assembly in search of acquaintance, and found it presently in the form of Henry and Eliza. I was astonished to discover the little Comtesse in attendance—for it is her usual custom only to *dine* at six or seven, and to her the Assembly's hours must seem shockingly provincial.

"Dear madam!" Eliza cried, with a salute to my mother's cheek. "This is courage, indeed, to venture the crush of the Lower Rooms, and on such a chilly night! And here are the girls—positively ravishing, I declare!" She stepped back a pace, the better to view my sap-

---

[1] Beau Nash was Master of Ceremonies for the Bath Assembly up to his death in 1761, and believed himself responsible for the regulation of public conduct. He forced those who frequented the Rooms—duchess and commoner alike—to a rigid standard of etiquette that survived him by fully fifty years.—*Editor's note.*

phire gown and Cassandra's spotted muslin, and turned to her husband for support. ''We must hope for a glimpse of Lord Harold, Henry, when Jane is in such good looks.''

I coloured—for some thought of the Gentleman Rogue *had* coun-seled me to put aside my cap this once, and run ribbons through my hair—and felt Cassandra stiffen beside me.

''I wonder you seek to press his lordship's suit, Eliza,'' she ob-jected. ''He cannot be respectable.''

''Pooh! And what should that signify to me? Or to Jane, for that matter? We shall leave such tedious fellows as have only their respect-ability to recommend them, entirely to yourself, my dear—and find contentment in the reflected glow of virtue.''

I reached a self-conscious hand to my throat, and fingered my topaz cross. ''You look very well this evening, Eliza. Purple is not a hue that many may wear—but it entirely becomes you.''

''Oh, this old thing,'' she said, with an indifferent shrug. ''I should not dare to attempt it in London, where it has already been seen this age—but in Bath—well—'' Her bright eyes roved about the room. They were filled with an animation that belied her three-and-forty years.

''Mrs. Austen!'' cried a tall woman with a long white neck, her hair done up in a bewitching demi-turban of Sèvres blue and gold. She reached down to the diminutive Comtesse and pressed her gloved hand. ''How delightful to see you! It has been an age!''

''Isabella Wolff, I declare!'' Eliza replied in kind, and seized the beauty in a determined grasp. ''You grow lovelier with every year. Jane, Cassandra—allow me to introduce Mrs. Jens Wolff, the wife of the Danish Consul. My sisters, the Miss Austens.''

Cassandra and I curtseyed.

''May I introduce Mr. Thomas Lawrence to your acquaintance, Mrs. Austen?'' Isabella Wolff enquired in turn; and peering over Eliza's shoulder I observed the handsome painter. He awaited Mrs. Wolff with an air of patient adoration. It seemed quite alien to his stormy, self-possessed features—but perhaps the more striking for its unfamiliarity.

Mr. Lawrence bowed, but showed no inclination to part with the attentions of his lady for even so short a space as an introduction; and we were forced to be content with an unintelligible word mut-tered into his neckcloth. If he recollected our introduction in Laura

Place, he gave no sign; and I thought it very probable that he did not—his faculties this morning having been entirely taken up with the effort of capturing Lady Desdemona's likeness.

"And is Mr. Wolff in Bath as well?"

"He is not at present." The Consul's wife seemed indisposed to elucidate the matter.

"But you do intend a visit of some duration?" Eliza persisted.

"As for *intentions*—I may never return to London at all! Everything about Bath agrees with me exceedingly." This, with a provocative smile for Mr. Lawrence, who had the grace to colour slightly. "You must call upon me in Bladuds Buildings, Eliza—or look in upon the meeting of the Philosophical Society. I quite depend upon it—" And so, with a flutter of her hand and a general nod, Isabella Wolff ran off, and spent the better part of the evening in dancing with Mr. Lawrence, to the scandal of the town.

"Now I wonder what *she* has got up to," Eliza mused, as she followed the pair with her eyes.

"A very handsome lady," my mother said with approval, "though I cannot like her taste in turbans. She might almost hail from the tent of an Oriental, I declare!"

"She was never happy with Jens Wolff, and Mr. Lawrence is decidedly handsome," Eliza went on, oblivious. "He has quite a brooding, stormy air as well, does he not? I might as readily lose my heart to him myself, were I disposed to wander."

My mother started, and surveyed the Comtesse narrowly. "I believe I shall go in search of Henry, my dear," she said with decision; and so she left us.

"But you are not disposed to wander," I reminded Eliza, who *would* giggle at my mother's departing back, "and I cannot think that Mr. Lawrence would be entirely agreeable, on closer acquaintance. I have it on reasonably good authority that he is nearly a bankrupt."

"And who among the fashionable is not?" Eliza retorted carelessly, as she fanned her flushed cheeks. "A man may run on for years in that fashion, owing huge sums to everybody, so long as he clings to reputation."

"I should judge Mrs. Wolff to risk far more in *that* quarter," Cassandra observed. "Her reputation is not likely to survive her visit to Bath."

"Mr. Lawrence does have a habit of throwing ladies into disaffection with their husbands, Jane," Eliza conceded. "You must have seen the recent letter in the *Morning Gazette*."

"It has been ages since I read a London paper," I replied, my curiosity roused. "To what letter would you refer?"

"Mr. Siddons's."

"The husband of the celebrated Sarah?"

"The same. He resides here in Bath, you know, for his gouty legs—and has quite broken off with his wife."

"I did not know it. But what of this letter?"

Eliza's eyes shone with delicious malice. "Mr. Siddons offered a *reward*, no less, to those who would expose the author of the slanders directed at his irreproachable lady—of having been detected in adultery with Mr. Lawrence."

"But she has always been reputed virtuous—and is of an age to be Mr. Lawrence's mother!"

"I quite agree, my dear. Isabella Wolff, at least, we may consider his contemporary. But Mr. Lawrence has painted Mrs. Siddons a score of times, to the greatest public acclaim—and in years past, seemed quite taken with the entire family. Excepting, perhaps, *Mr. Siddons.*"

"I think you had better convey this tale to your friend Mrs. Wolff," Cassandra observed, in a tone of gentle reproof.

"She is already aware of it, I am sure," Eliza said with a shrug. Then, leaning towards my sister, she said in a conspiratorial whisper, "Is not that Mr. Kemble, Cassandra? Your old friend from the Chilham ball?"

A portly officer in his thirties, not above the middle height and with receding brown hair, was advancing determinedly upon us; and I trembled for my sister. She is of so mild and unprotesting a disposition in general, as to be severely imposed upon by bores of every description—who find in her quiet beauty and paltry fortune a double advantage; for she is a lady who can neither fail to bring them credit as a partner, nor tempt them to abandon the single state. At the Chilham ball to which Eliza referred, my sister had consented to dance no less than *four dances* with Mr. Kemble—and had found both his conversation and skill to be sorely waning. He can claim no relation to the famous Kemble family of actors—tho' such a distinction might render even *his* tedium easier to bear—but is rather a member of the Kent militia, and an intimate of my brother Edward's home at Godmersham. Mr. Kemble is a great enthusiast for shooting and riding to hounds. He finds ample scope for discourse in the merits of his dogs and hunters.

"Now *there* is a respectable gentleman, Jane," my mother declared, reappearing with Henry in tow. "*There* is credit and propriety."

My sister audibly sighed.

"Shall we seek the cloak-room?" I enquired, but it was too late. Mr. Kemble had achieved his object.

"Miss Austen," he cried heartily to Cassandra, with a bow that brought him nearly so low as her knees. "Delighted! Capital! I am only just arrived in Bath—and here I find my old partner! You haven't changed a bit—and it has been all of three years since we met, I declare! I might never have left Chilham! I trust you are at liberty for the first?"

"I am, sir," my amiable sister replied with a curtsey.

"Excellent! Excellent! I shall look to partner you the entire evening, then—would consider it a favour to your excellent brother Edward!—for I cannot suppose a lady of your mature years to be very much in request. We shall deal famously together!"

Mr. Kemble offered his arm, and with a despairing look, Cassandra accepted it; and I heard him exclaim, as they moved towards the floor: "My setter Daisy's had two litters since you went away! Capital little bitch! No turning her from the scent!"

"How well they look together," my mother mused, in following her elder daughter amidst the couples. "Though she *is* perhaps too near him in height for convention's sake."

"That is very bad in Cassandra, indeed," Eliza said mischievously. "A lady should always attempt to be shorter than her partner, can she contrive it, and had much better sit down if not. But *you* shall not suffer a similar indignity, Jane, for Lord Harold is quite tall, indeed. Shall we dance, Henry?"

The first dance was struck up; I found Cassandra quite martyred among the couples; and felt a gentleman to loom at my elbow. I turned—and saw Hugh Conyngham.

He had left off his court dress, and was arrayed this evening in a plum-coloured coat of superfine cloth, a pair of dove-grey pantaloons, and a waistcoat of embroidered silk. The folds of his neckcloth were so intricate as to leave the eye entirely bewildered, and his collar points so stiff as to demand a permanent elevation of the chin. I smothered an unruly impulse to laugh aloud—the tragic Hugh Conyngham, a Dandy!—and curtseyed deep in acknowledgement. For all that he might affect the popinjay, Mr. Conyngham is nonetheless a handsome fellow, with his tousled dark head and his bright blue eyes—and I must appear sensible of the honour of his attentions.

''Miss Austen,'' the actor said with a bow. ''Your ankle is quite recovered, I trust?''

''Entirely, sir, I assure you. I may thank your excessive goodness—and excellent brandy—for the preservation of my health.''

''Then may I solicit this dance?''

''With pleasure.'' My surprise was considerable; but I followed him to the floor without a murmur, my thoughts revolving wildly. Had he discovered the plundered desk in the manager's office, and recollected the curious nature of my stumbling in the wings?

''I am all astonishment, Mr. Conyngham, at finding you present in the Lower Rooms,'' I said, as we entered the line of couples arranged for a minuet. ''I had thought the company engaged tonight in Bristol.''

''And so they are—but the play they would mount has no part for me.'' He moved well, with unconscious grace, and his aspect was hardly grim; perhaps I had misread his eagerness in seeking me for a partner. ''I had thought to find Her Grace's party at the Assembly—but must suppose their present misfortune to have counselled a quiet evening at home.''

''Perhaps. Though I believe they intended the Rooms.''

''Lord Harold is a prepossessing gentleman. I had not made his acquaintance before his appearance in Orchard Street last evening.''

''Very prepossessing, indeed,'' I carefully replied. ''And blessed with considerable penetration. He is highly placed in Government circles, I understand.''

A swift, assessing look, as swiftly averted. ''You are quite intimate with the family?''

''No more so than yourself, Mr. Conyngham.''

''I?'' He permitted himself a smile. ''As though it were possible! No, no, Miss Austen—not for me the pretensions of a Mr. Portal. I do not aim so high as a ducal family.''

"And did the manager truly entertain a hope in that quarter?"

"I must assume so. Portal was excessively attentive to Lady Desdemona."

"But—forgive me—I had understood him to be devoted to your sister."

"Admiration, perhaps—esteem and affection—but devotion? I should not call it such." He shook his head.

"No," I mused, "for the devoted do not look elsewhere."

"As my sister has long been aware. Maria has never been so incautious as to place her faith in the affections of a gentleman; and I cannot find it in me to counsel her otherwise. We are a reprehensible lot, where ladies are concerned."

"You are severe upon your sex!"

He smiled bitterly. "I have seen perhaps too much of our fickle nature, Miss Austen."

"But you can know nothing of light attachments yourself, Mr. Conyngham." I hesitated, then plunged on. "I have it on the very best authority that your heart is given over to one already in her grave."

He inclined his handsome head in acknowledgement, but seemed much preoccupied, and presently said, "I see that you have heard something of my sad history."

"Your affection for the late Miss Siddons? Yes—an acquaintance of mine, familiar with the story, did let something slip."

A flush suffused Hugh Conyngham's cheeks, and as swiftly drained away. Such acute sensibility should not be surprising in a man devoted to the Theatre.

"I must applaud your sentiments," I continued. "Such constancy in a gentleman—even unto death—is exceedingly rare."

His blue eyes held mine for a long moment, and then he moved around me in a figure of the dance. "It was Her Grace who happened to speak of the business, I must suppose?"

"On the contrary—an old friend of your family's. Madam Anne Lefroy."

"I do not recollect—"

"You are unacquainted with the lady, I believe, but may profess at least to have seen her. Madam attended Her Grace's rout in the guise of Queen Elizabeth."

tion with the Red Harlequin."

"Mr. Thomas Lawrence. Do you know the gentleman at all?"

"Our paths have crossed before," Hugh Conyngham supplied briefly. "But tell me, Miss Austen—how is it that your friend professes to know aught of my history? For I have assuredly never met her."

"She chanced to act in an amateur theatrical with your parents many years ago, I understand, at the Dowager's estate in Kent—and followed the course of your life with considerable interest for many years thereafter. Music, and theatre, and excellence in composition, are beyond all things Madam Lefroy's delight."

Mr. Conyngham's looks were abstracted, as though his mind was entirely fled, but he collected himself enough to say, "A lady of parts, I perceive. She is resident in Bath? For I should like to make her acquaintance, and hear her recollection of my parents."

"I regret to say that her home is in Hampshire—in the village of Ashe, not far from where I spent the better part of my childhood."

When the actor reached for my hand in the figure of the dance, I perceived that his own was trembling slightly. "But Madam Lefroy claims an acquaintance with both yourself and the Trowbridge family?" he enquired. "Then perhaps I may yet encounter her with time."

"I should do much to summon her again to Bath," I said with feeling.

We danced on some moments in silence; and then I thought it wise to revert to our first topic. He had certainly abandoned it for the slightest diversion; and such discomfort must be probed. "Even so cautious a lady as your sister, Mr. Conyngham, must place *some* credit in the affections of a gentleman. For she is happy, I believe, in the attentions of the Earl of Swithin. Lord Harold himself seems quite struck by the Earl's regard. He remarked upon it only last evening."

At this, Mr. Conyngham faltered in the dance. "They are the merest acquaintances, I believe. Maria possesses any number of beaux, who appear in the wings with all manner of tributes, and vanish as swiftly by morning. I cannot think what Lord Harold finds to remark in the offering of a few flowers."

"Nor can I," I cheerfully replied, "but after all, my dear sir, such a man must have sources of information of which we can know nothing."

He could hardly rejoice in the thought; that he knew the desk had been plundered, and by whom, I little doubted—and so, in the most desultory manner imaginable, our dance declined to its end.

"I AM HAPPY TO SEE YOU AGAIN, LORD HAROLD," MY MOTHER SAID with considerable effort a half-hour later, as we stood in the Tea Room hopeful of securing places. "You do not know Mrs. Henry Austen, I believe."

"On the contrary, madam—we have met in London. At the late Sir Hugh Walpole's, I believe." Lord Harold bowed.

"You have a remarkable memory, my lord," Eliza cried. "I have not seen Lady Walpole this age! But I believe we may have met at a rout or two, when she was more given to braving society."

"You are well, Lord Harold, I hope?" my mother enquired.

"I am, ma'am. And I find you in good health, I trust?"

"Tolerable, tolerable—though Mr. Austen's is not what I would wish. Mr. Bowen *will* have him walk out in the coldest weather, as you saw yourself when you were so kind as to call in Green Park Buildings Wednesday; and though the exercise may be beneficial, I cannot think the sharpness of the wind entirely salubrious."

"No, indeed. And did the Reverend determine to remain at home this evening?"

"He is playing at whist, sir. My son Henry attends him."

"Jane," my sister Eliza whispered, "I am *quite taken* with your Gentleman Rogue. I understand, now, Lady Walpole's utter enslavement to Trowbridge several years past. There was quite a scandal, you know, when she abandoned Sir Hugh."

"Eliza," I retorted in a quelling tone. "He will hear you."

The little Comtesse's dark eyes sparkled with mischief. "I do not care if he does. I should like nothing better than to have the whole history from Lord Harold himself. Sir Hugh shot himself in the midst of Pall Mall, you know; and Lady Walpole has not shown her face this age. Lord Harold has quite thrown her off, I expect."

"Eliza—"

But I need not have excited anxiety. Lord Harold was utterly transfixed by my mother's recitation of woe. In his dark blue coat and cream-coloured breeches, his head tilted slightly to one side, he was all politeness—and might rather have been attending Georgiana, Duchess of Devonshire, on the Whigs' prospects in Government.

"Reverend Austen has suffered a trifling cough," my mother continued, "though I *will* dress his chest in mustard and flannel; and I *cannot* be sanguine regarding his bowels."

"Now, Mamma," I protested. "Lord Harold is hardly a physician, and can have no interest in our . . . trifling coughs."

"On the contrary," he protested amiably, "I am frequently called to offer an opinion in my mother's case, and place the greatest trust in Dr. Charles Gibbs, of Milsom Street. He is a most excellent physician, and has quite preserved the Dowager Duchess against Bath's penetrating damps."

"I have not the honour of acquaintance with Dr. Gibbs," my mother replied.

"Then I shall make certain to send him to Green Park Buildings. You cannot do without Gibbs."

My mother curtseyed, and turned to me abruptly. "Jane, my dear, I long to be at home. Have you not had enough of dancing? Cassandra is greatly fatigued—the poor child suffered a trying injury to the head last summer, Lord Harold, while we were travelling in Dorset—and I cannot think the lateness of the hour good for her."

"I shall be quite all right, Mamma," I replied with equanimity. "For Henry and Eliza do not desert me. Do you attend Cassandra home, and I shall follow presently."

She would have protested—would rather have remained, than abandoned me to Lord Harold in her absence—but my brother was so insistent upon her leaving, and even went in search of my father for the purpose of speeding her departure, that her intentions were utterly routed. She turned from our little party with a swirl of her skirts, and I perceived that I should be subject to a scolding on the morrow.

"And now we may have our tea in peace," Eliza announced. She seized upon a table with remarkable energy, and awaited the appearance of a footman with the tea things.

"I did not expect the pleasure of meeting you this evening," I said to Lord Harold, when all the bustle of family business was over.

"I could not resist attending my niece to the Assembly, in direct opposition to the Earl of Swithin's views of propriety. I observe that *he* at least has not remained at home, in deference to my nephew. He is even now paying court to Miss Conyngham, and is careful that Desdemona observes it. Mona, for her part, is engrossed in conversation with a Colonel Easton. How diverting it all is, to be sure."

"Colonel Easton?"

"He is an officer in the Dragoon Guards, and has been in love with my niece this age. Mona rides with him tomorrow at Dash's."[2]

"I am unacquainted with Colonel Easton—but had heard that he is recently come to Bath. And that he was injured in a duel," I managed. "The result of an insult to Lord Swithin."

"And so he was. His right arm is still bound up in a sling, like a badge of honour. The Colonel and the Earl do not speak. We may presume this lends the flirtation a certain piquancy in Mona's eyes."

Lord Harold handed me a glass of wine punch, and secured himself another.

"Your family does not regard my attentions with pleasure, Miss Austen. I fear I have rendered you a disservice. Pray accept my apologies."

I coloured, and looked conscious. "I do not understand you, my lord."

"I beg your pardon, but I fancy you do. I quite ruin your reputation with every advance upon your doorstep, my dear." The Gentleman Rogue's words were couched in boredom; but I detected a wound. It is something, indeed, to be suspected of impropriety wherever one goes—the justice of the suspicion notwithstanding.

"My family may, perhaps, be a little overawed at your greatness, my lord."

"Then they are very unlike the greater run of Bath society." He surveyed the crush of pleasure-seekers jostling for places in the Tea Room, several of whom averted their looks as his lordship glanced their way, and an expression of bitterness flitted across his countenance. "Perhaps I should have attempted to speak to you in the midst of the street, and preferably at noon. For we should hardly draw greater interest in the public square, than we have done in the privacy of this corner. I have damaged you immeasurably, Miss Aus-

---

[2] This was a riding school located in Montpelier Street, where, for a seasonal subscription, the gentry might receive instruction in riding or hire mounts for their use.—*Editor's note.*

ten. First the theatre, and now the Assembly—it requires only an urchin to publish our assignation in the Labyrinth, to complete the ruin of your reputation! All of Bath will be detecting you in an intrigue, and pitying you when I turn my attentions to Miss Conyngham."

"I should rather thank than berate you, Lord Harold." I sipped at my punch and felt suddenly exposed to an hundred curious eyes. "Such interesting attention will at least ensure that my present life is less tedious than of old."

He was silent a moment. "Are you, then, unhappy with your lot? Bath, to be sure, lacks the superior society of London, but I have heard many ladies describe it as endlessly diverting. Is it so unequal to your amusement?"

"I have not the idleness of character to take pleasure in dissipation," I replied. "I sorely want to be doing something. And perhaps I have endured Bath's pleasures too long. Even Paradise, I suspect, will grow contemptible through eternal association."

"We are very much alike in this, my dear. I find the tedium of daily routine very nearly insupportable. It is the sole inducement to involve myself in—affairs of a delicate nature. Without the spur of variety, I should be a lost man, unfitted to good society."

And thus we find the root of your restless heart, I silently observed, *forever intent upon the next conquest.* But I only said, "In the present case, at least, you have the welfare of your nephew to lend urgency to the game. Your energies could never be brought to a similar pitch by mere *ennui* alone."

"That is true," he said, his grey eyes alight. "But tell me, I beg. Did you learn anything of Hugh Conyngham? For I observed you to dance with him an hour since."

"Nothing of what Mr. Elliot would deign to call *proof*," I said with a droll look, "but I would wager my life that he knows of the letters' disappearance, and misgives the nature of our recent visit to the wings. I took care to present you as a formidable fellow, alive with suspicion regarding his sister and the Earl, and happy in resources denied to others. I may fairly say we may expect the unfortunate Mr. Conyngham to move in considerable anxiety—and seek the protection of the only person available to lend it—the Earl of Swithin."

"And tomorrow I embark upon Maria Conyngham."

"Take care, Lord Harold, that she does not embark upon *you.*"

"That must be impossible, my dear."

"Forgive me, but I cannot be so sanguine." I met his eyes as steadily as I knew how.

"You do not believe me in danger!" He affected a careless good humour, but there was a wariness in his looks.

"I think you move at your very peril. Her motives and skill are of the most subtle; her charms, infinite. Have a care, I beg."

"I will promise to present the lady with a heart as duplicitous as her own appears to be," Lord Harold replied; but there was little of levity in his words.

And so he bowed, and left me to the significant looks of Henry and Eliza, and all the comfort of cooling tea.

Chapter 11

A Knife
at the Throat

*Saturday,
15 December 1804*
~

I PARTED FROM THE HENRY AUSTENS IN THE FOYER OF THE LOWER
Rooms not long thereafter, but I did not go to my chair in even
tolerable composure. My thoughts were entirely consumed with Lord
Harold Trowbridge for the better part of my journey home to Green
Park Buildings. He has ever been a man of coldest calculation, a
master-player at chess, and moving amongst a multitude of boards—
all of them quite chequered. I had thought the tender passions to be
his abhorrence; and indeed, with such a career as he has made, they
should never prove his friends. However many women he may keep
in style in Mayfair, his heart is unlikely to be touched. This containment of temper preserves him from the stabs of the impertinent, just
as it renders the exploitative without object. Moreover, I trace in its
lineaments the result of some great disappointment in early life—the
loss of a beloved to betrayal, or perhaps a crueller fate. My intimacy
with Lord Harold has never been of so great a kind as to permit the
exchange of confidences; and thus my conjectures must remain un-
satisfied. But his weakness in the present instance troubles me—I
detect an inclination to the challenge of Maria Conyngham's heart—
and I fear for the composure of his mind.

I cannot, however, find in this any possible hope of happiness for Lord Harold. He knows of her proximity to Richard Portal, and of that gentleman's blackmailing art; knows, too, that Maria is tied by affection or avarice to the Earl of Swithin. And though he cannot prove it was her hand thrust home the dagger, suspicion will curl in his very entrails—poisoning his thoughts, destroying his sleep, and turning his tenderest feeling the betrayer of his judgement. He will be flayed alive by the division in his soul—and that suffering will lead him to divine the truth.

And in seeking the truth, he can only destroy Miss Conyngham.

A sudden lurch to the chair thrust me strongly against the left-hand window, and I cried out in some alarm. I had barely time to observe that the forward bearer had set down his poles, pitching me to the front of my seat, before the aft man did likewise; and the two ran off without a word of explanation, quite impervious to my exclamations of outrage and dismay. Where was the link boy, with his flaring lamp?[1] The darkness enshrouding the chair was absolute, and in sudden, sharp fear, I fumbled at the door.

It was then I perceived a figure looming over me—and my breath caught hard within my throat.

"There now, ma'am, hand us your reticule, or we'll be forced to find it—and we've ways of looking you won't much like." A most ruffianly-appearing fellow stared down at me in the darkness, his face partially obscured by a handkerchief. "You shouldn't ought to travel when the night's without the moon, miss. Mortal dangerous it is."

I sank back into the chair, finding in its low-ceilinged space a hint of reassurance and protection, and saw that a second man, bearded and muffled to defy detection, had taken up position by the first. The chair had been abandoned in an alley—no doubt through the thieves' collusion with the dastardly chairmen—and the place was unfamiliar to my eyes. In such darkness, however, all of Bath might be disguised. I briefly considered screaming in a bid for assistance—surely the streets must as yet be populous—but recollected the habit of the most common footpad, of carrying a knife or a club. And so I handed the thieves my reticule without complaint.

<hr>

[1] A man or boy holding aloft a lamp—or "link"—ran before the sedan chair at night, to warn pedestrians and to illuminate the route.—*Editor's note.*

They were a curious pair—hulking and sturdy as farming hands, but dressed in the ape of fashion. Had I passed them on the street, and never heard them speak, I might have taken them for gentlemen, indeed—and could hardly believe their raiment won from the profits of petty stealing. The first man untied the strings of my little purse and probed within.

The second man peered through the doorway, and I quailed at the rage in his eyes. They were singular, indeed, as though the Devil's mark was upon him—for even in the gloom I could discern that one eye was light, and the other dark. Where had I seen a similar pair before? But I lacked time for all reflection—for to my extreme terror, he reached a hand to the collar of my pelisse, and the hand held a knife.

I rapped his knuckles sharply with my fan and screamed aloud at the full pitch of my lungs. The ruffian seized me by the shoulders, and endeavoured to bring the knife to my very throat—when his hand was stilled by the blessed sound of running feet careening around a corner.

With an oath and a slam of a fist to the sedan chair's roof, my assailant dashed back into the darkened alley. His companion followed hard at his heels. And it was then I remembered where last I had seen him—he was Smythe, the labourer from the Theatre Royal. I screamed again, and thrust myself out of the chair and into the arms of a burly fellow in the blue uniform and peaked cap of the chairmen—and recoiled in horror, as from a nightmare too quickly renewed.[2]

"Now, miss," the man said comfortingly, "what's the to-do?"

"I was abandoned in this place by some of your brethren, and set upon by thieves," I managed. "Pray to call the constable."

He turned and hallooed to some confederates, who dashed off in pursuit of my assailants; and trembling in every limb, I was conducted through a growing crowd to the safety of a coaching inn.

It was another hour before I achieved the stoop of Green Park Buildings, however, having been sent home in a hack chaise at the

---

[2] From their familiarity with the streets and their presence at all hours, chairmen served as almost a police force in Bath, although an unregulated one; they were known to occasionally hold their fares captive, for the extortion of money.—*Editor's note.*

constable's expense. I had lost my reticule and such coin as I possessed to my dedicated footpads. The constable had dutifully noted the abandonment of the chair, the seizing of my purse, and my description of a man with parti-coloured eyes, who I thought was named Smythe, and very likely to be found in Orchard Street. He was content to believe the incident one of common theft—but I knew otherwise. It was nothing less than murder that Smythe had attempted tonight; and that he was sent by the same person responsible for Richard Portal's death, I felt certain.

The question that remained, however, was *why*?

MY FATHER WAS SITTING UP WITH AN ANXIOUS FACE, HIS CANDLE NEARLY guttered and a volume of *Grandison* open on his lap. "Jane!" he cried, as I entered the sitting-room. "It is nearly one o'clock! The dancing cannot have been so excessively prolonged."

"No, Father, it was not," I wearily replied, and laid my bonnet upon the Pembroke table. "I have been waylaid and robbed in the neighbourhood of Westgate Buildings."

"Robbed? — But were you then walking alone? And how came you near Westgate Buildings?"

"I was not so foolish as to venture entirely alone into the streets on a night without moon." My voice was cross, but I had perhaps had too much of questioning. "I can only think the chairmen were in league with the thieves, for they brought me to that insalubrious neighbourhood and abandoned me to my fate."

My father said not another word, but enfolded me in his frail arms. We are almost of a height, he and I; and through the flannel of his dressing-gown, I could discern the light, rapid beating of his heart. "I fear for you, Jane," he said at last. "This is uncommon, indeed, for Bath at Christmastide, and the close of a respectable evening's entertainment. It would not have to do, I suppose, with a certain gentleman we all choose to despise?"

"I assure you it does not, Father," I untruthfully replied; but no further words could I utter.

"Very well." His looks were grave, and I detected a want of his usual confidence. He might almost have disbelieved me. "But you are not to summon a chair again, Jane, unless in the company of a larger party."

"I may safely promise you *never* to do so."

He bent to kiss the crown of my head in the gentlest fashion possible. "I am sorry for you, indeed, my dear. You will say nothing of this affair to your mother, I beg. Her fancies run quite wild enough, without the fodder of fact to lend them strength."

SLEEP WAS LONG IN COMING WHEN AT LAST I SOUGHT MY BED, AND MY dreams were racked with fear—so that I recoiled insensible from knives that pressed against my neck, and should have cried aloud, but for the choking length of pendant chain that twined around my throat. A glittering bauble hung almost to my knees, ringed about with pearls; and as I watched, its smouldering eye turned from blue to brown and back again—unblinking all the while.

I awoke in a shuddering torment, to find the dawn creeping at my window.

I took my father's excellent advice, and when at breakfast my mother condescended to enquire about my final hour in the Lower Rooms, I talked only of indifferent tea. She was satisfied with this, and soon abandoned us for the writing desk in her bedchamber, and a long-neglected correspondence. My father, however, lingered over his coffee and rolls, and seemed in no hurry to seek acquaintance in the Pump Room.

" 'Arrivals: Lord Harold Trowbridge, lately of St. James, resident in Bath at the home of Her Grace the Dowager Duchess of Wilborough, Laura Place, since Wednesday last.' "He twitched aside the sheaf of the Bath *Chronicle* from which he had been reading aloud, and gazed at me speculatively. "It has taken the editors of our noble broadsheet a good three days to record the gentleman's descent upon the city; but we may suppose them to have withheld this interesting intelligence until this morning, in order to supplement it with supposition and hearsay. For I observe, my dear Jane, in an adjacent column, the following delicious item. *What can have drawn a certain Lord* ———, *known for his fashionable intrigues, to so sedate a locale as Bath? The taking up of his nephew for murder? Or a clergyman's daughter resident in Green Park Buildings? The lady has recently been much remarked in Lord* ———'s *company, at the Theatre Royal and the Lower Rooms. We must suppose her possessed of startling naïveté—or a taste for dangerous gentlemen.*' "

I flushed, and set down my teacup. "How despicable!"

"You do not find it diverting, Jane?" my father cried with false astonishment. "We may then suppose naïveté, rather than a danger-ous taste, to be foremost in your character—and I shall convey the news to the editors of the *Chronicle* without delay. All of Bath is sure to be impatient for our reply."

I hastened to my father's side and snatched the paper from his unprotesting hands. "But this is abominable!"

"It is no more than you should have expected, I am sure," said Cassandra from her place by the fire. But her eyes, when they met mine, held no triumph. "One cannot engage in public display with-out drawing the notice of the most impertinent and voluble of gos-sips."

"Am I to be denied, then, the common right of privacy with re-gard to my personal affairs?" I retorted hotly.

"I believe you forfeited it when you undertook to receive Lord Harold," my sister replied.

"Cannot you put an end to the acquaintance, my dear?" my fa-ther protested. "The present publicity alone must convince your friend that he may only do you harm with his attentions; and no honourable man would require further explanation. You cannot de-sire so much notoriety, I am certain."

I hesitated, for the warmest sensibility has always warred with rea-son in my character, and the impulse was strong to champion Lord Harold at the expense of my reputation. But in deference to my father, I said nothing of the outrage bubbling in my breast, or of the regard I felt for the gentleman's character. I took refuge, instead, in prevarication.

"For my part, I have always believed Lord Harold merely hoped I might strengthen my friendship with his niece, Lady Desdemona—who lacks a broad acquaintance in Bath, and must feel her brother's present misfortunes most acutely. I believe, moreover, that Lord Har-old is much attached to another, and henceforth is likely to further his interest with the lady."

"Indeed, Jane? But what is this? Jilted by the Gentleman Rogue?" my father cried. "Pray to fetch my paper and pen. The *Chronicle* must know of it immediately!"

I attempted a smile at his unfortunate raillery; but an oppression of spirits must defeat the effort.

"My poor Jane," Cassandra murmured. She set aside her napkin and gazed at me with pity. "I feel for the disappointment of your hopes. But considering Lord Harold's character, we could not have hoped for better. For is it not to be preferred, that his falseness and levity be revealed in the present hour, than discovered far later, when a greater damage had been done?"

A comforting thought, indeed.

"I am sure I shall learn to see the matter as you do, Cassandra," I replied; but the words came only with effort.

I COULD NOT REFLECT UPON THE PREVIOUS EVENING'S MISADVENTURE without the greatest trepidation; there was no one to whom I might confide my distress, other than Lord Harold; and yet the sly calculation of the Bath *Chronicle* had rendered comfort in that quarter suspect. I stood some moments before the looking-glass, to study my throat with the most acute eye, and imagine the descent of a blade— and all attempt at composure remained well beyond my reach. And so, a few hours after the *Chronicle* had been burnt in the sitting-room grate for the deception of my mother, I set out on foot to Dash's Riding School. Lord Harold had said that Lady Desdemona would ride there; and perhaps he might make one of the party. I could think of nothing so calculated for the relief of my mind, than the relation of the whole to that gentleman.

My heart was heavy, however, and I moved as though under the scrutiny of all Bath. An absurd emotion, of course—did even half the citizens I encountered along my route peruse the morning papers, only a handful were likely to have read the speculative column, and none of them were familiar with my face—but a blow had been struck, all the same, and I laboured under the wound.

Cassandra had barely uttered a word, when I had declared my intention of walking into Montpellier Row, where the riding school is situated; but the diffidence of my speech, regarding my intention to remain on terms of intimacy with Lady Desdemona despite her uncle's probable defection, could not disguise my true misery. In my father's eyes I read the reflection of my sister's doubts; and the disapproval of the entire household must weigh heavily upon me. It is the Austens' considered opinion that I am entirely lost to Lord Harold

Trowbridge, and that my character now hangs in the balance; at the advanced age of nearly nine-and-twenty, I have consented to play the fool, and serve as pawn in the designs of the great. In vain have I pled the cause of friendship, and the lamentable misfortune of Simon, Lord Kinsell. These are weighed as nothing in the scales of feminine virtue, which have clearly tipped in the direction of impropriety, subterfuge, and deceit.

And so to Dash's I have gone, with lowered spirits and a fading courage; for we are never so confident in our activity, as when we move with the certainty of the world's approbation—nor so dragging of feet, as when the contempt of the beloved is foremost in our minds.

"Miss Austen!" THE DOWAGER DUCHESS EXTENDED A GLOVED HAND and smiled up at me from her chair. "How delightful to see you again! I see we may claim one friend at least!"

"The honour is mine, Your Grace," I replied, and pressed the offered hand. "Miss Wren. You are well, I trust?"

"As you find me, Miss Austen." She bobbed a curtsey, but did not trouble to smile. "I *do* fear the onset of an inflammation of the lungs—it is ever a danger at this time of year, is it not?—though I should never complain, when dearest Mona is bent upon her little pleasures."

I turned to gaze at the riders circling within the ring, and presently located a fresh-faced lady in a dark blue habit. "How well she looks!" I exclaimed involuntarily.

"Like a general advancing upon the field," the Duchess agreed. "The soutache and braid are cunning, are they not? I had the design of her habit myself. And the hat is a perfection!"

The article thus described was a shako with feathers, and completed Lady Desdemona's air of having emerged triumphant from the battlefield; her cheeks were bright, and her eyes sparkled, as she gazed up into the face of the officer riding beside her. I recognised her partner from the Lower Rooms.

"Is that Colonel Easton I see, Your Grace?"

"The Earl of Northcote's second son. A well-bred, gentleman-like fellow enough, and quite martyred to my Mona."

"He is very handsome."

"—and possesses not a farthing to his name," Miss Wren sniffed.

"You exaggerate, my dear Wren," the Duchess countered. "He has an excellent commission, and the pay of a colonel's rank—a thousand pounds a year, at least. He lives in very easy circumstances."

"Or would, did he learn to abhor the gaming tables," Miss Wren retorted acidly. "But he is *nothing* compared to Lord Swithin. Mona's fortune should be entirely thrown away on such a fellow—and he cannot even offer her a title!"

The topic, I judged, had been canvassed before; but it was allowed to dwindle away, at the advance of two very fine ladies, habited to ride. Their hair was golden, their smiles complacent; and they might as readily have been a pair of china dolls, for all the animation I observed.

"The Lady Louisa Fortescue! And Lady Augusta, too! I am happy to see you." The Dowager spoke with an amiable nod. "You do not yet brave the ring, I see."

"We merely await the appearance of our brother, Your Grace; but could not delay another moment in offering our deepest sympathies regarding the misfortunes that have plagued your household." The elder Fortescue arranged her features in a poor display of sincerity. "Our brother has told us of the stupidity of the local magistrate. We were excessively miserable! For what is the kingdom coming to, if an heir to a dukedom may be summarily thrown into gaol? When, I beg, may we expect Lord Kinsfell to be restored to the bosom of his family?"

"Presently, we have reason to hope. And is the Earl of Swithin to ride today as well?"

"We should not consider it without him," the younger girl cried, with a look for her sister. "I cannot think it would be proper."

"Your delicacy does you credit, I am sure," Miss Wren interjected. "I could wish that *all* young ladies might conduct themselves so becomingly."

The Earl's sisters bestowed upon Wren their condescending smiles, and sank with a languid air into some chairs at the Duchess's side.

"You are not, I think, acquainted with Miss Austen." Her Grace turned her affectionate looks my way. "Lady Louisa and Lady Augusta Fortescue—Miss Jane Austen, Lady Desdemona's particular friend."

"Indeed?" the elder said, with an appearance of interest. "And are you visiting, then, in Laura Place, Miss Austen?"

"I am so fortunate as to call Bath my home, Lady Louisa."

"Ah. And what part of Bath?"

"My family resides in Green Park Buildings."

"Green Park—" She turned and glanced significantly at her sister. "And are you, perchance, a clergyman's daughter?"

My traitorous cheeks grew hot. So the *Chronicle* was read in the Earl's household, at least. But the Dowager Duchess's smooth intercession saved me the trouble of replying.

"How long do you intend to remain in Bath, Lady Louisa?" Her Grace enquired.

The Earl's sister shrugged, with all the indolent charm of a lady educated privately and at great expense. "As long as it pleases Charles. We come and go entirely at his command, Your Grace, for he must have the society of ladies to lend his establishments elegance."

"But of course," the Duchess replied. "You were lately, I believe, in London?"

"We came down on Thursday, at our brother's request. Charles sent for us from Bristol, you know, having business there earlier in the week—and when the intelligence of Lord Kinsfell's misfortunes reached his ears, nothing would suit but that he should journey to Bath immediately. And so we were required to join him, at great trouble to ourselves, and very little notice."

My senses were all alerted at this intelligence. The Earl of Swithin, so near to Bath as Bristol, at the time of Mr. Portal's murder?

"The Earl's attention and concern for the Wilborough family does him credit," Miss Wren observed, beaming. "So thoughtful of every particular!"

"I am sure that consideration had little to do with it," Lady Augusta supplied, "for Charles is a very heedless fellow, and never acts without consulting his own wishes first. Poor Mona will suffer from it, by and by—but I own I shall be glad to give up my place to Charles's wife! It is quite tedious to be always dancing attendance upon a brother. Only think! I might have gone to any number of balls in such a season, had I been allowed to remain in London; but here I am, forced to rusticate in Bath, and all because some actor must get himself killed! It is quite provoking.''

"It is too bad of you, Augusta!'' her elder sister cried, "for you were complaining only last week that London was dreadfully thin, and pining for a change.''

The clatter of a horse's hoofs drew all our attention to the ring, and the interesting revelations of the Fortescue ladies were at an end.

"Good morning, Miss Austen!'' Lady Desdemona cried, drawing up before the rail. "Louisa—Augusta—how droll to find you here! May I have the honour of presenting Colonel Easton?''

He was a ruddy-faced young man of perhaps thirty, with bright red hair and an expression of cheerful good temper in his brown eyes that was immediately pleasing. An air of capability and strength surrounded his person; but I shuddered to consider him at twenty paces from the Earl of Swithin's duelling pistol. The ruthlessness of the one must make short work of the other.

"Lady Louisa Fortescue, Lady Augusta Fortescue, Miss Jane Austen—Colonel George Easton.''

That he knew to whom the Fortescues were related, was entirely evident from the subtle transformation of the Colonel's expression; but he was nothing if not a gentleman, and merely inclined his head in salutation. His right arm was as yet in a sling, while his left managed the reins of his mount. "Forgive me, ladies, for my rudeness in retaining my headgear, but a trifling injury—''

"Say nothing of it, Colonel, I beg,'' I replied for my part, and curtseyed.

Lady Louisa inclined her golden head. "We have known Colonel Easton this age,'' she said, "though he pretended not to notice us in Bath Street the other day. Thursday morning, was it not, Augusta? We were only just arrived.''

"I beg your pardon, ma'am—had I perceived the honour of your presence in Bath Street, I should surely have attended you; but it was impossible. I arrived in Bath only yesterday.''

"And had not even stopped to secure a room, before paying your respects in Laura Place,'' observed the Dowager. "Such gallantry!''

"Why, I declare, Colonel Easton,'' Augusta Fortescue cried. She had been surveying his visage most intently. "You have quite shaved off your whiskers—and they were so very handsome, too! I might never have known you! But you will remark, Louisa, that it cannot have been Colonel Easton Thursday in Bath Street. For that gentleman possessed whiskers—and the Colonel's are quite gone.''

The Colonel coloured, and made some slight remark of deprecation—the fashion being now for clean-shaven faces—himself a slave to ladies' good opinion.

''You are on leave for the Christmas holiday, Colonel?'' I enquired.

''A few days only, to my despair.'' This, with a glance for Lady Desdemona. ''But every minute is as gold stored up against the poverty of winter.''

She blushed, and covered her emotion in leaning down to caress her horse's mane. ''Colonel Easton has expressed a desire to visit Simon, Grandmère—and I believe I shall attend him to the gaol.''

''My lady!'' Miss Wren cried out in horror, and looked all her agony at the Fortescue sisters. ''It is not to be thought of!''

''Is there any small item for Kinny's comfort you should wish me to convey, Your Grace?'' Lady Desdemona continued hurriedly.

The Dowager did not answer her for the space of a heartbeat. Then she smiled. ''Send Simon my dearest love, of course—and my belief in his courage. He shall not remain there long.''

''No,'' Lady Desdemona said thoughtfully, ''for Uncle says he is to be conveyed to Ilchester on Monday.''

''You cannot condone such a foolish notion, Your Grace,'' Miss Wren protested. ''I am sure you cannot! For the daughter of the Duke of Wilborough, to be seen in such a place!''

''If the *heir* to the Duke of Wilborough is already in residence, I cannot believe it makes one whit of difference,'' Lady Desdemona retorted, flaring. ''Besides, I shall have Miss Austen as chaperone. Shan't I, Miss Austen?''

''But of course,'' I stammered.

''And with Easton to attend us, there cannot be the slightest objection. We shall travel in his phaeton, and go entirely unremarked. I am quite determined, Wren.'' She wheeled her horse with grace and dexterity. ''I tarry only to stable my mount, Miss Austen!''

With a smile and a bow, the Colonel cantered off at her heels.

''Only fancy, Louisa,'' Augusta Fortescue remarked. ''Dash Easton dancing attendance on Mona again. And without his whiskers, too! What *will* Charles say?''

It was unfortunate, I thought, that the Earl arrived too late for such a display; but his sisters had lost not a syllable of the conversation.

Chapter 12

Accusation of a Dead Man

15 December 1804, cont.

~

THE BATH GAOL—A SMALL AFFAIR HARDLY INTENDED FOR THE imprisonment of a criminal legion, since such were summarily dispatched to Ilchester to await the quarterly Assizes—sits within the old town walls, hard by the Pump Room and the Abbey. I am no stranger to the stricter forms of incarceration, having braved so stern an institution as Newgate itself, on behalf of my beloved Isobel; but the Bath gaol recalls more nearly the prison of Lyme, in being a white-washed hovel of a building, more fitted to the shelter of beasts than men. Colonel Easton's chaise drew up before the gates, and we descended to a spare courtyard from which the bustle of Bath's streets had thankfully been banished. It but remained to make ourselves known, and enquire of the constable where Simon, Lord Kinsfell, might be found.

The Colonel hastened immediately about this errand; and we were rewarded, in a very little while, with his reappearance in company with a constable—one of the two, I believe, who descended upon Laura Place the night of the murder. He was a jaded personage addressed only as Shaw, who possessed a broken front tooth displayed to advantage in leering at the Quality. I judged him to be full sixty years of age and unastonished by any of life's present vicissitudes; accustomed to the seizure of pickpockets, drunkards, and foopads of every description, but hardly equal to the elucidation of a murder. He was content to believe that Kinsfell had stabbed poor Richard Portal from inebriated rage.

Mr. Shaw surveyed us with a curious blend of contempt and sympathy, and urged us to reconsider our notion of conversing with so dangerous a man; but Lady Desdemona was admirably determined. She pled the duty and feelings of a sister, and when seconded by so imposing a presence as the uniformed Colonel Easton, could not be gainsaid. Presently we were conveyed to a low door in a wall, where a gaoler sat whitling a stick. The fellow jumped up at our appearance, and pulled his forelock in salutation, at which Constable Shaw cuffed him absent-mindedly and bent to his keys.

"I shall return in a quarter-hour, sir," he said with a bow to Easton, and an unfortunate exposure of the broken tooth, "a quarter-hour and no more."

"Very well," the Colonel replied.

Lady Desdemona drew a shaky breath, composed her features, and entered the dimly-lit room. I followed, with the Colonel behind. I had known these odours before—of musty hay, poor drainage, and human excrement—but was nonetheless tempted to secure my handkerchief beneath my nose in an effort to block them out. The door shut-to at our backs, and I heard the key grate in the lock.

"Kinny!" Lady Desdemona cried.

A shadow against the opposite wall struggled to its feet, and shuffled but a few steps before halting to peer at us through the gloom. The cell was lit only by a small window cut into the wall at ceiling's height, and so late in December the shadows outside were already long.

"Have you been riding, Mona?" Lord Kinsfell enquired easily. Upon closer observation, the gentleman was revealed as being in irons at his wrists and ankles. "I don't suppose you thought to exercise the Defender. He must be kicking down his box door from sheer boredom. And who is that with you?"

"You remember Colonel Easton, Simon?" his sister anxiously enquired.

"How could I possibly forget? I stood second to Swithin. Your servant, sir—and no ill feelings, I hope."

"None whatsoever," Easton replied. "I should be a rogue, indeed, did I extend my grievance to my enemy's friends."

"And this is Miss Austen, Simon—an acquaintance of Uncle's, and now a friend of mine."

"Your humble servant, madam—particularly in my present circumstances," Kinsfell said with a smile. He attempted to bow, but his shackles denied him something of grace; and I observed a wave of irritation to pass over his countenance, leaving it careworn and older than his five-and-twenty years. The weight of his fears—the ignorance of his fate—the enforced inactivity and misspent energy—all must eat away at his complaisance and tell upon his nerves. For I judged that like his uncle, Lord Kinsfell was a man who must be constantly doing *something*. To be confined was for him to be entombed alive.

I stepped forward and bobbed a curtsey. "We have already met, Lord Kinsfell. Indeed, we danced a half-hour in each other's company at Her Grace's rout."

"The little Shepherdess! But how delightful to meet again! Though I confess I am astonished to find you here, and Mona, too," he added, turning towards his sister. "The guv'nor will be fit to be tied, does he hear of it!"

"And what if he is? Papa has quite despaired of *me* already, I assure you, Simon. Are you well?"

"Well enough," her brother said diffidently. "I long for an exchange from hay, however—and the victuals my gaoler is pleased to offer fairly turn my stomach! Never knew how glad I should be for a fresh pot of coffee, or a pipe if it comes to that, until they were quite beyond my reach!" He reached a hand to his tousled head, as though to make the fair locks more presentable—but the irons at his wrist turned the effort awkward and ineffectual. A muttered oath, and he dropped his arms to his sides. "But tell me if you are able—how does Uncle get on?"

"As swiftly as the most cunning mind in the kingdom may," I assured him. "He is never idle on your behalf."

"It gladdens my heart to hear it—for I am to be moved to Ilchester soon, and shall have precious little hope of news." He hesitated, and looked from his sister to Colonel Easton. "At least that magistrate cove is done hanging about. He quite puts the wind up a fellow."

"The impertinence of the Law is not to be borne," Colonel Easton remarked, "but we cannot presume that impertinence will prevail. Have courage, Kinsfell—for I am certain matters will come right in the end." He bowed, and moved to the door. "I should not wish to presume upon such intimacy, Lady Desdemona. I shall await you in the courtyard."

"You are very good, Easton."

"Perhaps I should go with the Colonel," I remarked.

"No—stay, I beg of you," she cried, with a hand to my arm. Her brother did not speak until the door had closed behind the Colonel. "So Easton is dancing attendance again, Mona? And when did he arrive in Bath?"

"Only yesterday. He was so good as to call in Laura Place, and express his outrage at your cruel treatment."

"Then all the world must know of this business, if Dash Easton has left St. James on the strength of it," Kinsfell mused gloomily. "And did he shave his whiskers as a sign of deference to a family overset by misfortune, I wonder? Or has he learned that you prefer your *beaux* clean-shaven?"

"Never mind that, Kinny," she retorted in exasperation, and then stopped short. "'Dash' Easton? However did he come by that name?"

The Marquis smiled faintly. "He won it as his right—the result of a wager. Some of the fellows at White's said he couldn't dash from London to Brighton in record time without changing horses, and Easton said he could."

"And did he?" I enquired curiously.

"Oh, yes—though at the expense of the unfortunate horse. Poor brute expired not five minutes after achieving Brighton. But Easton thought it worth the toss—he had wagered a year's pay."

"Good Lord!" Lady Desdemona cried, though not without admiration. "But, Kinny—we did not come here to talk of Easton's pranks. Miss Austen is entirely in Uncle's confidence, and may hear whatever you would say."

"I can tell you nothing, Mona," her brother said wearily.

"You know that to be the grossest falsehood, Kinny," Lady Desdemona retorted impatiently. "Swithin attended the inquest, and he is convinced that you labour under an affair of honour—that you mean to go to the gallows rather than betray your trust. I did not sleep a wink last night for considering of it!"

"Swithin! But I thought you despised the fellow!"

"Oh, as to that—" She paused awkwardly. "He is the most odious of men, and throws poor Easton into quite a favourable light. Do you know that Uncle suspects Swithin of the murder? And of leaving you to bear the blame?''

"But he was not even invited to Grandmère's rout!"

"No more he was. But Uncle has found a pin we believe to be his—a snarling tiger, with rubies for eyes—dropped and forgotten in the anteroom passageway. You know it cannot have come there honestly, Kinny. Swithin must have crept in unannounced, under cover of a mask.''

"The Devil!" Lord Kinsfell exclaimed, and then looked to myself with comic anxiety. "I beg your pardon, Miss Austen. I hope I did not offend—"

"So you see, Kinny, there is no need to protect the Earl. You must tell us what you know," his sister persisted. Her face shone palely through the gloom, and I knew that the abandonment of her favourite was not accomplished without a struggle. "Whatever your loyalty to Swithin, you must certainly never hang for it. He does not warrant such regard.''

"I do not pretend to understand you, Mona. I have no intention of shielding Swithin.''

"Kinny—you must try to be sensible, my dear.'' Lady Desdemona reached a gloved hand for his manacled one. "Did you observe him, when first you entered the room and found Portal insensible?''

Lord Kinsfell shook his head. "I saw nothing of Swithin that night.''

"But perhaps you saw a Pierrot?" I suggested. "A broad-shouldered fellow, not unlike the Earl. Throughout Her Grace's rout, I observed a similar figure in conversation with Maria Conyngham.''

He started at this, and surveyed me narrowly. "And what should Maria Conyngham have to do with Mr. Portal's death? You saw yourself how destroyed she was by his end.''

I shrugged. "We know her to be allied in the closest terms with Lord Swithin.''

"I fear you are mistaken, madam," Kinsfell cried, with a conscious look for Lady Desdemona. "Lord Swithin is excessively attached to my sister!''

"Oh, Kinny," Lady Desdemona retorted in exasperation, "how *can* you serve Miss Austen so! She speaks no more than the truth. We have all been treated to a display of Swithin's attachment for my-

self—and it is nothing compared to his attentions to Miss Conyngham! He waits upon her at the Theatre Royal, and the Lower Rooms;
and she meets his attentions with the most lively sensibility."

The Marquis threw himself down on the dirty hay and put his
head in his hands. "I cannot believe it of Maria."

"But you must, my dear," Lady Desdemona said gently. "For it is
no more than the truth. Whatever we each might have chosen to
hope regarding the respective parties, I for one refuse to continue in
ignorance."

He was silent a moment, and his sister glanced at me uneasily.

"Kinny," she said, "was it *this* that caused your words with Mr.
Portal? Did he expose Miss Conyngham's character to you that
wretched night?"

"It matters nothing, now."

"It matters a very great deal, indeed. I have only one brother, and
I will not part with him for the sake of such a jade, for any inducement in the world!" Lady Desdemona cried stoutly. "You know
something, I am sure of it."

"Did you chance to observe the lady on your passage to the
anteroom—while her brother was declaiming *Macbeth*?" I enquired.
The Marquis's answer was drowned in the clamour of knocking at
his door. "Time, my lady!" called Constable Shaw.

Lady Desdemona looked about her wildly. "Tell us, Kinny, I beg!
Your life may depend upon it!"

"Very well," he said, with infinite weariness. "I now no longer
care what happens to myself. I did not observe Maria Conyngham,
nor Swithin either. If he killed Portal and availed himself of the
passage, however, it must have been at Miss Conyngham's urging—
for she knew of the passage's existence, where Swithin could not. You
will remember, Mona, how often the Conynghams dined in Laura
Place, in the weeks before Her Grace's rout; and any might observe
the servants to pass from drawing-room to kitchen, by way of the
anteroom passage."

"That is no more than the truth," his sister thoughtfully replied.
"But there is something, Lord Kinsfell, that you know regarding
the lady," I said.

He looked at me for a long moment, his eyes devoid of hope. And
then he nodded once. "It is a word only."

"A word?"

"*Maria,*" he said. "I heard it on Portal's lips, in his final agony."

We left Lord Kinsfell to the most melancholy thoughts, and found Colonel Easton pacing in the central courtyard. He very kindly escorted us both to his phaeton, and enquired of our direction; and at Lady Desdemona's declaring herself faint from hunger, agreed to set us down in Milsom Street, for the procuring of a nuncheon at Molland's, the confectioners.[1] There he was forced to part from us, being elsewhere engaged; but we assured him of our ability to walk the remaining distance home in the strongest accents possible.

A little while later we were established on a pair of stools in the bow-front window, well-fortified with chocolate and macaroons.

"It would seem that Portal named his killer in his last moments," I began. "We must inform Lord Harold without delay."

"May I beg you to accompany me to Laura Place, Miss Austen, and dine there with us? For the morning is much advanced, and you cannot return home without first advising my uncle. I should feel the deprivation of your understanding most acutely, I vow, in attempting to make sense of our interview with Kinny. You will not desert me?"

Having reasons of my own for wishing to consult Lord Harold—a consultation already too-long deferred—I readily agreed.

"Then do you jot a little note for the instruction of your family, and I shall send one of Mrs. Molland's messengers to Green Park Buildings," Lady Desdemona suggested, with admirable efficiency.

The paper was brought, the note written, and the messenger despatched in a matter of moments. Mrs. Molland refreshed our cups, and we settled down to indulge in a thorough canvassing of Lord Kinsfell's affairs.

"Poor Kinny," Lady Desdemona observed. "I fear he is sadly overset by the revelation of his beloved's true character."

"Had you any notion of your brother's regard for Miss Conyngham?" I enquired.

[1] Readers of *Persuasion* will be familiar with Molland's, where Anne Elliot re-encounters Captain Frederick Wentworth in a sudden Bath rainstorm.—*Editor's note.*

''No, indeed,'' Lady Desdemona exclaimed. ''You must compre-hend, Miss Austen, that Kinny is beset by the attention of ladies wherever he goes—and thus I suppose I have grown used to his general air of indifference. He is considered a most eligible *parti*, because of his title and Papa's estates; and his personal address is not unpleasing. And though he has always been mad for the theatre, I had not understood that *one* among the multitude had particularly caught his eye.''

''Perhaps he found a value in discretion.''

''Rather than risk Papa's disapproval, you would mean? I should not be greatly surprised. But I must reproach myself for failing to detect the change in his behaviour. For Kinny would never have been so ready to come to Bath upon Papa's errand, or so little desir-ous of dragging me back again to London, had Miss Conyngham not been in residence here. He abhors the stupidity of Bath above all things.''

''A man of taste and elegance, I see. Does his acquaintance with the lady, then, predate this visit to Bath?''

''He came down last Easter to stay with Grandmère, and may have met Miss Conyngham then. I must suppose Mr. Portal to have thrown her in his way—for Portal was an intimate of long standing in Laura Place. But what I cannot comprehend, is *why* Miss Conyngham should wish to murder Mr. Portal. I always believed them united by the strongest ties of affection.''

''Perhaps she misconstrued his attentions to yourself,'' I offered gently. ''The theatre alone can give an hundred examples of jealousy inciting a murderous rage.''

''But it is too absurd!'' my companion cried. ''I cared nothing for the fellow!''

''—Though you may have encouraged him, from a desire to pique the Earl of Swithin.''

Lady Desdemona flushed hotly. ''Perhaps I may—perhaps I did. I have never regretted a similar indiscretion so intensely in my life, Miss Austen. For if either Swithin or Miss Conyngham was driven to violence by the appearance of my regard for Mr. Portal, I shall never forgive myself.''

We were silent a moment, and toyed with our macaroons. I consid-ered my nightmares of early morning, in some confusion and vexation. Jealousy of Lady Desdemona—from either the Earl or Maria Conyngham—could not hope to explain the haunting pendant eye Lord Kinsfell had found on Richard Portal's breast. "Do not reproach yourself excessively, Lady Desdemona," I said at last. "I would warrant that the Earl—if indeed it was his hand that struck the blow—acted as much at Miss Conyngham's behest, as from a desire to despatch his rival."

She smiled faintly. "There is very little of comfort in *that* reflection, however. I cannot rejoice in the suspicion of Swithin's attachment to another."

I studied her narrowly. "You regret the Earl's defection, then?"

"I cannot help but do so. The sensation is nothing, however, to my horror at his lordship's being suspected of murder. The torments of the past few days, Miss Austen, have been extreme. You cannot have the slightest notion; for revolve the matter in solitude as I might, I can arrive at no very satisfactory conclusion. Lord Swithin is either a murderer, a deceiver, or both; and the knowledge can only give me pain."

"Then why, when he was eager to marry, did you refuse his proposals?"

Her countenance clouded. "Mamma does not admire him, on account of his being so much in the way of the Carlton House set. They are very fast, you know, as is everything to do with the Prince, and spend a vast deal of money; and Mamma suspects that Swithin sought me for my fifty thousand pounds."

I silently blessed Desdemona's Mamma; and concluded that the Duchess of Wilborough was less empty-headed than I had thought her.

"But Papa saw nothing wrong in Swithin—and said that with so vast a fortune at his command, mine should be the merest pin money. He was almost gratified, in fact, that I should have attracted the suit of a man who has spurned nearly every woman in London."

"The Earl is much sought-after?"

"Oh, Miss Austen—I have observed such doings in Town, as should curl your hair! Such barefaced flattery, and complaisant simpering, and obnoxious efforts to please! There are ladies who go about in nothing but puce, because they believe it to be his favourite colour—though I know he quite abhors it, and laughs at them all the while. And there are others who embroider his device upon their sleeves—" She stopped short, her eyes widening. "Oh, good Lord!"

I seized her hand. "Like Mrs. Fitzherbert, who carved the Prince's feathers in the lintel of her door in Richmond Hill.² The tiger! Of course!"

"A gift to a lady, and not his own."

"The *Maria* Portal named with his dying breath! Why did we not perceive it before?"

"And so it was Miss *Conyngham* who killed Portal, and fled through the anteroom passageway, and lost the tiger unbeknownst to herself," Lady Desdemona whispered breathlessly. "Oh, my dearest Miss Austen—we must away to my uncle."

We threw some coin on Molland's counter, called hastily for chairs, and were gone.

DINNER WAS EXCESSIVELY GRAND, AND I FELT MY WANT OF EVENING DRESS acutely; but the Dowager kindly assured me that a trifling affair of two courses, comprising some twenty dishes, should never incommode so dear a friend as myself. Lord Harold presided at one end of the long table, his mother at the other, with myself and Lady Desdemona ranged in between; Miss Wren's earlier presentiment of ill-health having been realised with a most tiresome cold in the head, she kept to her rooms and requested a little warm gruel on a tray, and a hot mustard bath for her feet.

Her Grace was suffered to offer an apology, at presenting so excessively stupid a table for my amusement. Before Lord Kinsfell's misfortune, they had been wont to see some thirty guests in Laura Place at dinner; but a festive mood was wisely deemed unsuitable at such a time, and the Dowager had desisted in entertainment.

Lord Harold had greeted me with a bow, and a countenance devoid of expression; no mention was made of the offending item in that morning's *Chronicle;* and I blessed the elegance of manner that

² The coat-of-arms of the Prince of Wales is a crown surmounted by three ostrich plumes. Both his acknowledged wife—Caroline, Princess of Wales—and Mrs. Fitzherbert, the Catholic to whom he had been previously married by an Anglican priest in 1786, sported the three feathers throughout their house-holds.—*Editor's note.*

allowed the preservation of my composure. The Gentleman Rogue is too accustomed to impertinence from a public quarter, to dignify it with outrage; whereas among the Austens, such notice is so unusual as to be met with dismay on every side.

Her Grace enquired anxiously after Lord Kinsfell, and Lady Desdemona was able to give a tolerable report of his spirits; but before the servants, some four of which remained in an attitude of readiness behind our respective chairs, she was loath to mention the interesting intelligence our visit to the gaol had elicited. In thus longing for the relative privacy of the drawing-room, we were encouraged to make short work of the sole, the pheasant, and the venison. But an hour and a half of steady application to the Dowager's table, in fact, was required before I was released to the comforts of tea and feminine society.

When Lord Harold had done at last with the duty of his solitary Port, and appeared in the drawing-room reeking of tobacco, Lady Desdemona fairly leapt to his side. In a breathless accent, she related the whole of our morning's endeavours.

Her uncle listened, and looked grave. "My errand in Orchard Street gains in urgency. I had intended the Theatre Royal this evening—both the Conynghams are to play—and now I believe I must hasten there without delay. It is unfortunate that Mr. Elliot bore the interesting pin away with him to London; for I might have made an addition to my attire, and displayed the tiger on the collar of my coat. It should never have excited too great a notice in general; but in one quarter, at least, it might have moved the guilty to betrayal."

"But you do agree, Uncle, that it is possible Swithin had nothing to do with Mr. Portal's end?" Lady Desdemona persisted.

He gazed at her an instant before replying. "I hesitate to declare Swithin innocent of anything, my dear, until our excellent Mr. Elliot has returned from London."

"We need not await the magistrate's intelligence on one point, at least," I broke in, with an anxious look for Lady Desdemona. "For Lord Swithin's sisters acknowledged only this morning that the Earl had business so near to Bath as *Bristol* the very morning after Mr. Portal's murder. Certainly it was from Bristol that his lordship sent for the Fortescue ladies, before journeying to Bath himself on Wednesday. They joined him here on Thursday, I believe."

"Did they, indeed? This is news of the first water." Lord Harold considered my words a moment, then wheeled to confront his niece.

"Would it comfort you, Mona, to know that Swithin was in the clear?"

"It would," she replied, with downcast eyes.

"Though in all probability Miss Conyngham wore his device—in the most public admission of his patronage? You persist in valuing a man of so dissipated a character?"

His voice had grown quite stern, and Lady Desdemona quailed; but it was the Dowager who replied.

"Leave her be, Harry," she said with a wave, "you need not fear she is abandoned to the reprobate. She merely hopes he is not entirely so past recall, as to have murdered Mr. Portal. There is nothing very singular in this."

"Very well, Mamma. If we must consider Desdemona's heart, I can see no alternative but to adventure Bristol on the morrow. There are only two inns I can conceive of Swithin gracing; and at one of these, he will be remembered. And now I must away, or Miss Conyngham will play without my admiration. Miss Austen? May I set you down in Seymour Street?"

"You may, my lord, with my deepest thanks."

I made my *adieux*, and was very soon established in Lord Harold's curricle.

"YOU ARE RATHER QUIET THIS EVENING, MISS AUSTEN. I HOPE MY NIECE has not overtaxed your fund of strength."

"Hardly—though I am, perhaps, a little oppressed in spirits."

A swift glance, as swiftly averted. "I very much regret the impertinence of the newspaper, Jane."

The gentleness of his tone, and his adoption of my Christian name, very nearly brought tears to my eyes—but I drew a shaky breath and attempted to affect a carelessness I could not feel.

"Oh, as to that—do not trouble to consider of it further. For what do we live, but to make sport for our neighbours, and laugh at them in our turn? It shall be forgot, and Green Park Buildings returned to its usual obscurity."

"Your complaisance does you credit. I must hope that Maria Conyngham possesses not half so much—or I shall be sadly thwarted in my efforts to provoke her this evening.''

''Provocation is all very well—but I would counsel, my lord, that you undertake it only with the most zealous care for your person. There is a danger in travelling alone. My chair was waylaid by foot-pads as I attempted a return from the Lower Rooms last evening.''

''Footpads! I had not an idea of it!'' Lord Harold turned to me in astonishment. ''They were after your purse?''

''—Though there was little enough within. I recognised one of the men, however, as he held a knife to my throat—and informed the constable of his name and direction. He was a certain Smythe, of the Theatre Royal. I had remarked him Thursday when we ventured to the wings, as a man quite subject to Hugh Conyngham's direction. And though his beard and headgear obscured his face, I could hardly have been mistaken—for Smythe possesses one blue, and one brown eye; and thus must be instantly known, even in darkness.''

I spoke with tolerable composure, but Lord Harold's distress was sudden and extreme.

''He held a knife to your throat!''

''Do not concern yourself, I beg. He very soon ran off, when I summoned breath enough to scream. But I should be interested to learn whether the constable succeeded in seizing him. You might find it out at the theatre this evening.''

''And you believe this villain was despatched by one of the company?'' Lord Harold enquired in the grimmest accent.

''I am utterly convinced of it—by Hugh Conyngham himself, perhaps. Our conversation in the Lower Rooms last night must somehow have excited that gentleman's anxiety; and from a fear, perhaps, of the letters' exposure—or a fear of my intimacy with yourself—he determined that I should be silenced.''

''But you cannot have betrayed our suspicions so completely, Jane! And yet you think the man Smythe intended your death?''

''I detected no gentleness in his look—only the coldest light of determination.''

Lord Harold snapped the reins over the back of his team, though the horses already moved smartly enough. ''When I think that *I* might have prevented it! Had I never urged you to deceive Conyngham, while I searched the manager's office, you should not have been exposed to this danger."

"You must not reproach yourself, my lord. I am no slip of a girl to require excessive protection; what I have done, was done of my own free will. I impart the particulars only so that you may be on your guard. For if you persist in baiting Maria Conyngham, you surely risk the gravest injury. Have a care, Lord Harold—and trust no one's appearance of benevolence."

"You could not have bestowed your warning on a less likely object," he replied with mirth. "It is many years, indeed, since I have trusted the appearance of anything like disinterested good."

We achieved the stoop of Green Park Buildings, and he jumped down to hand me to the street.

"Jane, Jane," he said with a sigh, "I regret your misfortune extremely."

"Not another word, my lord. I would not forfeit the thrill of this chase for a thousand footpads. And there is Lord Kinsfell to be thought of—is he to rot in gaol for the preservation of a man like Smythe? Never!"

Lord Harold surveyed me with a judicious air. "It is as much as I would expect of you, my dear. Having risked your life thus far, may I enquire whether you would accompany me to Bristol on the morrow? I should value your penetration extremely."

"Sunday travel? I should never hear the end of it, among the Austens," I mused with a smile.[3] "But I think I shall attend you, all the same. Tomorrow is my birthday, Lord Harold, and I shall regard the journey as in tribute to my natal day! But you *must* allow me an hour first for the observance of morning service. I might pray to be forgiven my family's poor opinion."

"Capital!" he cried. "Expect my carriage at eleven o'clock. We shall be returned in time for dinner."

---

[3] Those respectful of the Sabbath rarely traveled on Sunday in Austen's time.—*Editor's note.*

Chapter 13

A Confidential Nuncheon

Sunday,
16 December 1804

~

A QUIET SUNDAY SERVICE AT THE QUEEN'S CHAPEL, FOLLOWED BY A short turn in the muddy Crescent—and so the morning of my twenty-ninth birthday passed as many a Sabbath, while resident in Bath.[1] Though quite out of charity with all my beloved family, I was nonetheless treated to some small remembrances of the day—an embroidered needle-case from dear Cassandra, offered with an anxious look; from my father, a handsome set of Maria Edgeworth's *Castle Rackrent,* bound in vellum and tooled in gold; and from my mother, who learned somehow of the slyness of the Bath *Chronicle,* a lecture on the foolishness of impropriety in one so nearly beyond the marriageable age. Did I suffer my reputation to sink, no respectable gentleman would *ever* solicit my hand, and how my dear mother was expected to keep me once Reverend Austen was cold in his grave, she could not begin to think. She then exclaimed at length upon the subject of Lord Harold, and went so far as to solicit my father's authority, and beg that he should abhor the acquaintance—but the

---

[1] The Crescent refers not to the imposing houses of the Royal Crescent on Brock Street, but to the broad green immediately opposite, where all of fashionable Bath was wont to walk on Sunday afternoons.—*Editor's note.*

Reverend George, however uneasy in his own mind, refused to censure my activity so much. I was, he declared, a woman of some maturity, and must exert my own judgement in these and all matters; I should not have my father to look to, in a very few years more; and if the principles with which I had been raised, did not serve as friends in the present case, he could do nothing further with me.

I reminded my mother that our beloved Madam Lefroy had declined the wedded state until her twenty-ninth year, and had yet attained a highly respectable, if modest, condition, in the acceptance of her clergyman—but it would not do.

"For," the good lady darkly pronounced, "Madam Lefroy's excellent fortune is of no account, for there were many more eligible young men a quarter-century ago, before Buonaparte forced the country into regimentals. Cassandra I cannot reproach for tarrying in the single state, though she is several years your senior, for she would have got poor Tom Fowle if she could. But there—it was not to be. Let her misfortune be a lesson, my dear, and do not place your affections among such men as are likely to die of little trifling fevers."[2]

We were joined at breakfast by Henry and Eliza, who took notice of the day by pressing upon me a ravishing headdress of apricot silk and feathers, purchased no doubt in Edgar's Buildings, and quite admirably suited to my fashionable new gown.

Promptly at eleven the housemaid announced Lord Harold; he bid good morning to all the world, won an interesting sparkle from Eliza's fine eyes, presented me with a posy, and voiced the hope that I might be granted many happy returns of the day. This little ceremony of deception being well-received, and the weather continuing to hold fine, his lordship did not scruple to suggest a country drive; and to the astonishment and dismay of all my family, I readily acceded to the whole, and hurried into my warmest pelisse. The Gentleman Rogue assured my father I should be much improved from the healthfulness of the airing, and that I should be returned unharmed before nightfall; and so we drove off, with an agree-

[2] Cassandra Austen was engaged in 1792 to marry the Reverend Thomas Craven Fowle (1765–1797), son of the Austens' lifelong friends and a protégé of Lord Craven, whose naval expedition to the West Indies in 1795 Fowle felt obligated to join. He died of yellow fever in San Domingo in February 1797. He left Cassandra a legacy of one thousand pounds.—*Editor's note.*

able sensation of liberty on my part, and a distinct uneasiness behind.

"I expect to be arrived in Bristol by one o'clock at the latest, barring a mishap to the wheels," Lord Harold observed as we trotted up Charles Street towards Monmouth, and the turning for the Bristol Road. "I shall regale you in the interval with an account of last evening's adventures at the Theatre Royal."

"Miss Conyngham was in evidence?"

"She was, though her brother Hugh was not. Indisposed, according to the program notes—perhaps the result of your too-lively dancing, Jane."

"You do not think, that having failed in his efforts to silence *me*, he has summarily fled the city?"

"His sister assures me that he has not—but in her word I place the barest confidence. Upon quitting the Theatre Royal, however, I undertook to seek his lodgings—and was told that the gentleman was within, but was to see no one, under the strictest injunctions from his doctor. And so I had not the least glimpse of the fellow, and cannot say whether he was there or no."

"That is very bad."

"Less bad, perhaps, than it at first appears. Mr. Conyngham is unlikely to desert his sister. Of Mr. Smythe, however, I cannot say so much."

I drew the collar of my pelisse close about my throat, at the sensation of a sudden chill. "But you have some intelligence of Smythe?"

Lord Harold nodded. "I happened to enquire of an errand-boy in the wings, and for the price of a few pence was told that the constables had rousted the villain from bed in the small hours of yesterday morning. Being warned by his landlady, however, Smythe jumped from a back window, and made off through the alleyways unpursued."

"He jumped from a window, you say? And was it a *first-floor* window?"

"You think of Her Grace's anteroom! The same suspicion has animated us both. I eagerly enquired of the boy, and was told with the greatest pride and satisfaction that his hero Smythe disdained any distance under twenty feet. He is a tumbler by rearing, and was wont as a child to roam about the countryside with a band of performers known for their physical feats."

"But this is excellent news!" I cried. "Did we find the guise of Pierrot discarded in his lodgings, we might free Lord Kinsell to-day."

"I had expected you to feel some trepidation in the knowledge that the man was at liberty. Are you so careless of security, Jane?"

I lifted a gloved hand to shade my eyes from the brilliance of the morning sun. The countryside beyond the city's environs was blighted by the advance of winter—a brownish heap of rolling Somerset hills, dotted at random with the occasional beast; but my spirits would not be oppressed even by fallow fields. "I cannot rejoice in his escape," I admitted, "but must trust to Providence. Mr. Smythe is unlikely to adventure so perilous a town as Bath for some time to come. I will not indulge in excessive anxiety."

"All the same—" Lord Harold began.

"I shall promise you never to venture out-of-doors without the company of another," I said. "Now tell me of Miss Conyngham."

"She refused to see me, of course, and so I was reduced to storming her dressing-room. I thought it wise to inform her that Mr. Elliot was hardly as satisfied with the case against my nephew as had once been believed, and that the magistrate was even now embarked upon the errand of tracing a curious bauble discarded in the cunning passage, that might well prove to be the property of the murderer. I was deliberately vague; but Miss Conyngham was observed to pale, and stagger a little for support—and she agreed at last to the space of a conversation."

"And? Did she confess the whole?"

"Jane, Jane—would you have a woman go blindly to the scaffold? Naturally she did not. She intends to divine first how much I know. That I *suspect* a good deal—that I have perhaps learnt something to her detriment, from my researches or my nephew or both—she is completely aware. But she is confident I have not the conclusive proof; and so she intends to fence with me for as long as she is able.

"We sat down; and I found occasion to comment upon the Earl of Swithin's interesting attentions to my niece—our belief that he intended to renew his offer for Mona's hand—a few reflections on the disappointment of Mr. Portal's death in that quarter—Mona ready to be consoled by the attentions of another—even Colonel Easton much in attendance—and Miss Conyngham's visage was observed to darken. I then made my *adieux,* and left her to consider the intelligence conveyed; and I hope very soon to see my stratagems bear fruit."

"You are an incorrigible beast," I calmly replied, "but as the lady seems deserving of no very great solicitude, I cannot abuse you as thoroughly as I might. Did she betray anxiety? Guilt? The desperation of an abandoned character?"

"None whatsoever. A suggestion of grief, at Portal's passing—but we must believe that to be the grossest falsehood. It is a pity," Lord Harold reflected, "that such a degree of dramatic talent should be employed in so unfortunate a manner."

"You regard her as beyond salvation, then? As being devoid of every proper feeling?"

"I cannot reconcile her conduct in any other way," he replied, with an edge of harshness to his usual tone. "And I confess that it troubles me exceedingly. Real evil is rare enough in this world, my dear Jane—but when found in the form of a beautiful young woman, sobering in the extreme."

WE ACHIEVED BRISTOL IN LESS THAN TWO HOURS OF EASY TRAVEL, and immediately sought one of the city's principal inns—the ancient, half-timbered Llandoger Trow, which sits not far from Bristol's Theatre Royal. Lord Harold reasoned that if the Earl of Swithin had been present in Bristol so early as Monday evening—and moving in concert with Maria Conyngham—then he should have been likely to seek a lodging not far from where the actress played. Before we embarked upon our interrogation of the publican, however, Lord Harold was intent upon bread and cheese, in the quiet of a little parlour, while I should not say nay to a respectable pot of tea.

We pulled up on cobbled King Street and turned into the Llandoger Trow's yard. A stable-boy ran out to seize the horses' heads.

"Morning, guv'nor," the youth affably cried. "Will you be changing horses, or staying the night?"

"Neither," Lord Harold replied. "A bucket of oats, pray, and some water for the team."

"Quick as winking, guv. You just ask for Bob when you're wishful of having them sent round."

"Very good. Tell me, Bob, are there any travellers in the habit of hiring equipages of the publican?"

"Post horses, you mean?"

"I do not. I am wondering whether your master—"

"Mr. Twinkling," Bob quickly supplied.

"—Mr. Twinkling—keeps a carriage or two that he occasionally lets out for the use of travellers. Lodgers at the inn, for example, who might wish a morning's drive; or those whose equipages may have fallen into disrepair."

The boy's face cleared. "There's his old chariot, and the missus's tilbury, what he lets out with Nelly betimes."

"Very good, my lad," Lord Harold said, and tossed him tuppence.

The Llandoger Trow was a noble old pile, its casement windows secured against the draughts and a roaring fire in the massive hearth. I welcomed the tide of warmth, and its concomitant odours of roasting fowl and bubbling stew, and followed a woman I assumed to be Mrs. Twinkling into a private parlour at the broad building's front. A scattering of local townsfolk held place in the public room, their tankards clattering noisily on oaken tables; but here, all was quiet and removed, with a faint scent of beeswax that was not un-pleasing.

"You'll be wanting a nuncheon, I expect," the woman said kindly. "Half frozen you must be, miss, coming all that way and the sun not half so warm as it should be. A toddy, perhaps, or some wine punch?"

"Tea would suit me exceedingly," I replied gratefully. "Are you Mrs. Twinkling?"

"These thirty year or more, miss. You're a stranger to Bristol?"

"Yes." I drew off my bonnet and gloves and set them on a chair. "Though our acquaintance have often praised the city—and the Llandoger Trow in particular—most handsomely. The Earl of Swithin was recently your lodger, I believe?"

"And has been, off and on, a year and more. He's a great one for the theatre, is the Earl."

"Indeed! We are speaking of the same Lord Swithin, I collect—a well-made, fair-haired gentleman with a commanding aspect, and a very fine coach-and-four, with the device of a tiger on its door?"

"Aye, and he weren't half put out when his axle broke and old Twinkling couldn't set it to rights on Monday," she replied with energy. "Fair shouted the eaves of the house down around us, he did, with all his oaths about needing to be on the road as soon as may be."

"Mrs. Twinkling," Lord Harold said with a nod from the doorway. "Your excellent husband thought I should find you here. We should be greatly obliged if you could manage some victuals."

"I've bread and cheese and half a cold ham just waiting in the larder," she said, beaming, and left us with a curtsey.

"That was most unfortunate," I told Lord Harold crossly, "for she was on the point of revealing our Swithin's history. She remembered him in an instant, and said he was most put out by an injury to his equipage."

"Do not trouble yourself, madam." Lord Harold drew a chair to the fire and warmed his hands. "I have had the whole from our host Twinkling himself. It would not do to have us *both* appear interested to a fault. Lord Swithin was present, from late Sunday until early Wednesday morning, when he sped like hell-fire—excuse me, my dear, a thousand pardons for the liberty—to Bath itself."

"And the carriage?"

"A curious mishap, indeed; for the axle was unbroken upon his arrival, and appears to have acquired its injury while lodged in the carriage house itself. Mr. Twinkling suspects a band of local boys, who delight in the destruction of transient property. Though *we* might conjecture a more deliberate cause. The Earl should not have wished to drive his *own* equipage under Her Grace's window for the purpose of receiving a murderer."

"This is most illuminating."

"The necessity of repairs required our Lord Swithin to hire the missus's tilbury, about the conduct of some business on Tuesday."

"—When no doubt he sped like hell-fire to Bath," I finished absently, "about the stabbing of poor Mr. Portal."

"Perhaps. Although Mr. Twinkling believed his direction then to have been Portsmouth."

"Portsmouth! But what could possibly have occasioned so sudden a journey?"

"The Earl received news of a ship Monday—a homebound Indiaman, expected in Portsmouth the following day."[3]

"Good heavens!"

"Whether it was one of Swithin's vessels, miraculously returned, or merely another that brought news of his ships' fate, Twinkling could not tell me. Perhaps he lacked the particulars."

"Or perhaps Swithin never went to Portsmouth at all."

"In any case, the Earl returned to the Llanoger Trow in the wee hours of Wednesday, and departed for Bath later that morning in his repaired equipage."

"If so much is true, it is unlikely that his lordship broke his pressing return from Portsmouth to parade in Laura Place bearded and disguised as Pierrot," I mused.

"Unlikely—but not impossible. As you say, we cannot know whether he travelled to Portsmouth at all."

I sighed with vexation. "I must observe, my lord, that we possess an abundance of miscreants, all clamouring for attention, in this sorry business! There is Miss Conyngham, who probably discarded the tiger in the passage; Mr. Smythe, who is a proficient in tumbling, and might have jumped from the open window; and Lord Swithin, who hired a carriage—possibly intended for Portsmouth, or possibly so that he might halt it in argument beneath the Dowager Duchess's window in Bath."

"But unfortunately we have no proof of the latter," Lord Harold retorted, "and that is the one thing Mr. Wilberforce Elliot will undoubtedly require."

On the heels of this dampening remark, the parlour door swung open, and Mrs. Twinkling appeared with flushed cheeks and a tray of victuals held high. Behind her, to our extreme surprise and no little delight, stood Mr. Elliot himself.

"Lord Harold," he said, with a bow and a creaking of his considerable weight, "and the little Shepherdess."

"Miss Austen," I supplied.

[3] An Indiaman was a merchant ship transporting cargo from the East Indies. They were usually owned by the Honourable East India Company, but in this case, we may read the term to indicate one of the Earl's private vessels.—*Editor's note.*

"Imagine my surprise at finding you come to Bristol to greet me! I should not have looked for such a courtesy for all the world. How d'ye do? How d'ye do? And a fine, bright day for a pleasure drive it is!"

"Indeed," his lordship replied, with a speaking look in Mrs. Twinkling's direction. The magistrate winked, stood aside to allow her passage, and then eased himself into the little parlour.

"Would you require some fortification against the hard miles remaining to Bath?" Lord Harold enquired, with ironic solicitude, "or perhaps a seat in my carriage?"

"Thanking you kindly, my lord, but I've fortified myself already, and your lordship's funds have been so good as to supply a suitable conveyance."

"That is very well—for had you accepted, either Miss Austen or myself should have been obliged to remain behind."

Mr. Elliot laughed. "And isn't that just like a lord! No politeness is too great, even if it comes at a loss. I'm infinitely obliged, my lord—but just you tuck into the victuals while I bend your ear, as the saying goes, and we'll suit each other famously. I find you on the trail of a certain Earl, I expect?"

"As no doubt you are yourself."

Mr. Elliot settled himself on a stout wooden chair, thrust his toes towards the fire, and nodded at me affably. "The cold has brought roses to your cheeks, ma'am, and a picture you do look. I must suppose you are in his lordship's confidence?"

"You must," Lord Harold replied. "There is no one whose penetration I value more than Miss Austen's."

"And when am I to wish you joy, my lord?" Mr. Elliot enquired with an innocent air.

I coloured despite myself.

"When you have freed my nephew from his unfortunate predicament," Lord Harold concluded smoothly. He took up a spoon and attacked an admirable Stilton. "Tell us how you fared in London, Elliot. We are all agog for the news."

"I began my enquiries in Laura Place, as you were so good to suggest. When presented with the interesting tiger pin, the Earl of Swithin frowned—looked amazed—and unfortunately recovered his composure. He assured me he had never seen the thing before, and could only imagine that some sprig of fashion had adopted his device, from a misplaced desire to ape his lordship's style.''

''—Maria Conyngham, I suspect,'' Lord Harold offered complacently.

''Indeed?'' Mr. Elliot's black eyes widened. ''I perceive you are before me in this, my lord, as in so many things. But to proceed—I next travelled into London and adventured St. James. The cunning insertion into Fortescue House, of a designing male—in short, a constable by the name of Warren I carried in my train—through excessive flattery of the under-housemaid, elicited the information that his lordship has been absent from London some weeks. Since Saturday a fortnight since, to be exact. Early Wednesday last the Earl sent for the Lady Fortescues from Bristol, without so much as a by-your-leave, and bid them all to travel down to Bath without delay; and quite indignant the under-housemaid was, too, at the disarray this occasioned in the household. All on account of the master's ill-consideration, and his sisters in quite a taking. And so, perceiving as how I should never find my murderer in Town, I left Warren in possession of the cunning pin, and charged him with enquiring as to its origins among the principal London jewellers; and myself ambled along to Bristol. I have been enquiring of the inns these two hours at least.''

''Then you know, I assume, what we have recently learned.''

''That the Earl had occasion to hire an open carriage? Aye—though it took me a deal of trouble to get it out of old Twinkling,'' Mr. Elliot complained. ''Not to mention the publicans of the Hart and Dove, the Merry Milkmaid, and the Rose and Crown. There's a deal of inns in Bristol, my lord, and only one of them had the lodging of the Earl. I'll warrant any publican worth his ale can spy the Law from a mile off, and turn mute and deaf in an instant, though he'd shift to be of service to yourselves.''

''You know, then, that he is supposed to have gone to Portsmouth Tuesday.''

''And that I shall next be coaching that way myself,'' Mr. Elliot rejoined with resignation. ''It seems the Earl refused a driver, being intent upon handling the ribbons himself. I see how your thoughts are forming in *that* quarter. You think to find his lordship never went to Portsmouth at all. But tell me, my lord, your reasons for suspecting Miss Conyngham.''

Lord Harold was engrossed in consuming a very fine portion of ham, and seemed entirely given over to enjoyment; but after an instant, he reached into his coat and pulled out a sheaf of papers. "I believe you will find a few of your answers here, Mr. Elliot."

The magistrate seized them immediately. "Letters, my lord?"

"Taken inadvertently from Mr. Portal's theatre office. I might suggest, in future, that you search a fellow's place of business as well as his lodgings, my good sir."

Elliot perused the papers swiftly, his brow furrowed in an effort to make out the hand, and then raised his eyes to Lord Harold.

"Well, I'm blessed," he said succinctly. "The girl and Swithin hand-in-glove. I shall take them up immediately upon returning to Bath."

"Stay, Mr. Elliot," Lord Harold enjoined swiftly, and to me, "Pray pour out the tea, Miss Austen, and I should be very much obliged."

I did so, and offered a cup to the magistrate; but he declined it with an air of impatience. "And why should I leave these malefactors at liberty?" he demanded.

"In deference to a most interesting matter that is as yet in abeyance," Lord Harold replied. "I must confess a grievous sin, Mr. Elliot, on the part of my nephew Kinsfell. You will remember, I am sure, that he discovered the unfortunate Mr. Portal."

"Yes, yes—"

"But you are not aware, I think, that he discovered something else on Mr. Portal's person. A most intriguing miniature pendant, showing the likeness of an eye, and probably set upon Portal's breast by the same hand that drove home the knife."

Mr. Elliot turned to me in confusion. I smiled at him benignly.

"My nephew, from dubious motives, secured the portrait of the eye about his neck. He gave it into my keeping the following day."

"The Marquis made away with evidence?" Mr. Elliot exclaimed. "Why, the cunning rogue! I'll have his head for it." The uttering of this natural sentiment must immediately have struck him as being in poor taste, and he averted his glittering black eyes from Lord Harold's face.

"I applaud your feelings," his lordship observed. "They are commendable, if somewhat ill-phrased. But however reprehensible the act, my nephew feared it could not be undone; and I think it just possible that he acted from the noblest of motives—the desire to shield his sister. She is possessed of grey eyes; and the portrait revealed a similar orb. Poor Kinsell feared for her implication in Portal's death, and attempted to prevent it.''

I doubted the extent of this statement's truth, and thought it more likely Lord Kinsell had hoped to shield Maria Conyngham, whose name Portal had spoken as he breathed his last; but I knew that Miss Conyngham's eye was brown, and so forbore from disputing with one of his lordship's experience and perspicacity.

''I undertook to consult an artist of Miss Austen's acquaintance, an acknowledged expert in these things; and he, in turn, has applied for information to a quarter that might hopefully yield it. The token was left deliberately as a sign, and I cannot think Mr. Portal's murder unconnected to the identity of the portrait's subject. It is that subject's name we seek, Mr. Elliot, and until we possess it we cannot hope to comprehend the depths of this affair. The letters you now hold, and the fact of the Earl's presence in Bristol, are the merest fraction of your case.''

''That can be of little account,'' Mr. Elliot retorted. ''Far better to seize the pair and learn the whole from them at the Assizes.''

''But having acted precipitately *once*,'' his lordship countered, ''and taken up an innocent man, you should hesitate to do so a second time. It cannot inspire confidence on the part of the public, or ease in the breasts of your benefactors.''[4]

There was a feeling silence. Mr. Elliot availed himself of the Stilton, and chewed it ruminatively. At last he said, ''And when do you expect the portrait's subject to be exposed?''

''I am daily in expectation of intelligence. Having received it, I should not hesitate to impart it to yourself.''

''You must understand how irregular the business is,'' Mr. Elliot said. ''That portrait should have been turned over to me. As should these letters. You have been grossly behindhand, my lord, in your dealings with the Law.''

''I regret and acknowledge the whole. But you might admit, my good sir,'' Lord Harold observed with a smile, ''that you gave me little reason to confide in your sense and benevolence. You seemed most easy at the prospect of hanging my nephew, and but for the word of a chairman or two, should still be deaf to reason. I cannot be dissatisfied with my conduct of the affair, and must trust the healing effect of time to do away with your injury.''

Mr. Elliot sighed. "I suppose I must lose not a moment on the Portsmouth road, then.''

"It would seem the logical course," Lord Harold said comfortably. "Stilton, Jane?''

Chapter 14

An Unexpected Blow

Monday,
17 December 1804
~

M**Y HEART IS HEAVY, INDEED, AS** I **TAKE UP MY FAITHFUL PEN, THE BETTER** to comprehend the intelligence received so suddenly this morning—an intelligence at which my whole mind revolts. *Madam Lefroy is dead.*

She was suffered to depart this life on the very anniversary of my birth. And I was not at hand to comfort her, or to take a final leave.

We learned the news of my brother James, by express—in all the clatter of a horse's hoofs too hastily reined-in before the door of Green Park Buildings, and the apprehension of ill-tidings devoutly wished upon others. But it could not be put off; the letter was for ourselves; and the express desired to wait for an answer. Some injury to James we feared, or to Mary and the children, our remembrance of sudden death in that household being as yet too present.[1]

But it was of Ashe he wrote to us—and of my own dear Anne.

James had met with her on the Saturday, in the neighbouring village of Overton, intent upon her shopping with a servant in tow.

---

[1] James Austen's first wife, Anne Mathew, whom he married in 1792, died suddenly in 1795—after which he married Mary Lloyd, the sister of Jane's lifelong friend Martha. Martha would later become Frank Austen's second wife.—*Editor's note.*

Madam remarked in passing that her horse was so stupid and lazy, she could barely make him stir; and so they had parted, with kind wishes on both sides. With what horror, then, did brother James learn later that the horse in question had bolted at the top of Overton Hill! The servant missing his grip upon the bridle, Anne Lefroy careened away in utter chaos; and perhaps from fear, or from an unsteadiness in riding side-saddle, she fell to the ground with bruising force. A concussion was sustained; she remained insensible throughout Saturday evening, and slipped quietly away at three o'clock Sunday morning.[2]

Why did not the presentiment of her passing strike me hard in that dreadful hour? Why were the clocks not suffered to stop, and the rain to cease to fall, and the world entire fall hideously rapt, in acknowledgement of its loss? *Such goodness and worth as yours, I shall not meet with again.*

I have laboured and laboured to comprehend—to *reconcile* with her death; but still I cannot. Far beyond the usual repugnance and denial with which the human heart must meet such events, there is the outrage of my reason. For Anne Lefroy was an accomplished horsewoman—from the tenderest years she had mastered her mounts. It was a point of pride that she sat so neatly, and jumped so well, and feared neither hedgerow nor fence paling. She is the very last woman I should expect to be completely run away with; and my heart *will* whisper that all is not as it seems. For a horse may be frighted any number of ways, by malice or intent.

Is it too absurd? It *must,* it cannot be other, than the fevered conjectures of my brain, quite overpowered by the sudden loss. And so I will put down my pen, and make an end to activity, in the hope that silence may be as balm, and isolation relieve despair.

---

[2] This description of Anne Lefroy's death accords quite closely with that contained in the family memoir *Jane Austen: A Family Record* (by William Austen-Leigh and Richard Arthur Austen-Leigh, revised by Deirdre LeFaye, London: The British Library, 1989).—*Editor's note.*

Tuesday,
18 December 1804

~

A SLEEPLESS NIGHT, AND A TEDIOUS MORNING HAVE FAILED TO BRING relief; and tho' I thrust myself out-of-doors to trudge the Gravel Walk with Cassandra as silent companion, in brooding contemplation of mortality, no comfort could I find in exercise. I engaged in the melancholy review of my entire history with Madam Lefroy—the pleasant hours of companionship, in reading silently together in the library at Ashe; her delight in forming a sort of schoolroom, for the improvement of the poorer children in the parish, that they might with time learn their sums and letters; her ecstasy in conversation, and news of the world.

One episode only in our mutual acquaintance has still the power to cause me pain—and that is the part that Madam played in my ruined hopes of her nephew. Though at twenty Tom Lefroy was full young to fall in love, having neither profession nor fortune to recommend him, at nearly twenty-nine he now possesses both, and a wife into the bargain. Had Madam not interfered where interference was not wanted, I might have been happy these nine years at least; and I have never been disposed to consider her actions as anything but officious. Prudence, in matters of love, is all very well where character is lacking; but when two young people of sense and ability are *truly* attached, I cannot think it wise to speak only of fortune in the disposition of their hopes.

But Tom was sent away, and I was left to the derision of the neighbourhood, for having shewn too clearly my preference for his regard, and for having encouraged it on so little means as the twenty pounds per annum I may consider my own.

I have wondered, often, what the present Mrs. Tom Lefroy is like—how she looks, and behaves, and cares for her husband. But it does not do to dwell upon such things. There cannot have been too much affection on Tom Lefroy's side, or he should not have forgot me so soon—for he married Miss Mary Paul barely three years after he might have married *me*. That is ever the difference of sex, however—men have their professions and pursuits, to divert their

minds from sorrows of the heart; but *we* sit at home, quiet and confined, and our feelings prey upon us.[3]

My appetite is quite gone, and I find the enforced society of the
household insupportable. I do not pretend to suffer these emotions
alone—Anne Lefroy was as dear as family to all the Austens—but I
may claim a particular intimacy with the lady, a commonality of
spirit, that makes her loss decidedly cruel. I suspect my father to
suffer from a similar sensibility. His turn of humour, and his love of
wit, found always a ready ear in Madam Lefroy; and so he is grown
too silent, and looks the burden of his age. Does his indifferent
health permit, my father has very nearly determined to journey into
Hampshire for the funeral, which James is to perform this Friday;
but such activity being beyond the female members of the household, little of a cheerful nature may be derived from the event.[4]

We returned from our walk, and Cassandra retired to her room
for a period of silent reflection. I commenced to pace before the
sitting-room fire like a caged beast, but at length my mother's exclamations, and my father's look of distress, urged me to adopt a chair,
and open once more my journal for the recording of these thoughts.

THE CLOCK HAD STRUCK TWO, AND CASSANDRA HAD EMERGED FROM HER
solitary melancholy, when my mother bethought herself of her
brother, Mr. Leigh-Perrot, and his formidable wife. The Leigh-
Perrots have been acquainted with Madam Lefroy these twenty years
at least, and should certainly wish the earliest intelligence of her
untimely end; my mother was horrified at the notion of their learning it from anyone but herself; and between reproaches at having
formed no thought of them, in the earliest hours of her misery, and
the acutest anxiety to be with them directly, she would not be satis-

³ Jane ascribes similar feelings, in virtually the same language, to Anne Elliot of
Persuasion—a woman who, at twenty-seven, regrets the advice of her older friend,
Lady Russell, who discouraged her attachment eight years previously to a young
sailor without prospects. Jane allowed Anne Elliot to be eventually reunited with
Captain Frederick Wentworth.—*Editor's note.*

⁴ Women rarely attended funerals in Austen's day, it being considered the province of a family's male members to follow the body to both chapel and cemetery.
The best a bereaved woman might do was to read Divine Service in the privacy
of her home.—*Editor's note.*

fied until we were bundled out-of-doors, and intent upon the Perrots' lodgings in Paragon Buildings.

The brilliance of the sun stunned my eyes, while my ears were battered by the shouts of chairmen and the clatter of horses' hoofs, as yet greater parties of gay young men and ladies rolled into town for the celebration of Christmastide. I was as open as a fresh wound to this assault upon my senses—the wound being in my heart, and of Anne Lefroy's making. I could not free my thoughts of her; like an angel or a ghost, she shimmered just beyond the range of sight.

"How mad they all are for enjoyment, I declare," my mother cried, as two open carriages dashed by, each driven by a handsome young gentleman, and sporting ladies of perhaps sixteen, their bright faces huddled in fur tippets. "They shall be overturned in an instant, I daresay, and there shall be an end to romance."

I drew my mother's gloved hand within my arm. "Do not distress yourself, madam. Romance at that age is akin to health—it thrives on every stroke of abuse. An overturning can do no less than advance the engagement of the respective parties, where it should quite drive off affection in ladies of more mature sentiment."

"I wonder you can be so cheerful, Jane," Cassandra remarked. "It quite pains *me* to laugh."

My sister had yet to forgive or approve me, it seemed; and the knowledge of my disgrace pressed hard upon my spirits. Cassandra has ever been my dearest confidante, my most beloved companion, a second self; and her disapprobation was not to be dismissed, however much I might attempt it.

And so we walked on in silence.

My Aunt and Uncle Leigh-Perrot have maintained for some time a creditable establishment at No. 1 Paragon Buildings, in which they reside fully half the year, being childless and given over to the fancies of old-age and ill-health. No benefit can they derive from their imbibing of the waters, if one is to judge from the weight of complaints with which they daily unburden themselves; Bath is as useless to them in this quarter, as the moon; but in Bath they must remain for the duration of the winter, or suffer the most dreadful of reverses. Even my unfortunate aunt's being taken up for theft, and imprisoned some seven months before her trial and acquittal, has not dispelled the charms of the Leigh-Perrots' adopted city; and their society is one of the more tedious burdens of our residence here these three years and more.[5] For though possessed of considerable means, a small household, and no very great inclination to dress herself finely or entertain upon a lavish scale—my aunt is convinced she is on the point of penury, and makes a great to-do about every trifling expense. This parsimony in her nature, when taken with her cultivation of ill-health, makes her a difficult companion in the easiest of times.

"Well, girls!" my aunt cried, upon perceiving us at the door, "and so you have put on black gloves for Madam Lefroy! Aye, I heard it all from John Butcher, who is to marry the daughter of your Cook; and I wonder that you did not trouble to visit us before! It is very bad, to have the news of a person of that kind; they are all for puffing themselves up with importance, in a most unbecoming and insolent fashion! That veil is very fine, Cassandra—but I am sure you gave too much for it. You always do."

My aunt was established today on the sitting-room sofa, a lap rug tucked well about her, quite splendid in dressing-gown and cap. Jane Leigh-Perrot is possessed of the most manly features I have ever observed in a woman—a square chin, long nose, and frankly assessing eyes. Her countenance *must* convey an impression of vigour and health entirely at variance with her languorous airs; and I shall probably be guilty of abusing her on her deathbed, so little confidence do I place in her claims to ill-health.

"Good morning, Aunt," Cassandra advanced to offer her cheek.

"You look very well."

"I do not *feel* myself to be so, I assure you. Such palpitations of the heart! Such faintings and flutterings in my head and my bowels! Do you fetch my vinaigrette, Cassandra, and then tell me all the news."

[5] In August 1799, Jane Leigh-Perrot was accused by a shopkeeper in Bath Street of stealing a card of white lace, which was found wrapped with some black lace she had purchased in the establishment. She denied the theft—and was probably framed by the shopkeeper, who knew that the monetary value of the stolen lace—in excess of twelve pence—made the theft a capital crime, punishable by death or transportation to Australia. Blackmail was probably the object, and when the Leigh-Perrots refused to pay for silence, they were imprisoned together at Ilchester gaol for seven months before Mrs. Leigh-Perrot's trial and acquittal. Austen scholar Park Honan points out, however, that Mrs. Leigh-Perrot's defense attorney thought she was a kleptomaniac who got off.—*Editor's note*.

"Indeed we have none, Aunt—being quite sunk in mourning, and little disposed to society," I interposed.

The good lady snorted, and subjected my figure to the very coldest appraisal. "Do not be affecting modesty in *my* eyes, Miss Jane! I have heard it all from your mother these two days at least! I know that you are quite abandoned to pleasure and dissipation, and go about with a most disreputable set! No amount of black ribbon can deceive *me*!"

"That is very well, Aunt, for deception is hardly my inclination."

She snorted again, like a well-exercised horse, and rounded upon my mother. The poor lady had perched anxiously on the edge of a chair, in an effort to avoid my gaze. "Is she buried, then, Mrs. Austen?"

"The service is to be on Friday," my mother supplied, "and James is to have the performing of it."

"That is very singular—for she died in the early hours of Sunday, did she not? I fear the decomposition of the corpse will be highly advanced. There will be a stench. Most distressing to the unfortunate relicts."

We were saved the necessity of an answer by the appearance of my uncle, a spare, lithe, twinkling personage with a high forehead and ruddy complexion. He was today all smiles and affability. "Ah, there you are, sister!" he exclaimed, and advanced upon us with that mingled expression of pain and forbearance that generally marks the gout sufferer. "This is happily met, indeed! For I was just upon the point of seeking you in Seymour Street, and you have saved me the job of it! What do you think? I have taken a subscription to the concert tomorrow evening, and there are places for us all—if you will do me the honour of accepting!"

"It should be quite beyond our power, brother," my mother replied with an anxious look, "for you see we are in mourning, on account of Madam Lefroy."

"Well—and what is the point of mourning, hey, if not to be observed by all the world? We do not go about in black merely to sit at home quietly by the fire, and admire one another! I doubt Cassandra would wish to keep so fine a veil from the sight of the wondering public."

At this brilliant sally, he doubled over with laughter, and poked my sister in the ribs. Cassandra looked discomfited, and shifted uneasily in her chair. "Indeed, Uncle, I have no desire to parade my distress before anyone, I assure you."

"And Jane has never very much enjoyment in a concert," my aunt observed with conscious malice.

"No, indeed—she has the most wretched ear imaginable when it comes to Rauzzini and Mrs. Billington," my mother agreed. "The music should *quite* be wasted upon Jane."

"So I fear you must give up your tickets, Perrot," my aunt pronounced with decision. "They are not wanted at all; and do you be certain to retrieve your money from the ticket-sellers—they are all for what they can get, and will be pressing in their claim that you must exchange one concert for another! We shall stay at home tomorrow, and invite the Austens to make an additional table at whist. There is no harm in cards, surely, when one is in mourning?"

My unfortunate uncle looked crestfallen. "But this is too bad!" he cried. "I was as fond of Madam Lefroy as anyone, to be sure—but I do not think she would wish for us to endure the season with long faces. What is Christmas, without music or amusement? I had thought perhaps we might return here after the concert, Jane, for a game of charades. We cannot observe the holiday, without we have charades!"

"My Uncle Leigh-Perrot is a rare hand at the composition of these gentle conundrums, they having formed the chief part of the Leigh family's revels in his childhood; and he takes such obvious delight in the confusion of all his relations, that we none of us are at pains to guess his riddles too soon.[6] In nine-and-twenty years of observing Christmas, I have survived only a few without charades; I learned the art of their construction at my mother's knee, and all the Austens may profess a certain ingenuity in their devising. In considering of

[6] Charades formed a part of Christmas revels in England throughout the eighteenth, nineteenth, and early twentieth centuries. They took two forms—the recitation of a riddle, the first part of which defined the first syllable of a word, and the second its ending; or the presentation of a short play, designed to illustrate each syllable and the word as a whole. Several charades thought to be composed by James Leigh-Perrot and Jane Austen can be found in *Jane Austen: Collected Poems and Verse of the Austen Family* (David Selwyn, ed., U.K.: Carcanet Press Ltd., 1996). Mr. Leigh-Perrot's are sweet but obvious, while Jane's are brief and fiendishly clever.—*Editor's note.*

my uncle's disappointment, and my own dread of martyrdom to my aunt's affection for cards, I at last determined to speak.

"If I might venture an opinion, Uncle—"

"By all means, Jane."

"I must believe that a soul oppressed by misery and grief should far sooner find consolation in the strains of the violincello, or the airs of an Italian love song, than in betting and trumps. I shall be happy to accompany you, sir, should you wish to pursue the concert scheme; and stand ready to brave your most inveterate wit, upon our return."

"Capital! Capital! And perhaps we shall persuade your brother Henry and his little wife to make another couple!" He beamed all around, and reached for his fine black hat. "I shall invite them my-self—for I am bent upon the Pump Room this very moment, Jane, in pursuit of my glass of water, you know—and am sure to meet them there! There is nothing like Mrs. Henry for the Pump Room of a morning!"

But his energy was not required; the door was hurriedly opened, and the housemaid announced the Henry Austens, in a breathless accent that suggested they were hard upon her heels. And indeed, it required only an instant for Eliza to enter, beaming, in a ravishing blue silk gown and fur tippet, with Henry hurrying behind.

"My dear Mrs. Perrot!" she exclaimed, "and Uncle James! How delighted I am to see you all! But surely you are not on the point of leaving, Uncle—for we have had the saddest struggle in the world in adventuring the streets, and it would be too bad of you to run away now that we are come."

"It is the Christmas holiday," my aunt opined sagely. "Bath is ever a hurly-burly at such a time; and in a week it will be worse—what with mummers, and Waits, and singing bands, and children begging coins for the slightest service.[7] Good-for-nothings, all of them, intent on profiting by a sacred observance!"

"It was not the crowd, Aunt, but the chairmen! Only fancy! Our chairs were very nearly overturned! I was reminded of poor Mr. Law-rence, Jane, and thought of you extremely."

---

[7] The Waits were a group of carolers often paid by the mayor of a town to sing at public functions or holidays. Over time, the term evolved to mean any group of Christmas carolers who performed for tips.—*Editor's note.*

"Mr. Lawrence?" I said with a frown.

"Why, yes! Did you not hear of his misfortune? It was all about the Pump Room yesterday—though I had the news myself of Isabella Wolff, while attending service at the Laura Chapel."

"What news?"

"Mr. Lawrence was waylaid Saturday evening, upon his return to the Bear from the Theatre Royal, and not a stone's throw from our own lodgings. A band of ruffians set upon him, and very nearly exacted his life! The poor man was most shockingly beat about the head, and was several hours insensible, until the ministrations of Dr. Gibbs succeeded in reviving him."

"I am astonished!" I cried, my colour rising. I was devoutly happy, at that moment, that my father had elected to remain at home in Green Park Buildings, for his sensibility should have betrayed the truth of my own misadventure. "And did not the chairmen come to his aid?"

"They were all run off; and I believe the Mayor of Bath is to make a representation to the principals among them, protesting Mr. Lawrence's shocking treatment, for he *is* a figure of some note, and his misfortune cannot show the town to advantage."

"Assuredly not. Mr. Lawrence is recovered, I hope?"

"He is; but keeps to his rooms, and sees no one but my dear Isabella. She was much distressed, and attempted the Laura Chapel a-purpose to beseech Divine Providence for intercession."

"I wonder she did not find in his misfortune a visitation of Divine Judgement," Cassandra mused, "upon her reprehensible behaviour in encouraging the gentleman's attentions. She might more profitably have sought to mend her erring ways, and returned to London and her husband."

"Oh, pshaw!" Eliza cried. "You are become a sad stick, indeed, Cassandra, since your unfortunate overturning in Lyme!"

My brother Henry had been speaking in a low voice all the while to my mother; and at this, he made his way to my side, and folded me to his bosom. "My dearest Jane," he said, with a speaking glance, "I am made most unhappy by this dreadful news from Ashe."

"What is it, Henry?" his wife broke in. "Of what are you speaking?"

"Did you but observe my sisters, Eliza, even so headlong a wit as *yours* must endeavour to form a notion."

She gazed, her happiness fled; comprehended the sombre nature of our gowns, and the dusky colour of our ribbons and gloves; and entreated us for explanation.

"Our own dear Madam Lefroy," I said with difficulty. "She was injured in a fall from a horse on Saturday, and died but a few hours later."

"Oh, Jane! How desperate for yourself—and indeed, for all our dear family," Eliza cried, and sat down abruptly upon a footstool. "I had not an idea of it! But how melancholy for the unfortunate Lefroys! The youngest cannot be sixteen!"

"Thirteen," Cassandra supplied, and turned to my mother, who had commenced a quiet weeping.

"When I consider, that we spoke our last to her only a week ago, in Laura Place—with never a notion that we should see her no more!" Eliza pressed her little hands to her head. "La, this is a miserable business. And you should feel it most acutely, Jane, who were as another daughter to her. She will be very much missed."

"And so she is already."

"Even *I,* who knew her only slightly, can remember her with nothing but affection. Do you know," Eliza said with a small laugh through her tears, "that I credit Madam Lefroy with encouraging dear Henry to press his suit? Yes! It was she! For you know your mother should never have looked kindly on him marrying his cousin, and one full ten years his senior, at that. But Madam Lefroy had known us together in our youth—when we played at *The Wonder, or A Woman Keeps a Secret,* at Steventon one Christmas. Your brother James wrote an epilogue for it. Do you remember, Jane?"

"Vaguely—but I was very young."

"Not above eight or so, I should think. I was only just returned from France. Yes. It was the year '87, little Hastings was yet a babe in arms, and my husband established on his estates with his mistress— and I felt, as I gazed upon poor Henry, that I had never seen a boy so callow and yet so filled with every noble emotion. It was ten years, of course, and the Comte de Feuillide a victim of the guillotine, before I felt myself free to marry again; but I learned to my joy that it was Madam Lefroy brought dear Henry to the point."

"Madam believed in marriages of attachment a great deal more than marriages of prudence." —Though prudence had taken the upper hand in the case of her nephew.

"It is strange, is it not," Eliza mused, "that she should lose her life so hard upon the heels of the Duchess's rout? We must declare the evening ill-fortune'd in every particular, for it has certainly occasioned a tide of melancholy and loss."

"Madam's death can have little to do with the masquerade, my dear," I replied, with far more assurance than in fact I felt. "But I will admit the coincidence of events may bear so unhappy a construction."

"And now Mr. Lawrence is set upon at the doors of his inn," she reflected. "I cannot like the present aspect of Bath; it is but too reminiscent of my last days in Paris! I shall not trust myself to the streets, and must exert my energies to a swift removal."

I smiled and sat down beside her. "Eliza, Eliza—I cannot think an overturned chair, or a lady's fall from a horse in Hampshire, can recall anything of the revolt in France. Endeavour to compose yourself, my dear, and attend to my Uncle Perrot. He has a scheme devised solely for your pleasure."

She turned immediately to that affable gentleman; heard his proposal for the concert; and had only to learn that I intended to make another of the party, to accept in the most delightful accent possible—and so Eliza's mourning passed, as all her extremes of spirit must—with the force and transience of a summer shower.

WE MADE OUR MELANCHOLY WAY ONCE MORE TO GREEN PARK Buildings, and found my father had quite deserted us. My mother confessed herself somewhat exhausted by the emotions of the day, and the rigours of her sister Perrot's conversation, and sought her rooms in the hope of rest. Cassandra set about the instruction of Cook, in the matter of mince pies; and I returned in solitude to the little sitting-room. But I had not even attempted the composition of these few lines, when a knock on the door announced a visitor; and I very soon was presented with Mary the housemaid, a most anxious look upon her countenance.

"If you please, ma'am, there's a gentleman as wishes to see you," she said.

I studied her with irritation. "I am not inclined to visitors today."

Poor Mary's visage clouded. "I know that, ma'am. And so I told him. But he would have it as I should bring you his card, and so I have done." She crossed, and held out the offending object; and with a sudden exclamation I set down my pen.

"Lord Harold! Why did not you say so at once, unfortunate girl!"

I rose, and smoothed my hair; Lord Harold strode into the room, and tossed his hat carelessly upon a table. "Miss Austen." He bowed over my hand, but his eyes remained fixed on my own. "I fear I should better have stayed away. You are even now in mourning. My very deepest sympathies."

I nodded, too overcome for speech. Solicitude in the Gentleman Rogue is so seldom a mover, as to make its recipient almost uneasy.

"Your housemaid informed me of the loss. She had little inclination to allow my passage, but I confess I overruled her." He straightened, and studied my countenance. I knew it to be decidedly ugly with the effects of weeping. "I shall not presume upon your privacy long. You have other concerns that must render the affair in Laura Place of very little consequence."

"Nay—I beg of you, do not disturb yourself on my account," I rejoined with haste. "Pray tell me what has occasioned your journey into Seymour Street this morning."

I seated myself once more at my little table, but Lord Harold took a turn about the room, his hands in his trouser pockets. My brothers being prone as yet to the wearing of knee breeches, I had rarely seen a man who sported the newer fashion—and never one whose tailor had managed it so entirely to perfection. He came to a halt before a porcelain box reposing upon the mantel, and subjected it to the regard of his quizzing-glass.

"Tell me a little of your friend."

"Madam Lefroy? She was everything that was excellent in a woman. For this, you need seek no further than Her Grace's good opinion—for the Dowager was quite intimate with Anne Lefroy, I believe, and desired her presence at last Tuesday's rout."

"So much I had understood. I had rather you told me how she came to die." The quizzing-glass swung round, and was briefly fixed upon myself. I shuddered at the distorted grey eye its lens revealed, feeling touched once more by the shadow of nightmare; and then Lord Harold secured the glass within his coat.

"I hardly know how to consider the matter myself," I slowly said. "Madam Lefroy was thrown from a runaway horse—a mount she considered so lazy, as to make bolting the very last of her concerns.

And her skill as a horsewoman was celebrated throughout the country."

Lord Harold took up his customary position by the fire, one booted foot raised upon the fender. "You find in her end a disturbing tendency."

As always, he moved directly to the heart of matters.

"I do. Though it may be only the misapprehension of grief—a denial of the ways of Providence."

He smiled grimly and retrieved a small packet from within his coat. "I would have you peruse the contents of a letter I received this morning from France, my dear Jane—and only then judge of the ways of Providence."

I straightened in my chair. "A letter—from Mrs. Cosway? Regarding the malevolent eye?"

"Indeed. It was in the hope of soliciting your opinion that I determined to call at Green Park Buildings this morning. For I begin to wonder if we have not approached this affair from the wrong direction entirely."

He handed me the letter—a single sheet close-written in a feminine hand. I read hurriedly through the initial paragraphs, feeling acutely for Mr. Cosway, and the exposure of his most intimate affairs; but was very soon rewarded with an end to all suspense.

14 December, Lyons

My dear Richard—

I received your letter by express only this morning, and found in it yet further proof of your continuing regard for myself, despite our differences and the sad losses we have sustained. I have bade the messenger to wait, for I comprehend you require the most precipitate of replies, and every moment must be precious; but I congratulate myself that you shall have this letter in a very few days.

Your words were as water in a desert—and I thank you for their most cherished sentiments. I continue to make progress in my establishment for the education of young ladies; Father Benedict has been most helpful and kind, and I expect to have no less than twenty pupils when at last I open my doors. It is quite impossible, as you see, to contemplate a return to England at present, though your assurances of assistance in the event are always welcome.

Your enquiry regarding the miniature whose likeness you enclosed—a most excellent line drawing, my dear Richard, and quite of a piece with your accustomed skill—is readily answered. I do not need to send to Paris, or solicit the opinion of my acquaintance among the artists of this country, for I am cognisant of the pendant's origins myself, and should have recognised the painter's hand in an instant. Though done in the French style, I believe the portrait to have been painted by Mr. Thomas Lawrence, with whose technique I am quite intimate. You will recall, no doubt, that my brush was united with his a few years past in the execution of the portrait of Princess Caroline and her daughter, Charlotte.[8] Mr. Lawrence only rarely paints in miniature—the grandeur of his passions requires a broader canvas—but he does so on occasion at the behest of friends. If you require the name of the subject, you would do well to ask Lawrence himself; for of the sitter I know nothing.

Adieu, my dearest friend—do not prolong your silence, I beg—but send me the slightest intelligence of yourself and my beloved England.

Your Maria

"Another Maria," I murmured. "That name is destined to haunt our very sleep. And have you gone to Mr. Lawrence, my lord?"

"I have—and learned that he will not admit visitors, being shut up in his rooms after the most bruising attack upon his chair Saturday evening. It is singular, is it not," Lord Harold added, "how roughly our friends are treated?"

"Singular and disturbing in the extreme." I frowned in consideration. "I wonder if Mr. Lawrence knows to whom he owes his present misfortunes?"

"We must enquire of him ourselves. Will you consent to accompany me to the Bear tomorrow morning, Jane, for the interrogation of the man?"

I hesitated. "Nothing would pique my interest more, Lord Harold, but I am engaged to attend the concert in the Upper Rooms, and would not wish to be delayed for dinner."

"Then we shall undertake to pay the call at one o'clock, and

[8] Maria Cosway and Thomas Lawrence collaborated on the 1801 portrait of the Princess of Wales and her daughter, with Mrs. Cosway completing much of the portrait's ground, and Lawrence working on the principals' faces.—*Editor's note.*

remain not above an hour. But now tell me, my dear—was Mr. Law-rence at all acquainted with your friend Madam Lefroy?''

I started at his words, and felt my heart to commence a painful beating. ''A little, I must assume. For Madam Lefroy was much in conversation with a Red Harlequin at Her Grace's rout, and Lady Desdemona assures me it was thus Mr. Lawrence was disguised. Even Mr. Conyngham remarked their intimacy, for he spoke of it when we danced together in the Lower Rooms—'' I faltered as the implica-tion of this thought fell hard upon me. ''What would you intimate, my lord—that Madam was *murdered* for her acquaintance with Mr. Lawrence?''

''—Or was Lawrence attacked because of his acquaintance with Madam Lefroy?'' his lordship countered.

At this, my senses were thrown entirely into turmoil. From dismay and incredulity, I swiftly moved to conviction—and returned to doubt again. ''Impossible!'' I cried. ''It must be impossible! Dearest, most excellent, Anne Lefroy! That your life should be snuffed out like the merest taper—and for what? Where is the sense to be found in such evil?''

''Pray compose yourself, my dear Jane,'' Lord Harold advised me gently, ''and endeavour to think. Though I am no friend to magis-trates in general, and must consider even Mr. Elliot's conventions tiresome in the extreme, it is well to search for *proofs* before one contemplates the charge of murder—particularly when one is en-tirely without a culprit. Let us set about the ordering of our minds. What became of Madam's mount? The beast that threw her?''

''My brother assures us that it was destroyed.''

''A pity. But only to be expected. We might have learned much from its harness—whether the saddle, for example, was meddled with. But at this remove from events, all such discovery is unlikely.'' He commenced to pace again, the picture of brooding. ''Unless . . . your brother might serve our purpose.''

''James?''

''He is resident in Hampshire, I presume?''

''Yes—and will have the performing of Madam's funeral service in a few days' time.''

''A clergyman!'' Lord Harold's countenance lightened. ''But that is capital! He might well learn something to our advantage. I suggest you write to him with the desire for further particulars of your dear friend's tragic end. Say that you cannot rest until you are apprised of every detail of Madam Lefroy's death. This is often the way with ladies, I believe; they hunger for the minutest fact of a fellow creature's passing, the better to brood over it, and lament, and sigh in contemplation of their own more happy escape. Let it appear, at least, that such is your inclination—the better to deceive your brother."

"For *that* is required no undue exertion," I replied, with a thought for James's unfortunate Mary. "My brother has always inclined to the view that women are extremely foolish creatures; and it has been amply proved by his experience."

"All the better. He will journey to Ashe—and there he will interrogate the family, or even perhaps the groom who attended Madam Lefroy, and faithfully report his intelligence. Do you make certain to beg that he relate the exact circumstances of the horse's bolting. Was it a rook, calling too loud within a hedgerow? Or the sudden report of a gun? How came the servant to account for it? Depend upon it, all at Ashe will know; tho' they cannot place upon events the construction that *we* should do."

"And perhaps I may enquire," I added slowly, "whether any strangers were remarked of late in the village."

"A funeral is quite often an occasion for the exchange of gossip," Lord Harold observed delicately. "They may have remarked a handsome young man of distinguished appearance, putting up at the local inn; or worse yet, a transient labourer of brutish aspect—remarkable for his dissimilar eyes."

Chapter 15

Portrait of a Witch

*Wednesday,
19 December 1804*
~

I DEVOTED AN HOUR AFTER BREAKFAST THIS MORNING TO MY correspondence—a long-delayed letter of condolence to Anne Lefroy's daughter, Jemima, and a second note intended for my brother James's eyes alone. In this I begged him, with the most acute sensibility, to relate by return of post every particular of Madam Lefroy's death—not excepting the loose talk of the neighbourhood that had undoubtedly arisen, in the train of so hideous an accident. I went so far as to hint that he might satisfy my anxiety with an interrogation of the unfortunate groom. And at the last, I enquired whether he had chanced to encounter some gentlemen of my acquaintance in the neighbourhood of Overton—the actor, Hugh Conyngham, or his lackey, Smythe, a hulking, great fellow with one blue and one brown eye. I thought them likely to have gone into Hampshire, and would not wish them to suffer from a dearth of acquaintance.

Not even James could resist so patent an invitation to gossip.

Quite pleased with my efforts, I sealed the sheet with a wafer, inscribed the direction, and had only to await the collection of the post. I have never been so decidedly impatient for correspondence from my eldest brother in all my life—for we do not enjoy as happy

an intimacy as I might wish. I must hope that the oddity of my beseeching him for news, should not utterly rouse his suspicions.

I SET OUT NOT LONG THEREAFTER FOR LAURA PLACE; BUT HAD ONLY
achieved Pulteney Bridge, when I espied the figure of a woman in
conversation with someone in a phaeton drawn up near one of the
shops that line its length. Something in her elegant figure, the remarkable carriage of her head, seemed familiar, but the lady was so
heavily veiled, I could not make her features out. As I approached
she turned away, and hurried off into the marketplace that runs
along the river at that point; and I decided I must have been mistaken. My conviction was given considerable reinforcement as I drew
up with the carriage itself—and was hailed by none other than Colonel Easton.

"Colonel!" I cried. "And a very good day to you. Are you intending to call in Laura Place?"

"I am, Miss Austen—and should have been there already, had not
I chanced upon the wife of a fellow officer, Mrs. Grimsby, a most
excellent young woman, indeed. Grimsby is presently called away to
the North, and she is sadly without friends. All the world is abroad
this morning, I may say! But I am happy to find you here. May I carry
you to Lady Desdemona?"

With these words, the Colonel chanced to take the measure of my
sombre gown and black gloves, and his bluff good humour immediately faded. "I say—I hope I don't intrude unhandsomely—but have
you recently sustained a loss, Miss Austen?"

"I regret that I have."

"My deepest sympathies, ma'am. And in such a season!"

"You are very good, Colonel. I should be delighted to attend you
to Laura Place."

He jumped out with a glad smile, and showed me into the phaeton. "I had hoped to ride with Lady Desdemona this morning, but I
learned to my regret that she was a trifle indisposed."

"Nothing serious, I hope?"

He shook his head. "I fancy she's only blue-devilled by Kinsell's
entanglement. And that uncle of hers cannot be a comfort—Trowbridge is forever dangling after one woman or another. I saw him
myself in Orchard Street only last night, in such a display! Most

unbecoming, with the family's fortunes at such a pass; but the fellow never had the least discretion.''

Colonel Easton's tact might as readily have been suspect; but I assumed he had not yet adopted the habit of reading the Bath *Chronicle*. He handed me into his chaise, then stepped up himself as swiftly as his wounded right arm would allow; and in pleasantries on one side, and some absence of mind on the other, we soon achieved Laura Place.

"MISS AUSTEN!" LADY DESDEMONA CRIED, RISING FROM WHAT HAD obviously been a most interesting *tête-à-tête* with the Earl of Swithin. His long legs were stretched indolently towards the fire, in so comfortable an attitude that he might have claimed the Dowager's drawing-room as his own these many months; but at the sight of visitors the Earl propelled himself to his feet, and managed a bow.

Lady Desdemona's colour was high, and her eyes sparkling; and if she cast a guilty glance Lord Swithin's way, and looked too conscious when she met my gaze, I could not find it in me to reproach her.

"I am delighted to see you," she said, her hand extended. "And Colonel Easton—''

Her warmth *must* falter at the Colonel's advance, but she need not have discomposed her mind. Easton had only to observe his rival in possession of coveted ground, take stock of the force he might bring to bear, and determine upon a judicious retreat; and with the most correct of bows, and a wooden countenance, the Colonel declared himself sadly engaged among acquaintance in Rivers Street, and stopping only long enough to enquire after Mona's health.

"I chanced upon Miss Austen at Pulteney Bridge, and was so happy as to be able to bring her hither; but having seen her to your door, my lady, I fear it is beyond my power to remain.''

"How unfortunate," Lady Desdemona replied implausibly. "But we shall have the concert this evening.''

"Until then," Colonel Easton murmured—and so she rang for the footman.

"What an excellent fellow Easton is, to be sure," Lord Swithin observed, as the rattle of his carriage proclaimed him well upon his way. The Earl was decidedly dashing this morning, I thought, in yellow pantaloons and tasselled Hessians, polished to a fare-thee-well.

"He is correct almost to a fault—though one could wish his arm less encumbered by that wretched sling. It must decidedly reduce the effect of his regimentals."

"You are a beast, Swithin." Lady Desdemona rejoined tartly. "Easton is everything that is admirable in a man—his character must be beyond reproach."

"Yes—and he is the sort of man the whole world speaks well of, but no one remembers to speak *with*. But having bested him at twenty paces, my dear Mona, I should be foolish to attempt it a second time when his back is turned. Miss Austen, I am sure, would not approve; and for Miss Austen's approval I live in daily hope."

The Earl accompanied this sally with an archly raised eyebrow, and despite my doubts regarding his character, I could not quite repress a smile.

"To laugh at a man when he is incapable of justification would seem a paltry art," I observed, "but I see you have managed it in the same breath as you declare it to be unwarranted."

"Cleverness will out, despite one's better nature," he said with a bow. "But enough of Easton. I like him even less clean-shaven, than I did when he disguised his fawning looks with whiskers. I understand, Miss Austen, from my sisters that they had the pleasure of meeting you at Dash's Riding School on Sunday."

I should hardly have expected the insipid Lady Louisa, or the pettish Lady Augusta, to have recalled the face of an insignificant Miss Austen, much less her *name*—but I inclined my head in acknowledgement of the Earl's good breeding. "Yes, I was so fortunate as to make their ladyships' acquaintance. They were—most gracious, indeed. Though perhaps a little fatigued, at having been summoned so unexpectedly to Bath."

"It was very bad of you, Swithin, to throw all your sisters' schemes for the season into upheaval," Lady Desdemona said with an innocent air. "I cannot think what should draw you to Bristol—nor why, once determined upon Christmas in Bath, you gave your family so little notice."

She was, I observed, decidedly a Trowbridge.

The Earl seemed to hesitate, and then plunged unwillingly into explanation. "As for Bristol, Mona—I had matters of business that could not be put off. Bristol has long been the seat of a wealth of trade, as no doubt you are aware—and though it pains me to admit vulgarity, my dear, a Venturer in trade I have, of necessity, become. He arranged himself near the hearth, his gaze averted, as though drawn by the play of the flames. "As for Christmas in Bath—I had long determined to descend upon the place. I may date the decision from the moment of your having done so yourself, my dear Mona. I tarried in London some weeks after your departure, however, for the silencing of the gossips. Had I informed Augusta and Louisa of my intention, the news should have been all over Town in a thrice." He turned then, and studied her with amusement. "I may *be* your devoted servant, my dear—quite lost to every consideration, and willing to undertake any humiliation in your train—but I have no wish for the world to observe it. A trifling fatigue on the part of my sisters was well worth the preservation, however fleeting, of my reputation."

Lady Desdemona blushed, and avoided his eye. "Swithin, Swithin—what have I done to you?"

He said nothing for a moment, his countenance grown suddenly grave; then he reached for his elegant black hat. "What no other lady has managed, my dear; and therein lies the mystery of your charms. But perhaps you will find it in your heart to pity me, Mona— and allow me to escort you to Mr. Rauzzini's concert this evening."

"The concert! I had not thought—that is to say—I am to be escorted this evening by Colonel Easton."

"A pity. Easton cannot appreciate an Italian love song as I do, nor hope to translate it so prettily. But I shall have the pleasure of seeing you, at least; and such things may sustain a man a fortnight, with care. Miss Austen, your servant—" The Earl bowed, and quitted the room not a moment later.

"What an extraordinary man," I observed in puzzlement. "I cannot make him out at all. He has quite the air of command; and I might almost believe him to have walked a quarterdeck, in company with my naval brothers, than the more prosaic ground of Tattersall's betting room."

"Oh, Miss Austen!" Lady Desdemona cried, with a brilliant smile, "you *are* a caution! It is exactly that quality in Swithin that so outrages and enslaves me both! His air of command! Decidedly, it is his air of command! I shall be in agonies tonight on Easton's arm."

"You remain so sensible of the Earl's regard," I said carefully, "though your uncle believes him capable of the grossest deceit?"

"Whatever Uncle may choose to think—whatever, indeed, he may eventually prove—my heart *will* whisper that Swithin is honourable."

Lady Desdemona replied firmly.

"I could not remonstrate, or argue—for I had myself been urged by a similar conviction, not so very long ago, in the matter of Geoffrey Sidmouth; and had I ignored the counsel of my heart, and followed solely the evidence of others, he might eventually have hanged.

"But I am forgetting!" Lady Desdemona cried, and hurried to the little desk at one corner of the room. "You have come to enquire of Uncle—and he charged me most earnestly not to delay a moment. He left this note for you."

It held a few lines only—Lord Harold regretted the inconvenience, but he had been called out urgently on business—should be most happy if I might meet him at the Bear—Her Grace's carriage to be called for the purpose—he remained my humble and devoted, etc.

A glance at the mantel clock betrayed my tardiness; I could not stay for the harnessing of the horses; and so with a hurried farewell, I found myself once more in the street, and hastening in the direction of the Pump Room.

THE BEAR IS THE SECOND OF BATH'S FOREMOST COACHING INNS, WITH A broad yard fronting on Cheap Street intended for the regular accommodation of the London stages and the mail coach. The inn's frenzied activity at certain hours may be readily observed from both the White Hart and the Colonnade opposite; and it is not uncommon for young ladies intent upon the Pump Room to be nearly overrun at Union Passage by gentlemen too inept to keep their spirited teams in check. I never can approach the Bear without witnessing a near disaster, or hearing screams and oaths uttered together with a desperate lack of concern for the public view.

To the Bear I proceeded through the dirty streets—a typical Bath rain having quite blasted the morning's promise of sun, and occasioned my employment of a broad black umbrella pressed upon me by Lady Desdemona. I had set out in good time, but Lord Harold was there before me—leaning carelessly against the inn's iron gates, adjusting his gloves. The Gentleman Rogue was very fine this morning in a bottle-green coat and fawn pantaloons, with a greatcoat over all; and he bowed as I approached, and pronounced me most punctual.

We were informed by the Bear's landlady, a Mrs. Pope, that Mr. Lawrence was not at present within, but that she expected him returned at any moment, and would be happy if we condescended to await the painter's arrival in comfort upstairs.

Upstairs we were duly shewn—to a parlour attached to several commodious rooms, one serving, by all appearances, as bedchamber, and the other as temporary studio. Here we found Mr. Lawrence's assistant—Job Harnley by name, a lad of perhaps sixteen, who was awash in sweat and very red about the face. It seemed that Lawrence was set upon London at last—and would depart this evening in a post-chaise. Master Harnley was even now intent upon the stowing of his traps, and the arranging of his canvases; for though he should keep his rooms at the Bear in earnest of his return, there were clients in London whose demands necessitated the striking of the studio.

"Perhaps his brush with a band of ruffians has quite overset our Lawrence's spirits," Lord Harold murmured.

We assured the young man of our indifference to his continued labour, and charged him to proceed as though we were ourselves invisible; and sat some moments in silence, our eyes wandering the parlour's walls. Here there were sketches of every size and description—half-lengths, full-lengths, and three-quarters—that seemed to leap from the canvas itself, as though intent upon three dimensions. There were heads in profile, heads resting upon arms or drooping in melancholy abstraction—and they captivated the heart and fixed the gaze immediately.

Lord Harold had once told me that when Lawrence painted women, he contrived to convert them to pieces of confection; and as I surveyed the examples mounted on the walls, I understood what he had meant. They were, in the main, fashionable ladies displayed to decided advantage, of no very great interest to any but their originals. But when Lawrence undertook to paint a man—*here* was movement, expression, energy, power. The eyes glowed, the lips curled in misery or disdain; the features—freed from the burden of vanity—worked with thought and emotion. To one, in particular, my gaze was often turned; and this was a head of Mrs. Siddons's brother,

John Philip Kemble. Did he play at Hamlet? Or perhaps Macbeth? Some creature surely tormented beyond reason. The ghastly features were mere suggestions—broad strokes of the brush; the neck and chest were naked still in the charcoal of their underpainting; but the agony stamped on the half-finished head was palpable in the extreme. I was moved and horrified at once. As an artist, Mr. Lawrence clearly thrilled to the passion of the theatre.

"Do you observe the sketch on the wall opposite?" Lord Harold said, breaking into my thoughts.

I followed the direction of his eyes.

"That is Mr. John Julius Angerstein, I believe—a highly influential merchant in Town. He has recently undertaken to reform Lloyd's, the insurers, and is one of the most important collectors of Old Master paintings. In this he rivals the Prince of Wales, who has profited from the confusion in France to acquire the greatest paintings in Europe."

"It is a noble head, indeed," I observed, studying the sketch, "though hardly handsome. An honesty of expression—a forthright countenance—and the care of years of trial are stamped upon the features."[1]

A crash from beyond the studio door, where poor Master Harnley laboured, suggested the overturning of an easel.

"I recollect your saying that Mr. Lawrence rarely painted a woman in the truest light—or at least, that his feminine portraits lack a certain vivid emotion he never denies his men," I continued. "In viewing these, I comprehend your meaning. But I would direct your eye to the sketch of Mrs. Wolff. It is extraordinary, is it not?"

The portrait was as yet in charcoal on canvas, without a touch of paint; but the curve of her swan-like neck, and the aversion of her glance as she bent over a book, suggested an infinite silence and containment, as though she were a woman complete in herself.

"It is a classical pose," Lord Harold observed. "Taken, I think,

[1] Angerstein's extraordinary collection was purchased by the nation following his death, and formed the basis of the National Gallery in the structure newly built for that purpose in Trafalgar Square. The Lawrence portrait of Angerstein—a friend and patron of many years' duration—was painted between 1790 and 1795. It hangs in the National Gallery, London.—*Editor's note.*

from Michelangelo. One of his Sibyls, perhaps. Lawrence has managed it superbly. You are acquainted with the lady?"[2]

"She is intimate with my sister Eliza. And also, I think, quite intimate with Mr. Lawrence. In fact, I should not be surprised to learn that it is to Mrs. Wolff, in Bladuds Buildings, that he is presently gone."

"I see." Lord Harold bent to leaf through a collection of drawings propped in a huddle against the wall, his lips pursed and his eyes narrowing at a few. Of a sudden, however, his gaze was arrested— and the stillness of his entire form, together with the slight tremble in his fingers, fixed my attention.

"My lord?"

He turned and handed me the portrait without a word. Maria Conyngham, if I did not greatly mistake—her beautiful face turned fully towards the viewer, and her long-limbed form arranged upon a divan. She wore a dressing-gown of filmiest gauze, and her hair was unloosed upon a pillow; the expression in her superb brown eyes was dreamy, wanton, half-expressed and half-realised. The face of a creature moved by passion, if not by love.

"It is an excellent likeness," I observed hollowly. "Perhaps he intended her as Juliet. Mr. Lawrence delights, I understand, in portraying artists of the theatre in their greatest roles."

"He has portrayed her as a courtesan," said Lord Harold abruptly, and withdrew the portrait from my hands. "We might wonder when she sat for it. Or should I say—*reclined*?"

"Lord Harold—"

But his attention was already fled. He had set the revealing image aside and withdrawn another, his brows knit in a scowl. "And who is this, I wonder?"

It was the head of a girl—done in charcoal, with eyes like burning coals. They had been fixed on Lawrence with an expression of some intensity, but whether of love or hate I could not tell. A stormy creature, in any event, with a tangle of short curls about her face, a prominent nose, a pursed mouth, and the suggestion of a hectic flush upon her cheeks.

---

[2] The portrait of Isabella Wolff, begun in 1802, is patterned after the pose of the Erythraean Sibyl on the Sistine Chapel ceiling. It now hangs in the Art Institute of Chicago.—*Editor's note.*

But most extraordinary of all was the vicious scrawl of red paint—stark and mortal as blood—smeared across the surface. It partly obscured the girl's features, and rendered the whole slightly lunatic.

"Begging your pardon, my lord, but I would wish you didn't bother with those things," said Master Harnley in an anxious voice. We turned as one, and observed him in the doorway of the make-shift studio. "They didn't ought to be there, in truth, being intended for the rubbish."

"Mr. Lawrence is disposing of these?" Lord Harold enquired in some astonishment.

Harnley nodded. "So he told me himself this morning."

"Then I wonder if you might tell us something about this one." I displayed the image so violently defaced with red. "It is a striking countenance, is it not?"

Harnley's young face darkened visibly. "That's the witch what keeps him up of nights," he muttered, and taking a step backwards, he crossed himself. "Always crying and plaguing him in his dreams. Draws her over and over, he does, to rid himself of her evil charms—but it's no use. I've destroyed a dozen or more like that, and still she comes by night."

I glanced at Lord Harold, chilled and perplexed at once.

"How very singular," he said indifferently. "And Mrs. Pope admits the lady to Mr. Lawrence's presence?"

"Admits her? Lord, sir—she's been dead these six or seven year! That's the youngest Miss Siddons, what Mr. Lawrence intended to marry."

The parlour door was thrust open hard upon the heels of this extraordinary remark, and our three heads turned as one—to perceive none other than the painter himself, preceded by Mrs. Pope and her beaming face. The landlady brought with her a tray of tea and warm cakes whose heady scent quite filled the room; and as she set her burden down upon the table, and bustled about with napkin and cutlery, the unfortunate Harnley advanced upon his master. With a deft and silent movement observed only by myself, Lord Harold turned the drawings to the wall—though not all, I believe, for one at least was secreted in his coat.

"Miss Austen!" Thomas Lawrence cried, with an agitated look. "And Lord Harold Trowbridge, indeed! This is a pleasure quite un-looked-for, I assure you! Harnley will have informed you, I suspect,

that we are called away this very evening—upon urgent business."
He was almost prostrate with the effect of his haste; and I observed
the marks of his late misfortune everywhere about his person. Mr.
Lawrence's head was bound round with a neat linen bandage, one
eye was purple, and his expressive lips were bruised and swollen.
When he moved, it was with a hesitancy that suggested a cracked rib
or collarbone. "We cannot delay an hour."

"So we understand, sir," Lord Harold replied with a bow, "and
we should not presume upon your time were it not a matter of some
gravity that brings us thither."

Mr. Lawrence was all impatience. "If it is about Lady Desdemona's
portrait, I assure you it shall be attended to the moment she is returned to London. For though I may attempt a drawing with tolerable success at some remove from my studio, I cannot undertake a
finished portrait anywhere but in Town."

"I entirely comprehend. The matter on which we would consult is
wholly unconcerned with my niece."

Mr. Lawrence looked from Lord Harold to myself, and an expression of *ennui* overlaid his handsome countenance.

"Very well," he replied, gesturing to the table, "I shall spare you a
quarter-hour. Pour out the tea, Mrs. Pope, and then be so good as to
leave us. I shall ring for you presently. Harnley, see to the stowing of
my dunnage in the chaise, there's a good fellow."

The landlady bobbed her way to the door, in company with Master
Harnley, and when they had gone, Mr. Lawrence settled himself at
the table with a cup at his elbow. "How may I be of service?"

Lord Harold withdrew the eye portrait from his coat and placed it
upon the table. "This, I believe, was done by your hand."

An indrawn breath, and Mr. Lawrence turned white.

The painter reached out and dashed the stormy grey eye to the
floor. "Where in God's name did you find that thing?"

"You know it for your own?"

"Cursed be the day I painted it—yes," he cried. "I have had neither peace nor happiness since Maria Siddons died; and if I had
never met, nor believed myself to love her, I should be a better man
today."

"*Maria* Siddons?" I enquired eagerly. Was this, then, the Maria
Richard Portal had named in his final agony—the Siddons girl beloved of Hugh Conyngham?

A swift glance from Lawrence, while Lord Harold stooped to re-trieve the pendant. "The same. She was the younger of the Siddons daughters; and I was so foolish as to engage to marry her."

Lord Harold sought the ruined sketch of the spectral lady, and held it up to the light. Even at the distance of several feet, I could perceive the likeness of the eyes.

"I must entreat you to tell me how you came by this thing," Law-rence said again, with obvious trepidation. "I had thought it buried with her."

Lord Harold turned. "It was found on the breast of a murdered man," he replied, "who whispered *Maria* as he died. We may pre-sume that whoever stabbed him, uttered the name with conviction as the blade went home. A killing of revenge, perhaps, but visited upon the wrong person. For it was *you*, Mr. Lawrence, the assassin in-tended to kill."

"I?" The unfortunate painter looked all his bewilderment.

"You were dressed in the guise of a Harlequin at the Dowager Duchess's rout, were you not?" I observed.

"I was," Lawrence said, comprehension dawning, "and I shud-dered when another, so similarly garbed, was murdered in that hid-eous fashion. I gather you were also present that unfortunate evening."

"I was," I replied; and saw again in memory Mr. Lawrence's Red Harlequin, conversing with Madam Lefroy.

"Then I may tell you that I quitted the house before the consta-bles arrived. But you cannot mean that Portal's end was meant for me?" The horror of the truth overcame him, and he threw his head in his hands. "Then the attack upon my chair—the gang of ruffi-ans—was occasioned by a far more malevolent purpose than I had supposed."

"There can be no other satisfactory explanation." Lord Harold set the eye portrait before Lawrence; but the painter started with revulsion, and thrust his chair from the table.

"This is madness!" he cried. "It cannot be otherwise. We are cruelly imposed upon—for I know this portrait to have been held as sacred by one who should never have given it up."

Lord Harold's eyebrow rose, and he glanced at me. "Pray explain yourself, Mr. Lawrence."

The painter stabbed a finger in accusation at the offending miniature. "You must know that Maria was for many years plagued with the consumption that ultimately proved her ruin. I painted this portrait of Maria for her mother, Mrs. Siddons, who feared the girl's sudden end. The great lady's talents being so much in demand, and her family generally in want of funds—as who is not?—Mrs. Siddons was frequently burdened with engagements abroad. It was a comfort to carry some token of her daughter about her person."

Lord Harold retrieved the miniature and turned it delicately in his fingers. "And while painting Maria's grey eye—you fell in love with the lady?"

Lawrence shrugged and averted his gaze. "I was, at the time, pledged to Maria's sister—Miss Sally Siddons, the elder of the two. But you will understand, my lord, that Sally was a gentle creature, of unassuming aspect and mildest disposition—her temper was unmoved by storms of passion. Maria was . . . utterly different."

"Her gaze alone is smouldering," I observed.

"It is. Or was." Lawrence swallowed convulsively, his eyes averted from the pendant. "Maria was jealous of her sister—jealous of what she believed was Sally's stronger constitution and happier fortune—and she set about to ruin her life."

It was fortunate the young lady was prevented from any reply, I thought, since Mr. Lawrence saw fit to so abuse her in death. I could not like or approve him; but he was clearly never without torment—and in this, I deeply pitied him.

"Under the most desperate infatuation, I broke off my engagement to Sally, and caused *there* the greatest pain a lady may know," he continued. "Within a very few months, however, I realised the folly of my impulse. I begged dear Sally to forgive me, and attempt to love again; to Maria I explained the whole—but the result was most unsatisfactory. From disappointment or pique, Maria went into a decline from that day forward—and died not long thereafter."

"How dreadful!" I whispered. "And was she very young?"

"But eighteen." He was silent a moment, and touched the blazing pendant. "There was worse than mourning to come, however. For with her dying breath Maria exacted a promise of her sister, Sally—a sacred promise that must endure beyond the grave—never to unite her life with mine. And Sally agreed."

"A formidable girl, indeed," Lord Harold said drily, "like a figure from Greek tragedy."

"I will confess I felt it to be so, when I learned the truth in a letter from my beloved. I was never to see Sally Siddons the more—and though I raved, and went nearly mad for a time; threatened suicide or murder or both—she stood firm in her resolution. Maria had exacted her promise, and to Maria at least Sally might be true."

"She has never wavered?" I said, appalled.

"Never for an instant," he retorted, with a bitter smile. "I threat-ened, I cajoled, I wounded her with silence and attentions to others, including even her childhood friend, Maria Conyngham—but never a word did I receive. And last year, in the full blush of summer, Sally followed her sister to the grave, a victim of the same infirmity. The physician who attended her believes that she contracted the disease while nursing the dying Maria."[3]

We were silent some moments in horror. Mr. Lawrence's head was sunk in his hands. But at last Lord Harold broke the stillness. "Tell me, Mr. Lawrence, of Miss Siddons's childhood friend—Maria Con-yngham," he said. "You attempted to secure her affections?"

"Attempted—and succeeded," the painter retorted with con-tempt.

"But surely you must have known that her brother was once in love with the younger Miss Siddons?" I cried.

"I did not," Lawrence said, with faint surprise. "Maria Siddons would have it that she had never loved anyone before myself."

"And perhaps, indeed, she did not," I mused. "For certainly she gave up Hugh Conyngham without a pang. In the gentleman's breast, however, there were stronger emotions." I regarded the pen-dant eye portrait with mounting trepidation, as the murderous scheme declared itself in my mind. "Forgive me, Mr. Lawrence, for so invading your privacy—but can you tell us when you ended your attentions to Miss Conyngham?"

"The moment I learned of Sally's death. In August, perhaps, of last year."

Nearly eighteen months ago.

"And did she meet the affair's end with composure?"

[3] The details of the Siddons girls' love affairs with Thomas Lawrence, and their untimely ends—as well as the supposition that he sought them both out of a thwarted desire for their mother—can be found in *The Kemble Era: John Philip Kemble, Sarah Siddons, and the London Stage*, by Linda Kelly (New York: Random House, 1980).—*Editor's note.*

"Tolerably so. There was a period of recrimination—of tears and threats—but I am accustomed to these of old." The first horror of revelation being now past, Mr. Lawrence smoothed his dishevelled locks with a hand that barely trembled. "I have recently vowed, Miss Austen, to pay my respects in future to *married* ladies alone; they are far steadier in their attachments, and demand of one a great deal less."

Was Isabella Wolff, then, so retiring? I considered the turbanned beauty, and thought it rather unlikely. Mr. Lawrence's callousness should have enraged me, had I not seen evidence of its extent throughout the conversation; but for an instant, at least, I understood the emotions that had moved the Conyngham pair. The torment of brother and sister—the desire for revenge so heated in the bosoms of both—had grown and festered with time. They had waited for the proper moment; had secured their positions in Bath; and had plotted the scene of Lawrence's destruction, with the pendant eye as silent witness.

"You are aware, sir, that the Conynghams were raised in the bosom of the Siddons family," I observed. "Is it so unlikely that certain of Mrs. Siddons's possessions might have passed to Hugh or Maria?"

"With both of her daughters claimed by the grave, Mrs. Siddons might well regard the Conynghams as even dearer than before," the painter replied with a shrug. "It should not be remarkable for the lady to convey some *memento mori* into their keeping."

One thing only remained a puzzle. Given their intimacy with Richard Portal, *how* had the Conynghams mistaken one Harlequin for another?

"I wonder, Mr. Lawrence, whether you have recently received any communication from Miss Conyngham?" Lord Harold interposed.

"A single note, nothing more." Lawrence stood up, and fished among a pile of papers scattered upon a table. "Harnley has made a poor job of packing, I see—but he is greatly distressed about the attack in Cheap Street a few nights ago, and should have bolted to London before this, had I not restrained him. Ah, yes—here it is."

He held out an unsealed letter, crossed with a feminine hand. "Miss Conyngham required me most urgently to attend Her Grace's rout," he said, "so that we might converse privately. She was most pressing in her request that I should meet her in the little anteroom, while the attention of all was engrossed with her brother's recital."

As he spoke the words, a look of comprehension came into his eyes.

"The anteroom—but it cannot be that *Maria*—"

"And did you meet her there?"

"I did. But as soon as I entered the room, I perceived Miss Con-yngham slipping behind a door in the corner opposite, and so I followed her there. She returned to the drawing-room by a back hallway, and I did the same, on the assumption that she no longer wished to speak with me."

"And did you observe Mr. Portal in your passage through the room?"

"I did. He lay in a heavy slumber upon the settee."

Lord Harold pocketed the actress's letter, and retrieved the pen-dant. "Whatever Miss Conyngham's duplicity or malice, they can be as nothing to yours, Mr. Lawrence. Were I even remotely attached to the lady, I should be compelled to demand satisfaction. Your behav-iour to one in her circumstance and position is nothing short of outrage; though it is of a piece, I collect, with your general treatment of the fairer sex."

He reached for his hat and gloves, intent upon taking leave of the painter. His hooded eyes were inscrutable as ever, but in his tone I detected an admirable command of anger.

"But it is of no account," Trowbridge continued, as he escorted me to the door. "The lady has others to act in my stead. And much as I should like you to relate the whole to Mr. Wilberforce Elliot, the magistrate, I must undertake to speak on your behalf. Make for Lon-don with the greatest possible speed, by all means, Mr. Lawrence—for your life is not worth tuppence in Bath."

Chapter 16

The Importance of Appearances

"IT IS CLEAR, MY DEAR JANE, THAT WE HAVE BEEN CHASING THE WRONG hare," Lord Harold said, as we regained the street. "For all his ingenuity at blackmail, Mr. Portal was never the object of murderous attack. It was another Harlequin—a Harlequin arrayed in *red* instead of *white*—who was meant to end on the knife."

"But who, my lord, struck the murderous blow? For though he surely spoke *Maria* as he died, Portal could not have meant to name Miss Conyngham. She should have known him regardless of disguise; and Mr. Lawrence did not discover a murdered man in following her through the passage. *Maria* must refer to the eye portrait of Miss Siddons."

"So much is obvious," Lord Harold replied. "It was merely Miss Conyngham's role to lure the painter to the anteroom. She may have panicked, in finding a slumbering Portal already in command of the place, and fled immediately—Lawrence followed hard on her heels—but the man intended to kill Lawrence could not know of the mistake. He merely stabbed the Harlequin at hand, and left the portrait on his breast."

"Lord Swithin, perhaps, or the man Smythe," I said.

"But without a confession from one of them, we cannot hope to prove it." Lord Harold shook his head. "I intend, however, to place

Miss Conyngham's letter in the magistrate's keeping, and divulge to him the whole of this extraordinary interview."

"Mr. Elliot is returned, then, from Portsmouth?"

"He is. It was to hear the summary of his labours that I was called away from Laura Place this morning."

"Do not keep me in suspense, Lord Harold, I beg! What of Swithin's ships? Was either the man or his hired tilbury remarked upon the quay?"

"They were not," the gentleman replied. "From the experience of your brothers, Jane, I must assume you to be cognizant of the traffic about the Portsmouth slips—the embarkation of passengers and crews—the sudden mooring and as sudden sailing of a multitude of vessels. A wearisome business Mr. Elliot found it; and all for naught. At least three Indiamen had put in last week, but all belonged to the Honourable Company; their crews being dispersed on a hard-earned shore-leave, Mr. Elliot could discover nothing of whether any bore news of Swithin's ships. And of the gentleman himself, and his flying visit to the town, our magistrate saw no sign; for Swithin did not put up at an inn, and one fellow among so many is unlikely to be remembered."

"That is very bad for the Earl," I said.

"Mr. Elliot had other news, as well. His man Warren discovered something in London of the discarded tiger pin."

"And from the turn of your countenance, I should judge it equally unfortunate for Swithin's case."

"The brooch was fashioned for his lordship's mother, by Thomas Grey, the jeweller in Sackville Street a very reputable old firm. It has been in the family's possession some thirty years."

I sighed.

"But Warren learned something even more intriguing, Jane— from a pawnbroker in Cheapside. The tiger brooch was lately pawned, and then redeemed, by a man who called himself Mr. Smith."

"*John Smith*, no doubt."

Lord Harold smiled. "The man did not answer at all to the Earl's description. He was burly and bearded, by all accounts."

"Then perhaps he spells his name *Smythe*," I suggested, "or may be found in the person of Lord Swithin's groom. Can the Earl's fortunes be so reduced, as to require him to pawn his mother's jewels? It is incredible!"

"Incredible, indeed," Lord Harold said wryly. "But I have delayed already too long. I will conduct you to Green Park Buildings, my dear, and then away."

We turned in the direction of Seymour Street, our umbrellas raised high against the fitful gusts of rain.

"We are so much more advanced in our researches than a week ago," I mused, "and yet we come no nearer to our purpose. How do you hope to effect the murderer's exposure, Lord Harold? A confession would be everything—but how to provoke it?"

"I do not know, Jane—or at least, not yet. But I think I shall attend the Rauzzini concert this evening, and carry the Conynghams in my train. Brother and sister are unnecessary to the company's performance in Bristol, it being a Christmas pantomime; and they are shrewd enough to profit from the chance to learn just exactly how much I know."

"Hugh Conyngham consents to quit his rooms, then?" I cried.

"He does; and shows no inclination for flight. No doubt he will enjoy the little diversion offered by Mr. Rauzzini's music."

"I understand that Lady Desdemona is to be escorted by Colonel Easton."

"Yes—we shall happily make a crowd in the Wilborough coach. You spoke with Mona this morning, then?"

"And with Easton himself. The Colonel carried me to Laura Place, but soon retreated, upon finding the position already held by his enemy."

"Swithin?"

"The redoubtable Earl." I hesitated, then plunged on. "Lady Desdemona seemed most happy in his lordship's attentions, and excessively sorry to refuse his offer of escort to the concert. Unfortunate girl—I feel for her most exceedingly. The Colonel is excellent in every respect, and yet—"

"And yet, Jane?" Lord Harold enquired keenly.

"And yet she cannot love him." I managed a smile. "We are a perverse race, are we not, my lord, in being given to the bestowal of affections upon the least worthy of objects?"

"It is certainly a family failing," he mused. "So the Earl is to be treated to the spectacle of *both* Miss Conyngham and my niece ac-companied by his rivals! We may expect Swithin to look daggers at the Colonel, and toss a challenge at my feet, before Mrs. Billing-ton has accomplished half an aria. I begin to enjoy the prospect of this evening's entertainment all the more. To assemble so many of the principals, in one place! What an invitation to scandal and display!"

"But how should the mere public appearance of the Conynghams and the Earl hope to gain your point?"

He dismissed me with a wave of the hand. "You have lived long enough in the world, my dear, to know that appearances are every-thing."

"Even, perhaps, when they are meant to deceive." I added thoughtfully; and we walked on some moments in silence. Presently, however, Lord Harold observed, "You are melancholy, Jane."

"I cannot but believe, my lord, that Anne Lefroy died because of my indiscretion."

He frowned. "I do not pretend to understand you."

"Had I never spoken of Madam Lefroy to Hugh Conyngham, she might well be alive today."

His lordship's footsteps slowed, but his gaze remained fixed upon the glistening pavement at our feet. "When did this interesting dis-course occur, my dear Jane?"

"At Friday's Assembly in the Lower Rooms. Mr. Conyngham chanced to speak slightingly of a gentleman's constancy, at which point I reminded him of his enduring attachment to the late Miss Siddons. It was Madam Lefroy who imparted the history of the affair to me, in the midst of Her Grace's rout. She was privileged in know-ing Mr. Conyngham's parents, you understand, many years ago—and had followed their childrens' careers ever since. I freely owned as much to Conyngham while we danced."

"And as a consequence," Lord Harold murmured, "you were waylaid in your chair later that evening—and Madam Lefroy was sent to her death."

I nodded painfully, all but incapable of speech. "The coincidence of events is not to be dismissed."

"As for that—you know my opinion of coincidence."

The rain dripped mournfully from our black umbrellas, as though all Bath must lament my dear Madam's passing. "We learned, moreover, that Mr. Conyngham kept to his rooms throughout Saturday and Sunday, in respect of an indisposition—but might not he rather have found occasion for a journey into Hampshire?"

"About the startling of Madam's horse."

"Exactly. I admit it seems a tissue of the most fantastic construction—"

Lord Harold gave me a long look, as honest and pitiless as one of Lawrence's heads. "Would that it were, my dear Jane. Would that it were. But it rings, rather, with undeniable truth. Imagine Conyngham's agitation, upon learning that Anne Lefroy had published his childhood passion for Maria Siddons! *Anne Lefroy,* whom he had observed the night of the murder in closest conversation with the regrettable Lawrence! What if the painter had recounted his own affections for Maria Siddons, or even his portrait of her eye? The eye that was left on the wrong man's breast, and so mysteriously disappeared! Mr. Conyngham should be a fool not to perceive that events had moved beyond his ordering of them. And so he attempted to silence you and Madam Lefroy both—and Mr. Lawrence into the bargain. I may count myself fortunate, I suppose, that I am walking about unbattered."

I had not energy enough to summon a reply; and the oppression of spirits—the uneasy sensation of complicity in Madam's end—dragged bitterly at my heart. Of a sudden I was infinitely weary.

"But you must reflect, Jane," my companion added gently, "that yours was not the hand, or the murderous intent, that effected her death."

"No more than the unfortunate horse," I retorted angrily, my countenance flushing, "but he was equally destroyed."

MR. RAUZZINI'S CONCERTS ARE ALWAYS HELD IN THE UPPER ROOMS, which are of recent construction and happily situated between the Circus and the portion of the Lansdowne Road known familiarly as Belmont.[1] Here one may find the Ballroom and the Octagons, Little and Grand; the Card Room and the Tea Room, where our concert

[1] The Upper Rooms, as they were called in Austen's time to distinguish them from those in the lower part of town, are now called the Assembly Rooms.—*Editor's note.*

tonight was to be held. These are large, high-ceilinged spaces, done up in pale hues and Adam Fretwork and cream, ideally suited to either a Cotillion Ball or the presentation of an aria; and as they sit but three or four blocks from Paragon Buildings, my uncle's gouty disposition need be indisposed very little, in pursuit of his enjoy-ment.

We had agreed that Eliza and Henry should meet us at the con-cert itself, while my uncle should call for me in his comfortable carriage. I was a little anxious for the arrival of the Henry Austens, in fearing that Mr. Leigh-Perrot—who is most prompt on all occa-sions—should never comprehend the effort at dress required by so fashionable a lady as Eliza. But at a quarter 'til eight, the Austens assembled in considerable style by the hearth in the Grand Octagon; and despite the persistent oppression of my spirits, and some little agitation on Lord Harold's account, I was very well pleased at the sentiment that had counselled me to forgo my aunt's insipid card party.

Besides, my uncle had stood me the price of the ticket.

"Well, Jane, you are very fine," my brother Henry said, as he surveyed my sapphire muslin. "The black gloves and shawl look very well, indeed, with that delicate colour. It quite becomes you. I am sure Lord Harold will approve."

"You must have your portrait taken in exactly that shade, my dear—it brings out the grey of your eyes exceedingly," Eliza ob-served.

"Is she to have her portrait done, then?"

"Or perhaps her eye alone. I forget which. Jane has been to con-sult with Cosway."

Henry frowned. "But isn't he rather dear?"

"Your eyes, Jane?" my uncle enquired, catching the latter part of Eliza's meaning. "Are they troubling you again? It is the effect of too much writing in very poor light—you must have a lamp entirely to yourself, if you will persist in scribbling of an evening. I have often remarked as much to Mrs. Perrot, and she *does* intend to make you a present of a lamp on some occasion or other—Christmas, perhaps—but there it is. You know that her health is indifferent at present, and she cannot be running about in search of the cheapest shops."

I was capable of only partial attendance to his words, for my thoughts would wander, and my eyes search fruitlessly for the Wilborough party. But I managed a smile, and said, "Should not we go in? There is a considerable crush, and I should not like to be left at the rear!"

My uncle was all affability; the Henry Austens permitted themselves to be wooed from the warmth of the flames; and so to the cream-coloured Tea Room ablaze with an hundred candles we proceeded, in company with most of Bath.

The musicians appeared, and sought their places before the Tea Room hearth, Rauzzini himself progressed to his position at the fore, and Mrs. Billington condescended to grace the company with her smiles and her elegant bronze satin. All discussion of such things as portraits and eyes was at an end; and I breathed a private sigh of relief. For though I may profess no very ardent love of concerts, I must declare them an admirable sedative for an agitated heart. Not even the most satiric eye should detect anything like apprehension in the countenance of Miss Austen, once beguiled by an Italian air.

"MISS AUSTEN!" LADY DESDEMONA CRIED, WHEN THE CONCERT HAD done, and we had fled the heat of the room for the relative comfort of the hall. Lord Harold's niece stood before one of the marble columns that flanked the Little Octagon, like a single rose displayed to advantage, and her face was alive with pleasure. "I am happy to see you! I did not know you intended the concert. Uncle *will* be pleased. He is only now gone off with Easton in search of claret— although how the poor Colonel shall manage it with his wounded right arm as yet in a sling, I cannot think. But that is Easton all over—he is gallant to a fault." She sighed; from vexation, I should judge, rather than pity.

I searched the length of the hallway's parquet floor, intent upon Lord Harold's silver head, but no glimpse of him did I seize. "I did not know that your uncle was fond of music, Lady Desdemona."

"He is a proficient himself upon the pianoforte—so proficient, in fact, that I have never attempted to master the instrument, for fear of comparison with my betters. But come! I have such news!" She drew me close with a secretive air. "You will never guess whom Uncle has brought to the concert!"

"Indeed, I cannot," I replied with false innocence.

"The redoubtable Conynghams! Uncle has certainly effected a change in their sentiment towards the Trowbridge family; though perhaps in this we should credit the tokens he wears about his person."

"Tokens?"

Lady Desdemona smiled. "I thought Miss Conyngham should all but faint when Uncle took off his greatcoat; and indeed, she is remarkable even now for her pallor. See—they are over there, by the bust of Caesar."

I gazed in the appointed direction and observed a creature so unlike the Medusa of memory, that I was quite struck. Miss Conyngham was arrayed tonight in virginal white, with a wreath of flowers in her dark hair. The slightest hint of grief about her eyes lent interest to a countenance already formed for beauty, and her pallor was exceptional. She stood near her brother in the closest conversation, oblivious to the crowd surging about her; and the classical effect of a velvet drapery behind—so suggestive of the dramatic muse—was unconsciously lovely.

I looked once more about the room, and found, inevitably, Lord Harold himself. He stood idly at some little remove from the crowd, two glasses of claret suspended in his hands—and he was engrossed in the study of the Conynghams. On the lapel of his coat was the golden tiger; and around his neck, the pendant bearing Maria Siddons's eye.

You have lived long enough in the world, my dear, to know that appearances are everything.

As I watched, the Gentleman Rogue forced a passage through the crowd to the actors' side. They accepted the claret with tolerable composure, and the slightest appearance of effort; but Hugh Conyngham's gaze was feverishly intent, and his sister's fingers shook. I observed her eyes to stray towards his lordship's coat, and judged that she found Lord Harold's society taxing, and a strain upon her nerves.

"Ah, Jane." My uncle's voice recalled me to my situation. "We wondered where you had got to. Would you care for an ice, or perhaps some little cakes?"

"No, Uncle, I thank you. Lady Desdemona, may I have the honour of introducing Mr. Leigh-Perrot to your acquaintance? Mr. Perrot is my uncle."

Lady Desdemona murmured a politeness and curtseyed; but her eyes were on me, and their expression was anxious. "I fear you are unwell, Miss Austen."

"A head-ache, nothing more. It is so excessively hot in the Rooms!" I forced myself to smile, but my eyes *would* return to Lord Harold. My anxiety was intense; for had he moved anywhere but in so public a throng, his life would already be at an end. It required now only the appearance of the Earl, for the mixture to prove volatile.

"Would you wish to depart, Jane?" my uncle enquired. "I will forgo the punch, and summon the chaise this instant, for we cannot have you decline the charades, on account of a head-ache!"

"You may rest easy on that score, sir. I should never disappoint you."

"Charades?" enquired Lady Desdemona, her eyes alight with fun. "How cunning! I should dearly love to play—and Easton, I am sure, would be very droll!"

"Then you must certainly make another of the party, my lady," my uncle said affably, "for one cannot have too many at a game of that sort, you know. We are to return to Paragon Buildings, where Mrs. Leigh-Perrot is presently entertaining friends, and I am sure she should be most happy to see you."

I little doubted the Trowbridges' reception; for though my aunt may be mean in her habits, and crushing to her acquaintance, she is beyond everything a most frightful snob. The capture in Paragon Buildings of the Wilborough set—however disreputable Aunt Perrot might profess to find it—would be the season's triumph.

Lady Desdemona accepted his invitation with thanks, and then craned on tip-toe to peer amidst the crowd. "And there is Easton at last!" she exclaimed. "I thought I should die of thirst before the interval was out. And look—he has brought a waiter with claret enough for all of us! Do you take a glass, Miss Austen—for I am sure it should do your head a world of good."

I bade the excellent Colonel hello, and made yet another introduction of my uncle—who immediately solicited the gentleman for charades, and his opinion regarding Buonaparte's intentions towards the Channel coast.

"Uncle!" Lady Desdemona cried, with a wave of her fan. "You shall never guess what fun! We are all to play at charades this evening, in the company of Miss Austen!"

"Charades?" Lord Harold enquired, as he appeared with his party at my elbow. "But how appropriate to the season! And how exactly suited to my inclination! Your servant, Miss Austen."

"Lord Harold. May I have the honour of presenting my uncle to your acquaintance?"

They exchanged their hellos, with a twinkle of amusement and a significant look on Mr. Leigh-Perrot's side; and then Lord Harold remembered the Conynghams.

The brother bowed, and the sister curtseyed deeply to my uncle. "Charmed, madam," Mr. Leigh-Perrot said with a flush. "I have long desired to convey to you my extreme appreciation of your talents. This is your first season in the Theatre Royal, is it not?"

"It is."

"And before that, you studied with Mrs. Siddons?"

"I have had that privilege," Maria Conyngham replied, with a quick look for her brother. "You are quite knowledgeable on the subject of the theatre, I see. A devotee of the Dramatic Muse, perhaps?"

"A frustrated player, I own. As a lad at Eton I took the breeches parts in Shakespeare; and I have never quite got over my turn as Viola."

"But she is one of my favourites!" Miss Conyngham offered graciously.

My uncle's good humour was at full flood, and he was on the point of inviting the actors to make an addition to our post-concert party, when Eliza's voice was heard above the throng.

"Look who I have found, Jane!"

I turned—and observed my sister advancing excitedly, with Henry and Lord Swithin in tow.

The Earl's strong figure loomed over our little party, and his eyes went first to Lady Desdemona, still and silent at Easton's side; and then to Lord Harold's coat, where the tiger and the pendant gleamed dully in the candlelight. His lordship's countenance turned first white, and then red with suppressed emotion; but he managed a creditable bow. "Lord Harold. Lady Desdemona."

"Good evening, Swithin," Lord Harold said. "I see you have come to pay your respects to dear Mona at last. You remember Miss Conyngham, of course?"

"Who could not?" Lord Swithin's tone was easy enough, but his eyes *would* fix on Lord Harold's tiger.

"We were on the point of carrying her off to play at charades," observed the Gentleman Rogue, "but now I come to think of it, Mr. Leigh-Perrot, we are become a shocking great party, indeed! It should never do to incommode your excellent wife with the addition of so many. May I propose our removal to Laura Place instead?"

My uncle hesitated, and looked to me; and I rallied tolerably to Lord Harold's purpose.

"What better place for diversion? I quite long to see that noble drawing-room alight once more, and explore the cunning passage! And I am sure Aunt's unfortunate indisposition must render the suggestion a welcome one."

My gentle relation gave way. "To Laura Place, then, without delay!"

"*In confinement I'm chained every day,*" UNCLE LEIGH-PERROT began with a mischievous twinkle,

> "*Yet my enemies need not be crowing*
> *To my chain I have always a key,*
> *And no prison can keep me from going.*

> "*Small and weak are my hands I'll allow,*
> *Yet for striking my character's great,*
> *Though ruined by one fatal blow,*
> *My strokes, if hard pressed, I repeat.*"

Our side received this sally with a mixture of emotions—tolerance for my part, who was familiar with my uncle's wit, and puzzlement among those less adept at word-play than the Austens. There were five of us ranged to the right of the drawing-room fire—Lord Swithin, the Conynghams, my brother Henry, and myself—while Lord Harold and my uncle anchored the opposing team of Eliza, Lady Desdemona, and Colonel Easton. The Dowager Duchess had elected to serve as audience, with Miss Wren disapproving at her side.

"A clock," Hugh Conyngham suggested.

"No, no," Henry objected. "Though the notion of striking is apt, I grant you, you must endeavour to comprise the whole of Uncle's meaning. It is a repeating watch. Consider the chain."

"Capital, dear boy!" my uncle cried.

"But should we accord them the victory?" Lord Harold enquired. "For surely the immediate response was inaccurate. Should not the team present a unified face, and reply with one accord?"

"Very well—in future we shall do so," said Swithin. "But let us consider the last point as unplayed."

"Unplayed!" my uncle cried indignantly. "But it was a most ingenious riddle!"

"Then let me propose another," said Lord Harold smoothly; and after a moment's consultation, presented the following:

"Divided, I'm a gentleman
In public deeds and powers;
United I'm a monster, who
That gentleman devours." [2]

An absolute silence greeted this offering, and with a sidelong glance, I saw that Maria Conyngham's countenance was as death. She reached for her brother's hand, and he clutched it close.

"Could it be," Henry mused, his eyes on the elaborate plaster carving of the Dowager's ceiling—"but no, that makes three syllables—now I wonder—"

"*'United I'm a monster . . .'*" Miss Conyngham whispered, and declined into silence.

"Agent," the Earl spat out, with a venomous look in his eye. "It is *agent.*"

[2] This charade has long been attributed to Austen's pen, but we learn here it was actually created by Lord Harold.—*Editor's note.*

"Very well played." Lord Harold applauded lightly. "The one who strikes on behalf of another, and in so doing, involves them both in ruin. I had thought the notion might possibly thwart your penetration."

"I may *employ* such men, Lord Harold, but I am hardly thwarted by them," Swithin rejoined.

"Indeed? Your turn, I believe."

We consulted in a group, and agreed upon a word I suggested, having had occasion to compose a riddle on its meaning before; and then I turned to the others, and said:

> *"When my first is a task to a young girl of spirit,*
> *And my second confines her to finish the piece,*
> *How hard is her fate! But how great is her merit,*
> *If by taking my all she effects her release!"*

"Sew—cook—wash—what other tasks must be onerous to a girl of spirit, Eliza?" my uncle enquired, puzzling it out.

"Visits to elderly relations?"

"No, no—it must be one syllable!"

"Darn? Mend? Do you exert your energies towards the first part, Mr. Perrot, and I shall endeavour to make out the second." She closed her eyes in a pretty attitude of concentration. "Might you repeat that section, Jane?"

" '*And my second confines her to finish the piece,*' " I said, with a casual air; but I thought Maria Conyngham's looks grew more pallid still.

"Confine. Yes. Now, then—chain? Bond? Tie?"

Colonel Easton's voice, in a tone of quiet amusement, superseded the little Comtesse's. "Darnchain? Mendbond? Cooktie? I do not think we shall progress very far in such a fashion. Let us declare ourselves at a loss."

I bowed. "Miss Conyngham? Will you relieve their ignorance?"

"The word is *hemlock*," she said, in a voice barely above a whisper.

"Of course. Suicide, that happiest of releases from tasks both onerous and unmentionable," Lord Harold observed.

"Excellent! Excellent, indeed, my dear Jane," my uncle cried merrily. "I must exert myself to another. Unless, that is, someone else on our side—" He looked about.

"I believe I may offer a small diversion," said Colonel Easton. He stood, and would have posed for oratory, his hands clasped behind his back, but for the impediment of his sling.

"*My first has the making of honey to charm,*
My second brings breakfast to bed on your arm,
My third bores a hole in leather so fine,
while united the whole breaks a heart most kind!"

"Well, I know for a fact that the third is an awl," Henry said with satisfaction. "It cannot be otherwise."

"And the first is a bee," Hugh Conyngham said.

"So the whole must be *betrayal*," I concluded briskly. "You are no match for us, Colonel. We have routed you entirely."

"Well played," Lord Harold observed with a nod. "Now let us have our revenge. I am quite a man for revenge, you know—though I cannot quite decide against whom I must direct it. All of you present such tempting objects." He moved towards the drawing-room fireplace as he spoke, fingering the eye portrait absently; and I instantly felt the tension in Hugh Conyngham.

His sister rose unsteadily to her feet. "I do not think I like your manner of playing, my lord. It resembles too closely a cat with a cornered mouse."

"Maria!" her brother said abruptly. "Sit down!"

"—What? Hey?" enquired my Uncle Perrot in confusion. "It is only a game, after all."

And at that moment, Lord Harold reached for one of the massive porcelain vases that stood regally at either end of the mantel, hefted it in his arms, and tossed it at Colonel Easton.

Miss Wren screamed; Lady Desdemona shied; and without an instant's hesitation, the Colonel caught the priceless object—employing for the purpose his injured *right* hand.

There was an instant of shocked silence; and then, with a rustle of muslin, Maria Conyngham slid to the floor in a faint.

"Appearances, you will remember, are everything, Miss Austen," Lord Harold observed drily. "We had taken for granted that Colonel Easton could never have stabbed a man; for his arm was assuredly useless. That was excellently caught, Colonel—or should I say, *Pier-rot?*"

Easton seized a fire tong and leapt at Lord Harold with frightening savagery, amidst the horrified screams of the ladies. But in a moment, the Earl of Swithin had thrown himself into the fray, thrusting Lord Harold aside and battering Easton with his fists. The two toppled a delicate little table, pitched headlong into the anteroom, and came to rest in a heap before the opening panel door.

"Gentlemen! Gentlemen! I beg of you—have a care for Her Grace's furnishings!"

Mr. Wilberforce Elliot, looming in the cunning little passage.

Chapter 17

God Rest Ye Merry, Gentlemen

19 December 1804, cont.

~

"I SEE HOW IT IS, YOU BLACKGUARD," HUGH CONYNGHAM TOLD THE Colonel bitterly. He was bent over his insensible sister, the Dowager's vinaigrette in his hand. "These riddles are easy enough to comprehend. You have betrayed us to the agent of our ruin, and all attempt at prevarication must be as so much hemlock—a release, perhaps, but hardly happy!"

Easton struggled to his feet, but was quickly overpowered by the Earl and Mr. Elliot. "I, betray *you*?" the Colonel cried. "That is a fanciful tale, when your jade of a sister has already divulged the whole to Trowbridge! She has been parading about on his arm this week or more. Enquire how much he pays for her charms, I beg—for I am beyond all caring!"

"Perhaps you will explain how the same man came by that curst portrait," Conyngham retorted hotly. "if not at your hand! For it was you who had the keeping of the eye, not Maria. I gave it to you the night of the Dowager's rout!"

"That is a lie!"

"A lie? You would deny the whole? Reprehensible coward!"

Mr. Conyngham might have continued in recrimination, had his sister not come to her senses at that moment; and so it was Lord Harold who satisfied the curious.

"The pendant was found by my nephew, Lord Kinsfell, and hidden within his clothes at the moment he was seized for Portal's murder," he coolly said. "I must congratulate Simon on his perspicacity; for this single act has proved the undoing of those who would have seen him hang."

"But, Uncle," Lady Desdemona said faintly, "how could you possibly have known the murderer was Easton?"

"I did not *know*, my dear Mona," he replied, "but the suspicion has been growing upon me. I told Miss Austen only this morning that appearances are everything; and she replied, *even, perhaps, when they are meant to deceive.* I must credit my excellent friend with starting the notion of Easton's guilt, for he was the sole person among us whose appearance had greatly altered in recent weeks, and I found that fact intriguing. Once started upon the trail, I proceeded rapidly to its end—for one aspect of this murder has puzzled me from the start, and Easton answered the purpose admirably." He wheeled about and faced us as implacably as a judge. "*Why was the murder committed in Her Grace's household?*"

"Why, indeed?" the Duchess echoed.

"To throw blame and ruin upon *Easton's* enemies. Mr. Portal—or Mr. Thomas Lawrence, the intended victim—might have been killed as readily elsewhere. But the murder was designed to despatch several birds at a single stone. To implicate Swithin—whose attentions to my niece had threatened the murderer's suit—and possibly Lord Kinsfell, whose interest in the murderer's *mistress* had outraged his reason."

"Miss Conyngham? Easton's *mistress?*" I cried; and remembered, of a sudden, the figure I had glimpsed on Pulteney Bridge, in conversation with the colonel's phaeton. Mrs. Grimsby, he had called her—but the familiar grace of her carriage and form had been entirely Maria Conyngham's.

Lord Harold looked to the lady. "Well, my dear?"

Maria's wonderful head came up, as regal as Cleopatra's. "I will not deny it."

He bowed. "You retain one claim to honour, at least. I suspected Easton only lately, Mona. I fear that for the better part of this sad affair, my suspicions were turned against Lord Swithin—as they were intended to do. For it was Swithin's device that was found in the anteroom passage—found, most curiously, *after the night of the mur-*

der, when Mr. Elliot had summarily searched it. I reflected on that point at length, and thought it too curious for plausibility. Colonel Easton had visited Mona on Friday, just before I searched the passage myself; and it was Colonel Easton who dropped the tiger behind the door."

I started up at this. "But the tiger belongs in the Fortescue family!"

"So it does—and was lost by the present Earl, I think, in a game of cards or some other wager. Am I correct, Swithin?"

"You are, my lord. At Carlton House, a twelvemonth ago at least."

"And did you lose it to Easton?"

"No—but I would imagine the man who won it, did not possess it long. He is notoriously unlucky at games of chance, and must soon have given up the brooch to another."

"The Colonel was certainly in possession of it a few months back, when a man calling himself Mr. Smith—a bearded fellow of some bearing—pawned the object in Cheapside. Easton redeemed it only a few weeks ago—just after the affair of honour, in which you injured his right arm. We may conclude that his desire for revenge, and his incipient plan, dates from that unhappy event. It was fought in respect of Miss Conyngham, was it not?"

Swithin inclined his head. "Easton believed me to have designs upon the lady—but I assured him that whatever my past attentions might have been, my heart was *now* engaged by another. He called me a blackguard and a liar. I could not allow such accusations to rest."

"Your sisters thought they had seen the Colonel in Bath Street on Thursday, but were later confused by his clean-shaven appearance." Lord Harold looked to me. "Did Pierrot sport whiskers, Miss Austen?"

The image of a burly, bearded figure of motley in converse with a scarlet Medusa rose before my eyes.

"Easton!" Lady Desdemona cried. "It *was* you!"

Throughout this explanation, Colonel Easton had stood mute and white-faced in the magistrate's grip; but now he burst out with venom, "You shall never prove it, Trowbridge!"

"I do not have to," Lord Harold replied easily. "For that is Mr. Elliot's task."

•   •   •

AND SO OUR MISBEGOTTEN PARLOUR GAME WAS AT LAST COME TO AN END.

"Despicable man," Maria Conyngham whispered, as she passed before Lord Harold's gaze. "I shall damn you from my grave."

He inclined his head with exquisite grace; and at Mr. Elliot's behest, the lady quitted the room. But I observed Lord Harold's eyelids to flicker as he watched her go, and his countenance become even more inscrutable; and read in these the extent of his self-loathing. His mother observed as well, and understood; but the Duchess said nothing—merely reached for his hand.

"Well, my dear Jane—here's a to-do," my Uncle Perrot mused in a whisper. "It will be all over Bath on the morrow; and what I shall say to your aunt, I cannot think!"

"Lay the whole at my feet, my dear," I advised him, "for she has quite despaired of my character these three years at least."

Monday,
24 December 1804
Christmas Eve
~

TIME PASSED; LORD KINSFELL WAS RELEASED, AND RETURNED TO THE bosom of his family. The spectacular fall of the interesting Conynghams was a three-days' wonder, and Eliza's account of it much solicited in the Pump Room. My mother soon forgot her younger daughter's scandalous taste for blood in a more consuming anxiety for her son's financial well-being—and grew seriously vexed when no commissions for Henry materialised from my intimacy with the Wilborough family. I cast about for solace—and found it in the unlikely form of the Leigh-Perrots. For, as I told my mother, the very evening of the infamous Rauzzini concert my uncle had excessively valued Henry's sage advice regarding the 'Change.

"Then it is fortunate, indeed, Jane, that you took him up on the concert scheme, for I am sure he should not have thought of Henry and Eliza otherwise—and I know it was a sacrifice for yourself, disliking music of that kind. You were always a good sort of open-hearted girl. Cassandra is nothing to you." She busied herself about her work a moment, humming fitfully in snatches of disconnected song, and presently warmed once more to her subject.

"Perhaps now your uncle may place some funds at Henry's disposal—for Lord knows he has enough lying about at Scarlets, and even here at Paragon, to keep your brother in commissions a twelve-month. I cannot think what he contrives to do with it all—for my sister Perrot hardly spends a farthing. She is of a saving nature, is sister Perrot—very saving indeed, and the housekeeping is the worse for it. The soused pig tasted decidedly ill the evening of her card party, and I could not find that she had even so trifling a confection as a seed-cake about her. The claret was tolerable, however—but I suppose that Mr. Perrot is vigilant about the laying-down of his cellar. No, Jane, you did not suffer at all in your sacrifice of the card party—and your willingness to oblige your uncle did you credit in his eyes, I am sure. Perhaps there may be a legacy in it, by and by."

I left her happy in scheming how the various Austens might best contrive to exploit their more comfortably situated relations, and trusted that the patronage of the ducal family might never be mentioned again.

ONE SENSATION WAS SWIFTLY SUCCEEDED BY ANOTHER, AND THE MURDER of Richard Portal gave way to news of far happier moment, with the announcement of Lady Desdemona Trowbridge's betrothal to the Earl of Swithin. The gossips of the Pump Room would have it the redoubtable Earl had once fought a murderer at pistol-point in defense of the lady's honour—but in support of so broad a claim, even Eliza very wisely said nothing.

"Jane," my sister Cassandra said, as I lingered over the notice in the Bath *Chronicle,* "the post is come. You have a great letter from James. Is it not singular, indeed? For he never writes to *you,* if he can help it. I cannot think what he has found to say—and at considerable length, too."

I jumped up from the sitting-room table and turned eagerly to the packet she held in her hands. "This is despatch, indeed! I must admire my brother the more, when that spirit of industry and rectitude—so generally tedious in his person—may contribute at last to satisfying my concerns. I expect this to contain news of Ashe."

Cassandra stood very still, and a change came over her countenance. "Jane, there is a something you have not disclosed, that is troubling you deeply. I am certain of it. You have been comporting yourself in the strangest manner—most unlike yourself, indeed—from the moment we learned of Madam Lefroy's death."

I settled myself once more at the table, James's letter slack in my hands. "And should you expect me to behave as myself, in the midst of so dreadful a grief?"

"As yourself in mourning, perhaps. But instead you go about like a lady of the *ton*, embarked upon her first Season! Madam Lefroy is all but forgot—and then, *this?*"

"Poor brother James! He would be no end offended to hear you speak so of his letters!"

"Do not sport with me, Jane." Dear Cassandra's voice held an unaccustomed ferocity. "I have always been privileged to share your smallest cares, as you have shared mine; but of late I must feel that you are entirely closed to me." She sat down beside me and reached for my hand. "Your behaviour pains me, I will not deny. I esteemed Madam Lefroy as much as did you, and her death has quite destroyed my peace. You are not alone in your melancholy. Or perhaps you have not observed the torment of our dearest father? It galled him so to be unfitted by poor health for the journey to Ashe. But he was told that all travel must be impossible, with the delicate state of the lungs—Mr. Bowen feared an inflammation, it seems—and so Father was frustrated in his desire to show some small respect of friends cherished the better part of a lifetime. It is not fair in you, Jane—it is most unkind—to exclude your family from your counsels, and turn instead to strangers."

"And is James, then, become a stranger?"

Cassandra sighed. "You know that I do not speak of James."

I took up the letter and broke open the seal. There were two full sheets, quite written through and crossed.

22 December 1804

Steventon Rectory

My dear Jane—

I was gratified to receive your letter of Wednesday last, and found it most proper in every expression of condolence and respect for the Deceased, though perhaps a trifle wanting in the form of its composition. You shall never be a truly accomplished writer, dear Sister, until you have studied the art of orthography and attempted consistency in its employ. In point of length your missive was not deficient, but in the organisation of your ideas—! The postscript alone was a mere jot, and entirely unconnected to the previous subject of your thesis. A sad muddle altogether. But of this, it is perhaps wiser not to speak. I may credit the fullness of your heart—that becoming depth of feeling so natural in the Female—for the unfortunate flow of your words, and the lack of stops to your sentences. I recollect that our excellent Father did not see fit to have you tutored in either Latin or Greek—quite rightly, too, for it should have burdened a mind remarkable for the weaknesses of its Sex!—and that you must be regarded, accordingly, as only half-educated.

I was so fortunate as to accompany my esteemed colleague, the Reverend Isaac Peter George Lefroy, to the carpenter's last week, about the ordering of the coffin. I had offered this little service, of attending him in the arrangements for the burial of the Deceased, and I may assure you that he was excessively quick in his acceptance. The Reverend Lefroy was gratified, I daresay, by my expression of respect and willingness to act in the guise of Son, to one who has always behaved with Paternal Affection. His own boys, I may report, behave abominably; young Ben has not left off crying since the Unhappy Event; and even Mr. Rice, whose assumption of Orders should have taught him delicacy and advised him to stand in a Son's place, to the father of his Chosen Companion, has failed utterly to lend support. He has taken, in fact, to Spirits, and spends the better part of every evening in throwing dice among the stable-boys.[1] But I was enabled by your letter, my dear Jane, to convey the Austen family's warmest sentiments of regard and feeling to the Reverend Lefroy, and can extend to you in turn the melancholy gratitude of a Man reduced to nothing by Grief.

The carpenter resided in Broad Street, in the neighbouring village of Overton; and as we progressed thither, our hearts could not fail to be oppressed by the dreadful memory of the Unhappy Event, in being forced to review again the site of the tragedy itself. You will recall that Madam Lefroy was in the act of quitting Overton, and had attained the top of Overton Hill, when her horse bolted and precipitated her injury. As we drew near the Fatal spot, Reverend Lefroy would not be gainsaid by the most earnest entreaty—he drew up his horse at the hedgerow itself—and holding aloft his whip, he pronounced the awful words.

---

[1] Henry Rice, Madam Lefroy's son-in-law, although the curate of Ashe, was a confirmed gamester who ended his days in flight to the Continent, pursued for debt.—Editor's note.

"Here, my dear Austen, is the very ground of her unmaking. Here did the poacher sit, under cover of winter's early dusk; here, he aimed his gun, and fired upon the partridge, that should have gone to Sir Walter's bag"—for you know, Jane, that Sir Walter Martin has always held that hedgerow in fief, and is sadly plagued by poachers—"and here the horse took fright, and ran away with my Beloved, to her tragic ruin." At this juncture he dis-mounted, and tore at the hedgerow's branches, and commenced a fearful weeping; and I must believe that had he proceeded alone, the carpenter should never have received him at all.

In consideration of Reverend Lefroy's behaviour, indeed, I begin to compre-hend the excesses of his offspring—but will allow no hint of remonstration to fall from my lips.

I apprehend, from the tenor of your missive, Jane, that you wish a full recital of Madam Lefroy's misfortune, and some account of her final hours. I might caution you, perhaps, against the over-indulgence of a morbid sentiment, and the feverish immersion in all that pertains to the Passing of the Flesh; but I believe you to be a lady of some sense, Jane, and will trust in Providence and the excellent example of our beloved father, to preserve you from excesses of Emotion and Thought.

I encountered Madam Lefroy myself on that fateful day, as our father has no doubt informed you from the intelligence of my late express. She re-marked at the time that her mount was so stupid and lazy she could hardly make him go, and so we parted—I to return home, and she to conduct her business among the tradesmen of the town. At about the hour of four o'clock, however, Madam Lefroy was in the act of quitting Overton with her groom—when at the summit of Overton Hill, her horse was frighted by the report of a gun fired from the hedgerow not ten paces distant from the animal's withers. The horse bolted, and the groom failed in his attempt to seize its head. From fright or unsteadiness, Madam Lefroy then threw her-self off, and sustained the gravest concussion. After some little delay about the conveyance, she was carried home to Ashe, and there lingered some twelve hours. Mr. Charles Lyford of Basingstoke—you will remember him, I am sure—attended her; but she slipped away quietly in the early hours of Sunday morning. I do not know whether she stirred or spoke before the End.

The shot that startled the horse has been imputed to the carelessness of a poacher—a poacher who remains at large, and will probably be far from his *native turf at present, for the preservation of his neck. A just horror at the ruin his shot had caused, should undoubtedly have urged the rogue to flee under cover of the falling dark. His apprehension must go unaided by any report from Madam's groom, who was necessarily engrossed in the pursuit and recovery of his mistress's mount, now sadly destroyed—and so we must impute the Disaster to Him whose ways are hidden, and accept it with the propriety and grace becoming a Christian.*

Propriety and grace, however, are sadly lacking among the Lefroys at present, and I may congratulate myself at having borne my own Dear Departed's passing with a more commendable fortitude, as my present Wife is quick to recollect. The Lefroys are a family destined to be plagued with misfortune, as Mary has also condescended to point out; the heedlessness and injury to young Anthony's back, and his subsequent death, were almost a presaging of this fresh tragedy.[2] *They had much better avoid the horses altogether in future. But, however—I could not find it remarkable in any of them to behave most lamentably throughout the service, and was duly resigned to demonstrations of grief on every side.*

You enquired, at the last, whether I have remarked the appearance of any strangers recently in the neighbourhood. There were a great many come for Madam Lefroy's service—and I congratulate myself that I did not disappoint their expectations!—but I take it you would refer particularly to your acquaintance from Bath. How you come to know such disreputable persons as the man Smythe, I cannot begin to think, my dear sister; and when I mentioned the matter to my beloved Mary, she joined most vigorously in my opinion. For the full extent of his history, I was forced to enquire of the housemaid, Daisy, who was so unfortunate as to encourage the man's lingering in the vicinity of the parsonage, through the offering of table scraps; and I have learned to my horror that he is a most dissolute person. If Daisy is to be credited, Smythe caroused in the Overton inn, meddled with the tradesmen's daughters, and performed certain high jinks in the public lanes—tumbling and jumping for such pennies as the curious might afford him. We were only too glad to learn that he had quitted the vicinity as

---

[2] James Austen refers here to the death of Anne Lefroy's second son, Anthony Brydges Lefroy, who was injured in a fall from a horse at the age of fourteen, and endured a lingering decline of some two years before dying in 1800.—*Editor's note.*

suddenly as he came; and must wonder at your having noticed him at all.
Where he is gone, I cannot tell you.

Daisy I have dismissed for her impertinence and want of proper discretion,
with full pay and her character, of course.

I remain, your most respectful Brother,
Rev. Ja. Austen

I set down the letter with hands that *would* tremble. Smythe had been in Overton; and Madam's horse had been frighted by a shot from the hedgerow at Overton Hill's summit. James could tell me nothing of dates; but I remembered Lord Harold's opinion of coincidence, and knew that though I should never possess what Mr. Elliot should describe as *proof*, I had learned the name of Anne Lefroy's murderer.

Nothing should be simpler, than the achievement of the deed. Smythe had only to conceal himself in the hedgerow for the purpose, and fire a gun lent to him by Hugh Conyngham. For the precarious seat of ladies forced to ride side-saddle was everywhere acknowledged—and Madam's ruin was certain. He might as readily have pointed the gun at her heart.

"What a commendable letter, Jane," Cassandra observed, "in its closing passages, particularly. I can never like my brother's style or sentiments—he has grown too pompous with the advance of years, and his preferment in his profession—but his concern for your reputation is quite honestly expressed. He might have been altogether a different man, perhaps, if—that is to say—" Her voice trailed abruptly away.

"Altogether different, had Anne survived," I finished for her. We had all of us loved the elegant and well-bred Anne; her character was steady, her understanding excellent. And though we could not like Mary Lloyd half so well, our affection for her sister Martha would generally make us silent upon the subject.

"Can you not confide in me, Jane, the reason for your attention to Madam Lefroy's passing?"

I avoided my sister's eye. "There is nothing very extraordinary in it, surely? We must all of us feel the most lively interest on the subject."

"I cannot dismiss it soon enough. To dwell upon such matters is intolerable, and quite unlike your usual activity. You do not brood, Jane. I am quite confounded at the impulse that should solicit such a letter."

"You must not importune me, Cassandra," I replied. "We all of us have different ways of grieving, and of making our last farewells. And now I think I should like to walk a little in the Crescent, and take a breath of air. Would you consent to accompany me, my dear?"

WE SAT DOWN TO AN EARLY DINNER, AS IS USUAL WITH THE AUSTENS; but a pull of the bell not long thereafter brought a note addressed to myself, and in Lord Harold's crabbed hand. I was summoned to drink the season's cheer and Lady Desdemona's health, in Laura Place at eight o'clock.

"Tea!" my mother exclaimed. "Had they considered you this morning, it might as well have been dinner. This is no very great honour, Jane, in being left so late—and on Christmas Eve, too! They have been disappointed in another of their party, I expect, and require your presence *now* merely to make up a table of cards. You had much better decline the invitation—for it will not do to seem grateful for so small a consideration."

"Indeed, ma'am, I am sure you mistake," I calmly replied. "At her time in life, the Duchess has no very great love of distinction; and being formerly of less than the first rank herself, is more inclined to show interest than disdain for ladies with modest prospects. I would be gratified to drink her tea, I assure you."

"Oh, well—if you must throw yourself in his lordship's way, it cannot be helped, I suppose," my mother replied with an appearance of indifference. "Only tea! However, they *may* desire you to remain for supper, Jane, and I will not have you sitting down with a duchess in your brown cambric. Run along and exchange your gown for another, my dear, and do not neglect to leave off your cap. Mary will dress your hair."

IT WAS A SELECT AND EVEN ELEGANT PARTY THAT GATHERED IN LAURA Place this evening—the Duchess seated in comfortable intimacy with Lord Harold, while Lady Desdemona provoked the Earl and her brother to rueful laughter at the opposite end of the room. Miss

Wren held down the middle part, established over her finger—and at first I feared I should fall victim to her desire for a confidante, and learn every syllable of the abuse she must suffer, now Mona was to go away, and leave Miss Wren quite at the Dowager's mercy—but at length, the young lady herself condescended to open the pianoforte, and required Miss Wren to turn the pages. Lady Desdemona commenced a Scotch air, her sweet voice swelling with pathos; and as if drawn by an invisible chord, the Earl moved close to the instrument to gaze upon his beloved.

"You will recollect, Jane, that I said I would not have my Mona thrown away," Lord Harold observed as he came to stand by my side. "I cannot now think any other man so deserving of her. My sources tell me that Swithin has entirely left off the opium trade, by the by, and indeed, has spent the better part of the years since his father's death, in extricating the family fortunes from that dubious business." A glint of amusement flickered in his hooded gaze, then vanished abruptly. "He is a ruthless fellow, but he has a character of iron; and men of that stamp are rare enough in any age. Mona is quite resigned to the Colonel's infamy, happy in her brother's release—and looks only to the future."

"But you, however, cannot," I said.

A swift look, as swiftly averted. "No," Trowbridge replied. "I have had news this evening, my dear Jane, that must weigh heavily upon me. Maria Conyngham is dead."

"Dead!"

"She hanged herself at Ilchester—tore the flounces from her gown, it seems, and wound them into a noose. Her brother is said to be mad with grief, and screaming vengeance on my head."

We were silent a moment; and in the confusion of my thoughts I heard Lady Desdemona's voice—simple, pure, and joyous without reckoning. "You cannot feel yourself responsible, my lord," I told Lord Harold, "for what Hugh Conyngham has done. The ruin of his sister's life, and his own, was inspired by his lust for vengeance against Mr. Lawrence; and had he never been moved to violence—had he allowed Maria Siddons to rest in her grave—his sister might yet be treading the boards in Bristol this evening."

"I wonder, Jane," Lord Harold mused. "I wonder. When I consider the Colonel, willing to risk everything to murder such a man—

I cannot believe the plotting to be entirely Conyngham's. Easton would not have lifted a finger for *him*. But for Maria Conyngham, he would have done much—even married a lady he did not love, in order to keep them both in fortune. No—the revenge against Mr. Lawrence was planned, I believe, by Maria alone; and now she has cheated even her brother, and left him to shoulder the blame."

"So much of ruin, for a girl already gone three years to her grave, and a man not worth speaking of," I mused.

"I imagine Maria Siddons would be gratified, did she know of it. She was, like Miss Conyngham, a creature formed for vengeance; and if Mr. Lawrence's peace has been even a little disturbed by the threat to his person, she will be dancing tonight in heaven."

"And what of the portrait, my lord? Maria Siddons's malevolent eye?"

"It shall be returned, of course, to her mother—though I must admit to the temptation of tossing it in the river. Such ill-fortuned baubles should be entombed with their subjects."

"—Excepting, perhaps, Mr. Lawrence's sketch of Maria Conyngham?"

Lord Harold's eyes failed to meet my own. I had observed him to secure the impassioned likeness within his coat the morning of our visit to the painter's rooms, and I must suppose his lordship to retain it still; but I could hardly expect him to declare as much. Impertinence is usually met by Lord Harold with an impenetrable silence, as I had occasion to know; and the present instance would not warrant an exception.

He sighed, and reached for my cup of tea. "This is hardly Christmas cheer, my dear. I shall fetch you some claret."

"My lord—"

He turned, and lifted an eyebrow.

"You must learn to endure it. As I have learned to endure Madam's death," I said softly.

"I shall, Jane. I shall—as the hangman submits to his calling; with revulsion, and anxiety, until the grave is filled. It is a dreadful presumption to serve in judgement on one's fellow men. It is to play a little at God—and though I have been accused of such a score of times before, I only now admit to approaching it."

"When justice is done, you may sleep in peace."

"Yes." He hesitated. "And until then, I believe I shall go away for a time."

I knew better than to enquire his direction.

THE HOUR OF MIDNIGHT STRUCK; LADY DESDEMONA THREW WIDE THE drawing-room casements, and looked down into the street below. "Look, Grandmère! The Waits are come!" Her glowing face turned affectionately to Lord Kinsfell. "How happy I am, dear Kinny, that you are with us to hear them sing!"

The Dowager cried out to Jenkins to conduct the Waits hither; and they very soon assembled before the drawing-room fire, cheeks flushed and eyes bright with cold. They were a rag-tag group of common folk, dressed for warmth rather than style, some of them no more than children—but the sound of their singing, when once they commenced, had the power to lift the heart. The very soul of Old England, rife with Yule logs and roasting mutton, good fellowship and love. I thought of Anne Lefroy, divided forever from her comfortable hearth, the table surrounded by children, and shivered with a sudden chill.

God rest ye merry, gentlemen, let nothing ye dismay . . .

I lifted my voice, and sang aloud with the rest.